Sugar and Spice

Sugar and Spice

A NOVEL BY

William Gill

LITTLE, BROWN AND COMPANY

BOSTON · TORONTO · LONDON

First Edition

This is a work of fiction. Any similarity to real persons, living or dead, is coincidental and not intended by the author. Names, characters, places, and incidents either are the product of the author's imagination or, if real, are used fictitiously.

Library of Congress Cataloging-in-Publication Data

Gill, William, 1946–
    Sugar and spice: a novel / by William Gill. — 1st ed.
    p. cm.
    I. Title.
  PR6057.I567S8 1990
  823'.914 — dc20   90-6161
  ISBN 0-316-31391-2

10 9 8 7 6 5 4 3 2 1
MV-PA

Published simultaneously in Canada by Little, Brown & Company (Canada) Limited

Printed in the United States of America

To Clare, for a million reasons

Prologue

Punta del Este
January 1, 1989

"GO faster!" Pandora urged the driver. The moon was covered by clouds. Only the road ahead was visible in the car's headlights as they took the sharp turn leading up into the hills. The evening breeze had become an ocean wind, bending the plumes of pampas grass at both sides of the narrow country lane. The trees yielded to it, and the sound of summer foliage, beaten and blown, muffled the roar of the engine at full throttle.

The wind suddenly broke the cloud, and at last she saw "La Encantada" ahead of them, the fairy-tale palace that had been brought from Spain stone by stone, a monument to the money and the madness of Simón de la Force. The walls shone a watery silver in the moonlight, but behind the trees that concealed the tower from sight Pandora could see an orange glow in the sky.

The car drew up outside, and Pandora stared at the tower, its top completely wrapped in flames. "Call the firemen!" she screamed to the driver. Then she ran to the house and opened the huge front door. Inside was complete darkness. The wind blew in, making the Flemish tapestries flap against the stone walls of the hall.

Pandora pressed the light switch, but the lights did not come on. Only the moonlight filtering through the landing windows faintly outlined the stairs ahead of her through the haze that was rapidly filling the vaulted passage. She could hear Arianne's cries of terror from her room at the top.

Pandora rushed upstairs. Her eyes began to stream, and she could feel the grittiness of the smoke in her throat as she approached the final flight. It seemed forever until she reached the top. Blinded by smoke, she crawled toward the door somewhere in front of her. She *had* to save Arianne. A blinding line of orange light at the bottom of the door guided her through the last few yards of smoke-filled blackness. The Moorish tiles on the wall around the door were cracking from the heat, the faint noise transformed to pistol shots by her fear. The only other sound was the sinister hiss of the fire beyond the closed door, nothing else. The screams had stopped.

Pandora fumbled in the darkness until her fingers gripped the door handle, her skin blistering at the touch of the incandescent metal. She had to open the door. A banal, everyday action, a reflex almost, had become the most important thing in her life. She desperately pushed at the heavy door. It gave a fraction, and a slap of heat rushed through the opening, singeing her eyelashes. Her lungs ached for air, sweet, cool air. Will and instinct clashed for a second. Her friend was almost within reach, but Pandora found herself turning back toward the ocean wind just a moment away. She staggered a few steps, and then collapsed at the top of the stairs.

All she could see now was the glint of the heart-shaped diamond on her finger. Ted Carson's ring, the ring that had caused her so much doubt, just as Charles's behavior over the last ten days had fueled Arianne's suspicions. Yet they had both disregarded their instincts. They were separated only by a burning door, a sheet of Spanish oak that had been lovingly carved four hundred years ago, now slowly crumbling to ashes.

As her consciousness faded away, she remembered her own home as it had been long ago, its horizon immense and new to a child's eyes. But it was all irrelevant in the end; she realized that she had misunderstood so many things. . . . Perhaps millions. Yes, maybe millions . . .

Part One

1

New York
April 1987

"FIFTY-TWO million," the auctioneer said, as the woman's hand rose. The spotlights caught first the gloss of her nail polish, then the mat finish of the gold pencil she was holding, and finally the square-cut emerald of her ring. The gesture was precise, just enough to be noticeable from the dais, no more.

Murmurs filled the room while the electronic board above the rostrum converted the figure from dollars into yen, Deutschmarks, sterling, French and Swiss francs. As expected, Manet's long-lost *Portrait de Madame Claire* had become the world's most expensive painting.

Displayed next to the auctioneer on a velvet-lined stand, as if on a shrine, its calm beauty contrasted with the commotion around it. The painting depicted an unknown sitter, supposedly one of the models for the *Déjeuner sur l'Herbe,* standing in front of a gilt-framed mirror. She was seen from the back but her head was turned over her right shoulder, as if her attention had just been caught by someone behind her. The face was partly in profile and partly reflected in the mirror, two incomplete images adding to a whole in the viewer's eye.

It was this counterpoint between reality and reflection, what we see and what we believe we see, a mature development of the painter's earlier *Bar au Folies-Bergère,* which had caused such a sensation in the art world when the painting had been discovered a few months before in the attic of a house in upstate New York. The old woman's great-uncle had been the painter's assistant, and she had inherited the house from him. The rolled canvas had laid forgotten in a dusty closet for decades, and it had been found only after her death. The woman had died in poverty.

But poverty was unimaginable tonight, in Christie's main auction room. Famous paintings were being fought over by the famously rich in an atmosphere of almost erotic tension, where money ceased to matter and possession became all-important. The excitement was now at a new peak after the woman's offer.

Pandora Doyle's professional interest was stirred as soon as she heard the bid and caught sight of the emerald on the woman's raised hand. She had no idea who this woman was.

At first, a number of people had taken part in the bidding, but once the price had reached thirty-seven million, it had become a two-man contest between Jacob Kugler, the New York dealer, and someone who was bidding on the telephone. Pandora heard the man next to her whisper to his companion that the call was surely from Tokyo, and that Kugler was acting on behalf of Ted Carson, the Anglo-Australian tycoon whose eagerness to collect paintings had earned him the nickname of "King Kong" within the art world. From forty-eight million on, the Tokyo bids had been more cautious, and they had finally stopped when Kugler offered fifty-one million. At that point, the tension in the room had slackened: the hand had been played. Pandora was about to leave to beat the rush to the door, when the woman's bid stopped her.

Pandora stretched her neck, trying to catch a glimpse of the bidder, but the rituals of money are ruled by strict codes, as polished as court ceremonial, and the woman was close to the auctioneer's dais, while Pandora stood near the very back of the room, the difference between a budding journalist and someone who could bid fifty-two million. Pandora had phoned Christie's that afternoon to reserve a place in the magazine's name, otherwise she would have been outside, among the crowd of celebrity-watchers. She could not see much of the woman from where she was: very shiny black hair pulled tightly into a chignon, a long neck, the collar of a sable coat, and, almost tangible, the aura of opulent wealth.

There was a story here, and that was exactly what Pandora needed. She had been at *Chic* for almost five weeks and had by now realized that the "Shopping List" section was the magazine's Siberia. Her predecessors had been either Upper East Side girls killing time until they found a husband, or rich divorcées waiting for their settlements. As soon as one or the other materialized they moved on, leaving behind them a brief memory of Chanel suits and spelling errors, both displayed in awesome quantities. Pandora badly needed a story.

Now she watched as Jacob Kugler hesitated for a moment, then raised his catalogue. The auctioneer was about to say "Fifty-three million," but the woman raised her gold pencil before he could even acknowledge the bid.

"Fifty-five million," she said, and a frisson of excitement ran through the room. Bidders do not normally announce their bids, let alone double their last increase, unless prompted by the auctioneer. Both the impatience and the foreign accent were just noticeable in her voice, but the message was clear: "Get out of my way."

All eyes were on Kugler, waiting for his next move. Pandora decided to break the rules of polite behavior at million-bid auctions: she left her place and, after treading on the feet of the man next to her and ignoring his icy look, she walked slowly down the side aisle until she reached the woman's row. Pandora stood against the wall, looking at her.

The face combined handsome Latin features with British aloofness, something that Pandora had previously noticed in rich Italians or South Americans. The nose was slightly aquiline, the golden-brown eyes slanted upward, and the smooth olive skin was tight against perfect cheekbones. The woman was neither young nor old, the early-thirties look of women just past forty who have a magnificent bone structure, and perhaps a great plastic surgeon as well.

The man next to her was about her age. Framed by his prematurely silver-gray hair and deeply tanned skin, his sky-blue eyes were almost luminous. He was dressed in the standard uniform of the international rich, a navy-blue double-breasted suit, crisp white shirt, and red silk tie. He was supremely attractive and, from his constant attention to the woman's smallest gesture, clearly not her husband.

"I have fifty-five million dollars on my left, fifty-five million." The Hon Henry Lyndhurst-Smythe had come from London to conduct the auction, a polished performance in eagle-eyed nonchalance that managed to make the actual bids slightly insignificant, almost trivial in the presence of Art, an infallible formula for achieving a record price. He paused now, apparently scanning the room but never losing sight of Kugler, who remained silent.

"Fifty-five million; any more bids?" This time he looked directly at Kugler. His eyes moved on after a few seconds, enough time for him to know that the dealer was beaten.

"All done? Last time," he said. "Fifty-five million dollars once, fifty-five million twice" — he raised the old ebony gavel a few inches, paused, and then brought it down.

"Sold for fifty-five million, thank you. For you, madam."

Pandora noticed the woman's eyes light up for a moment, but the impassive expression soon returned. She left her seat, followed by the man, and moved swiftly to the nearest exit, where she was quickly surrounded by well-wishers and dealers, complimenting her on her wise choice, her courage, her vision. A nod from her well-coiffed head was all they got in return. She paused for a moment to shake hands with Christie's Impressionist expert, while a uniformed porter held the door open for her. Once outside, the woman took no notice of the waiting TV crews; even under the hard glare of the lights, both her beauty and her stance were flawless. The small crowd of onlookers cleared a path in front of her, partly in recognition of her icy grandeur, but mostly because of effective push-and-shove work by her chauffeur and a bodyguard, both in gray uniforms. She got into a light-gray Rolls, seemingly unaware of the flashbulbs exploding around her. The man waved at the crowd and then walked around the car to climb into it from the street side.

Pandora, no chauffeurs or bodyguards to clear her path, had some difficulty in following them. She managed to reach the front line, and caught a glimpse of the man getting into the car. Their eyes met, his automatically sending out an instant flash of sexual charm.

The car pulled out. The crowd moved forward and pushed her into the road. She had often dreamed about a moment like this: a taxi would instantly appear, she would climb in, push a large note into the driver's hand, and say "Follow that car!" Then they would fly off in pursuit, tires screeching. But there was no taxi. She just stood there, breathing the cool April air and the warm traffic fumes, and watched her would-be story slowly vanishing into the New York night.

Fighting disappointment, Pandora turned into Fifty-ninth Street toward Madison Avenue and began to walk home, a few blocks away. It did not feel quite like home to her, though: it would always be her father's apartment. His sudden death from a heart attack last year had rattled her, but the simultaneous collapse of her marriage had prevented her from fully grasping its implications at the time. She had come to New York then to attend his funeral and deal with the lawyers, but had kept her visit as short as possible. It was suggested to her that the apartment should be sold, but she could not bring herself to do it. She just cleared out her father's clothes, burned his personal papers, and locked the door behind her. She was strengthened by the thought that she could now have a second home, the chance of a new life somewhere else, but that had been only part of the reason behind her decision. The apartment was still evidence of her father's presence, and she could not part with it when, after all those years, she was finally realizing what he had meant to her.

It was still difficult for her to accept that so much had changed since Christmas. She had always looked for certainties, for life to be safe, organized. Like the little pigs' houses, her certainties had been blown away. After eight years as Mrs. John Lyons, she was once again Pandora Doyle.

She stopped by the Laura Ashley window, and stared at its nostalgic reconstruction of English life. The window dummies were set up as mother and daughters in a scene of Edwardian domestic bliss. When Pandora was little, Viyella nighties and dresses with sailor collars from Liberty's had failed to make up for a father who had decided to return home to New York when she was only five. Her mother had never been able to disregard the polite scorn of her friends when her marriage failed, scorn which could have been anticipated from their equally polite surprise when they had first heard she was going to marry a handsome American serviceman from the nearby base, rather than one of the local elder sons with lots of fertile acres. Pandora had grown up in the loneliness of a rectory in Norfolk, within her uncle's estate. She had longed to go to boarding school, dreaded by many, because for her it was the chance to be with other girls who would not know that her father had left.

But school underlined her isolation. She was too posh for the girls sent to Benenden by nouveau riche parents in order to improve their prospects, too diffident for those whose mothers had gone there, and generally too odd for either group, this half-American girl with little money and no Daddy. Only with Geraldine Freeman, also considered odd by the other girls at school, because of her striking but very singular looks, did she feel at ease during those difficult years.

As she entered adolescence, Pandora had become more and more torn between her father's hopes for her, constantly preached in his letters from the other side of the Atlantic, and the aspirations of her mother. Her father wanted her to embrace a career as a marriage; her mother saw marriage as a career.

Partly because of Pandora's unadmitted resentment towards her father for his desertion, and partly because of her own need to belong, her mother's values had prevailed. A worshiper taking up a faith for reasons other than true belief, she had embraced it without allowing herself any doubts. At school she could not wait to grow up, leave, and fall in love, as people did in books. She got her dream, only to see it end in disaster. Johnny was gone.

Not only was he gone, he had shattered her life. During the last years of their marriage she had been cook, valet, and once-a-week lay during the commercial break just before the "News at Ten," not allowed to have children, "not yet," because they would interfere with his progress. His career at the bank required her full-time support, he said, and while she gave it, he was having an affair with some power-dressed trader who dealt in Japanese securities. It was the final episode in a long line of disenchantments. At least she knew it had been hurt pride, not love, behind her explosion when she threw him out. Love had died long before.

After school, she had wanted to develop a career in interior decoration, and a friend of her mother's introduced her to Mrs. Ogilvy, London's Queen of Chintz. She took her job very seriously, but she wished Mrs. Ogilvy had been equally serious about her, instead of putting Pandora in charge of atrocious jobs for rich Arabs, which kept the cash flow rolling while Mrs. Ogilvy took the kudos for her much-publicized country-house work for the National Trust.

Pandora had found it easy to give up work for Johnny, but soon after their marriage she had opened a small shop of her own. It had ended in failure, to Johnny's not-so-silent satisfaction.

She turned into Sixty-fourth Street, almost bumping into a jogger, oblivious to the world around him thanks to his bright yellow Sony Walkman. The distraction broke the bitter, brooding mood into which the subject of Johnny inevitably cast her. "Don't brood, darling" had been Geraldine's advice when Pandora had told her the story two months ago in London.

Geraldine had been asked by the Sainsburys to the Royal Gala at Covent Garden and was staying with Pandora for the night, her first houseguest in the new flat in Campden Grove. She had sold the house in Fulham as soon as Johnny left: the rooms had become unbearable, stage sets for a play suddenly without the male lead. Thanks to the housing boom and her father's inheritance, Pandora had ended up a modestly rich woman. "If you must cry, it's better to cry in a Rolls than in the Underground," Geraldine had told her a long time ago. She would prefer not to have to cry at all.

Ever since they had met, sixteen years ago, Geraldine had either done all the things that Pandora would have liked to do but didn't, or done them better, or simply first. When they left school, Pandora had drifted into her Season while Geraldine had had a well-publicized affair with a famous columnist, at least twenty-five years older than she was. Her own column soon followed, a stepping-stone toward the editorship of *The Diary,* a moribund magazine that even Pandora's mother found rather old-fashioned. Geraldine turned it into the Bible of London glitz in just six months. Her success had been the springboard to her appointment as editor of *Chic* in New York, with a salary and perks that were unimaginable in London. She had been even more successful in America, and three years ago she had married Solly Goldschmidt, a very rich real-estate man.

"Don't brood; just think about what you'll do from now on. You're bright, you're young, you're beautiful in spite of what you do, or rather don't do, to yourself, and there are no children to tie you down. The world is yours," Geraldine had said. "What you need is a break, something completely different. Come back with me to New York and help me at the magazine for a while. You were very good at writing at school. We'll fly back tomorrow, early morning Concorde, my treat, don't say a word. You have dual nationality, no immigration problems: use what you've got; that's the secret."

Was it? She wasn't sure, but it had been better than sitting in London doing nothing. At least it gave her a chance to try a different road. As she let herself into her apartment, her thoughts returned to the auction; if she could only find out who the woman was, and if there really was a story there . . . Geraldine would know. She would ask her tomorrow.

2

New York
April 1987

THE elevator stopped at the thirty-seventh floor. Pandora glanced quickly in the mirror. She knew that her clothes were all wrong. Everything she owned had seemed charming in London, variations on the early Princess Diana theme. Here they made her feel ready for the Salvation Army. She had to go shopping for clothes, but she didn't feel in the mood.

That morning *The New York Times* had reported the auction on the front page, but it had said that the buyer was an anonymous woman. No one that rich could be totally unknown unless she wanted it that way.

The receptionist showed her into Geraldine's office. Pandora was no longer startled by the walls covered in newsprint, the 1950s furniture, or the tiger-skin-print velvet curtains framing the New York skyline. The room had been one of Terry Cappello's landmark interiors, a brief moment of glory just before the onset of AIDS and his premature death.

Geraldine greeted her by the door, and Pandora, as usual, felt dwarfed by her height. Geraldine had been six feet tall since the age of fourteen, a laughing matter at school, but now a key ingredient of her stellar presence. Geraldine believed in making the most of what she had: her very high heels and the short skirt of her tight dress emphasized her superb legs and the starved leanness of her figure. Her straight flame-red hair reached her elbows, her bangs covering the top of her glasses.

Smiling warmly at Pandora, Geraldine kissed her on both cheeks. In a city where capped teeth are as common as dyed hair, only her outsize self-confidence could explain why she had not felt it necessary to do anything about hers, once described as the dental equivalent of an earthquake.

"Dearest, I forgot to ask you to come to my party tonight. It's for Paloma and Rafael, they arrived yesterday. Come around eight-thirty." Geraldine scanned Pandora's clothes. "Maybe you could treat yourself to something nice for tonight, and get out of those things you wear. You're not ready for the pyre just yet. Come and sit down." She pointed toward a kidney-shaped sofa, the gesture accompanied by the clanking of her huge crystal bangles.

Pandora glanced at Geraldine's portrait by Andy Warhol hanging over the sofa. The strong face had been glamorized but, even behind the huge glasses, it was impossible to conceal the shrewdness of her narrow eyes.

"What can I do for you, darling?" she asked.

"Last night I went to the Christie's sale — " Pandora began, but Geraldine interrupted her.

"Arianne de la Force," she said, glancing at the claret-colored polish on her nails.

"How did you know what I was going to ask you?"

"I know lots of things, my darling, and one of them is that you are desperate for a story. There's a good one there."

Pandora had at least a name, a lead to follow.

"Do you know her?" she asked hopefully.

"I've come across her a few times, but we are not friends. If you are going to write about her, be careful. She doesn't give interviews, and she sues if the copy isn't factual. It is difficult to be completely accurate when writing about someone who can conceal her past behind a mountain of money, and Jaws might vacillate before biting the kind of lawyers she employs. What do you want to know about her?"

"She looks South American. Do you know where she comes from?"

"The CIA might — just — find the answer to that one. She told me once that she had been born in France and brought up in Brazil, but then she said the opposite to somebody I know. She is one of those people who have an accent in every language they speak. I've also heard her say that she is Argentine, which could be true because of her husband."

Pandora remembered the handsome man at the auction. He did not look South American and he did not act like a husband, but she was eager to keep the conversation going before Geraldine became distracted, and she did not want to appear totally clueless.

"He was with her last night. He is very handsome," she said.

Geraldine raised one elegant eyebrow.

"Darling, if you really saw them together last night, I am going to make a lot of money out of you." She chuckled, then went on. "She married a much older man, Simón de la Force, an incredibly rich Argentine. He died very soon afterwards."

Pandora blushed at her misfired attempt to appear knowledgeable, Geraldine's amusement adding to her embarrassment. But she was finding the story more and more interesting.

"How did he die?"

"I think he had a good old-fashioned heart attack. Not surprising if you think about a man in his fifties, before aerobics and non-smoking, trying to impress the divine Arianne. She was one of the three top models in Paris when she married him. I wonder what she does to look so damn good still. Must be that wizard surgeon in Rio."

The secretary came in to say that a Mrs. O'Connor had arrived, but Geraldine was obviously having a good time, and waved her hand in a dismissive gesture.

"Tell her to wait." She continued talking. "All I've told you is gossip, and anyway you and I were playing lacrosse at the time it happened. She must have married him at least fifteen years ago."

It was difficult for Pandora to understand a woman like that, and she could not help feeling a twinge of disapproval. It was the old, old story of a wonderful-looking woman marrying a very rich man.

"What does she do?" A stupid question, she thought. What do rich women do? Have couture fittings and get bored.

"When he died she took over his business and ran it extremely well. She has apparently doubled its size. It is the largest everything-to-do-with-sugar in South America, or something like that, plus much else all over the world, and no shareholders anywhere. Some say she is worth nearly a billion, others insist that two billion would not shake her. She lives most of the time here or in Europe now; something to do with guerrillas in Argentina in the seventies."

The woman was not quite as predictable as Pandora had thought, but if she was so able, so powerful, why wasn't she in the public eye?

"Why is she so secretive?"

Geraldine smiled. "You *are* sweet. Privacy is the ultimate luxury. Any greaseball can go to the South of France, but only the really rich or the penniless can live without being seen unless they want to be. Besides, there were all kinds of stories when Simón de la Force died, then the guerrilla episode. She has good reason to dislike journalists."

"What kind of stories?"

The clock on the side table struck the hour. "I can't keep that O'Connor woman waiting the whole afternoon. My time is too expensive to use it for research, anyway. If you want to write about Arianne you'd better do some work yourself. But remember those lawyers."

Pandora stood up. She had heard enough to confirm her interest, and she instantly made her plan. She would go to the library and look up any available information on Arianne de la Force. As she followed Geraldine toward the door, she felt excited by the prospect. She had found her story at last.

Geraldine stared at her, obviously amused.

"I can see you are looking forward to the chance of playing Sherlock Holmes, but perhaps you should wait until my party this evening before spending hours breathing dust in libraries. I thought that a bit of South American glamour was necessary for the occasion, and Arianne is coming. I'll introduce you, and we might be able to arrange an interview with her. It's always better to hear it from the horse's mouth, even if it's a lie. And be nice to Charles Murdoch. In the magazine I would call him her 'constant companion,' but to you I would describe him as her regular, and very expensive, lay. He is gorgeous to look at, and he might provide you with some interesting angles. Don't be too nice, though: she doesn't take competition kindly, and I'm using the best silver tonight. I hate bent knives. Mind you, Arianne is too polished for that. She'll probably send you poisonous orchids from one of her plantations. And try to buy a new dress, darling. Your mother is a lovely lady, but you've dressed like her for long enough."

On her way out, Pandora felt full of anticipation. She would go and buy the new dress right now. She had always been careful about money until now, but to hell with it. . . .

THE apartment had cost $6 million to buy, and $3 million to decorate, not counting the antique furniture or pictures. It meant a price of half a million dollars per window for the pleasure of looking at Central Park from high above Fifth Avenue, but the last thing on Arianne de la Force's mind as she stood in front of one of her expensive windows was the cost of anything other than Charles Murdoch's silence. They were in the library. The fire in the Louis XVI fireplace threw a red glow on the green-and-gold tooled cordovan leather on the walls, and brought out the gilded outline of the picture frames.

The night before, on the way back from the auction, Charles had said that he wanted to talk to her. Alone, he had added, pointing at the chauffeur and the bodyguard in the front seat.

When they arrived home she felt tired and had gone straight to bed after checking her calendar for the next day's engagements. Her personal trainer was coming at 8:00 A.M., Michelle would arrive at 9:30 to do her hair, then a fitting at Oscar de la Renta which would take some time, lunch with Pat Buckley, and she was seeing Ted Bosco at Shearson Lehman in the afternoon to review her bond holdings. They agreed to talk early in the evening, before changing for Geraldine's party.

Charles was already there when she walked into the room, standing by the drinks tray and pouring himself a whisky.

"Would you like anything?" he asked.

"The usual," she said, sitting down on the Thomas Hope chair by the fireplace, her back to the fire. He poured a glass of Salus, the Uruguayan mineral water she had shipped to wherever she was, brought it to her, then sat facing her.

"Are we alone?" he asked.

"Yes."

"Where is Gloria?"

"She is long past the age of telling me where she is going. I don't know. She went out. I probably ask less about what Gloria does than I could, but you've been asking about her a good deal more than you should lately. I don't like it."

She looked at her watch. "Before you tell me anything, Charles, phone Rick and remind him to have the car downstairs in an hour. We still have to change, and Michelle is waiting to dress my hair for tonight."

Charles walked to the desk, picked up the phone, dialed, and waited for a while. "He isn't there," he said, putting the receiver down. "I told him earlier anyway, but I'll try again later." He went back to his seat and took a sip of his whisky, his eyes on her.

"You are lovely," he said.

She noticed his eyes on her body, and pulled the hem of her skirt down over the top of her knees.

"I thought we were long past all that."

"Don't you miss it?" asked Charles.

"If what you wanted to tell me is that we should screw again, once in twelve years is enough for me. Why are you suddenly getting so romantic?"

He smiled ruefully.

"I'm concerned about my future. I've reached the age by which most people have arranged some pension scheme. I have none."

"You know that for as long as you keep your mouth shut, I will look after you. There can't be a better pension scheme than that."

"Probably not, but what will become of me if, perish the thought, something ghastly were to happen to you in ten years' time? It's not easy to rearrange your life when you are over fifty."

Arianne smiled. "No, particularly in your profession." Her contempt showed in her voice.

He glared at her.

"Since keeping my mouth shut is what this is all about, I will not remind you of the details, but don't get holier than thou, Mrs. de la Force. Or is it *Madame? Señora?* You are so international. . . ." He smiled. "But there's no point in getting angry. Old couples do that, and we are not old yet."

"And we are not a couple," said Arianne. A long silence followed, his eyes on hers.

"But we can be one," he said at last.

"What are you talking about?" She tried to conceal her fear.

He walked toward her and leaned down, his hands on the carved arms of her chair, until their faces were inches apart.

"I am talking about Mrs. Arianne Murdoch, the former Mrs. de la Force. I think it sounds very good."

She stood up, pushing him aside, and walked toward the window.

"Why?" she asked, her back to him.

"I told you why. Fear of old age, a perfectly reasonable motive. I am sure you will outlive me, but imagine my position if you don't."

"I can provide for you in my will."

He helped himself to another whisky.

"Don't think that this is a rash proposition, because it isn't. I know that you could provide for me, but the problem is that you are not just a rich woman, you are enormously rich, and I'm used to your life-style now. If you were to provide for me, but made me merely rich, I would have to drop my standards; not easy at any age and cruel when you are getting old. If you were to leave me enough money to continue to live like this, any lawyer worth his fee will advise Gloria to contest your will. I know the caliber of the lawyers you employ: they will be Gloria's lawyers, spurred on by endless money."

He took a long sip from his glass, then went on.

"No, there is no acceptable alternative but to get married. Then the law would be on my side, and I will keep to the deal. I promise you I will never leave you."

Arianne laughed. "I am sure you won't. The gossip columns always say that the only women richer than me are the Queen of Holland and the Queen of England. Neither is likely to leave her husband for you."

Her face hardened. "You've obviously thought carefully about your situation. We have been together for twelve years, and neither of us is the hurrying type. Not about things that matter, at least. I'll think about what you've said, and let you know in due course."

She stood up, and walked toward the door.

"I don't want to be late. Please phone Rick again," she said over her shoulder as she left the room.

*   *   *

PANDORA was applying Chanel's Ombre Couture Jersey Ambre to her right eyelid while struggling to keep the magazine open with her left hand, when the phone rang. After many attempts, she was at last managing a passable imitation of the model's makeup in the photograph. It had taken quite a while to achieve a perfect porcelain finish with Teint Naturel Fluide and La Poudre de Chanel in Lumière Midi, and then she had tackled her cheeks, gently contoured with Rose Turbulent Joues Contraste. She had already applied the Ombre Couture Jersey Pêche to both eyelids, and then it would only be a matter of brushing on the Cils Lumière Brune.

While looking for her new dress at lunchtime, she had walked through Bloomingdale's cosmetics department and realized that her makeup was hopelessly basic. Not knowing what to do about it, she had bought *Vogue:* the coloring of the dark-blond, blue-eyed model on the cover was similar to her own. She had then gone to the Chanel counter at Bloomingdale's, and bought all the cosmetics listed in the caption, plus a few other suggestions from the salesgirl as well. Her heart stopped when the bill came to $384, but she was too embarrassed to ask the girl to take anything back. The experience prepared her for the next step, a short, wonderful black faille Valentino dress. She was full of excitement after her conversation with Geraldine, and was spurred on by the store's atmosphere into a sort of hypnotic shopping abandon, made easier by her credit card.

A few hours later, she was cruelly aware that she had spent nearly three thousand dollars for the sake of one evening, and she had been standing in front of the mirror for the last hour to achieve an apparently effortless look. It had been worth it, though; the carefully applied makeup brought out her blue eyes and her cheekbones, while the lipstick underscored the softness of her mouth and the golden streaks in her dark-blond hair. But she was horribly late, and now the damned phone was ringing. As she put the eye-shadow box on the bathroom shelf, her hand brushed the foundation bottle, which crashed to the floor, splashing liquid makeup all over the tiles. Shit shit shit. She ran to the telephone, only to find out it was a wrong number.

Pandora rushed back to the bathroom. She applied a last coat of mascara, and decided to leave the mess until later. She walked to her bedroom, took her dress off the hanger and put it on, her high spirits cheered on by the rustle of new silk, and stood in front of the mirror; for the first time in months, she was pleased by what she saw. She picked up her black wrap from the armchair and walked to the door.

THE man was lying on his back, his coarsely handsome head propped up by pillows, watching the girl sitting on top of him, astride his thighs. The phone rang and he tried to pick it up, but the girl leaned down, her small breasts just touching the hairs of his belly, and grabbed his wrists to stop him. Her tongue encircled one of his nipples first, then the other, faster and faster, until they were taut, smeared by her lip gloss, the hard edge of her teeth against the soft flesh moistened by her saliva. Her fingers encircled his swelling cock, her thumbnail gently following the thick vein along the shaft. He gasped in pleasure.

"Let me fuck you, please, baby, please."

She raised her head, smiling. "Not yet. You always want it too soon, and I'm not ready yet."

He watched her hands cup her breasts, her thumbs rubbing her nipples, her eyes closed and her teeth biting her lower lip. She then lifted herself up, just enough for the head of his cock to slip between her thighs. She moved up and down very gently; he arched his spine in a desperate effort to enter her, but she raised herself slightly to prevent him. A drop of semen appeared on the tip of his penis: she quickly wiped it with her finger, and licked it greedily.

"Oh, I like it, I want it," she sighed, "but not yet, naughty boy, not yet." She eyed him slowly, taking in the strong body, the broad shoulders, the arms almost as thick as her thighs. "Baby needs to calm down, he's so impatient. Baby needs something sweet."

She looked at the bedside table. Next to his keys and his wallet, there was a Mars bar. She picked it up, tore the wrapping off, rubbed it against his lips until it was soft, and then slipped it inside her, pushing the Mars bar in and out, her fingers smeared by the slowly melting chocolate.

"Baby's going to like this," she whispered. She pulled the moist chocolate bar out and slowly moved her body forward, until she could feel the grittiness of the five o'clock shadow on his cheeks rubbing against her inner thighs, his breath on her skin.

"Now have some nice warm chocolate. Lick me, baby, I'm all sweet for you."

The tip of his tongue touched her, first gently, then faster and more firmly until she felt herself begin to melt. Suddenly he caught the soft ridge between his teeth, and she screamed.

"Oh, yes, baby can have me now." She leaned down and kissed him deeply, her tongue rubbing against his, her nails digging into his chest. He suddenly rose, one arm around her waist, and pushed her onto the bed, face down, the weight of his body crushing her. Slipping his arm under her belly, he entered her from the back, his fingers digging into her rear. She felt the rush swelling inside her, bit her lips, and buried her face in the pillow as his animal roar filled the room, the waves of her pleasure in unison with his hot out-pouring.

As he lay on her back, panting, his body pinning her to the bed, the phone rang again. He picked it up.

"Yes, sir, immediately." He jumped out of bed. "That was Mr. Murdoch. Sorry, Gloria, I've got to drive your mother to a party tonight," he said, pulling on his chauffeur's uniform as fast as he could.

3

New York
April 1987

THE taxi swerved across two lanes of Park Avenue traffic in a crescendo of enraged hooting before turning into Seventieth Street. Pandora slid along the back seat, then clung to the window handle to regain her balance as the cab slowed to a halt outside Geraldine's house.

Pandora got out, took a deep, steadying breath, and walked up to the double doors, their glossy black paint reflecting the streetlights. The brass doorbell was the size of a side-plate, and polished to a mirror finish. As she waited, her eyes wandered along the beautiful street, its mansions and brownstones softened by the tracery of the large trees, taking in the lovely house nearby, a Parisian toy in New York. "We live just a few steps from the Mellon house," Geraldine had told her proudly when she had given her the address. Pandora, at that time completely ignorant of the finer points of New York society, thought she meant a very expensive East Side grocer. By now she knew better.

The door opened and the English butler let her in and took her wrap.

"Good evening, Compton. Am I terribly late?"

"Good evening, Miss Doyle. No, you're not. I believe that Mrs. Goldschmidt has asked forty guests, and only about half are here so far. If you'll excuse my saying so, Miss Doyle, I think there's nothing prettier than a good-looking English girl."

Compton's voice was pitched at the right tone of cheerfully polite deference. Pandora felt both flattered and uncomfortable, her usual reaction to compliments.

"Thank you, Compton, but I think that you are just being patriotic. I'd better join the others before you start singing 'God Save the Queen.' "

Her guess was that Compton was not the name he had been given at some church in Derby but Geraldine's choice, another facet of her clever strategy to conquer New York by combining outrageous idiosyncrasies with upper-class British mannerisms.

The house was typical of her approach. It was the perfect New York Upper East Side residence from the outside, but as soon as the door was opened, another of Terry Cappello's interiors engulfed the visitor. The circular foyer had industrial flooring in steel plate, its walls pockmarked with dents and scratches, covered in graffiti and painted to imitate the rotting walls of a slum in the Bronx. Two plasterers had been brought from Italy, at a rate of a hundred dollars per hour plus expenses, to achieve the distressed surface. It had taken three attempts, and four weeks, to please Terry, and only then had the painters moved in. The ceiling, a nineteenth-century French canvas, combined nymphs, cherubs, and clouds. Opposite the entrance door, two huge Ron Arad panels in gashed steel sheets slid silently to the sides as Pandora approached them, revealing the crowded hall.

Here, the decor was in faultless Regency style, down to the staircase copied from Sheringford Hall, and the elaborately swagged drapes, which, according to Geraldine, had been inspired by the Brighton Pavilion. The room was carefully lit by uplights behind huge arrangements of quince branches and leaves in terra-cotta urns in the corners.

Pandora noticed at first glance that most of the women were blond and ageless, their hair and their diamonds glowing brighter than the dimmed lights. Geraldine was close to the door. Not close enough to give the impression that she was standing there to greet the guests as they arrived, but sufficiently close for her not to miss anyone coming in. Like most of the women in the room, she was wearing Lacroix, hers in yellow and black and very short.

She was talking to a small group of guests, and quickly introduced Pandora to them. Paloma Picasso looked ravishing in red and black, with enormous jewels. The others in the group were equally famous: Marco Bellini, the film director laden with Oscars and Palmes d'Or, Nick Abrams, the anchorman, Roz Rittner, whose picture seemed a permanent feature of American glossies, and a man whose name she did not catch, because Geraldine's voice was momentarily drowned by a sudden burst of laughter from somewhere nearby. After the brief interruption of her arrival, they continued their conversation. They were discussing *The End of Dreams,* the recently published novel about life in New York which had become the success of the decade.

"I found it too exaggerated," Roz Rittner said, wrinkling her nose.

"Exaggeration, like beauty, is in the beholder's eye," replied Bellini.

In spite of her social smoothness, it was clear from her face that Mrs. Rittner did not like being contradicted, and Geraldine intervened.

"I wouldn't know, Marco; I'm always beautiful but never exaggerated," she said. They all laughed politely, relieved that the moment had been saved, then launched into further praise of the book. Pandora cut in.

"I thought it was marvelously well observed, and . . ." She realized no one was paying any attention to her, and stopped. Their simultaneous monologues finally ran their course, and a brief silence followed.

"Pandora has just arrived from London. I've been begging her to do some special writing for me. She's fantastic, everyone wants her. She has agreed to do Mrs. Thatcher for us; the Prime Minister is very particular about who she'll give interviews to," Geraldine said. Her tone underlined the importance of the secret she had just revealed, and Pandora could sense the group's attention suddenly turning to her for the first time.

"Do you know Mrs. Thatcher? I admire her enormously," said the man whose name she had missed. He was in his fifties, with a face as shrewd as his watch was expensive. Although amused by Geraldine's fabrication, Pandora felt annoyed at being turned into the center of attention on the back of a lie, but she could not deny it without embarrassing Geraldine.

"I don't know her at all, but I once did a profile of Mrs. Gandhi for a journal which may have caught the Prime Minister's attention." Geraldine's almost imperceptible wink confirmed to her that she also remembered Pandora's contribution to the school magazine many years ago.

"English girls err on the side of excessive modesty," Geraldine said. Then, casting her eye around her, she turned toward another group nearby.

"Solly darling, please be an angel and show Pandora your new Schnabel before everybody arrives. Ever since I told her about it she's been dying to see it."

A terror to the world, chewing up deals and people for twelve hours a day, Solly Goldschmidt yearned for domestic peace, and had learned soon enough that the easiest way to have it was not to contradict Geraldine. He excused himself from his guests, and led Pandora toward the library.

Relieved to be taken away, she smiled at Solly. Everything about Solly was solid: his head, his body, and his views. He was short and compact, his bright brown eyes and black curly hair his most noticeable features.

"I never would've guessed that you are such a fan of Julian Schnabel," he said.

"I've no idea who he is."

He stopped and stared at her, obviously nonplussed.

"What the hell is going on?"

"I don't know. Geraldine launched into a fantastic story about me, and then asked you to take me away. Maybe she was trying to make me look more important than I am, and then sent me away before the others could find out."

He smiled, picked up a glass of champagne from the tray presented by a waiter, and handed it to Pandora.

"She was probably right. Nobody listens to details at parties; after five minutes all they'll remember is that you are somebody worth knowing. Have a drink, and I'll show you my Schnabel anyway."

They walked into the empty library and Solly pointed at the huge painting above the sofa: dozens of broken white plates embedded into a thick crust of paint in vibrant colors.

They stood silently in front of it. Uncertain what to say, Pandora hesitated before asking: "Do you like it?"

Solly gave her a sharp look.

"What's that got to do with anything? Geraldine told me that I must have it, and I beat the shit out of the dealer on the asking price. He was selling for a guy in real trouble and wanted the money quick. I don't look at paintings, I only go to museums for the parties. But do *you* like it?"

Pandora inspected the painting for a moment.

"I don't think so, no, I'm afraid I don't," she finally said, almost apologetically. She knew that it would have been wiser to flatter Solly, but she also knew that she would not have been able to sound sincere about what, to her, looked like a mess of broken crockery.

"You Brits are funny. Why are you 'afraid'? I ain't gonna kill you for it. Just say 'No, I don't.' Life is easier if we know where we stand. Come on, let's go back; I'm supposed to be the host here."

They left the library and walked up the wide staircase to the second-floor landing leading to the drawing room. The big double doors were open, and they heard the sound of party laughter. As they walked into the room, a woman rushed toward them.

"Solly! Solly daaarling!"

Pandora was pushed aside by a swirl of rustling silk, bare shoulders, tempestuous black hair, and dramatic eyes made up in Maria Callas style. Solly disentangled himself from her embrace, and introduced them: "Pandora, this is Maria Dimitrescu; Pandora Doyle."

The woman's eyes scanned Pandora from top to bottom, and then she focused on Solly with extraordinary intensity, as if he were the only person in the room.

"You are *méchant,* so naughty. When are you going to come to my encounters? It's just a weekend, and you'll discover a new dimension to yourself, a deeper meaning to our life in communion with our brothers and sisters." Solly's black tie was perfectly straight, but she straightened it while she talked, her eyes on his. "Promise me that you will come. And Geraldine, of course. I *adore* Geraldine, she is my best friend." A minute ago they had been three people chatting at a party; now Maria had turned the scene into a couple in intimate dialogue, and Pandora had become an intruder.

"I don't know," said Solly. "You'd better ask her."

"Ah, how you love each other. You are both a-dorable! Geraldine told me that I should ask *you*. Why don't you come the first weekend in May? La duchesse de Brie-Montval will be there, and Barry Leen is coming specially from London. Do come, Solly." She smoothed his lapels. "*Please* do." There was a sly expression in her eyes now. "David Blomfield will also be there."

David Blomfield, or Lord Blomfield, as he had been for a few years, was a financial titan who had recently surprised everybody by unloading all his stocks in spite of the buoyant markets. He was now sitting on a mountain of cash, and was supposed to be interested in property deals.

Solly's voice softened a fraction. "We may have something to do then, but I think we can get free."

The change in Solly's tone obviously pleased Maria, and she flashed a huge smile, her capped teeth shining in the half-light. "I'll drop you a little note, not a billet-doux, just to remind you."

The corners of her mouth turned up into a coquettish smile. "*Au revoir,* darling." She then turned her face just a fraction toward Pandora, murmuring "Nice to meet you" as her eyes checked out the other guests.

"Who is she?" asked Pandora as soon as Maria left.

"Oh, someone who turns up everywhere. Her parents fled from Romania to Paris when she was little. They struggled to educate her, and eventually she got a degree in something or other. When she was in college she fucked some very old professor who knew everybody, and got herself launched in Paris society. Hasn't stopped since. She moved here when she realized it's where the real bucks are. She's probably learning Japanese by now."

"She doesn't seem to waste much time. What was she inviting you to?"

"There isn't any point in wasting time if you know what you want. She has some method of talking to God, direct line, or some crap like that. She's done very well with it."

Stung by his reference to wasted time, Pandora looked sharply at Solly, but realized from his face that there had been no personal edge to his remark, and was as annoyed by her own insecurity as by Maria's brazenness.

"At least she knows what she wants," she told Solly.

"Don't you?" There was genuine surprise in his voice. Pandora smiled.

"I thought I did, but I was wrong." She sensed that Solly might think she was asking for sympathy. "But I'm finding my way now," she added quickly.

They were halfway down the stairs when the doors to the hall opened, and Arianne de la Force came in.

At the auction, Pandora had been struck by her beauty, but there Arianne had been surrounded by a quietly elegant audience. Now Pandora saw her among the most glamorous women in New York, and realized that this woman was truly unique. She stood as straight as a plumb line, shoulders thrown back, her long neck and exquisite head slightly tilted. Yet there was nothing contrived or rehearsed about the way she moved, just instinctive grace.

Her perfection was underlined by her dress, the simplest long-sleeved, body-skimming sheath in thick satin the color of ice. In a room full of frills and bows, her refined elegance pushed every other woman into the background. Her shiny black hair was pulled back in the same style as the night before, and even at a distance Pandora noticed the size of the pearl studs in her ears. Charles Murdoch was one step behind her. As Geraldine greeted them, she glared over Arianne's shoulder at the nearest waiter, who rushed to offer drinks to the newly arrived guests.

Solly led Pandora back to Geraldine's group.

"Ah, there you are, my darlings. Arianne, this is Pandora Doyle, my oldest friend in the world. Pandora Doyle, Arianne de la Force and Charles Murdoch. Pandora is going to write a series of profiles of the world's leading women for the magazine, or at least I hope so. She's so hard to get."

Charles Murdoch's eyes were on Pandora.

"Are you?" he asked pointedly. The flirtation was so blatant that it was obviously for the benefit of the company as much as for her. Maybe it was his retaliation for being relegated to Arianne's shadow.

"Pandora should tell us about Mrs. Thatcher," said the man with the shrewd face to the group at large, then he turned toward Arianne. "She is one of her favorite journalists." Pandora guessed that at this rate she would become Mrs. Thatcher's *éminence grise* before the evening was over.

Arianne gazed at him, an amused expression in her eyes.

"You are always very well informed, Bob. Miss Doyle reminds me of that lovely-looking secretary you used to have a long time ago." Her voice was soft and very low, a mixture of Brazilian lilt and French cadence in her accent.

Geraldine cut in. "I've been desperately trying to talk Pandora into writing your profile, Arianne. I would be delighted if you would consider helping her."

"I love those foliage arrangements, Geraldine. Who does them for you?" Arianne asked, as if she had not heard her.

"A marvelous girl I found in London; she used to be at school with Princess Diana. I fly her in when we have a party. Much more sensible than paying New York florists' prices." Pandora wondered if either woman really knew the price of flowers, in New York or anywhere else.

"I know. I fly orchids from Brazil for my parties if I can, but here it's so difficult to bring plants in," Arianne said, and then took a sip from her glass of sparkling water. Pandora noticed that she was wearing identical square emeralds on both hands.

"What wonderful rings."

Arianne smiled. "You are very observant, like a journalist. But how unusual for an English person to comment on one's possessions." The silky rebuke was delivered in an equally silky voice.

"England is no longer what it used to be, darling," said Geraldine, "but your jewels get better and better." She showed Arianne her massive gilt and faux-pearl cuff bracelets. "I don't wear real jewelry anymore; I can't be bothered with the insurance. These are by Mercedes Robirosa; she is absolutely the best designer around now."

"I gave up costume jewelry a long time ago," replied Arianne.

"It's understandable, with emeralds like yours," Geraldine said acidly.

"Simón gave them to me sometime before our marriage. He said that he could see no reason why he should favor one of my hands over the other." Arianne's eyes wandered over the room, an almost constant smile of recognition on her lips as she came across one familiar face after another.

"I wish Solly had heard that," said Geraldine. "I might ask you to repeat the story when he's around. Where is Solly, anyway? We should sit down to dinner now. Please come with me, Arianne. Paloma and you are sitting at Solly's table." She led Arianne away.

The guests began to drift toward the just-opened gilt and mahogany doors at the back of the room.

"Have you checked where your seat is?" Charles Murdoch asked Pandora, offering her his arm. She did not like the man, but his charm was evident, even in trivial conversation.

"No, I haven't." It had not crossed her mind to do it. She was not used to going to dinner parties at friends' homes with forty guests or more and seating plans.

Charles stopped by a gilded console between the doors leading to the dining room. New York hostesses went to great efforts of imagination and money to display seating plans for their guests, but Geraldine considered them common. A sheet of white paper, typed by her secretary and pinned to a cork board, rested on the marble top.

"We are sitting next to each other. Well done, Geraldine," said Charles.

Looking at the plan, Pandora noticed the name on the left side of her seat.

"Who is Sheridan Crabtree?"

"I don't know, but don't waste your time," he said, escorting her into the dining room.

Pandora had been here before, but the transformation for just one night amazed her. The huge French doors to the garden had been removed, and a conservatorylike structure had been added on, doubling the size of the room. The whole space was tented in pale silver gauze shimmering in the candlelight. On the tables, candles burned in Empire silver-gilt candlesticks in the shape of Egyptian goddesses, forming a circle around the mass of wild flowers in the center; more candles burned in the huge Waterford chandelier hanging from a tasseled silk rope, their light refracted by the faceted drops into miniature spectrums. The floor was strewn with kilims, adding to the opulent atmosphere. A row of veiled girls, dressed up like harem slaves, was lined up against the rear wall of the room.

There were two tables, for twenty each. Pandora was at Geraldine's, within the room, while Solly presided over the second table, in the conservatory. As they sat down, she was at first disappointed not to be at the same table as Arianne, but then she realized that she would not have been able to talk to her anyway: there would have been at least one man between them. Geraldine had done the best possible thing for her, placing her next to Arianne's lover.

Pandora glanced briefly at Sheridan Crabtree as she picked up her napkin from the side plate. The most remarkable things about him were his extremely old dinner jacket, and a pungent smell of rancid sweat, drowning the combined strength of the world's most expensive perfumes. Pandora turned away from him.

The conversation around the table was at that fragile stage when people are still sitting down and finding out about their neighbors. As the line of waitresses started to move around the tables pouring Puligny-Montrachet 1971 in the first of four St. Louis crystal glasses, Charles Murdoch asked Pandora if she had been in New York for long.

"I've been here for a few . . ." She was going to say "weeks," but it would have been at odds with Geraldine's version of her non-existent career. Star journalists don't stay anywhere without a definite purpose.

Another slave presented a huge silver dish. Grateful for the distraction, Pandora helped herself to lobster and Burma lettuce salad.

"I've been here for a few days. Presumably you came here with Mrs. de la Force. She seems such a fascinating woman. How did you meet her?" she asked abruptly.

He glanced at her, amused.

"I thought this was dinner-party conversation, but you seem to be writing your profile already."

Pandora smiled, regretting her impatience.

"I'm sorry if you thought I was interviewing you. It was not at all my intention. I use a tape recorder when I'm on duty, and it would be very difficult to hide it under my dress."

"I wouldn't mind checking that later," he said.

"I thought this was dinner-party conversation, not a seduction," she laughed.

"You seem old enough to know that that's what most dinner-party conversations are." He picked up his knife and fork.

"Odd that Geraldine, who is such a perfectionist, would not know that one needs fish cutlery to eat lobster," he added.

His pretentious remark brought out the worst in Pandora, already grated by his smugness.

"Fish cutlery is a Victorian invention. Only nouveau-riche people inherit *that* kind of silver," she said, sounding exactly like her mother.

He gave her a sharp look.

"I can't imagine Solly's family bought much silver in the eighteenth century," he replied, and then carried on as if the exchange had not taken place. "Have you been to the Liechtenstein exhibition? It's fascinating. We went to the Benefactors' viewing." He launched into a long description of the exhibits. Pandora was certain that he was not the type to care about art collections: he was steering the conversation away from the one subject she was interested in. She had to regain the initiative.

". . . and apparently his Titians are fabulous." He paused to take a sip of his wine.

"You seem amazingly knowledgeable about paintings, but I can't imagine that you are an art dealer. What do you do?" she asked, then went on eating her salad, which was delicious. Once again, Charles seemed amused by her question.

"I run a very lengthy educational course. The subject is 'how to have a good time,' and the only student is me. By and large, it's running very well." He stopped talking and watched Pandora as she took another bite of lobster. He smiled.

"You must be the only woman in New York who actually eats at dinner parties. Stop eating and tell me more about yourself. Are you married?"

"Separated," she said tersely. She hated to discuss her personal life.

"You ought to be more expansive, otherwise I won't have time for even one mouthful myself."

"My husband and I . . ." It did not sound right, and she started again. "We separated five months ago. We were married for eight years. We married very young." She knew that perhaps she ought to expand on the subject. Making this man feel she was confiding in him might encourage him to talk about himself, but she drew the line at using her personal life to entice confidences.

"Where are you from?" she asked. "Your accent is almost American, but not quite."

"I lived in Europe for a very long time. Your accent changes if you live abroad."

"You sound like a character in a Henry James novel. Where did you live in Europe?" She had to get the subject back to Arianne, but at least the conversation was now on personal ground. The slaves began to take away their plates.

"South of France, mostly. Very good place for educational purposes."

"I haven't been to the South of France for years. It must have changed so much," she carried on glibly, to put him at ease. "Did you meet Arianne there?"

He smiled.

"No, I met her at Formentor, many years ago."

The main course, very pink *noisettes d'agneau* garnished with courgettes, minute carrots, and infinitesimal potatoes cooked to perfection, was presented to Pandora. She helped herself, and Charles Murdoch turned toward the woman on his right. As Pandora turned her head to her left, she caught a snippet of conversation across the table.

"You shouldn't be so cruel about poor Nathan," a woman wearing rubies said to the man next to her. "I know him well. He's one of my best friends, in fact, and he's really a sweetie when he's sober." Pandora decided to concentrate on the man next to her.

THE "bombe glacée à la délice des Indes" was served, and Pandora thanked God for his mercy. For the last half-hour she had been listening to Sheridan Crabtree's adenoidal voice. He had informed Pandora that he was an architect, but that he really did not practice because buildings today were not worthy of his talent. Instead, he was the editor and founder of *The Palladian Gazette,* an exquisite architectural journal of limited circulation, which he ran from his home in Wiltshire. He was in New York because of work: he explained that he was "chief design consultant for a large historical reconstruction project," adding that his wife was Geraldine's cousin.

Pandora remembered Geraldine's mentioning his arrival and describing him as a pompous bore. She had also said that his visit was to advise on the decoration of a new club called Boodles, where the aim was to re-create an English country house atmosphere.

During the conversation, Pandora had noticed that suddenly Charles Murdoch's leg was beside hers, not touching, but close enough for her to feel the texture of his trouser leg through her stocking, the warmth of his body reaching her skin. She looked at him, but he seemed to be completely immersed in conversation with the woman on his right. She moved her leg away, and kept on listening to Crabtree.

As the Roederer Cristal 1976 was poured, Charles turned toward her and said: "Where were we?"

"Mrs. de la Force."

"You can call her Arianne. I'm sure she won't mind, not here at least."

The edge of sarcasm in his voice was evident. An embittered lounge lizard, she thought.

"I've heard that she had a problem with the guerrillas in Argentina."

"That was a long time ago. I met her after she and Gloria went to live in Europe."

"Who is Gloria?"

"Her daughter."

Pandora was nonplussed.

"I thought her husband died very soon after their wedding."

"Simón de la Force was not Gloria's father. Gloria was two or three years old when Arianne married Simón."

"Who was she married to before?"

"You'd better ask her." He smoothed over his terse reply, adding, "I don't know; I think he was a Frenchman. I am sure Arianne told me all about him, but I've forgotten. I'm sorry that I make such a poor gossip, but I never remember other people's personal stories. And now that you know that I am reliable, or at least that my discretion is, perhaps you will tell me more about yourself?"

"What could you possibly want to know?" Her guardedness was more genuine than she would have liked it to be. There was little in her life at the moment she felt at ease about.

"What are you doing tomorrow, for instance? The afternoon is better, but mornings can be fun."

Pandora was not attracted to him, so it was easy to exaggerate her annoyance. She gave him a frosty look.

"I do something rather unusual: I work. My mornings and afternoons are busy, and I'm very tired in the evenings."

Her right hand was on the table: he moved his left hand until they almost touched. She took her napkin to her lips, and then rested her hand on her lap.

"You are exceptionally unfriendly," he said. "Is it because you are having an affair with Solly, or something like that?"

Amazed by his brazenness, Pandora felt her cheeks burning with rage.

"How dare you say something like that, here of all places? Geraldine is my oldest and best friend."

Charles seemed genuinely puzzled by her outburst.

"Please excuse me if I have offended you, but I don't think that you should take it like this. Speaking for myself, going to bed with the wives of my best friends is what I have done all my life. Let's not get upset about trivial things."

She was about to reply when the slaves reappeared with minute gilded cups and antique Turkish coffeepots. Perhaps it was better to drop the subject.

Pandora noticed that Geraldine was talking to the man Arianne had seemed to know, the man with the shrewd face whose name she had missed earlier.

"Who is the man on Geraldine's left?" she asked.

"Bob Chalmers. He's a financial genius: got most of the Third World into debt, then got huge fees for suggesting ways to get them out of it. He now advises just a few private clients; Arianne is one of them. Since Geraldine seems transfixed by everything he says, I would guess that he has something to do with Solly as well."

At that moment Geraldine left the table and led the way to the drawing room upstairs. Her red hair glowed in the candlelight as she walked across the room, quickly surveying the scene, the success of her dinner party confirming to her, once again, that the richest, the brightest, and just a very few of the most boring had been awed by her style.

As soon as Charles and Pandora left their table, they were joined by Bob Chalmers.

"We haven't played tennis since Lyford Cay, Charles. How about Piping Rock next Saturday? I hope your serve has suffered during the winter; otherwise it will be very boring for you." He smiled at Pandora and, as they approached the marble staircase, he offered her his arm. Charles stayed behind to talk to some people at the bottom of the stairs.

"I am very impressed by someone as young as you being so successful," he said. "You must be very good. Have you published something recently?" After dinner with Charles Murdoch, Pandora was wary of men's flattery, and Bob Chalmers's interest seemed excessive. On the other hand, she had been introduced to him as a successful journalist.

"I have a few things in the pipeline," she said, "but only one of them will be in *Chic*. The rest will be published in England. Right now I am doing research on some new material."

"I'll ask my secretary to keep an eye on *Chic*." He pulled out a gold-trimmed card case from his pocket and gave her his card. "I would be delighted if you would send me a copy of your English features as soon as they're published."

"Of course," she said with a smile, slipping his card into her evening purse. They walked into the drawing room, which was buzzing with conversation. Geraldine was sitting at the end of one of the two black and gold Regency chaises longues by the fireplace, with Rafael López Sánchez in the middle, and Arianne at the other end.

As Pandora and Bob walked in, Geraldine saw their reflection in the huge gilded mirror above the fireplace. She waved at them.

"Come here. Rafael is telling us about his theater days in Buenos Aires in the sixties." She pointed toward the huge tapestry stool by the fireplace, and asked them to sit down.

". . . and they were halfway through the play when the general's wife in the audience couldn't restrain herself anymore: she climbed on stage, pulled a rosary out of her bag and whipped the actors with it, shouting 'Blasphemy! Blasphemy!' It was so awful. . . . The play was banned the following day. I left for Paris soon after."

He turned toward Arianne. "Were you in Buenos Aires then? I can't remember; it's such a long time ago."

"No. Simón and I got married in 1969. I missed the sixties there."

"Where were you in the sixties, Arianne?" Geraldine asked. "Mind you, now that Pandora will be doing your profile, I should save the answer for my readers."

"There's no point in boring your readers." Pandora noticed that Arianne had clenched her left hand, the thumb folded under her fingers, and she was turning the emerald ring round and round.

Geraldine raised her hands in mock horror.

"Goodness me, I've never come across anyone so uncooperative. You are worse than Garbo, darling, but at least she wants to be alone. You must be used to talking about yourself at parties. Conversation would be so boring otherwise."

"Where is Charles? We have to go soon," said Arianne, picking up her purse from the coffee table.

"Pandora dear, I think that I will have to fly you to Rio on a research trip, your interviewee is so *very* unhelpful. It's beginning to look as if she may have something to hide."

Geraldine's tone made the phrase sound like a joke, but she stared at Arianne with a deadpan face.

Arianne stood up. She smiled at her hostess.

"I'm not as interesting as all that." She turned toward Pandora. "Please phone my secretary to make an appointment. I'd rather talk to you for half an hour than be cross-examined by Geraldine every time we meet. Goodnight, everybody."

A man dashed across the room and approached Arianne. He was Simon Heinegger, a Swiss art dealer who had been extremely successful in selling Impressionists to the Japanese. He stood in front of her, blocking her way.

"Arianne darling, I must congratulate you on your buy. Marvelous picture. It's so bold of you to buy something like that without getting the best advice available." His voice oozed condescending admiration.

Arianne raised her eyebrows. "Thank you for the compliment. I use my own judgment."

Heinegger looked puzzled, and then he blushed.

"But Thomas Winters told me that he was advising you." Thomas Winters was his main rival in Europe.

Arianne smiled. "You shouldn't believe dealers' talk," she said before turning away from him.

Geraldine left her seat. "I'll walk with you to the stairs. You're my favorite guests, but I've been sitting here for far too long. I must mingle," she said.

The two women walked toward the door chatting and laughing like old friends, as if their contretemps just a moment ago had never happened.

4

New York
April 1987

THE gray sky was getting darker, and Pandora hurried along Fifty-seventh Street. She began to cross the road as the first drops hit the ground. By the time she reached the other side the rain was crashing down on the sidewalks, and the gutters had turned into streams. Damn it, she had the best of her Fulham-princess wear on and her favorite shoes. Neither would survive this monsoonlike storm. She took shelter in the doorway of Hammacher Schlemmer just in time to avoid the sheet of water sprayed over the pavement by a bright red delivery van.

She scanned the street for a taxi. It was twenty to three, and she was supposed to be at Arianne de la Force's apartment in twenty minutes. Unless she found a taxi soon, she would have to walk in the rain.

Her mood and the weather had run parallel that morning. She woke up full of anticipation of her meeting with Arianne, arranged last Friday. She had asked Geraldine's secretary for Arianne's number as soon as she arrived at the office the morning after the party. She had expected Arianne's secretary to have a sharp voice and the polite kindness of a cheetah. She was right. But the cheetah had not put up any further struggle than to say "Madame de la Force is going abroad on Friday; she is terribly, terribly busy. Let me see if she has any gaps in her diary, but it is so unlikely," and then abruptly added, "She can see you next Thursday at three P.M."

Pandora had walked to the office under a blue sky and in high spirits. She loved early morning in New York: the buzz of the street life, the traffic, the street salesmen creating a miniature bazaarlike atmosphere at most corners. The short walk was a pleasure, although she knew her morning meeting with the advertising manager was not going to be one of the day's joys. As she entered into the chrome, black marble, and mirror 1930s foyer of the *Chic* building, she suspected that this second meeting with the advertising ogre was likely to be as unpleasant as the first, which had occurred two weeks after she had started work at the magazine.

Pandora had arrived in New York with a very vague notion of what her job entailed. She had thought that her relationship with Geraldine at work would be an extension of their friendship, but she soon realized that while Geraldine was genuinely trying to be helpful, she now lived in a world of Concorde flights and lunches with Nancy Reagan. Only crucial matters concerned her, and then only those critical to either the success of the magazine or her personal career.

It was true that on her first day Geraldine had received her warmly, asked her to come up for a cup of tea in her extraordinary office, and given her a lurid account of who was screwing whom, but she soon cut the meeting short because she had an urgent engagement. When Pandora asked for some briefing on what she was supposed to do, she was told to wait for "someone to contact you, and explain the ropes. It's really quite simple, you can do it in your sleep. I'll call you, darling. Maybe you can come for dinner tomorrow. Sam and Jessica are in town; you will adore them." She had gone to dinner at Geraldine's home the following night, with fifteen other people, but she still had no idea what she was supposed to be doing in the office.

The next week boredom began to overwhelm her, and she started a list of possible subjects for feature articles to discuss with Geraldine. It was during one of those afternoons, as more and more pages of her notepad were becoming slowly covered in doodled daisies and crossed-out beginnings for the article that would bring her to the attention of New York, that her phone rang for the first time. It was Connie van Naalt's secretary, asking Pandora to come up to see Miss van Naalt in her office in an hour's time.

The reputation of Connie van Naalt, *Chic*'s fashion editor, was formidable. She had discovered struggling designers in the Bronx and made them Seventh Avenue superstars, turned girls glimpsed in the street into international models, and started more fashion trends than she had swallowed ginseng tablets. Obsessed with perfection, she was known to rip dresses off the backs of her terrified assistants if she found them "common," an expression picked up during a brief stay in London during the sixties. After years of cleverly hopping from one job to the other on an ever-upward route, she had joined *Chic,* eventually achieving the prize of American fashion journalism, second only to the editorship itself.

Some of this Pandora knew from her sessions at her Fulham hairdresser's. What she did not know was that when the previous editor-in-chief had retired, Connie had made a bid for the succession, and made no secret of it. She was sure that her legendary sense for the most subtle fashion vibrations ensured her right to it.

However, Mrs. Greene, the owner of *Chic* and many other journals, had an equally legendary nose for profits, and she had not failed to notice the magazine's disappointing balance sheet and static circulation. She needed someone who understood how to make money through style, not a fashion legend. She had heard of Geraldine Freeman, and had flown to London for an overnight visit, where she asked Geraldine to dinner in her suite at Claridges. Geraldine's appointment was announced in New York the following week.

Connie's silence was as elegant as everything else about her because there was nowhere to go but down from *Chic,* and she was too skillful to antagonize Geraldine in any way or show the slightest sign of dissatisfaction. But when she heard that a new girl had been appointed for the "Shopping" section, a protégée of Geraldine Freeman's without any previous journalistic experience, she felt the joyous expectation of a vulture who has circled the sky for hours and suddenly notices a limping rabbit on the ground.

"Another new girl for the 'Shopping' page?" Connie had asked Geraldine casually.

"Yes, that idiot Bibi Sohnnental had a skiing accident in Gstaad two weeks ago. She has to stay in a clinic there for God knows how long. I asked Pandora Doyle, a girl I know from London, to stand in. She is very competent. I've sent a memo to Tony to brief her," replied Geraldine crisply.

"I'm sure she will be fabulous, Geraldine," said Connie enthusiastically. Geraldine was momentarily nonplussed by the sudden change in Connie's usually haughty demeanor, but put it down to a sporadic impulse to show her willingness to please her successful rival. Perhaps the back-stabbing phase was over.

"You know Tony. He is always so worried about figures that he will take as little time as possible over the briefing. If you agree, Geraldine, I could have a chat with Pandora to brief her, and explain our total concept, our philosophy." Nothing but constructive concern showed in Connie's voice, and Geraldine agreed to her kind offer.

Back in her office, Connie spoke briefly to Tony Andreotti, the advertising manager. She then called up the draft "Shopping" section for the forthcoming issue on her PC, and the facing editorial advertisers for the following issue, already approached by Bibi Sohnnental before her multiple fractures. The subject of the feature was to be Italy on the East Side. She asked her secretary to make a copy of the advertisers' list, and then call Pandora to her office.

An hour later, her secretary announced Miss Doyle. Connie went to her light box and switched it on, pretending to look at the shots of the American summer collections taken in the Maldives by Anahi Paivakis, the sensational Greek photographer she had discovered while in Paris for the last collections.

"Please sit down," she said to Pandora without turning around, pointing at the chair facing her desk. Connie inspected the transparencies for a few minutes, and then turned toward her visitor.

At the sight of Connie's blue-black hair cut into a severe bob, shaved eyebrows, black-and-white Kabuki makeup, black skin-tight dress, and steel jewelry, Pandora's first impression was that she was facing Cruella de Ville. However, Connie's mortuary look was belied by the warm smile that flashed briefly on her lips; a month later, Pandora would have been able to appreciate the very special honor of a smile from a higher-ranking colleague in an American fashion magazine, but she was still unaware of such fine points.

"My dear, I've heard so much about you from Geraldine that I was dying to meet you," said Connie, fixing an admiring glance on Pandora. She leaned forward, her elbows on the desk, her chin resting on her hands, a look of warm complicity in her eyes. "I'm supposed to brief you about your job, but I feel it's almost embarrassing. It reminds me of that charming saying in your country, 'teaching mother to suck eggs' or something like that, so expressive. Please tell me if you want me to explain the basics, but I really don't dare. One look at you is enough to make me realize that I would be insulting you."

Overwhelmed by the compliments, Pandora could not bring herself to contradict Connie. Geraldine had vaguely explained to her that her job was very simple, and would entail writing about interesting shops. Pandora just hoped that it would all become clearer in the course of the conversation.

"Here is the list of the F-E . . . ," as she uttered the abbreviation for "facing editorial," the code word for advertisers that have to be specifically mentioned in the text, with their ads placed on the opposite page, an expression that might justify a request for clarification from Pandora, Connie coughed violently and the initials were almost lost in the noisy spasm. ". . . Oh, I'm sorry, excuse me, advertisers for the next issue. As you can see, the subject is Italy on the East Side." She handed a sheet of paper to Pandora.

"I so regret that people have just not been willing to be more imaginative or creative with your section," Connie went on. "The scope could be immense. Just imagine, Italy, for instance . . ." She stopped for a moment. "I must restrain myself, and not put impossible ideas in your head, but I know that Mark Brody, our advertising director, is always keen on new angles." Fond memories of their affair a few years ago flashed through Connie's mind. "But it may not be easy with that section. Perhaps your predecessors gave little thought to the possibilities. I don't know, maybe a real journalist could do something much more exciting with it, but I will not bother you with my boring views, and I shouldn't. You must report to Tony Andreotti, the advertising manager, as soon as your material is ready. He is a very dynamic man." She did not consider it necessary to inform Pandora that his flashes of temper could justify the evacuation of the building, and the most frequent cause for them was work at variance with his expectations.

Connie then launched into an enraptured vision of what fashion meant in people's lives, putting much emphasis on the fact that fashion, far from being frivolous, was perhaps as important an aspect of culture as music or literature. Her passionate delivery was accompanied by much fluttering of hands and rolling of eyes. After ten minutes, she let Pandora go, and sent a memo to Geraldine confirming that the briefing had taken place.

Pandora could hardly wait to get back to her office and start planning the new section. Over the weekend, she checked old issues of the magazine, and understood what Connie had meant. The section was predictable, month after month going on about restaurants, clothes, and other everyday necessities, expensive but trivial. Pandora considered a number of options, and finally decided that her subject would be Italian music.

She spent the next three days in a fever of excitement, combing antique dealers and rare-book traders, from cozy little shops on Second Avenue to grand galleries in stone town houses in the Upper Seventies. It took her a day in the office to draft the two pages of copy, further polished at home in the evening and then redrafted the following morning. After much agonizing, she decided that she had done her best, and phoned Andreotti's secretary. She was asked to bring the copy upstairs immediately, because they were very close to the deadline.

She walked into Andreotti's office, terror clamping her stomach and anticipation of his praise making her heart jump. He did not stand up when she came in, just waved his hand toward the chair facing his desk, cigarette ash dropping on the papers in front of him. Pandora guessed that he was not very tall, but his one continuous eyebrow, the scowl and the deep lines on his face gave him a fearsome presence. As soon as she sat down, he held out his hand. Pandora gave him her draft, and waited.

He began to read it, then stopped and looked at her, his continuous eyebrow knotting into a frown. Pandora saw his face go red as he raised his closed fist and then brought it down, rattling the desk with terrifying force.

"Who the fuck cares about Puccini's desk or Aida's gold bra from the 1879 Milan performance, and who would want to buy them? How do you imagine I'm gonna get ads out of the jerks who sell them, you smartass?" Pandora began to mumble some explanation, but his ranting was unstoppable. He stood up and leaned across the desk, his hands flat on the desk top. His face almost dusky now.

"I'm fed up with all you cocktail-party queens who can't even write a fucking shopping list. Where do they find you? None of you has ever been good for anything other than acting snooty, but you're the tops, Miss Puccini. You've even put on a Brit accent!" He flung the papers onto Pandora's lap. "You'd better appear tomorrow at the same time with something the advertisers will appreciate. Now get out."

She collected her copy, stood up, and coolly walked out of the office, her head high as she swept past the giggling secretary, but as soon as she was outside the department she felt the hot flush on her face, and the tears pricking behind her eyelids. While waiting for the elevator she lost her control at last, and began to sob quietly.

Back in her office, she reread the section as published over the previous six issues, and suddenly realized that virtually all the shops mentioned had ads immediately adjacent to the text, or within the next few pages, and at last she understood the implications of the advertisers' list Connie had handed to her. She rushed out of the building and managed to visit all the shops on the list before closing time. The following morning she typed the copy in two hours flat and rushed it upstairs, where she left it with Andreotti's secretary.

A week went by. Finally Pandora phoned his secretary, who told her that if there had been any problems she would have heard from Tony. Pandora then checked past columns, wrote a list of possible subjects and city areas to cover and sent it to the advertising ogre for his approval. His secretary phoned to say that Tony had approved the list, and he liked the open-air party theme for her next article. Now the advertisers were lined up, the deadline was close, and this morning she had to face Andreotti for the second time. Their meeting was scheduled for 11:30.

She walked into her office, a larger than average stationery store with a superannuated desk in it. Its proximity to the copy editors' room gave it some credibility as office space, but the boxes of computer printout paper and the decor (a 1977 Revlon calendar) denied it. Still, it had a telephone. After checking her mail, an assortment of invitations to a few of the shops she had been to as well as many she had never heard of, she began to write a letter to her mother to take her mind off the imminent meeting. She had long lost the habit of making her mother party to anything that really mattered to her, and New York's small talk of the kind Geraldine excelled in would be incomprehensible to someone whose weekly highlight was an evening of bridge at a friend's.

She looked at the photographs of her mother and of Walsham Hall in the faux tortoiseshell frames on her desk. The frames were two of her many wedding presents and the only objects she had brought over from London. She preferred to keep them in her office; this was alien territory, and she needed family support.

To anyone else, the photographs would have seemed incongruous, lost in the impersonal room. They were meant for a little round table draped in Colefax & Fowler chintz, to be surrounded by a bowl of potpourri, miniature boxes, and Herend china. But to Pandora they were a link with people, things and times she loved.

She dropped her notepad on her desk, and stared at the photograph of Walsham. The Queen Anne brick house had been photographed in the afternoon, the sun shining on its graceful white turret with the weathervane on top, and the wisteria climbing up at the east corner. That was the magical house of her childhood, when her uncle Harold had been a kind eccentric, fond of his niece within the limitations of his stunted affections. His expressions of love were a sweet after Sunday lunch, permission to look at the pheasant chicks with him in the spring, and a doll for her birthday, always bought at Bond's in Norwich by Hayward, the driver.

Occasionally, Uncle Harold would take her for a walk with Whisky, his West Highland white terrier. They would always take the same route, up the path to the stables, then alongside the kitchen garden, its crumbling brick wall covered in honeysuckle, and into the wood until they came to the small Greek temple folly by the lake, a ruin almost buried in the rhododendron bushes. He would hardly say a word, other than perhaps to comment on the shrubs, trees, or birds they came across, and then they would walk back to the house. She had never been at ease with Uncle Harold when he was silent, and she was always slightly afraid of his gruff voice when he spoke because it seemed to her to imply disapproval, but she had loved those walks.

They had been the only semblance of a father-daughter relationship in the long gaps between holidays and Christmas, when her father would appear with a mountain of toys from F.A.O. Schwarz. She would not admit then that she looked forward to his visits, because doing so would have been a betrayal of her mother's martyrdom. Once he was there, the long silences and stilted conversation between them confirmed to her that Daddy was not easy, a point stressed by her mother often enough.

Uncle Harold was now a recluse living in shuttered rooms, dust settling on his models of great ships of the 1914 war. The only thing that brought some shine to his Parkinsonism-dulled eyes were cricket matches on television, and Mrs. Thomas's bubble-and-squeak. Mrs. Thomas had been the cook at Walsham for nearly forty years, and Uncle Harold had never tired of her overcooked nursery food.

Pandora glanced at her watch and realized that she had to be upstairs in five minutes. Relieved, she abandoned her letter and rushed out of her office.

The scene began as a rerun of their first meeting. She handed over her copy, Tony Andreotti waved his hand in the direction of the chair, she sat down and he began to read. He read through the whole piece, then smiled.

"This is great, Pandy, really great." He was genuinely pleased by her witty style, and by now he was also aware that he was dealing with a close friend of the Great Bitch Upstairs. He stood up, came around to her, and patted her on the shoulder.

"It's really good, honey. You and I are gonna do good things together in the future."

Pandora thought that perhaps he was more bearable when he was unfriendly.

She was about to ask if there was anything else to discuss when the door opened, and a Richard Gere look-alike walked in. He was tall, in his mid-thirties, broad-shouldered, and he had obviously been in the sun recently. Pandora found him very attractive and purposely kept her eyes on the framed photograph on the wall, a view of New York by night.

"Hi, Tony, I'm back from the Comores. You won't get many ads from there, but it's a great place." The visitor patted Tony's stomach. "You could do with some healthy living yourself. Maybe you should go there."

"The only good thing for my health is getting more ads," said Tony sourly. "Paying for your expenses during your fancy travels for nothing really kills me."

"Don't worry, I've also been to Sri Lanka and Tahiti. Lots of flabby credit-card holders on vacation there and a long list of multistory hotels to tap for you. Let me show you. . . ." He put a folder on Tony's desk, and opened it.

Pandora stood up.

"Excuse me, but I have another appointment," she said. If she hurried, she might be able to get a sandwich before there was a long line at the counter.

The man looked at her, then back at Tony.

"I have to go, too. Have a look at the file, and I'll phone you later." He held the door open for Pandora, and they left together. He began to talk as soon as they were out of the room.

"I'm Tom Cansino. I'm the travel editor; that's why you haven't seen me very often. Who are you? You are the first real-looking woman I've seen in this place for a very long time."

She hesitated for a second, wary of his instant charm but also of that particular reaction she had had since Johnny's departure whenever she came across an attractive man. There had to be life after Johnny. She kept her reply as terse as possible, but she adorned it with a friendly smile.

"I'm Pandora Doyle. I am in charge of the 'Shopping' section," she answered. They reached the elevators and, conscious of his proximity, she purposely averted her eyes from his.

"I'll take the stairs. It's getting late for me," she said, and began to walk toward the door.

"Don't walk so fast; I only go to the gym three times a week," he said, coming up behind her. As they reached the stairs, he bowed in an exaggerated way.

"I'll show you what a gentleman I am. First, have the handrail side, and second, please be my guest for lunch."

She smiled, and began to descend on the handrail side.

"I'm sorry, but I have a lunch engagement already, and I'm late."

Her voice echoed up the huge stairwell, just as she noticed through the windows that the sky was getting dark. She began to run.

Tom dithered. He had already run behind her once; twice in a row was once too often. She was great-looking, but she was not the next Calvin Klein girl.

Pandora realized that she had been too abrupt. He was nice, he was attractive, and she did not have many friends. She stopped at the landing, two floors below, and turned around.

"I would love to have lunch any other time." She beamed up at him, and rushed on.

ARIANNE de la Force answered the internal phone.

"The doorman just called to say that Miss Doyle is on her way up, Madame."

"Thank you, François. Show her to the library. No, perhaps it's better if you take her to the drawing room instead." It would be more difficult for this mousy journalist to ask probing questions while sitting in one of the grandest rooms in New York. Keeping your distance, putting people in their place, *de haut en bas:* these were useful tactics when dealing with bothersome small fry.

She took off her emerald rings and put them on her dressing table, then opened a drawer of her jewel case. After a quick look at the velvet tray where gems sat edge to edge, she picked up a diamond ring. The flawless stone was an inch square: Simón had surpassed his high standards of ostentatiousness when he had chosen it. She never wore it, but this girl seemed to notice jewelry. The ring would awe her, and could help to divert the conversation, if necessary. She slipped it on while glancing at the clock on the mantelpiece, then sat down and picked up a magazine from the pile on the low table. She looked at it until she was exactly fifteen minutes late, then left the room.

Sitting in one of the gilt armchairs ordered by Catherine the Great for the Winter Palace, Pandora felt as if she were waiting in the Wallace Collection. She had seen a few rooms like this in England, also full of exquisite furniture and paintings, but those were put together by generations of privilege; she was now staring at the raw power of money. Pandora was usually able to read many things about the owner by looking at a room, but not in this case, other than the fact that the mistress of the house was immensely rich and fond of eighteenth-century decor at its most magnificent. There were perfect flower arrangements where they should be, obviously placed by experts, but there were no photographs in silver frames of either loved ones or mighty personages, no piles of artfully arranged picture books on the low tables hinting at private predilections, no slip of taste betraying an object favored by the owner for personal reasons. There were none of the touches that even interior decorators allow to give the illusion of life to rooms meant to be used only for entertainment. Like Arianne at the party, the room was expensively elegant, impeccably mannered, and gave nothing away.

At last, one of the double doors flanking the fireplace was opened, and Arianne walked in. As Pandora stood up and watched her walk across the vast room, an enchanting smile on her face, she thought that most people take second place to their possessions; only a few outshine them.

"Sit down, please," Arianne said as she approached, her left hand outstretched in a casual gesture toward Pandora's seat, the diamond sparkling in the light for a second. "I'm so sorry to have kept you waiting, but I was on the phone and I couldn't get away." They sat, and the butler walked in with a silver and ivory tea set. He placed it on the table between them.

"Would you like a cup of tea? Or anything else?"

"I'd love some tea," said Pandora. "Thank you so much for seeing me. I've asked the photographer to be here at quarter to four."

Arianne poured the tea, and the butler took a cup to Pandora.

"Would Madame need anything else?" he asked.

"No, François, that will be all, thank you. When the photographer arrives, please show him in." Arianne stirred her tea, then raised her eyes. Her impassive face was a clear indication that she expected the interview to begin now.

Pandora opened her bag and pulled out a miniature tape recorder. "Do you mind if I use it? It's easier than taking notes. I wouldn't want to use up more of your time than necessary. I understand that you are going away soon."

"Of course I don't mind, and I appreciate your concern for my time. I'm leaving for Buenos Aires tomorrow. I am not involved in the day-to-day running of my business anymore, but I like to keep in touch. The sugar industry is at a difficult moment now."

Pandora was too polite to mention the curious contradiction between the purchase of a fifty-million-dollar painting and an industry in trouble.

"This room is magnificent. How did you start your collection?"

"I inherited most of it from my husband. He had agents all over Europe buying for him immediately after the war. He was like a magpie, but I don't think he ever saw most of the pieces; they were just stored away in warehouses. I only buy paintings. In fact, I only buy portraits."

"Why?" asked Pandora. She felt excited: this was an angle worth exploring. It gave her an opening into what this woman found interesting in people, or at least their painted images.

"I like them. I'm sorry that I cannot be more articulate about it. I just like them."

"Perhaps it might be easier to concentrate on one picture," Pandora said. "Why did you buy the *Portrait de Madame Claire?*"

Arianne stared at her.

"Who said I bought it?" she asked.

"But I saw you there!"

Arianne smiled. "You may have seen me, but you must have read the papers the following morning, and I was not mentioned. As a journalist, you should trust your colleagues. Sometimes I bid for friends who want to remain anonymous, and they do the same for me. Things are not always what they seem."

Arianne leaned forward, picked up her cup of tea, and took a sip. She turned her head toward the windows.

"The storm has cleared up, thank God. Would you like some more tea?"

"No, thank you," said Pandora, conscious that she was getting nowhere. She tried again.

"Were you born in Brazil?"

"I grew up there." Arianne was going to leave it at that, but then remembered Geraldine's comment about sending Pandora on a research trip. This girl was beginning to look like a pushover, but

Geraldine wasn't; better to feed her what she wanted rather than letting someone else scavenge over her past.

"My father had a *fazenda* not very far from Bahia. He grew spices. I can still remember the smell in the house, the cedar floors and the spices in the air." She proceeded to give Pandora a long description of life on the estate, the black maids dressed in white flounced dresses, the horse-drawn carriages. For a second she wondered if further embellishments were necessary, but Pandora's attentive expression reassured her, and she carried on for a while with her evocation of her childhood in rural Brazil. ". . . and I did all my schooling at home, with private tutors. It would have been unthinkable for us to go to school, my sister and I were so sheltered from the outside world. When I was eighteen, I was sent to finishing school in France. My mother was a favorite client of Balenciaga, and he offered me the opportunity to model his last collection. Then I met Simón. As perhaps you know, he died soon after our marriage. It was a terrible, terrible blow." She paused, her voice trailing away, as if the memory overwhelmed her, then she smiled. "Otherwise, I have had a very protected, privileged life." She crossed her arms, her left hand resting on her upper arm, the diamond in full view.

Pandora realized that this woman was more than apt at glossing over any subject while giving the impression of a personal conversation. Her sheltered childhood would make entertaining reading, but it was not enough for a profile. She decided to probe cautiously.

"I have been told that you had some serious trouble with guerrillas in Argentina. . . ." Arianne seemed unruffled by the reference, and Pandora went on. "It must have been a traumatic experience for you. Did it have any lasting consequences?"

Arianne picked up her cup of tea.

"That's a very old story. It couldn't have been so serious, since you see me here, in one piece. There were many similar episodes in Argentina at the time. If you want more details, you will find them in any newspaper library." She gave Pandora an apologetic smile.

"I know I'm a difficult interviewee, but you journalists seem to think that I have some fascinating story to tell. My life is about running my business. It might be of interest to the *Wall Street Journal,* but I fear I'm rather dull for *Chic.*"

Difficult maybe, but dull unlikely, Pandora thought. There had to be some way of cracking her glass cage. She decided to try a round-about approach.

"Is there a particular aspect of your work which interests you?" she asked, concealing her impatience. Arianne rolled her eyes.

"So, so many . . . ," she sighed. She suddenly leaned forward in her seat. "I'll tell you one particular aspect I'm sure you will find fascinating. . . ." She paused, as if to allow Pandora to take in fully the implications of what she was about to hear, then continued. "I'm very interested in Eurosterling bonds, and the future relationship between U.K. government and nongovernment stocks. There are major questions there. Are we going to see long-dated corporate issues maintain their value, or will the spread widen to dangerous levels? There could well be a flight into liquid, quality stocks; it all depends on the relationship between swap rates and bond spreads against gilts. . . ." She went on and on, until Pandora tried to stop her in desperation.

"Mrs. de la Force, perhaps our readers — " Arianne interrupted her with an imperious wave of her hand, balanced by a disarming smile.

"You must listen to this; it is very important. If we look at five-year swap rates . . ." The torrent of financial wisdom poured forth, and Pandora gave up. It would take time to crack Mrs. de la Force's facade, and hers was running out. The door opened and François came in, followed by a street-worn photographer carrying an aluminum case, his camera and flash dangling at the end of a wide shoulder strap.

Arianne stood up. "We'd better do the pictures now. I would be delighted to continue talking to you, but unfortunately I have so many things to do."

While Pandora switched off her tape recorder, Arianne struggled to conceal a grin; life would be so easy if all journalists were like this one. Arianne quickly posed for the photographer, standing next to the fireplace, her arm resting on the mantelpiece. Her elegance gave new life to the cliché pose of a society woman at home.

The photographer took several shots. He was in the process of explaining a different setup to Arianne, when a magnificent ormolu clock struck the hour. Arianne looked up.

"Oh dear, I am very sorry, but I'll have to leave you now. I hope you've got everything you need." She walked briskly toward the door and waited until the photographer packed his case, then held the door open.

They left the drawing room and Arianne led her visitors through the marble foyer. Pandora and the photographer stopped by the front door to say good-bye; Arianne felt almost magnanimous. She held out her hand.

"If there is anything else you need, just . . ."

She was interrupted by a crescendo of screams from the other end of the long gallery. A door opened and a naked girl burst through, followed by Charles Murdoch shouting at the top of his voice: "You little whore! You slut! So that's what they taught you in Switzerland, to suck the chauffeur's cock!" He threw a dog leash and collar on the black and white marble floor. ". . . And don't forget your props, you little pervert!"

The girl was sobbing violently, almost hysterical. ". . . and who are *you* to teach me anything? You are nothing, just a paid cunt-licker. . . . Where would you be if you didn't fuck my mother? I hate you, you shit!"

Pandora glanced at Arianne: her face was white, but her eyes were fearsome.

"Gloria!" screamed Arianne, walking toward her. "Enough! Behave yourself! You disgust me!"

The girl was now completely out of control. She turned toward Arianne, her eyes blazing.

"Oh, I disgust you, Mummy dearest. I'm so sorry! . . . Sorry to upset your stud . . . You, hypocrite, *you* are disgusted. . . . Tell me, my wonderful *mother,* what does Nana know about you and your precious secrets? I despise you . . . I loathe you . . . !" Her voice became higher and higher until, in a frenzy, she picked up the huge Ming vase on the console and smashed it onto the marble floor.

"François! François!" called Arianne. Charles tried to restrain Gloria, who bit his hand until it bled. He roared with pain, then punched her in the stomach. Gloria fell on her knees, gasping for air.

Pandora was repelled by the sight. "Let's go," she whispered to the photographer, who was leering at Gloria's nakedness. He did not budge. She tried to touch his arm to catch his attention, but he moved suddenly, and her hand fell on his camera instead, pressing the shutter. The brutal white light from the flash filled the gallery for a blinding second, bathing the smashed vase, the naked girl, and Arianne's horrified expression in its glare. The butler put his jacket over Gloria's shoulders, and led her away. Pandora found the ensuing silence even more difficult to stand than the scene before.

"We'd better go now. . . ." Her timid voice echoed down the gallery. Charles Murdoch looked at her, then turned around and walked out, slamming the door behind him. Arianne rushed to Pandora.

"My dear, I'm so embarrassed. I hope you will forgive me for this awful incident. Perhaps the best thing is if we all forget that it ever took place, don't you think? I'll call you as soon as I am back. We must get together. Would you like to come to Venice with us? Or maybe do the Aegean on the yacht?" She seemed to be getting no response: what the hell was this girl going to write? She had heard about Nana, God damn it, she had heard about Nana. . . . And that picture. It would probably be in every tabloid from coast to coast by tomorrow morning.

Arianne felt fear growing in her. She thought of grabbing the camera to pull the film out, but the last thing she wanted was this obnoxious man suing her for assault: she was in America. She carried on in an ingratiating voice. "I'm sure you don't want to take those pictures back to your office. Why don't we take better ones tomorrow morning? I could wear my new Valentinos. Would you like to give me the film now?" She got no reaction. Fear grew into panic, shattering her control for a moment. "I noticed you admiring my ring while we talked," she went on. She took the ring off and held it out to Pandora. "Would you like it? I hardly ever wear it, I've got so many. . . ."

Pandora wondered why this icon of perfection was shaken to the point of making ridiculous offers. It could not just be the picture. It had to be something else, but she no longer cared to find out; she could not stand this place a second longer.

"No, thank you," she said. She gently pushed the photographer, and they stepped into the waiting elevator.

Arianne heard the elevator's door shut behind them. She began to shiver violently. Shoulders hunched, she closed her eyes and wrapped her arms about herself tightly as if protecting herself from an imminent blow. Then suddenly she opened her eyes in a ferocious glare, ashamed of her performance, ashamed of herself. Enough self-pity. Head high, she walked to the nearest telephone.

GERALDINE switched on the intercom to her secretary.

"Vanessa, get me the reception desk downstairs, please. Immediately. And find out who the photographer was who went to Mrs. de la Force's apartment with Pandora Doyle."

She leaned back in her chair. Her ear was still buzzing from Solly's outburst over the telephone. Bob Chalmers had phoned him to say that Arianne was so upset by a *Chic* journalist and photographer that she was reconsidering the Los Milagros deal, and had asked Bob to approach Lord Blomfield. The incident had just taken place. Arianne would review her decision only if the undeveloped film shot at her apartment was returned to her at once, and nothing was published about the incident.

Los Milagros was to be Europe's largest shopping mall, outside Madrid, on land that belonged to a de la Force company. Solly had been looking for the right opportunity to branch into Europe, and Bob Chalmers had put him in touch with Arianne. After a year of careful negotiations, the deal was almost signed. The dinner extravaganza had been a covert attempt to strengthen the personal contact between them. Paloma Picasso was wonderful, but Solly would not have spent thirty thousand dollars in one evening to entertain the Twelve Disciples, let alone her, unless it would show a profit somewhere.

Geraldine had played a role in these maneuvers, by underlining to Arianne the potential nuisance value of her magazine. Pandora had been perfect for the charade: a real journalist would have been dangerous, and difficult to control if the scent of blood was in the air. Geraldine had no intention of shattering her relationship with Arianne; a slight rattle was enough for her purpose. Two days after the party, Bob had phoned Solly to say that Arianne would sign the agreement before going away but now, obviously, she had to be appeased.

Geraldine's phone buzzed.

"I've got Luke at the reception desk for you, Miss Freeman. The photographer is Robert Lopinski."

"Thank you, Vanessa." There was a click in the line, then she heard the Southern drawl. "Good afternoon, Miss Freeman."

"Good afternoon, Luke. As soon as Miss Doyle and Mr. Lopinski come through the door, you bring them straight here. Don't just *send* them here; you accompany them, and see that they don't stop anywhere on the way up."

"They are coming through the door right now, Miss Freeman."

A moment later Vanessa showed them in. Geraldine stood up behind her desk, her hand outstretched, palm upward. Pandora had never seen Geraldine looking so stern.

"Now, Bob, you don't say a word, and you give me the film you shot at Mrs. de la Force's apartment. You then go back to your lab, and I'll do my best to forget this episode."

While he rolled the film back and took it out of the camera, she addressed Pandora, ice in her voice.

"I cannot tell you how displeased I am by what has happened." She took the film from Bob, dismissed him with a nod, and turned to Pandora. "You must learn that there is no point in upsetting people unnecessarily. I am telling you I will not tolerate . . ." As soon as the door closed behind Bob, she left her desk and rushed to Pandora.

"Sweetheart, as they say in the best circles, you must have her by the snatch!" She roared with laughter. "Let's sit down. I can't wait to hear all about it. What the hell did you find out?"

5

New York
April 1987

$\mathcal{T}$HE photograph showed the most beautiful evening dress Pandora had ever seen, a sculpture in fabric as stunning as the woman modeling it. The caption pasted at the bottom read: "N° 30 — *Robe du Soir en satin bleu* — *Collection Printemps/Eté 1968*," and the back of the picture was stamped "*Balenciaga — Reproduction interdite.*"

The pictures in the photo-library file were spread on her desk. There were a few others from the last Balenciaga collection in 1968, and an agency picture of "Arianne, Paris' latest star model, and Simón de la Force, South American magnate, arriving at Maxim's — December 1968." The other photographs, four or five in total, had all been taken during the summer of 1976, on the South of France social circuit.

Pandora was trying to replace the photographs returned by Geraldine. Arianne's archive pictures were dated by her clothes and hair style but not by her looks, which had barely changed over twenty years. Pandora's eye was caught by a head-and-shoulders shot of Arianne looking entrancing in a fruits and flowers headdress: "Bal de têtes, Villa Alexander, Cannes, July 1976." The costume gave a timeless quality to the photograph, and she set it aside.

However, it was the picture with Simón de la Force that really interested her. It was a standard paparazzo shot: the couple surprised as they were stepping out of a shiny black limousine. Simón de la Force's right hand was stretched toward the camera in an attempt to block the lens, an enormous cigar between his fingers, and an angry expression on his face.

The face would have been awesome even when smiling. There was an Indian cast to the features, and the hooded eyes blazed an iguanalike malevolence. The superb cut of the Savile Row suit was defeated by his barrel-chested body, a vicious fairground wrestler ill at ease in his Sunday finery.

Arianne was behind him, but this did not conceal the fact that he was noticeably shorter than his companion. She looked impossibly thin in the simplest of black dresses and a chinchilla jacket, a string of huge pearls around her neck. The festive air, suggested by the smiling doorman and the edge of the canopy with its Art Nouveau lettering, was denied by the absent look in her eyes.

The library pictures had been Geraldine's idea. After she had heard the details of the incident, she had been as helpful as ever. She encouraged Pandora to draft the piece, but suggested that they wait for a couple of days.

"I may not hear anything else from dear Mrs. de la Force, in which case we write a nice flattering profile, but if there is any more damning criticism of you from her, darling, then we do a hatchet job. We keep mum about her little darling's pastimes, but you could just hint at the starving peasants while Madam shops. Nothing heavy duty, of course, gloves on all the time." In the meantime, Pandora could check the library for pictures, or any additional information useful for the piece. She had felt grateful for Geraldine's support.

She was putting the pictures back in the folder when the phone rang.

"Are you free for lunch, or shall I join the line?" She recognized the voice, and smiled. "It's Tom, Tom Cansino. Please say yes."

She was flattered. She found him attractive, but that worried her. She could probably do with a little flirtation but she feared involvement, and she was too vulnerable still to get involved. Loneliness could be reassuringly snug.

"I'd love to have lunch with you, but I have to finish something for Geraldine. Thank you very much for the thought though; it's *so* kind of you." She masked the nagging edge of regret behind her punctiliously polite refusal, delivered in her best British-style apologetic manner.

"My goodness, that *is* heavy-duty name-dropping. Maybe I should learn to keep my place. Don't work too hard," he said cheerfully, and hung up.

As soon as she put the receiver down, she wished she had been less cautious. She thought for a moment, then impulsively picked up the office directory, and dialed Tom's extension. Somebody else answered it. "He has just left for lunch," the voice said.

She grabbed her coat and bag, and ran downstairs as fast as she could. She rushed through the door, and saw him walking down Madison Avenue. He turned into Fifty-third Street.

She caught up with him, and he contrived to retain his moody countenance.

"I thought you were working," he said acidly.

"You would be amazed at how *incredibly* fast I work," she replied with a smile. He looked at her, and then he smiled too.

"Sure," he said, "but I was going to take you to Le Cirque, and I canceled my reservation when you turned me down. The best I can offer now is Between the Bread."

"I've never been to either, so they are both the same to me," said Pandora. It was a crisp New York day. As they walked past Paley Park, the waterfall was sparkling in the sunshine. She glanced at him for a second, and was glad to have changed her mind. They stopped at the traffic light, and she was suddenly full of excitement at the sight of the palisade of buildings lining into the horizon, and the sudden expanse of sky over the park. She had had this feeling the first time she saw Fifth Avenue just before Christmas, as a little girl holding her father's hand; by now it was difficult to say if she still reacted to one of the world's great city views, no matter how familiar, or to the memory of a simple, wondrous emotion, only possible when places are still seen through unjaded eyes.

The light turned green. Tom held her arm, and they crossed the avenue. She was conscious of his touch.

"I will now tell you my favorite story for tourists," Tom said as they walked past Saint Thomas' Church. "This was the smartest church in New York at the turn of the century, and a lot of those

American girls with trunkfuls of greenbacks married here. There was an Italian stonemason working at the church when it was rebuilt, and he carved a dollar —" Two small boys ran up to them from behind, and hugged Tom's legs.

"Daddy! Daddy!" they shouted, jumping up and down.

"What are you doing here?" asked Tom incredulously. "I was going to phone you tonight. I thought we could go fishing on Sunday." He picked them both up in his arms.

"Mommy brought us to see Grandma. She's taking us to the movies this afternoon." A slim and, to Pandora's eye, very American-looking, girl caught up with them. She quickly scanned Pandora, then turned to Tom.

"Hi, this *is* a surprise," said Tom.

"Yes, it is. Tommy, Ben, please get down; it's time for lunch now."

The boys did not move. One of them hugged Tom. "Daddy, please have lunch with us. Please, Daddy, *please.*"

The woman seemed amused by Tom's obvious discomfort. Noticing it, Pandora glanced at her watch. "It's getting late. I think I'd better go." One of the children had begun to mess up Tom's hair, while the other pulled at his tie.

"I'll talk to you later," said Tom. "Maybe we can go to the movies one evening."

Pandora turned around and crossed the avenue again. And maybe not, she thought.

THEIR meeting at an end, Bob Chalmers collected his papers and locked his briefcase. Arianne led the way out of the room.

". . . and that settles Los Milagros. Please phone Solly, and arrange to sign the agreement today, Bob."

"I will. I'm glad that the problem with the magazine was solved. I thought the girl seemed very nice at Geraldine's party."

Arianne looked at him knowingly.

"It was pretty obvious that you did, and I think Betty noticed it also. It must be difficult to be your wife, Bob."

"Not at all. Every time I'm found out after a one-night stand, Betty goes to Bill Blass and buys a couple of evening dresses. She's told me that if she had to really start worrying about it, then she'd go to Bulgari, for the heavy-duty stuff. I can't afford to have a serious affair, but now you're putting ideas into my head. Maybe you can organize a small lunch when you are back, and ask that charming girl. I must be entitled to some gratitude for the brilliant deal I organized for you at Los Milagros."

Arianne raised her hands in mock horror.

"Are you suggesting that I become your procuress? You know how fond of Betty I am." She smiled slyly. "But maybe I ought to give a lunch for you when I come back. I haven't done much entertaining lately."

"I'll look forward to it." As they approached the door, Bob stopped in front of an elaborate flower arrangement on top of a marble console. "Where is your beautiful vase?" he asked.

"With the restorers. One of my idiotic maids must have been thinking about her boyfriend while dusting it. She dropped it on the floor," Arianne said casually.

"I'm sorry to hear that. Such a marvelous piece."

Arianne patted him on the arm, and smiled.

"You will have to make me an extra million, Bob, and then I will be able to buy another one." Her tone indicated that the subject was closed. He opened the door, and leaned forward to kiss her cheek.

"Have a good trip. I'll call you tomorrow morning." She closed the door behind him.

She returned to the library and sat at her desk, absentmindedly toying with the ivory letter opener. She closed her eyes and sighed. For almost twenty years she had never looked back. Her money had become her shield. But it was just a greenhouse, an exquisite world protected by a layer of thin glass, and now Charles was throwing pebbles at it.

She picked up the phone, and dialed Charles's bedroom extension. He answered, with a somnolent voice.

"Come to the library immediately. I have to talk to you."

"What's the time?" he asked.

"Late enough. I'm leaving in half an hour."

Charles appeared a few moments later, dressed in his silk dressing gown. A handsome man wearing only his dressing gown can be a sexual turn-on or an endearing picture of everyday domesticity. To Arianne, he was simply repellent.

Charles picked up the phone, asked for coffee, and sat down on the sofa. Arianne fixed her eyes on him.

"I've been thinking about your proposal . . ." Someone knocked at the door, and she stopped. After a moment, François came in with a silver coffee service. He placed it in front of Charles and left the room.

Charles poured coffee into the gilt-edged Sevres cup, and then concentrated on Arianne, waiting for her to go on.

"I have given a lot of thought to what you said. We know the facts, and I have to admit that you have a very strong hand." Both her head and her voice had dropped as she spoke. When she raised her face, she noticed a gleam of triumph in his eyes. She might enjoy this conversation, after all.

"Your analysis was entirely correct with regard to your position, but you forced me to think about mine and, much more important, yours in relation to mine." He sensed her impending answer, but had lost his grasp on her thoughts.

"There is one real threat you hold over me. Not publicity, because what you would get paid for the story is nothing when compared to what you already get by remaining silent. Your only option is to go to Simón's family. They can claim my money once they know what you have to tell them, but they cannot pay you the sort of figure you would want until they win the case. You'll have to drop your trump card before the bets are on the table."

She glanced at the clock on the mantelpiece. She had to leave in fifteen minutes.

"You are worried about your chances of upholding your rights in court if I were to change my will now and provide for you. Maybe you are right, but they are certainly higher than your chances would be if you have to fight Simón's family in court, if they decide not to honor whatever unsavory agreement you might strike with them. If they have any sense, they will not sign anything outside Argentina, and I would not rate your chances in court there against the de la Forces very high, once they became the richest family in the country."

She checked the time again; she ought to go now.

"Alternatively, we carry on as if these conversations had never taken place, except that I will change my will. You mentioned your concern about the passage of time, and I can understand it. But you shouldn't worry about the future, my dear, and you've never struck me as the worrying type. I'll see you in a few days." She turned around and walked out of the room.

"Give my regards to Nana. I'm sure you two will have a great time talking about the good old days," Charles said venomously as she left, but Arianne did not hear him.

Charles stood up, walked to the drinks tray, and poured himself a large Scotch. Arianne was right: he was not particularly keen on a dubious deal with the de la Forces. Only Arianne's fear had made their bargain possible at the beginning, but apparently she had learned to live with it after twelve years, enabling her to call his bluff. But he had not been bluffing when he had told her about the vulnerability of his position, *his* fear of time running out.

It was worse than that, though. He still had sufficient years ahead of him to find another rich woman, more than likely far less glamorous than Arianne, certainly less rich, but equally capable of providing the life-style he coveted. But he could no longer stomach the chase, the perpetual pretense. With Arianne, he was able to make love to any woman he fancied as long as he kept it quiet. His relationship with another woman would have to be based on the fallacy of her attractiveness, his daily praise of her beauty and the nightly evidence of his admiration. His years with Arianne had made him lose the dedication required to make a woman feel wanted if he didn't mean it.

Only his own money, or somebody else's under his control, was the answer. He stopped in midthought. The solution was so simple, so pristinely simple. The realization warmed his blood as effectively as the Scotch.

Arianne was right. Charles needn't worry about the future. There was Gloria. Young, screwed-up, silly Gloria.

NANA walked slowly up the stairs. It took her quite a while to reach the top, and she was breathing hard. She was getting too old for this task, but Arianne did not allow anyone but Nana to come into her bedroom here at "La Encantada," her favorite room in her favorite house. It was locked while Arianne was away, but she would be here any moment now, and Nana wanted to make sure that everything was tidy. Her task ahead of her, she sat in the armchair by the fireplace to catch her breath.

The bedroom occupied almost the whole of the top floor of the tower. It was very plainly decorated. The paneled walls matched the dark wood of the carved ceiling and the wide floorboards. The furniture was Brazilian, from colonial days: a large bed, a wardrobe, and a dressing table, all in solid mahogany almost black with age, waxed by Nana every week. A few chairs, a bookcase, a bedside table: that was all. No curtains at the windows, no pictures on the walls, just two photographs in silver frames on the dressing table.

Nana struggled to stand up again. She began to dust the room. It was unnecessary, because she had done it in the morning, but at her age routine had become almost obsessive, a day-to-day process to keep death away.

She had never asked why she was the only one allowed in the room. Nana already knew too much. Arianne needed her silence, she needed Arianne's protection. That was their bargain, and they had both kept it.

Nana polished the rock crystal toilet set on the dressing table. As usual, her eye was caught by the carved monogram "A." She had accepted so much and yet the name, even the initial, still distressed her.

She picked up one of the silver frames, gently rubbing it with her cloth. She had seen the picture a million times but she looked at it again. Little Gloria, so happy. She did not want to think about Gloria; it was too painful.

She polished the other frame on the table. It held a cracked old photograph in fading grays, the work of some street photographer. The mountainous background had the unmistakable outline of Rio de Janeiro's *morros*. The scene had been shot in a large public square, its paths lined by tall, slim palm trees, an equestrian statue in the center. On the monument's steps, a poorly dressed woman held two children by the hand. Her faintly mulatto face would have been beautiful, even stunning, if she had looked less worn. The children were very young. When she had first seen the photograph, Nana had guessed that the older girl was about five years old, the other one perhaps three or four. Both girls bore a striking resemblance to their mother. The woman wore a tattered dress outside fashion, but judging from the people in the background, the photograph must have been taken sometime around 1950.

She had never asked about this photograph, not even when she saw it for the first time in Paris, many years ago. Then, as now, she did not want to know any more. It was difficult enough to live with her own ghosts.

WHILE she was being driven through the airport, Arianne studied the back of the new chauffeur's head. François had found him through the Christian Welfare Association; the man had both an impeccable record as a driver and a speech impediment. She took in the gray hair, the wrinkled neck, and the narrow shoulders. This man was obviously much more suitable than the last one, and she made a mental note to raise François's pay on her return to New York.

Out of the window, she could now see the familiar shape of *Sugar One*. Of all her possessions, the plane and "La Encantada" were the ones she valued most. The key to her life had been to run away: from what she was, from where she was, from her husband. Then it had been necessary to stand her ground, and she had won. She did not need to run away anymore, but she enjoyed the knowledge that she had the means for flight. "La Encantada," the absurdity of a Moorish castle by the Uruguayan coast, was her refuge from reality, *Sugar One* her magic carpet.

The driver managed to get out of the car slowly and open her door. Arianne waited impatiently. It had taken her years to get used to having small things done for her by servants. She had learned to adapt her own tempo to it, but any change in the usual pace reawakened her old instincts.

She rushed up the steps and walked into the plane. As usual, María and José were waiting for her. As soon as she was inside, María closed the airplane's door. By the time Arianne had reached her private quarters at the front of the cabin, the ground staff had removed the steps. As soon as he heard Arianne was on board, the pilot started the engines.

In the cockpit, the copilot confirmed to the control tower that they were about to taxi toward the runway holding point. Arianne was now in her leather armchair, her seat belt on. José informed the cockpit that they were ready.

As Arianne sprayed a thin mist of Evian mineral water on her face to protect it from dehydration, the mixture of kerosene and air compressed to its limit flared inside the combustion chambers, the searing exhaust rushing out of the engines. Inside the cabin, Arianne felt a slight chill, and asked María for her cashmere shawl. Then she flicked through Italian *Vogue.*

The Boeing 737 began to move very slowly. Ninety-eight feet long, with a wingspan of almost ninety feet, the huge machine burned nearly two pints of fuel per second just to cruise along the tarmac while its solitary passenger admired Gianfranco Ferre's sashed shirts, so amusing for holiday evenings. The airplane reached the holding point and stopped. Engines running, the Fowler flaps and slats in takeoff position, the captain waited for the control tower's clearance.

Arianne did not like the moment just before takeoff: it made her feel vulnerable. Her whole life was about being in control, and now she was not. Anxious for distraction, she noticed that Charles's Walkman was in one of the pigeonholes by her seat. She picked it up and put the headphones on. Turning the volume knob up, she pressed "Play" and closed her eyes. She did not bother to look at the tape; any music would do. She just needed to close her eyes, and let her mind drift away for a few minutes.

Beethoven's Ninth Symphony, the great choral setting of the "Ode to Joy," burst within her head. She tore the headphones off as if they had burned her, trembling uncontrollably for a moment. For a moment she thought that Charles had set the whole thing up to hurt her, a diabolical plot to hit her with one of her worst memories at the moment when she would be most vulnerable, but then she realized that it was not possible. Only Nana could know what nightmares were unleashed by that particular music.

At last, the pilot received takeoff clearance from the tower. Engines at full throttle, brakes released, *Sugar One* rushed forward. The outside world began to shoot past Arianne's window like a speeded-up film, but she paid no attention. Her eyes tightly shut, she was sobbing quietly, as her memories ricocheted in her mind.

The plane roared forward at vertiginous speed now. The pilot carefully eased back the control wheel, and *Sugar One* began to climb toward the cloudless sky. Her back pressed to the seat by the acceleration, Arianne's eyes were also fixed on the sky, but she did not see it, nor the ocean below, the same ocean that thousands of miles southward washed the beaches of her childhood. The carefully built fortress in her mind, untouched for so long, had been demolished in seconds by her fear of flying and the "Ode to Joy." A prisoner on her magic carpet, she remembered. She remembered Florinda, she remembered Silvia, she remembered Brazil.

Part Two

6

Rio de Janeiro
March 1957

"Mamãe! Mamãe!"

The terrified shriek broke the quiet of the night. Carlota Souza jumped up from the rags spread on the dirt floor, and fumbled in the dark until she found the torch.

Aiming the light at her sleeping children, she saw an enormous black rat run toward a dark corner. But it was Silvia's leg, bleeding where the rat had nibbled at it, that made her cry out in horror. She picked up the bottle of *cachaça* from the upturned crate, and rushed to the girl.

Silvia flung her skinny arms around her mother, sobbing hysterically while Carlota poured rum on the wound, then held the child tightly against her, kissing her head again and again.

Florinda had also been wakened by her sister's anguished scream. She leapt to her feet and lit a candle. Then, eyes blazing, she picked up two long sticks, and cornered the scurrying rat. She pinned it to the dirt floor with one of the sticks, and savagely hit it with the other. She beat the repulsive creature until one of its eyes popped out of its socket, and blood dripped through its sharp, clenched teeth. The furry body twitched in its last convulsions, then its squeals ceased. Florinda picked up the limp remains by the long tail, pushed aside the corrugated sheet which served as a door, and flung the dead rat down the hill. She hoped it would land in the garden of one of the nice houses at the bottom of the almost vertical cliff. Florinda was only ten years old, but she had already learned to hate.

She went back inside, into the damp heat of the shack, and lay down again on her pile of newspapers and rags. Her sister was still weeping. "Shut up, you sissy, I want to sleep!" Florinda shouted at her before closing her eyes.

In the dark, holding her moaning child, Carlota prayed for rain. Only a downpour would cool the overheated *favela*, wash away the turds on the dirt paths, make life a bit more bearable.

Life had never been kind to Carlota. She looked like a middle-aged woman, but she had been born only twenty-seven years ago, on an estate in Pernambuco, the daughter of one of the women who cooked for the workers in the estate's *cantina*. Her mother had not been able to tell her who her father was. In fact, she had been able to tell her very little about anything, and Carlota had not had much schooling either. The local priest attempted to run a school on Sundays, but she was rarely able to attend.

She grew up to be a stunningly beautiful girl, as her mother had once been. Carlota's looks and unusual height were the result of hundreds of years of racial mixing. The Indian blood showed in her straight blue-black hair and her slanted eyes, her black ancestors in the high cheekbones and the slenderness of her body, and generations of white Portuguese masters in the pale honey color of her eyes and her olive skin. But beauty was a handicap for women like Carlota; hard work would destroy it before it could be used as a tool of escape from her miserable life and, for a brief period, it would make her too noticeable to the men around her.

In Carlota's case, eleven years ago it had brought her to the attention of one of the gangs of migrant laborers seasonally hired to harvest the sugarcane. Their job finished, most of their pay went into a last-night celebration at the dusty local bar, a few miles down the road to Natal. After many rounds of drinks and tales of sexual prowess, they walked out into the hot, damp air of the tropical night. Singing and shouting obscenities, they went to the hut where Carlota and her mother lived and kicked the door down.

Her mother tried to resist. It was a mistake. Her struggle did not save Carlota, and one of the many blows she received broke her neck. The men threw Carlota onto the bed, where she was a toy for the use of the drunken gang until the morning, when they finally left, after tying her up and gagging her.

It was while waiting for someone to come and release her, the bed damp with her own blood, the smell of men burning her nostrils, that Carlota made up her mind. After her mother was buried in the small cemetery by the whitewashed chapel, she went home and removed the slim wad of cruzeiro notes hidden in a tin. Her mother's savings would pay for her trip to Rio, to a new life, to freedom.

The savings barely covered the cost of the third-class train fare, and it took Carlota four days to make the journey. She finally arrived in the enormous city; she had no idea what to do or where to go, and her money had run out.

It was nearly dark when she left the station. Terrified, she crossed the wide avenue outside the station, and wandered into a park which reminded her of the scenery she knew, the fichu trees with their huge roots above the ground, the little agoutis playfully running on the grass. "Campo de Santana," said the enameled metal sign, but she could not read it.

She settled down on a bench, but was awakened in the middle of the night by a torch shining in her eyes. A policeman, his coarse face barely visible in the dark, asked for her papers, and began questioning her. When she had finished her story, he pulled out a notebook, gave her the address of a domestic employment agency, and let her go.

The following morning she went to the Vargas de Moreira Agency, and by the afternoon she was employed as a maid in a beautiful house in the Rua Redentor, near Ipanema Beach. The family was very nice. The *senhor* was an executive in a big company with a difficult name; the *senhora* slept late in the morning, and took the children to the beach in the afternoon. Carlota did all the housework other than the shopping, cooking, and kitchen work, which was done by Otilia, the cook.

For the first time in her life, she had a small room to herself and the use of a bathroom with running water. It was her job to clean the bathroom; Otilia, who shared it, purposely splashed water on the floor every time she used it, but Carlota did not mind. She was happy. When she was paid at the end of the month, she spent a considerable sum on a bathing suit, and she was then able to go to the beach with Otilia on Sundays, their day off.

In the joyfully sensual atmosphere of a Rio beach, a girl like

Carlota would not go unnoticed, but no matter how friendly the invitation, how funny the remark, she was not interested. The pervasive samba beat, the primevally shaped mountains, the oiled bodies under the sun, everything was redolent of sex, but not for Carlota. When smiling men leaned down to talk to her, the sight of their hairy chests frightened her.

Her monthly bleeding stopped. Her mother had told her once that this bleeding was something that happened to women: she guessed that its disappearance must be due to the change of place, that women living in big cities were smart and did not have the same troubles as women in the countryside.

Her breasts swelled up, and she began to have difficulty in doing up the buttons of her uniform over her waist. One morning the *senhora* told her that she wanted to talk to her. Carlota was nonplussed at first, then embarrassed by the *senhora*'s questions.

That evening, one of the *senhor*'s many cousins, a doctor, was asked to dinner with his wife. Just before dinner, Carlota was told that the doctor was going to check her over. She found the examination unpleasant, but it did not take long. The doctor told her she was expecting a baby.

The following morning the *senhora* told Carlota that she was shocked by her irresponsibility, and that she could not employ someone so unreliable in her home, but she was kind and did not want to upset a girl in Carlota's condition. Carlota could stay until the *senhora* found a reliable replacement for her. Four days later, the new maid moved in.

Her few belongings in a cardboard box, her wages in her pocket, Carlota walked back to the agency. The woman at the desk took one look at her and told her that she was no longer suitable for their clients.

She left the building, the midday crowd rushing around her, feeling desperately alone. She walked for a long time until she found the station. She had decided to go back home, but she was told that there was no train until the afternoon.

Longing for a familiar place, she went into the park across the avenue, and found her bench. She sat down, stretching her aching legs. Suddenly the full extent of her predicament became obvious to her.

There was nobody waiting for her back home. She did not even have a home; she had nothing. How would she be able to look after her baby? Lonely and very miserable, she burst into tears.

The sight of this unhappy young girl caught the eye of many passersby; some were moved, some were intrigued, most were indifferent. But one of them took one look, and accurately assessed the situation. Chico Ribeiro had seen this scene many times before, and he knew exactly what to do.

He sat next to Carlota and said, "Come on, there's nothing to worry about," again and again, wiping away her tears with his heavily scented handkerchief. Carlota had never seen a young man with so many gold chains, wearing such magnificent white crocodile shoes with beautiful Cuban heels.

Chico patted her hand, and her relief at another human being's concern for her was overwhelming. Carlota buried her face in his shoulder, crying out her despair. He put his arm around her, and helped her to sit up again. It was the easiest thing in the world to take her money from her pocket.

Chico muttered soothing words until she calmed down. Then he glanced at his gold watch, said, "My God, I must rush," and left, wishing Carlota good luck. He did not go far, just far enough to find a bush to hide behind while keeping watch on Carlota. After a while, she stood up and walked away, disappearing from his sight. It didn't matter; Chico knew she would come back.

He only had to wait for fifteen minutes. Her face was a mask of fear; she crawled on her knees around the bench, looking at the grass behind it, raking the gravel under it with her fingers. He could almost hear her sobs. At last, she sat down, her hands covering her face.

Chico walked toward her.

"You're still here! *Tudo bem?*" he asked cheerfully. The traditional "Everything all right?" Rio greeting felt like the stab of a knife to Carlota.

"Don't go, *senhor*, please don't go," she begged him.

He did not go. Far from it; he took over her life. When he heard about Carlota's problems, he immediately suggested that she move in with his fiancée until she found a job and somewhere to live.

Carlota could not believe her luck, and followed him to his car, clutching her cardboard box.

The fiancée lived in a small apartment near Maua Square, in the dock area. She greeted Carlota warmly, and told her that her name was Lula. She asked Carlota to come with her to the kitchen, where she was cooking supper. She emphatically refused Carlota's offer to help with the cooking, and listened sympathetically as Carlota told her her sad story. When they sat down at the table, Carlota was suddenly aware of her hunger, and immediately dove into the steaming plate of steak, rice, and fried bananas in front of her, a feast inconceivable a few hours ago. Lula said that since Carlota had had experience in domestic work, maybe she would be interested in a job in the exclusive institute that she managed. The girl who was in charge of domestic chores had just left. Carlota accepted immediately, full of gratitude for Chico and Lula's kindness. That night, Carlota slept on some cushions on the sitting-room floor.

The next morning, Chico drove them to a house in a run-down section of the district. Lula quickly scanned the street before opening the door, and pushed Carlota inside. The narrow hallway led to a steep flight of steps, harshly lit by a naked bulb. The cheap scent in the air hardly concealed the miasma of cat piss, and they could hear the sound of samba from a radio somewhere in the house.

As they climbed the stairs, a mulatto girl walked across the first floor landing. She was wearing very high-heeled sandals and nothing else, her large breasts partly concealed by the enameled wash bowl she carried with both hands. She looked down the stairs, and warmly greeted Lula without stopping. Carlota heard her open a door, followed by the splashing of liquid in a sink.

A moment later, the girl returned, holding the empty bowl. Lula introduced her to Carlota; her name was Nerinha. A door at the end of a corridor opened and a blond sailor appeared. He shyly said "Good-bye" as he walked past. Nerinha pursed her lips and held her breasts up, blocking his way and thrusting her bosom against his chest.

"*Ingrato,* make present, dollars, Nerinha all night, *sim?*" The boy pulled out a note from his pocket, handed it to Nerinha, and then left as fast as he could.

"These American boys . . . ," she said, rolling her eyes. Nerinha folded the note carefully. She was about to tuck it under her left breast, when Lula snatched it away with a smile, and put it in her pocket.

Carlota settled in quickly. There were two other girls in the house: Mimosa, who came from Ceará, and Magnolia, who had been born in Pelotas and kept two cats, Café, a brown mean-looking tom, and Leite, a fat, placid white. Each girl had her own room off the second-floor corridor, the glazed doors obscured by flowered curtains. Carlota's was a small attic, accessible by steep stairs next to the kitchen. It was impossibly hot at night, even when the breeze blew in from the harbor, but Carlota was proud to have her own room again. Her job was to cook for the girls, wash the floors, and make the beds.

Carlota's gratitude was the first step in Chico's plan. At present, she was not very useful to him. But he could afford to wait until she was able to offer the full range of services to his customers. And the baby would be useful for his other business, the beggars' ring. Once the child was born, and under Chico's control, Carlota would be willing to do whatever he wanted her to do.

Life settled into a routine for Carlota. The mornings were very quiet. The girls slept late and went to the beach around midday, when Carlota would do their rooms. They would come back around three or four in the afternoon and have a siesta; then they would all get together in Nerinha's room and listen to her new RCA Victor radio, speculating endlessly about the plots of the soap operas while they knitted or sewed clothes for Carlota's baby.

Some nights Lula would let the customers in. She would sit in a bentwood rocking chair in the hallway, waiting for them, while chain-smoking Dourado cigarettes; on other evenings they were greeted by Chico or Morena do Sul, a friend of Lula's who worked at one of the bars near the docks. Carlota stayed in her room in the evenings. She was afraid to go out on her own, worried that something might happen to her baby.

One night Chico and Lula asked her if she wanted to come with them to their *terreiro*. Carlota had been deeply religious, but she had not been to a place of worship since she had left home. Lula allowed her to make a white dress from an old sheet. She sat in the car in silence as they drove through a very long tunnel, then uphill, until the road turned into a dirt track. They stopped by a wooden fence. The house behind it was barely visible through the banana trees.

There was no moonlight, only the stars, the fireflies, and the city lights in the distance. They walked into a large shed where a small crowd of worshipers sat around the room, their white clothes reflecting the yellow glow of the candles on the floor. A large crucifix on a table dominated the clear area in the middle of the room. It was flanked by the statues of the Jesus-like Oxala, the beautiful Iemanja, goddess of the sea, and other images, a glass of water and a large conch shell. Also on the table there were many glasses or small vases holding flowers.

The singing started and Carlota joined in, losing herself to a feeling of abandon and well-being. In the clear space by the altar the *cavalhos,* in their white priestly robes, swayed to the music, humming loudly. Suddenly one of them grunted, and his face contorted into a mask. He fell to the ground and rolled backward and forward, hissing and muttering in an incomprehensible language. Soon the two other *cavalhos* followed, and the *macumba* rite began.

During the long night, in the constant dialogue between spirits and worshipers through the *cavalhos,* Carlota came to terms with her current circumstances. When her turn came to interrogate the spirit, her *cavalho* shook violently, until a beatific calm overcame him. His eyes suddenly opened and, looking at Chico, who stood next to Carlota, he made an unmistakable sign. The spirit had chosen Chico as a force for good in Carlota's life. The *cavalho* reinforced the bond with special herbal mixtures, and the cleansing ritual sealed it. The spirit had clearly said that Chico was to guide Carlota, and she accepted it. They returned to the house soon afterward, the peaks of the *morros* on the horizon outlined in gold by the rising sun. She did not know that the *cavalho* was Chico's cousin.

Very soon Chico gave her a new job. She and Morena do Sul were to travel in Rio's crowded buses. Carlota was to stand next to the most prosperous-looking passenger, her huge belly thrust forward. The man would then give up his seat out of kindness. If he didn't, Morena would lecture him in a very loud voice about people's lack of politeness. In either case, the man would leave his seat. In the ensuing commotion, Morena would pick his pocket. She would then get off the bus immediately, and Carlota would meet her at the following stop, where the two would wait for the next bus.

One afternoon, they were working the bus route along Nossa Senhora de Copacabana Avenue. They had just completed their routine, and Morena was elbowing her way to the door through the standing passengers when the man she had robbed shouted at her to stop, and began to call her a thief. Morena jumped out of the bus, the man in pursuit. Carlota began to wonder what she ought to do when she felt a flash of pain and water poured out of her, flooding the seat and the floor. Deeply embarrassed, she left the bus, ignoring the many offers of help from the other passengers.

She started to walk aimlessly, when the pain came again. Gasping, she stumbled and managed to balance herself against the trunk of a huge palm tree. She could feel the sweat on her face.

A woman came up to her, a woman with a kind face. She began to question her, but Carlota felt her strength flowing away. The woman asked her a question she could not hear, and she passed out. An ambulance took her to the Rocha Maia Hospital. Seventeen hours later, she was holding a newborn girl to her bosom. She had never felt so much love in her life; her baby needed her, and she would protect it.

During her stay in the hospital, she became friendly with a cleaning woman who came from Recife. The old woman's interest made Carlota wish that her own mother could be there to see her beautiful granddaughter, Florinda. Carlota had named her daughter after her favorite soap opera character. She hoped that her baby would one day be rich and famous, like her namesake.

Chico did not bother to look for Carlota; he knew that she would return. And he was right. A few days later, Carlota came back. The house was in commotion as Lula, Nerinha, Magnolia, and Mimosa cooed over little Florinda until the first customer arrived. Then they quickly cleared Mimosa's bed, and got back to work.

A month later, Carlota was cooking *feijoada* for supper, slowly stirring it with a fork, when Chico walked into the kitchen. He was smiling, and holding Florinda in his arms.

"The little one is ready for some fresh air," he said. "Tomorrow morning I'll take her out with some friends of mine." Carlota did not understand at first. She walked with Florinda in her arms every afternoon, and they went around the square at least twice before coming back. Her baby had plenty of fresh air.

"But I can't go tomorrow morning, I have to help Lula here."

"You don't need to come. In fact, from now on you will see Florinda only when I say so. I am taking her away."

Months of coexistence with Carlota had accustomed Chico to her meekness. But he had misjudged her. Carlota leaped at him, her eyes wide open. While grabbing Florinda with her left hand, she gashed Chico's face open with the fork from eyebrow to chin. Chico's pain was unbearable, and blood covered his eye. His screams brought the girls rushing downstairs. The front door was open, and Carlota and Florinda were gone.

Mimosa and Nerinha ran after them, while Magnolia looked after Chico. They turned into the Avenida Venezuela, but wolf whistles and hooting cars made them realize that they had left the house dressed in their work clothes, high-heeled sandals and black underwear. They could not afford to be stopped by the police, so they returned home in haste.

Carlota kept running. Sweat trickled down her neck, and her heart beat wildly, but she did not stop. After a while, Florinda began to cry. Carlota stopped in the doorway of a church, and fed her, the baby's soft mouth on her breast soothing her fears. Looking at Florinda, she remembered her first feeding in the hospital, and she thought of Maria, the old cleaning woman who had befriended her. Maria was her only hope.

Florinda went to sleep, milk dribbling down the sides of her mouth, a placid smile on her face. Carlota kept her watch for as long as she could, until she too fell asleep, just after hearing the church bells chime two o'clock.

When she woke up, it was still dark, and her body ached all over. She was hungry, desperate to find a toilet, and Florinda's diaper was soaked and dirty. The baby stirred, and began to moan. Carlota lifted her up gently and began to walk down the empty streets. She saw a small alley by the side of a house. Looking in every direction to ensure that nobody was watching her, she walked into the alley and relieved herself on the pavement. She noticed an open window nearby, behind ornate bars. The edge of a curtain was just visible.

Carlota scanned the ground around her, and saw a piece of broken glass. She placed Florinda on the sill of the adjacent window, then swiftly pulled the curtain out through the bars and slashed a square piece from it with the sharp edge of the glass. Holding the piece of fabric, she picked up the baby and ran away.

She ran for two blocks, until she found a sheltered doorway. Folding the piece of curtain into a triangle, she improvised a clean diaper for her baby. Farther down the street, she rinsed the dirty diaper in a kidney-shaped ornamental pond outside a new apartment building. The water lilies had just begun to open in the early morning light.

People were beginning to appear on the street. She asked for directions several times, and at last she found the hospital. She waited outside until she saw Maria. Calling her name, Carlota felt safe for the first time since leaving Chico. She burst into tears and explained her predicament. Maria went into the hospital; after a while, she came out with coffee in a paper cup and a roll. She told Carlota to wait for her outside until the end of the shift.

Carlota sat on a green wooden bench under a palm tree, holding Florinda. At last, exhaustion took over, and both mother and daughter fell asleep in the warm morning air.

Inside the huge white building, Maria thought about Carlota while mopping the tiled floor of an interminable corridor. She could do with help at home, and Nelson, her son, needed a woman. Carlota seemed a nice girl. She also produced beautiful, healthy babies. Nelson would be pleased.

When she left work, Maria told Carlota that she could come and stay with her; she also mentioned her son, and said that she was sure Nelson would like her. She explained that they lived in a nice part of town, overlooking the Jockey Club and the lagoon.

After a long bus ride, it took them nearly an hour to climb the steep hillside. It was difficult for Carlota to walk up the rocky path holding Florinda in her arms, the ferns and lianas growing on the rocks brushing against her. Maria offered several times to carry the baby, but Carlota refused.

At last they reached the *favela,* and began to walk among the hovels built at random, wherever it was possible to get a hold on the mountain face. Carlota could hold Florinda with just one arm, because she needed the other to wave her way through the clouds of flies swarming over the piles of rubbish and excrement. She did not particularly notice the naked children playing here and there, their scrawny bodies caked in mud. They were a familiar sight from her childhood.

Maria pushed open the tin door of one of the shacks. Inside, Carlota saw a young man, wearing only his trousers. He was snoring on the floor, an empty bottle beside him.

"Nelson . . . Nelson," called Maria. The man did not move. Maria shook him until he woke up. He struggled to stand, and Carlota noticed his lame leg.

"Nelson, this is Carlota," Maria said. "She is going to live with us. Her baby is called Florinda."

"Fine," said Nelson, eyeing Carlota's body under the cotton shift. He did not need further explanations. His mother kept him, and she had now produced a fine woman; Nelson was pleased.

Ten months later, Carlota gave birth to Silvia. She named her second daughter after Silvia da Costa, the movie star who had rocked Brazil.

On Silvia's third birthday, Maria fell ill. They had planned to go to the square and have their picture taken as a memento of the girl's birthday, but at the last moment Maria developed a terrible headache, and preferred to stay at home. Nelson announced that he would look after his mother. Shortly after Carlota and the girls left, Maria went to sleep and Nelson rushed off to the racetrack.

The next day, Maria was checked into the hospital where she worked. A brain tumor, they said, and she died a short while afterward. It took an even shorter time for Nelson to leave Carlota and the children. With Maria's savings he took himself to São Paulo, where he had been told that living was easy.

Carlota never saw him again. She had to make a living, but she could not go to work and leave Florinda and Silvia alone. If she did, she knew that, sooner or later, she would not find them there on her return. Begging became the only way for her to earn a few cruzeiros, and sifting through garbage cans the usual way of feeding her children.

No, life had not been kind to Carlota. Sometimes she wished that she had been luckier, but then she thanked God for her girls. She loved them, and had given them all she could.

She also worried about them. Not so much about Florinda; the girl was tough, and would survive anything. But she could not bear to think what would become of Silvia if she were not there to protect her.

At last, the child fell asleep in her arms, and Carlota gently moved her to her bed of rags. She kissed Silvia on the forehead, and then lay down on her own pile of rags. She felt feverish, but did not think much of it: it was to be expected after such a commotion.

She looked at her sleeping children. As usual, she was struck by their beauty, and proud of it, and yet she feared for them. Her own beauty had been no protection. She made a point of taking the girls to school every morning. At least they would learn to read and write. They would not be illiterate like her, but what would they become?

Closing her mind to disquieting thoughts, she tried to sleep.

7

Rio de Janeiro
December 31, 1962

*T*HE sun had just gone down over Copacabana beach. The purple-blue darkness had almost rubbed out the pink light from the horizon when Florinda and Silvia joined the vast crowd of worshipers on the sand.

It had taken them the whole morning to prepare the beautiful flower wreaths for the sea goddess, Iemanja: white roses from Florinda, red bird-of-paradise flowers from Silvia. Florinda had stolen the flowers early in the morning from the stall near the Jockey Club while Silvia, following her sister's instructions, had distracted the owner's attention.

The crowd stood away from the water's edge, and the sand glowed in the light of thousands of candles. The singing muffled the sound of the waves, but the noctilucas turned the breakers into a festoon of light in the darkness, a sign to the faithful that the goddess of the sea would visit them at midnight.

On one side of the Avenida Atlantica, the world's most spectacular sweep of seaside apartments shone in the night. Servants could be seen on the terraces setting candlelit tables for the New Year parties that would begin in a few hours. On the other side, past the wide pavement of black and white stones that formed a ribbon of undulating lines, one million people gathered by the sea to honor its goddess, a ritual brought over from Africa four hundred years before. At midnight, men in black tie and women in Dior and diamonds would toast the New Year from their penthouses while they watched, like benevolent gods from the clouds, the dancing crowd below them.

On the beach, Silvia and Florinda joined in the festivities, singing and dancing to the rhythmic beat of the drums. They were nearly the same size, both exquisitely proportioned, their long narrow bodies giving the impression of weightlessness, so supple were their movements. They both looked strikingly like their mother.

The music made them forget their worries. They had always come to the beach with Carlota, but now her health prevented it. For the last few days she had been running an extremely high temperature, but she refused to let the girls bring a doctor from the local dispensary. The herbal remedies from the *macumba* were all she needed, she said, and she insisted that the children should go to the beach that evening, otherwise the goddess might take offense.

Carlota had been unable to make a present for Iemanja. The effort had been too much for her. At the last moment she explained to Silvia what she wanted. At the bottom of a beer carton full of assorted pickings from garbage cans, Silvia found the square of material her mother had asked for. The edges were roughly cut as if a primitive tool had been used, and there was a large stain in the middle, which had caused the floral pattern to fade.

Carlota stared at the piece of material for a long time, before focusing her eyes on her children.

"Please bring me two of your flowers, both of you. And needle and thread as well." She made an effort not to let her tiredness show in her voice.

She stitched the flowers to the corners of the fabric, then gave it to Silvia.

"When you bring your offerings to Iemanja, put this next to them. She knows what my wish is." Her head sank onto the rags spread on the floor. In spite of the heat, she shivered constantly.

"Go now, children, go," she managed to say.

Silvia did not want to leave her mother, but Carlota insisted they should go. Even now, dancing under the stars, she worried about her mother.

The sisters' dancing caught the attention of others, and soon there was a circle of people around them, clapping their hands to the obsessive beat of the drums. Suddenly, the ring of people around them broke up and everybody joined the dance. The girls found themselves dancing with ever-changing partners, until two men held their stretched-out hands around them, shielding them from the crowd. The whole beach was now covered by a swaying ribbon of people dressed in white, folding and unfolding to the rhythm of the tribal sounds.

Just before midnight, the crowd rushed to the shore with their gifts. Lace cloths were spread along the tide line, and were instantly covered by the offerings of the faithful: flowers, fruits, ornaments, silk ribbons, a million gifts for the goddess of the sea. If Iemanja accepted their presents, she would send the tide to get them at midnight and grant the donor's wish.

Silvia and Florinda gave their presents, Carlota's cloth and their own floral offerings, to Iemanja. Then, holding hands, they faced the sea, and stood with the rest of the crowd, shoulder to shoulder along the water's edge.

As the surface of the water swelled in the distance, a murmur passed among them. The swelling became a huge wave, then it crashed into an explosion of phosphorescent foam, which rapidly approached the beach in a tidal surge. The foam-edged water rolled toward the spectators, covering their feet. The goddess had come to them, and the crowd cheered in their joy.

The receding surf carried away the offerings, and the roar from the crowd silenced everything, including the explosion of fireworks which, precisely at midnight, covered the skies of Rio de Janeiro in a shower of gold. As the tide continued to wash the shore, the people began to disperse. Soon the endless stretch of wet sand was clear. Only Carlota's offering, entangled in some driftwood trapped by the sand, was a reminder of the gifts that had been collected by the sea.

An incessant incantation ran from one end of the beach to the other: "Happy New Year!" "Happy New Year!" "Happy New Year!"

"Happy New Year," said the older of the two men next to Silvia and Florinda. "I'm Carlos, and he is Omar," he said, as he produced a hip flask full of Scotch. Omar, just a few years older than Florinda and very good-looking, smiled at her.

"Let's toast the year in," said Carlos, taking a swig from the flask.

"Welcome, 1963!" He passed the flask on to Silvia. Trying to conceal the fact that her only experience with drinking was an occasional beer, she gulped a large mouthful of whisky. She choked, and tears came to her eyes. Carlos slapped her on the back, while Omar took the flask and offered it to Florinda, who took just a small sip.

"You have to be careful with this stuff," said Carlos. He slapped Silvia's back once again, then his hand slid carelessly down her spine.

"Why don't we try to find somewhere to sit and watch the fireworks in peace?" Carlos asked. "We could go back to my apartment. I can drive you home later. You ought to see my car; it's very nice." He began to walk toward the road, his hands resting lightly on the sisters' shoulders. Omar took Florinda's hand in his. She recoiled slightly at his touch, but she noticed the gold watch on his wrist and said nothing.

They walked along the avenue, zigzagging their way through the crowd. Carlos and Omar cracked jokes and constantly offered the flask to Silvia. Florinda had declined it after a second tasting, but Silvia had accepted every offer. She was impressed by the men's conversation, their constant reference to cars, yachts, and famous people, their obvious ease in a world she longed for. In the meantime, Florinda studied them. The fit of their clothes made it obvious to her that they were not carrying wallets.

Omar suggested they take one of the side streets to get away from the crowd, and Florinda readily agreed. As they turned the corner, Omar held her arm and began to walk faster, until they were a few yards ahead of Carlos and Silvia. Omar talked to her without a break, trying to take her attention away from his arm, which now was encircling her waist. She pretended not to notice.

The lights hanging from wires across the road cast their pale yellow glow on the empty street ahead, and Florinda could see the square at the end. As they got farther away from the main road, the noise from the crowd became progressively fainter, and she could now hear Carlos chuckling and whispering to Silvia behind her.

They crossed the road and walked into the square, under the jacaranda trees. They were completely alone, the darkness all around them. Florinda gave Omar a coy look. "I feel dizzy. I would like to sit down somewhere very quiet," she said, placing her hand on his bare forearm, as if to keep her balance. "I'm so tired," she muttered, her head now resting on his shoulder.

Omar pointed at a gazebo, smothered by a bougainvillea in full bloom. He almost had to carry her inside, her eyes half-closed, her body limp against him. He could feel her full breasts pressed against his chest, her hand carelessly rubbing against his groin. Florinda noticed that his breathing had become quicker. Her eyes were half-closed, but she was able to see Carlos steering Silvia toward a nearby bush, his hand on her sister's buttock. The sight pleased her; she had work to do, and it would be easier if she and Omar were left on their own.

She collapsed on the bench inside the gazebo, Omar next to her. He took her in his arms. Florinda moaned softly, as he began to caress her breasts through her thin blouse, and guided her hand to his bulging prick.

While moaning and sighing, Florinda was methodically running through the lessons she had learned from Mario, the boy next door in the *favela*. His price had been one blow job per lesson; she would soon find out if it had been worth it.

Omar stood up to undo his belt, and Florinda saw her chance.

"Oh, you drive me crazy," she whispered, falling on her knees in front of him. She pulled down the zipper of his trousers, got hold of the top of his shorts and pulled his clothes down to his ankles. Gasping, she took his cock in her mouth. While her lips moved slowly up and down, she could sense him tremble with pleasure, oblivious to anything else. She slowly caressed his legs until she reached his feet. Then, as rapidly as she could, she tied his shoelaces together.

She took his wrists in her hands, as if to retain her balance, and began gently to caress the ridge between the head and the shaft of his penis with the edge of her teeth. Omar grunted with delight, and she felt a salty taste in her mouth. Time for action, otherwise this pig was going to shoot.

Suddenly she sank her teeth into his flesh. Overwhelmed by the horrendous pain, Omar did not feel her fingers unfastening the watch from his wrist. Florinda ran out of the gazebo. Screaming with pain and rage, Omar tried to follow her but he fell flat on his face, his feet tied together.

"Silvia, let's go! Police! Please help me! Police!" Florinda screamed at the top of her voice, running toward the street. She saw Carlos appear from behind the bush, his clothes undone; Silvia was behind him, tears in her eyes. Florinda grabbed her sister's hand and pulled her away. She ran as fast as she could, and kept on shouting for the police until she noticed that Carlos was running in the opposite direction, Omar stumbling behind him.

Florinda did not stop until they reached the main road. After making sure that they were not being followed, she turned to Silvia.

"You are a revolting whore, a shitty little slut. Wait until we get home, and I tell Mamãe," she said angrily.

"No, Florinda, don't tell Mamãe, please. You know she is ill," Silvia pleaded. Florinda felt a surge of pleasure; her sister was in her power.

"I'll think about it, but I don't know if I can ever look at you without feeling sick," she said. She dropped the watch inside her blouse, where she felt it come to rest against the tight waistband of her skirt.

Silvia walked in silence, her eyes on the pavement. Sex was as much a fact of everyday life in the *favela* as the grinding poverty, and Silvia had long been aware that men found her attractive, as attractive as Florinda. But that night, for the first time, she had come across a man who not only was attracted to her but who could offer her the opportunity to escape from a life of squalor. Men could be a way out of poverty, certainly the only one available to her. But she did not have Florinda's ruthlessness, her complete disregard for anything other than her own objectives. She often wished she could be more like her sister.

It was nearly morning by the time they reached home. As they walked in, the pale light of dawn coming through the door caught Carlota's body on the floor. Her pained expression had been replaced by a look of serenity, restoring her features to their original beauty.

"Mamãe, Mamãe . . . ," Silvia said, kneeling down and taking her mother's hand. Even in her ignorance, the cold skin confirmed her fear. She looked up at Florinda in despair.

"Mamãe is dead." Tears came to her eyes in sorrow for the person she had loved most and who had truly loved her. She stood up, sobbing uncontrollably, and embraced Florinda. Her sister remained motionless, looking at their dead mother. Things would be easier now: *she* was in control.

8

Rio de Janeiro
February 1966

"*LA plume de votre tante est sur la table,*" said the voice.

"*Non, la plume de ma tante n'est pas sur la table; elle est sur le dre . . . dre . . .* Oh, shit!" Florinda slammed her fist down on the coffee table in front of her armchair. She switched off the record player and closed the book on her lap.

"How long are you going to go on with that?" Silvia shouted from the kitchen. "I know it far better than you by now." She stood in the doorway, languidly leaning against the doorframe, her hand on her hip.

"*Voulez-vous du café?*" she asked in a mocking tone.

Florinda glared at her.

"I'll go on for as fucking long as it takes me to speak it. I may not be as clever as you, but I'm going to be a model in Paris while you're stuck here, still being screwed by your fat car dealer who will probably give you some rotten pox, if he doesn't get you pregnant first." She looked into Silvia's eyes. "I've told you a million times that I don't like you wearing my eye shadow. You have your own; leave mine alone."

Silvia pursed her lips and blew her a kiss.

"I'm sorry, but yours is such a lovely color. And don't get so upset. Some of the things you say *might* be true, but if it weren't for my fat car dealer, you would still be skidding on the turds in the *favela*. I would wait until that photographer of yours lives up to his promise to make you famous before making too many plans about Paris."

She walked across the room and turned on the radio.

". . . General Castelo Branco received a delegation of . . ." Silvia rolled her eyes, and changed the station. The voice of Astrud Gilberto singing "The Girl from Ipanema" filled the room.

"*Ah que coisa mais linda, mais cheia de graça, e ela menina . . . ,*" Silvia sang, dancing around the coffee table, her hips swaying to the tune.

"You ought to tell your Ruben to try to sell more cars, or be less stingy," said Florinda. "You are not living in Ipanema yet."

Silvia paused for a moment.

"Maybe, but at least Ruben pays the bills, and you live here thanks to him. If you don't like it, you can climb up a *morro* anytime and stay there." She sat on the arm of Florinda's seat, and put her arm around her sister's shoulders.

"I don't like fighting with you; I love you more than anyone else in the world. You know, Florinda, I've always envied you, wanted to be like you, and now we are bickering about stupid things. You shouldn't be nasty about Ruben, and I won't say anything about Marco. When am I going to meet him? You are very secretive about your photographer."

Florinda said nothing. Silvia leaned forward, and picked up a packet of Kent cigarettes from the table. She lit one, blew several smoke rings in the air, and continued.

"And my Ruben sells a lot of cars, you know. He's just done a big cash deal with someone who's bought a Jaguar," she said proudly. "You should see it, Florinda, such a lovely car. White, with red leather seats. The man's coming to pick it up on Friday at six o'clock, on his way to Cabo Frio. He must be one of those guys who think they're so important they can't stay for Carnival with people like you and me on the street. If you want to, I can take you to the showroom tomorrow, and you can see the car before it goes."

Florinda stood up, her eyes wide open, staring at Silvia.

"You know I can't stand the smell of cigarettes; put it out!" she screamed. Shaken by her sudden outburst, Silvia stubbed her cigarette out in the ashtray. Florinda walked toward the door.

"I'm going to have a shower and get ready," she said. "I can't waste any more time with you. Marco is taking me to the Copacabana Palace. He's picking me up at seven, because he wants me to have a drink with some film producer he knows."

"I'm sure you will look beautiful, and you must have something new and lovely to wear; you always do. You know how I get my money, but I'm never quite sure how you get yours, Florinda. I'd better not ask, I suppose." Silvia instantly regretted her words. She knew that only undiluted flattery kept Florinda under control during one of her moods.

"It's none of your business," Florinda said curtly.

Silvia quickly changed the subject.

"Promise not to come into my room," she said sweetly. "I have to finish my costume for tomorrow night, and I don't want you to see it before then. I think you'll like it."

Florinda shrugged her shoulders and walked across the hallway into her bedroom, closed the door, and leaned against it. Eyes closed, she bit her lip. She could not go on like this, not for much longer.

During the first year after their mother's death, Florinda had been in charge of their survival. She thieved when necessary and prostituted herself if she needed money quickly, while Silvia stayed at home, listening to the transistor radio Florinda had stolen for her. Silvia refused to go out. She lay at home in a daze, day after day, numbed by her mother's death. Her vulnerability was soon obvious to the gangs of young louts in the *favela,* and her fear of them increased her reluctance to leave their shack.

One afternoon, Florinda went past a group of men on her way back home. They cracked jokes about her little sister. She just kept on walking, but one of the boys followed her. He began to describe in detail what he would like to do both to Silvia and to her. Suddenly she stopped and picked up a dog turd from the road. She turned right around and smeared it over his face, kicking him in the balls for good measure. She had no further trouble.

Soon after the first anniversary of Carlota's death, Silvia regained her spirit. She began to frequent the beaches, where her looks made her as noticeable as Florinda, even more so. Silvia craved admiration, and she got it. It was during one of those lazy afternoons that she came across Ruben. They began meeting every day, and eventually the middle-aged car dealer rented a furnished apartment in the Rua Palmeira, not far from his office. Silvia insisted that she would live there only if Florinda could move in with her.

Sometimes Ruben stayed for the night, but not always. He was in the process of separating from his wife, and he had to keep up appearances until all the legal matters were settled. He lived with his mother in a house near São Conrado.

The apartment was small, but it had two bedrooms, one of them big enough for a double bed, a sitting room, kitchen, and bathroom. To Florinda and Silvia it was a world of inconceivable luxury, with hot and cold water coming out of the taps, and electricity in every room.

Their life appeared to have changed only for the better, but not from Florinda's point of view.

In the *favela,* she had been in charge of their lives. Ruben was the benefactor now, and, for Silvia, the source of love and money. It was only a matter of time before Florinda became a secondary factor in Silvia's life, a possibility that Florinda found intolerable. She wanted to be first in anything she did, and for anyone around her. Always.

There was also another, deeper layer to her dissatisfaction. Florinda had used sex for her own purposes since she was thirteen. Men meant nothing to her, and she felt nothing with them. She knew that her beauty made her irresistible to them, and she used it. Someday she would find a really big catch.

But in the meantime she had to carry on, a quick grope here and there to pick some sucker's pocket, occasionally a night in a hotel to get some decent money. Most of the men were fairly repulsive, with soft bellies and varicose veins, but she did not look very closely at them.

Silvia's affair with Ruben had shaken her. Her sister had achieved all the material benefits she wanted, and had found someone who adored her, for whom she was everything. It was this last aspect which aggrieved Florinda most.

She had invented Marco out of hurt pride. She had picked up his name from the captions in fashion photographs in O *Cruzeiro* and other glossies, and then told Silvia that a photographer had stopped her at the beach in Leblon and asked her to pose for him. She described him as tall, broad-shouldered, with blue-gray eyes and blond hair, the proud owner of a red Ford Thunderbird. Silvia had actually seen the car when the photographer came to pick up Florinda. What Silvia could not see from the window was that the man inside the car was Epitacio Barbosa, a fifty-four-year-old scrap dealer in non-ferrous metals with a flourishing business in the gritty industrial northern section of the city. The man was bald and overweight, and had difficulty in controlling his wind. He had picked up Florinda from his car one evening as she purposely strolled up and down the Avenida Atlantica. It was easy for Florinda to hook the podgy businessman into a weekly meeting in the evening, when they would spend an hour together in a hotel before he went back home to his family. She would then go to a late movie alone, preferably a musical or a romantic comedy. The following morning she would tell Silvia about the fabulous places she had been to the night before.

While watching *Charade* at the Joia Cinema, the sight of the exquisitely dressed Audrey Hepburn walking along the river in Paris had given Florinda the idea for her next fabrication. Over breakfast she had announced that Marco had told her that she was too classy for modeling in Rio, and that he was going to get her a job in Paris. When Silvia had asked how she would manage when she couldn't speak the language, Florinda had replied that she would learn it in no time at all. Later in the day, after spending most of the afternoon applying for a passport, she had used part of the money Epitacio had given her the previous night to acquire a "Teach Yourself French" record set.

She regretted her idea after the first lesson, because she found the exercises intolerably boring. But she could not face Silvia's predictably smug look if she appeared to give up on the project, so she sat every evening listening to the records, exercise book in hand.

Now she was trapped in her own story, pretending to learn a language which was useless to her, feted by a nonexistent admirer, supposedly on her way to an imaginary job. Epitacio had warned her, now that Carnival was upon them, that he had to be home early, so tonight he would pick her up at seven. She didn't even bother to dress up for the sake of her story. She decided to ask Epitacio to drive to a quiet spot in Tijuca, and they could have a quick screw in the back seat. She could then be back home in less than an hour, in time for dinner with Silvia. She would even cook the meal; she had not done so in a long time.

She left her room and opened Silvia's door just a fraction.

"I'm going now. I think I'm getting the curse, so I'll be back home after drinks. Don't go out tonight; I'll cook for you," she said.

"For Ruben too. He was taking me out, but I'll tell him we'll eat here. Don't come in; my costume is all over the bed."

Florinda left the apartment without replying. The sound of samba bands playing and singing in the streets came through the open windows.

FLORINDA walked into the sitting room carrying the tray with the coffeepot and cups. She saw Ruben holding Silvia's hand, and felt a stab of jealousy.

"That was a delicious dinner, Florinda," Ruben said, carefully picking his teeth. He slid his hand inside his shirt, almost undone to the waist, and patted his stomach to corroborate his compliment. "I haven't had such good *vatapá* for a long time."

"It's the only dish my mother taught me how to make," Florinda said. "She used to cook it once a year." Memories of the open fire inside the tin shack, the food cooking in discarded oil cans found in garbage dumps, the stench of the slum temporarily masked by the smell of shrimp frying in *dendê* oil, the rice simmering in coconut milk, flashed through Florinda's mind. Her eyes involuntarily drifted for a moment to the solid-gold identity bracelet on Ruben's wrist. She knew how easy it would be to slip back into the hell they had left behind, and she knew she should be grateful to Ruben. But she was not.

"I have a very worried man here," Silvia said. She patted Ruben's cheek affectionately. "I'm going to change and then we're going to go out and dance all night. You shouldn't worry so much about a broken safe," she added, finishing her coffee.

"What's the problem?" Florinda asked after Silvia had left the room.

"It's nothing. The lock in my office safe doesn't work. I would like to have it fixed tomorrow, but you can't get anyone to do work on Carnival Friday. It doesn't really matter." He began to tap a rhythm with the tip of his fingers on the edge of the table, a smile on his lips. "Carnaval-Carnaval, Carnaval-Carnaval," he sang, his fleshy shoulders moving in rhythm with his beat. He suddenly stopped and glanced at her. "You look fabulous tonight. Why don't you come out with us?"

Her arms crossed under her breasts, she leaned forward across the table. Her silky tank top slid downward as she moved, and her bosom was almost fully exposed. "Maybe *you* could amuse me later," she purred, pursing her lips.

She sensed his surprise, and acted upon his uncertainty. She swiftly left her chair and sat on his lap, putting her arms around his neck.

It suddenly became clear to her that at the bottom of her disquiet was the fact that she wanted Ruben for herself. She wanted him because he had money, because taking him away from Silvia would reinstate her sister's dependence on her. After all, if Silvia could love him, so could she.

"It's so nice of you to ask," she said softly, stroking his cheek, just as Silvia walked into the room, wearing a gold lamé bikini and a feathered headdress. Florinda was pleased to notice the anger in her eyes. She stood up and walked toward the kitchen.

"I'm going to do the dishes," she announced cheerfully, exaggerating the sway of her hips as she walked away.

Silvia glared at Ruben.

"You must be sorry that I interrupted you, you pig!" She tried to keep her voice low, so Florinda would not hear, but she could not hide her distress. "Leave my sister alone!" she said as Ruben led her toward the front door, vainly trying to explain what had happened.

Florinda heard every word of their exchange, pleased to know that she had ruined at least the early part of Silvia's evening. She felt more cheerful, and began to whistle as she tackled the pile of dishes by the sink. In her new mood, she briefly considered going out, joining the merry crowd on the streets, but she decided to stay at home. She had a lot of planning to do.

THE Jaguar XK-E stood in splendid isolation in the middle of the showroom, the high gloss of its perfect finish distorting Florinda's and Silvia's faces like a fun-fair mirror. Florinda slid her hand along its side, the cold metal giving her more pleasure than the touch of any man. Opening the wide door, she looked inside the car; the heady smell of brand-new leather upholstery enveloped her as she slid onto the low red seat. She was wearing shorts, and the feeling of the soft leather on her naked thighs sent a shiver up her spine. She caressed the knob at the top of the gearshift, then set her hands on the steering wheel, looking at the instruments on the satin-polished walnut dashboard. She did not know how to drive; she did not know so many things. It did not matter; soon she would be on her way. She affectionately patted the dashboard as Ruben leaned down to look at her inside the car.

"It's not a horse, you know, and I won't take you for a ride. The owner is picking it up tonight, and I can't take any risks with a beauty like this one."

Florinda got out of the car and closed the door. Even the solid "clunk" sound made by the lock gave her pleasure.

"Someday I will own one of these in every color," she said.

Over breakfast, while listening to Silvia's stories about all the places she and Ruben had been to the night before, Florinda feared that her sister might have forgotten her offer to bring her to the showroom to look at the car. Eventually, Silvia asked her if she would still like to see it. Florinda pretended not to be very interested, and went to the kitchen to make some more coffee, because she knew that Silvia would insist. She enjoyed showing off the evidence of Ruben's money.

"Come on, Florinda, we'll never get to the beach at this rate," said Silvia, looking at the clock on the showroom's wall.

"I need to go to the toilet," Florinda said. Ruben pointed toward a door at the other end. In the small hallway off the showroom, Florinda rapidly checked the ladies' room. No good. She then inspected the room marked "Gentlemen," and found what she wanted. She locked herself in.

THE almost vertical rock face of the Sugarloaf glowed in the sunset light. The thimble-shaped mountain stood out like a cutout against the sky, but neither Florinda nor Silvia took any notice of the extraordinary sight. For them it was familiar, a backdrop for the Carnival frenzy that had just begun, and would last for five days, until Ash Wednesday.

They had walked from the center of town to Leme, at the begin-

ning of the long arc of Copacabana beach. They had danced most of the way; as soon as they left Ruben's office they had come across one *banda* after another. Near the showroom the *bandas* were small, ten or twenty people, but as they approached the beach both the bands and the crowds following them got much bigger. Now, among thousands of other dancers, the girls followed the Banda do Leme as it progressed along the Avenida Atlantica. The tops of the palm trees rivaled some of the extraordinary headdresses among the dancing crowd. They had not said a word to each other; they did not need to. They just danced to the music of the bands, samba after samba, both carried away by the fantasy of Carnival, where millionaires were dressed in loincloths, beggars from the *favela* were covered in silks and feathers, and reality and identity faded away. But they had been dancing for five hours now, and Silvia suddenly felt very thirsty. She touched Florinda's shoulder as she twirled next to her.

"Let's sit over there," she shouted, pointing toward the awnings of a bar on a side street. "I'll buy you a beer." She had to say it again, Florinda reading her lips in the roar of the music and the singing around them.

They elbowed their way through the thick crowd and, suddenly aware of their tiredness, walked to the nearest empty table, and collapsed on the green metal chairs. "Two *chopes*." Silvia gave their order to the waiter standing by the door as they sat down. The waiter went inside, and soon returned. In the fierce February heat, the coarse glass beer mugs on his battered round tin tray arrived already covered in a dew of condensation.

Silvia took a long drink, then licked the white foam from her upper lip.

"I needed this," she said, and burped. "Excuse me," she muttered, covering her mouth with her hand.

"Oh, 'Excuse me.' You've become a real sissy! Ruben has turned you into a doll." Florinda laughed.

"What's wrong with you?" Silvia asked. "I know that tone; you're trying to pick a fight. But I'm not going to have a fight while the *banda* plays like this. Listen, Florinda," she said, her fingers tapping on the table to the rhythm of the samba being chorused by ten thousand voices a hundred yards away. "Just listen, and don't think about anything else."

"He has turned you into a whore," Florinda continued, her voice full of venom.

Silvia glared at her. Angrily, she took Florinda's wrist, her fingers clenched into hard prods.

"Listen to me, you bitch, I'm fed up with you going on about Ruben and me. Yes, Ruben keeps me and you benefit from it, but he has not turned me into anything. I have always needed someone to protect me, to look after me, and you don't, or maybe you just think you don't. If a guy you loathe gives you a present after screwing you, then you are clever, but if I'm given things by a guy I love, then I'm a whore. Sometimes you are a shit to me, or maybe you just see things as they suit you. But" — she paused — "you ought to realize how lucky you are, and how much easier things are for you. You're stronger than me."

Florinda pretended to be enraged.

"Do you think I'm lucky because a fat car dealer screws my sister, or that things are easy for me because you pay the rent with your ass? You are an idiot, and maybe we should split. I've had enough!"

She stood up and walked away. Silvia threw some money on the table, and ran after her.

"Florinda, please, you don't understand, I wasn't criticizing you. Please, Florinda, stop and listen to me."

Florinda began to run. Silvia followed her, but in a second Florinda had disappeared into the crowd.

Florinda walked on through the dancers until she reached Princesa Isabel Avenue, where she waited for a bus to take her home. She was in no hurry anymore. The first part of her plan had worked to perfection, but the knot of tension inside her tightened. It was always easy for her to quarrel with Silvia: the really difficult task was still ahead.

NAKED except for a silver-sequined G-string and bra and silver high-heeled shoes, Silvia looked in the mirror and put the final touches to her eye makeup. She heard Ruben hooting his car horn outside. She spent a few more seconds putting on her long black gloves, then picked up her headdress from the bed, turned off the light, and left the room.

As she walked past Florinda's empty bedroom, she wondered

where she could be. After their argument a few hours ago, she had gone to see Ruben at his office, arriving at the same time that Ruben was saying good-bye to the happy owner of the beautiful Jaguar. Silvia waited until the man climbed into the car and drove away, and then she told Ruben about her argument with Florinda. At first she refused to tell him the reason for it, but Ruben pressed her until she eventually said that Florinda was very upset because she occasionally borrowed her eye shadow. Ruben raised his eyebrows, but said nothing, then suggested that they have dinner together at a nice new restaurant he had found at Barra da Tijuca, where it would be cooler than in the city.

During dinner, Ruben told her that he thought it was time they had a proper vacation together. They would go to Europe either in April or May, and they would stay there for a few weeks. The excitement of planning and discussing their holiday made her forget the earlier incident with her sister. She felt so happy and safe with Ruben that she almost told him of her suspicions, but she decided not to break the news to him yet. She did not know how he would react, and she did not want to upset him, not now. She was not even sure if she was pregnant; she was only three weeks late. Better to tell him once Carnival was over.

Now, as she left the apartment, she quickly cast her eye toward the full-size mirror on the wall by the front door. She was sure that she would be noticed that evening.

She rushed toward Ruben's parked car, put her headdress on the back seat, and got in. As they drove away, the car lights just missed Florinda, who had been hiding in the doorway of one of the apartment buildings nearby for the last hour, waiting for Silvia and Ruben to leave.

Florinda rushed upstairs. She stood by the window for ten minutes to make sure that Ruben and Silvia were not coming back. Then she walked into her bedroom and changed her clothes. She picked up her passport and the airplane ticket she had bought that afternoon, and slipped them into a bag she had stolen the day before. She added the old photograph from the shelf and a plain cotton dress from her closet. Nothing else. A new life was waiting for her in Paris. She would not lack for anything there, and her success tonight depended on moving fast.

She scribbled a note on a piece of paper: "Silvia, we cant liv together. I am going." She stared at it for a moment, decided it could not be improved, and then left it on the sitting-room table.

She walked around the rooms for a last time. Maybe she had been happy here, but she was not sure. She picked up her bag and left the apartment without looking back.

THE noise in the Avenida Rio Branco could be heard from half a mile away. The parade of the *escolas do samba* was now in full progress, and a million people cheered on their favorites.

For months, the poor people in every district of Rio had gathered at their local *escola do samba,* an impromptu social club where the miseries of everyday life would temporarily fade in the elaborate preparations for the Carnival parade. Routines for hundreds of dancers had to be rehearsed, songs written, costumes made. Now it was parade day, and tens of thousands of people from Rio's poorer districts had descended on the Avenida Rio Branco dressed as Versailles courtiers, mandarins, Thousand-and-One-Nights princes, birds of paradise. Miles of satin and velvet had been turned into crinoline skirts and coronation robes, tons of sequins and rhinestones stitched into intricate patterns, mountains of feathers shaped into towering headdresses, all paid for from some of the world's lowest wages. Only by scrimping from the day after Carnival is over is it possible to pay for next year's costume and next year's dream.

The parade had been going on for hours. Several *escolas* had already appeared, filling the wide road from edge to edge with thousands of people. Each *escola* developed a theme set by the huge float at the front, a fantastic construction as dazzling as the costumes of the dancers and the beautiful girls on it, followed by standard-bearers, waves of dancing children and a crowd of older women in the traditional white costume from Bahia.

More floats went by, and then the *bateria,* the enormous percussion orchestra drowning the city with the sound of its own samba, sung by two or three thousand people in the road and eventually by a million voices as the *escola* unfolded its magical procession down the boulevard. People danced on the road, in the stalls, on the balconies of the tall buildings along the avenue, singing and laughing, sweating in the heat or soaked by the torrential rains that sooner or later burst upon the city, completely unnoticed, just another permutation in an incessant kaleidoscope.

Portela, Silvia's favorite *escola,* went past at last, float after float in the shape of golden gingerbread ships, their silver sails and banners floating in the breeze, the Louis XV costumes of the crew repeated in infinite variations on the squadrons of dancers filling the avenue. As yet another wave of black women dressed as Madame de Pompadour in silver satin and blue ostrich feathers went past, it was clear to Silvia that the magnificence of the spectacle had outdone all the other *escolas.* Every year she expected them to win, but this time she was sure they would. Her shouting and dancing became frenetic, and she turned toward Ruben.

"Look, Ruben, aren't they beautiful? I love them!" She noticed that Ruben was looking at his watch, a worried frown on his face.

"I think we ought to go to the ball," Ruben said.

"Why?" asked Silvia. "It's only two o'clock. Nothing happens until three."

"I'd rather go now," said Ruben, taking Silvia's arm and leading her away from the front row.

They walked in silence for a few minutes, until they came to the car.

"Why are you so worried?" asked Silvia once she had settled in the back seat, lying on it as if it were a bed. She did not want to take off her headdress, and it was impossible to sit in the front while wearing it.

"I hired a security guard to keep watch on the office because I have all that cash in my broken safe, but I suddenly thought that maybe the guy is dancing and fucking somewhere else instead of doing his job. I just want to make sure he's there."

"You worry too much," said Silvia, and she began to whistle Portela's *samba de enredo.*

FLORINDA stopped in her tracks just before she reached the forecourt of the building. She could hear the sound of samba in the distance. She kept watch for a while, until she was certain that she was alone. Then she ran quickly across the open area outside the building, and walked along the narrow passageway at the side, her back to the wall, her eyes nervously darting in all directions. She found the small window she had unlocked that morning. Her hands on the windowsill, she pushed herself up until her head and shoulders were through. She dropped her bag on the floor inside, and inch by inch she slid her body through the opening. She was glad that she had decided to wear trousers; otherwise it would have been impossible to maneuver her legs through the narrow opening. Supporting the whole of her weight on her arms, she brought her legs down, her feet against the wall, until they rested on the edges of the toilet seat. Sighing with relief, she stood up on the tiled floor.

She moved into the lobby next to the showroom. All the lights were out, but her eyes were now used to the dark. She quickly scanned the empty room through the half-open door before moving on. She heard no sound. Nonetheless, she walked across the showroom on tiptoe. The sound of samba from distant streets was too faint to drown out the pounding of her own heart. She was terrified, but there was no stopping now; tomorrow she would be on her way to Paris.

She reached the door to Ruben's office, and tried the door handle. It was open. She thought she heard the faint sound of a bell ringing somewhere, and she waited for a minute. Silence. She closed the door and walked to the desk.

Florinda turned the desk lamp on. In the soft light she could see the safe in the corner, under the picture of the Nossa Senhora da Conceição, the Holy Mother. Florinda quickly crossed herself before kneeling in front of the safe. She pulled the handle next to the combination lock, but the door did not move. She felt panic at her throat, but then the handle yielded to the weight of her hand. She opened the door.

There were two shelves inside, full of documents and files. On the first shelf, resting on top of the binders, she noticed a bulging brown envelope. As she pulled it out, the revolver balanced on top of it fell off the shelf. Florinda tore the envelope open, and saw the three wads of hundred-dollar bills bound together by paper bands. It was more money than she had ever seen. She was about to take it out of the safe when the door opened, and the beam of a flashlight fell on her.

The security guard, just wakened by his alarm clock, was still suffering the aftereffects of the bottle of rum he had finished off during the evening. He turned on the light and his hand went immediately to the gun on his belt, but not as fast as Florinda's reached for the revolver. The sound of the shot was deafening, but the guard did not hear it. The bullet went through his brain, killing him instantly. Florinda watched in shock as he collapsed to the floor, blood spurting out of a small hole in his forehead.

As Ruben parked the car in the yard outside, he and Silvia heard the shot. They ran into the building, saw the light coming through the open door of his office, and rushed in. The horror of the scene froze them: the dead man on the floor and Florinda next to the open safe, a vacant look in her eyes, the gun in her hand, now pointing at them.

"What have you done!" cried Silvia, walking toward her sister.

"Don't move, or I'll shoot you!" screamed Florinda.

Silvia leaped forward and tried to grab the gun, and Ruben moved to restrain Florinda. Silvia gripped the butt and felt her finger slip over the trigger, Florinda's hand on hers, pushing her finger inward. Their frantic struggle came to a sudden halt when the blast of the gun deafened them.

They recoiled away from each other, their eyes fixed on Ruben. He opened his mouth, but his lips froze before he could utter a sound. He collapsed to the floor. His blood squirted on Silvia's gloved hand, and slowly spread over his chest as it soaked his white shirt. Silvia let go of the gun, and fell to her knees by Ruben's side. She leaned down to kiss him for the last time.

Her world had been shattered. A moment ago, she had two protectors to keep the world at bay, and she loved both of them. Now one was dead, and the other had betrayed her. She was filled with sudden rage. Ruben had died because of Florinda. It was her greed, her envy, that had been the cause of both his death and her misery. Silvia's savage scream echoed in the empty building as she hurled herself toward her sister.

Florinda did not hesitate. Someone might have heard the shots, and the police could be on their way. Survival was her only priority now. As Silvia drew her hand back to slap her face, Florinda picked up the heavy glass paperweight from the desk and brought it crashing down on Silvia's skull with all her strength. Stunned by the blow, Silvia stumbled, and Florinda struck again and again, until her sister fell to the ground, her feathers spread around her as if she were a dead white bird. Then Florinda ran. She did not stop running until she joined the Carnival throng in the Avenida Presidente Vargas, far away from the little room where three bodies lay together on the floor.

9

Paris
April 1967

SILVIA came out of the Métro at the Place de la Porte d'Auteuil. She stopped at the ornate iron archway at the top of the stairs, and looked about in all directions. It was not necessary. She was no longer in Brazil and the nightmare was behind her, but the habit remained.

The streets were deserted. It was too late at night for the respectable bourgeoisie of the XVIieme district to be anywhere but in bed; only Silvia and her kind walked in the Bois de Boulogne after midnight. She crossed the square and began to amble down the Avenue into the Bois, toward the Allée de la Reine Marguerite. After three months, it had become a familiar routine.

She had fled Rio over a year ago, leaving behind the horror of that Carnival night. She had regained consciousness the following morning, and left the room without looking back. Her only thoughts were to get away from the bodies and the memories, and to remove any evidence of her presence there. If she were found, she knew the police would charge her with Ruben's murder. She had to leave Rio at once. She had picked up Florinda's bag and run away.

After a few minutes she stopped, suddenly realizing that she had no money, and that she was still wearing her costume. She did not dare to go back to the showroom to take some money from Ruben's wallet; the police might have arrived after she left. She had to go to the apartment, even at the risk of finding Florinda there. Not only did she need clothes, but she had to get her bag, with her wallet and her identity card.

As she approached the apartment building, she noticed the smoke coming out of the windows, and the fire engine outside, surrounded by a crowd of onlookers. Florinda had obviously been as keen as she was to remove all traces of their presence there. She ran away before anyone noticed her.

Only then did she check Florinda's bag, and discover the dress inside. She put it on and dropped her blood-stained gloves and her feathered headdress into the gutter. She also discovered Florinda's passport and the ticket to Paris in her name, and decided to keep them. The passport was specially valuable. She closely resembled Florinda, and someone was bound to ask for her papers sooner or later.

Clutching the bag in her hand, she walked all the way to the northern part of the city, until she stopped at a major crossroads. She did not have to wait long for a truck driver to offer her a ride to São Paulo. What she had to do to humor him once they were away from Rio was yet another memory she had erased from her mind.

In São Paulo, it soon became clear to Silvia that there was only one way she could earn a living: Florinda's way. She could not apply for a proper job. She had no work experience, no references, and she did not dare to produce Florinda's passport as proof of identity unless it was unavoidable.

After two nights, she had made enough money for the deposit required on a room in one of the many seedy hotels to which her clients took her. The owner had seemed friendlier than the rest, and had made it clear that no questions would be asked as long as the rent was paid.

It was not long before she realized that her period was late again. She had suspected it in Rio, and now she was sure. She was carrying Ruben's baby. She tried not to think about it. She could not have the baby. It would mean going back to the *favela*. When they had moved to the apartment in Rio, she had promised herself that she would never go back there, no matter what. She confided in one of the girls she met regularly on her rounds, who gave her the address of a reliable woman she knew.

The abortion did not take much time, but the woman warned her that there could be some bleeding afterward. When Silvia got back to her room it took four towels to soak up the hemorrhage. The owner of the hotel called a friendly doctor who attended to the ravages of the old woman's knitting needle in the best way he could, gave her a massive supply of antibiotics, and told her that he would come by the following day to see her. She would pull through, he said, but she would never be able to have children. Silvia cried the whole night, thinking about Ruben and what her future might have been.

Day by day, she began to believe that the news was a relief in some ways. She convinced herself that she did not want children anyway, and it would make her work easier. It also helped her to overcome her guilt about Ruben's death. She knew that it had been Florinda's fault, but it had been her hand, forced by her sister's, that had pulled the trigger. She saw her sterility as an expiation for her action, a way of coming to terms with her grief.

Silvia lived in perpetual fear of being caught by the police. Ruben had always been very careful about keeping her away from friends and relations. As far as she knew, his world was not aware of her existence, but this did not mean that the police would not be able to trace the connection between them. On the other hand, Ruben's murder might well be seen as just one of many during Carnival, another case of a burglar being disturbed at work. But she could not be sure, and the sight of any policeman revived her apprehension.

After a week she was able to leave her bed. Most of her savings went into buying a new mattress to placate the owner of the hotel. But now her luck changed. Her very first customer told her that she was too good-looking to be hanging around in the streets. He suggested that she apply for a job as hostess in the Papillon, a bar at the seamier end of town. The customer knew the owner, and told her to mention his name. He gave her only his Christian name, but the introduction was successful.

She soon had a string of regular clients, and the owner took only a reasonable cut from her earnings, leaving her enough to live on. She even managed to save some money. The bar would be a temporary stage, she told herself. She would soon find a protector, someone very rich. Then one evening she was told the owner wanted to see her.

"The police were here today," he told her. "They are looking for a girl in connection with some murder in Rio. Does it mean anything to you?" She just managed to keep an impassive expression on her face.

"No," she replied, "why do you think it should?" She took a cigarette from her bag and lit it, her eyes shifting away from his.

"Because they gave me a description of the girl. It could be you. I run an establishment for a respectable clientele, most of them married men who don't want any trouble. I told the police I hadn't seen anyone who looked like that, but if you're still here tomorrow my memory will start coming back. . . ."

She walked out of the dingy office and left the bar immediately, fear gripping her stomach. She had been using a false name, but time was running out.

One of the girls at the bar had worked for a while in Paris, and she had told Silvia that it was easy to make a living there, at a park called the Buadeboolon or something like that. She had earned good money for nearly a year, until she was caught by the police and thrown out as an illegal immigrant. Silvia mentioned that she spoke some French, and the girl insisted that she ought to give Paris a try. She even wrote down the address of the hotel where she had stayed, and the name of the best road in the park to ply their trade.

Silvia had kept the addresses. She also had Florinda's passport, the plane ticket, and the money she had saved. Now, in desperation, she decided she would go to Paris. It was a way out. But it was not quite as simple as going to the airport and taking the next flight. Passport control in Brazil was a risk she could not afford.

She went to the bus station and took a coach to Chuy. Two days later, she arrived at the small town on the border with Uruguay. She left the town on foot at midnight, clutching a map of the region she had bought at the gas station. She walked all night along country roads, until she was well into Uruguay.

It had been both exhausting and terrifying to cross open country at night, the only light from the stars of the Milky Way, a glowing ribbon across the dark sky. There were noises everywhere; some from creatures she could identify, like crickets and owls. There were many others she could not recognize, and she began to imagine what they might be. Soon every noise resembled the sliding of snakes across the paved road. Even more sinister was the silence, when the empty road across the immense countryside stretched toward nothing, only the blackness ahead.

She reached La Coronilla early in the morning, and slept on the bus to Montevideo. Once there, she spent some of her carefully treasured savings on two minidresses, a pair of white boots, a small suitcase, and a complete beauty treatment at a hairdresser. She then went to Air France, and presented Florinda's ticket. The girl at the counter told her it was valid for just another two weeks, and Silvia booked herself onto the Paris flight for that evening, paying extra for the Montevideo-Rio leg. She arrived in Paris the following day, with fifty dollars and a desperate will to survive. She told the immigration officer that she was on vacation. As he stamped her passport she suddenly realized that, from now on, her name would have to be Florinda.

The thought filled her with revulsion at first, but as she began her work, she was glad of the impersonation. It gave her a fragile shield against an appalling reality, as if it were her sister, not she, who was forced to earn a living through men. Three months had passed, and now at last she knew that it was going to work.

Her thoughts were interrupted by the lights of a car driving toward her. The car was cruising very slowly. Silvia stopped and took off her raincoat. She was wearing nothing but stockings, a garter belt, and a thin chain around her slim waist. She stood in the light, displaying her breasts to the driver, the length of her exquisite legs emphasized by her very high heels, but he did not stop and she let out a stream of her best French insults, her breath turning into vapor in the cool April air. She caught a glimpse of the man at the wheel. He was heavily made up, with dyed blond hair and a long white scarf around his neck. *He needs one of the studs at the Avenue de Saint Cloud,* she thought, quickly pulling her coat back on. She shrugged; there was trade for everyone in the Bois at night. She would be luckier next time. She turned into one of the Bois' many allées when she came across an extraordinary sight.

Visibly pregnant women were standing under every light, their coats open to display their bulging bellies and their swollen breasts. Two or three cars were parked next to various lights along the road; trade was obviously good. *Some men have really sick taste,* she thought. While she surveyed the scene one of the girls left the curb, and began to walk a few yards ahead of her. A car stopped by her side. The girl kept on walking, and the car followed her, the driver addressing her through his half-open window.

"I'm going home now, leave me alone," she said.

The man got out of the car and grabbed her arm. The girl screamed, and he punched her in the face. She stumbled, but he hauled her up and twisted her arm behind her back, pushing her toward his car while she moaned, calling faintly for help. Her lip was bleeding badly where he had broken it.

Silvia noticed a discarded bottle on the roadside, and did not hesitate. She picked it up and rushed toward the struggling couple. The man never saw her. He heard the tip-tap of approaching high heels, and then a flash of light exploded inside his skull. He collapsed on the road. Silvia helped the pregnant girl regain her balance and guided her away, an arm around her shoulders. They left the Bois, and Silvia stopped a taxi at the Boulevard Lannes.

"Where do you live?" she asked the girl. "I'll take you home."

"Near Pigalle," she replied.

"So do I," Silvia said.

The girl smiled. She took a second look at Silvia and realized they were both in the game.

"I thought you wouldn't live around here." The girl gave the address to the driver.

The incident created a momentary bond of companionship between them, something missing in Silvia's life for too long, and she suddenly hoped they would become friends.

"I'm Silvia," she said, using her real name for the first time without hesitation.

"I'm Arianne," the girl replied, and smiled wanly. "Thank you for helping me. You know what some of these shits can be like."

"You shouldn't be working if you are . . . like that," Silvia commented.

"You get a lot of money when you are pregnant; it's a specialty." She paused for a moment. "But you are special too. Where are you from? You are much too good-looking to be working the Bois; you should try the Avenue Foch."

"I'm from Brazil. I've been here for only three months." She looked at Arianne's broad face. Her features were coarse but her eyes were kind, and there was warmth in her smile. She liked her.

Arianne laughed. "Yes, I've heard that you Brazilians are very popular, but I'm not jealous. I have my clients, and you have yours." She tapped her belly. "We may be in competition when I've had the baby, though," she said with a mischievous smile.

"When is the baby due?"

"In June, two months from now. I hope I don't get too big, so that I will be able to work until the date. You can charge a lot during the last two months."

"Do you have to?" asked Silvia. She felt sorry for the girl and disgusted at the same time. She would never have children, and a part of her longed for a baby. In spite of herself, she felt envious of Arianne, and disturbed at the risk she was taking for herself and her unborn child.

"I have to support my mother, and I won't be able to work for a while after the baby is born. The rent doesn't stop when you have a baby, love," said Arianne, her hands on her belly. She had taken off her shoes, and was flexing her swollen toes. "I had a couple of guys tonight but then I didn't feel very well, and decided to go home." She peered out of the window. "We are nearly there, thank God." She struggled to control her dry retching.

Silvia noticed that Arianne's face had lost color as she spoke. The taxi pulled up outside a miserable-looking building facing the railway depot. Arianne pulled a fifty-franc note from her pocket, and gave it to the driver.

"Take my friend to her home, and give her the change." Arianne stumbled out of the car, and held on to a lamppost. She was suddenly sick.

Silvia rushed to her. As soon as she was out of the car, the driver slammed the door and drove away at high speed.

"Go to hell, whores!" he shouted through his open window.

"Anyone with a prick is a shit," muttered Arianne.

"Not always," said Silvia. "You may have a boy. Come on, I'll help you to the door."

She pressed the bell, and pushed the door open. She found the light switch in the hallway. The naked bulb threw harsh light on the dirty cream paint flaking off the walls. The place reeked of ammonia, and urine stains were visible on the gray tiled floor.

"How far up do you live?" asked Silvia, holding Arianne by the arm as they began to climb the rickety stairs.

"You do ask dumb questions. The top floor, of course. And the lights are gone from the second floor up."

After a few minutes, they reached the top of the stairs. Arianne opened the door, and turned on the light. A table, three pine chairs, and a mattress on the bare floor, near the wall, were the only furniture in the room. A curtain track ran across the ceiling. Arianne quietly closed the door to the adjacent room.

"I have some *pastis* here, but I can't give you anything else. The kitchen is in my mother's room, and she can't go back to sleep if she wakes up in the middle of the night," Arianne said.

"I don't want anything. I'll go now," Silvia replied.

"You can't go. It's nearly four o'clock, and you are not going to get a taxi around here." She glanced at Silvia's naked body under the raincoat. "Anyway, the police are going to ask you what's happened to your dress. They look the other way in the Bois, but not here. My mother's bed is wide enough for two. I'll sleep with her, and you can sleep in my bed."

After living on her own for more than a year, Silvia was delighted with the offer, and she readily agreed.

"I'm beginning to feel better now," said Arianne. "Let's have some *pastis*." They sat down at the table; Arianne poured the Ricard into two glasses, and then water from the jug next to it. She handed a glass with the cloudy mixture to Silvia.

"*Santé*," Arianne said, taking a large gulp from her glass. Silvia sipped her drink, and grimaced. The taste was not unpleasant, but she was unused to it.

"Don't make faces; it tastes better than most clients!" Arianne said. "Now tell me about yourself."

Silvia gave her a highly edited version of the last three years of her life. She explained that her mother had died, and she had moved away. Aware of her sketchy explanation of her recent past, she went into more detail about her years in the *favela* and the great sadness of her mother's death.

Arianne then told her about her childhood in the country. She explained that her father had died during the war, and that her mother had never recovered from the blow.

"The *Boches* did it, dirty pigs. He was a good man, and they shot him in front of my mother. I was a few months old. She was like a zombie for years. She had to leave the farm after a while, and we came to Paris. She thought it was going to be easier . . ." Arianne laughed bitterly.

"*Merde*, it's nearly five o'clock, and I wanted to go to bed early," she said. "Let's hit the sack. If you want a leak, the toilet is out there, on the landing. I'll go first; we mamas-to-be have priority." She came back after a moment, said goodnight to Silvia, and drew the curtain across the room, hiding the mattress from view.

Silvia went to the bathroom. It was filthy, but no more so than the one at her hotel. She returned to the room and found a long T-shirt on the makeshift bed, obviously left there for her by Arianne. She nearly cried at the idea of someone looking after her, concerned about her well-being. She got into bed and was asleep almost instantly.

She woke the following morning to the smell of fresh coffee and warm bread. She could hear the noise of crockery as the table was being set on the other side of the curtain. She pulled on her coat, and drew the curtain open.

"Ah, there you are! You had a good sleep, I hope. Nana has just been downstairs, and we've got fresh bread. Breakfast will be ready in a minute."

When Silvia came back from the bathroom, she saw a middle-aged woman in the room. She was frail, and at first glance seemed older than Silvia would have guessed Arianne's mother to be. Her almost white hair was pulled into a bun, and she was dressed entirely in black.

"Silvia, this is my mother. You can call her Nana. That's what she likes to be called."

"*Bonjour*," said Silvia. She felt ill at ease. There was something about Nana, her air of fatalistic acceptance of whatever life might throw at her, that reminded Silvia of her own mother. Nana was the first person Silvia had met outside her trade to whom it was clear that she was a whore, and she was embarrassed by the old woman's understanding look.

"*Bonjour,*" said Nana, as they sat down to breakfast. Arianne's chitchat bridged the awkwardness of the first moments of intimacy among three people who have just met, and by the end of breakfast Silvia felt more relaxed.

"I'll deal with the dishes, and then we must do some shopping. I hope you'll stay for lunch with us. You pay for your share," Arianne said as she cleared the table.

Silvia was delighted. At last she had made a friend. "I'll buy the food," she said. "I'll cook you *vatapá;*' it's my favorite Brazilian dish. I think you'll like it."

"You cook," Arianne said, "but we split the cost." She was also delighted. Silvia was exactly what she had been looking for: someone with her heart in the right place, who would help and, if necessary, deal with whatever problems had to be faced. It was not easy to find someone like that in the Bois.

When they had first moved to Paris, and things did not work out the way she had expected, her mother had lost her will, unable to face the world. Arianne had been forced to earn a living for both of them. There was only one way in which a girl of fourteen could make enough money to keep two people in Paris. Her mother had accepted her choice as yet another adversity, or at least that was what Arianne had assumed, because nothing had ever been said by Nana.

After years of living with the risk, her pregnancy came as a surprise to Arianne. She thought briefly about having an abortion, but as soon as Nana discovered her condition, it became impossible. For the first time, Arianne saw a glimmer of hope in her mother's eyes.

But she also recognized the problems. Life had been difficult enough with one dependent. It would be much harder with two: the burden had to be shared. A man was the obvious choice, but Arianne could not face it. Men were her work, not something she wanted to take home. Now Silvia had unexpectedly come into her life, and things would be easier.

While they did the shopping at the local market, Arianne asked

Silvia if she would like to move into a bigger place with them. It would cost Silvia less than the hotel, and she would only have to pay her share of the expenses. Silvia agreed immediately.

The Brazilian lunch was a great success. In the afternoon, Silvia checked out of the hotel, and brought her few possessions to the apartment. The girls went together to the Bois that night. As time went on, they were both certain that the arrangement was a good one.

Arianne found a bigger place almost immediately, not far from where they lived. It had four rooms, enabling each of them to have her own bedroom, and a basic kitchen. There was a toilet on the second-floor landing, and a bathroom on the ground floor.

Silvia tried to use the bathroom the day after they moved in, but the door did not lock, and the drunk who lived on the ground floor burst in as soon as she had taken off her clothes. She managed to push him out and jam the door with a chair, only to discover that there was no hot water. She remembered the bathroom in her Rio apartment with nostalgia; now she had to make do with a quick wash in the kitchen sink, and a visit to the municipal baths as often as she could manage it. But she enjoyed the two women's company, and she longed for the baby to be born. At last she was beginning to find her stride again.

FLORINDA walked into the darkened bedroom on tiptoe, and waited by the door for a moment until she confirmed that her entrance had not disturbed the couple's sleep. She was still wearing her maid's uniform, just in case she came across somebody on her way to the master suite, but she was wearing her clothes underneath, ready for her flight to Rio.

After a moment, she swiftly walked to the dressing table. As she expected, her employer had not bothered to put her jewelry in the safe. Florinda, the newest member of the staff, had been in the house for nearly five months already, and she had managed to impress her employers favorably soon after her arrival by engineering the disappearance of one of her mistress's gold bracelets during the night, then returning it the following morning, claiming to have found it while plumping up the cushions of one of the drawing-room sofas. No, there was no reason for the lady of the house to bother to open the safe again after a long dinner party. Her staff was reliable, the burglar alarm was on, and three Alsatians roamed the grounds of her villa in one of São Paulo's richest neighborhoods. Florinda put the jewels in her pocket, picked up the master's key ring from the top of the chest of drawers, took one last comtemptuous look at the sleeping rich pigs, and walked out of the bedroom.

She went to the entrance hall and turned off the burglar alarm with the master's key before returning to the staff wing. She listened for a moment to make sure that the rest of the staff was asleep, then went to the kitchen and tore off her maid's uniform, dropping it on the floor. She suddenly felt an urgent need to go to the lavatory.

She squatted over her crumpled uniform and relieved herself, wiping herself with the Venetian lace tablecloth she had removed from the dining room table after the party. It would be a nice parting gift for her mistress.

Picking up the case she had left by the kitchen door, she walked out of the house. The dogs would be no problem: they knew her. She crossed the garden, opened the side gate, and looked up and down the empty street. Not a soul in sight.

She looked at her watch. Santos would be waiting for her in the car, two blocks away. By the time the bastards woke up and called the police they would be in Rio de Janeiro. She was used to the routine by now. Two or three weeks of sun and fun on the beaches with Santos, then another "honest" domestic job in Rio for a few months, during which she would behave impeccably, her mother would then become suddenly ill, and she would have to leave. The glowing references from her Rio employers would get her a job with some really rich pigs in another town, she would clean them out, Santos would fence the stuff in Rio, and the cycle would start again.

As always after a successful job, Florinda found her thoughts drifting to her sister and that night at Ruben's office. She hated Silvia. It was because of her that Florinda had been forced to become a thief, to support them both when their mother had died. It was all her sister's fault, otherwise Florinda would have been a nice girl, married to a rich man, living like any of these rich women she was now forced to wait on. Yes, her sister had a lot to answer for.

If it hadn't been for Silvia, Florinda would not have needed to go back to the slums, to hide from the police. At least she had come across Santos there.

Florinda's only consolation was knowing that, without her, her sister had no hope of getting anywhere. She was probably living in some hell-hole God knew where. Maybe she was dead. She ought to be dead. It would be fair punishment for ruining Florinda's chances.

She saw Santos's car parked ahead, and ran toward it. As they pulled out, she put her sister out of her mind. She had better things to think about: the beach tomorrow, then the evening celebration of yet another success. Santos would probably get drunk, he would probably beat her up before screwing her, but Florinda didn't mind. She liked it, in fact. She was proud that he was a real man, and she considered herself a lucky girl to have found him.

10

*Paris
May 1967

SILVIA scanned the *allée* in both directions; she could see no cars. It was a bad night; the spring showers and the blustery wind made it unpleasant to be outside, and the clients did not like coming to the Bois in bad weather. She had thought of staying at home, but Arianne had not been able to work lately, and money was badly needed. The baby was due in two weeks.

Her thoughts were interrupted by the roll of thunder. Shit, it was going to rain again. It was nearly four o'clock. She had just decided to go home, when she saw the lights of an approaching car. She stood by the curb, her arms akimbo, her raincoat open. Her black vinyl corset pushed up her breasts, and emphasized her narrow waist. The car stopped by her side, and the window rolled down.

She had seen many men's faces, but this one was unusually unpleasant. He was not bad-looking, but his eyes were cold, and there was something cruel about the thin lips. He wore a black silk polo shirt, and he drove an expensive car. She had seen worse, she decided, and she had had no clients that evening.

He looked at her appreciatively, ignoring the other whore who had suddenly appeared from behind a bush.

"Do you suck?" he asked.

"Yes," she answered, glad that he didn't waste any time in embarrassed conversation. It had begun to rain hard, and she wanted to get into the car as soon as possible.

"How much will it cost me?"

"One hundred francs," said Silvia. *The man will bargain if he has any sense,* she thought.

"Get in," he said, opening the door. She sat next to him and held out her hand, palm upward. He paid her, and then started driving toward the lake, making conversation about the weather and the unpleasantness of the night. At last they reached a lane that led into the wood and he stopped, parking the car out of sight from the road.

"Here," he said. He reclined his seat until it was almost horizontal, and unzipped his trousers. "Now do a nice job," he muttered, lying back.

Silvia lowered her head onto his lap, closed her eyes, and started work. She let out the occasional moan and exaggerated sign of pleasure, thinking about the shopping she had to do in the morning. She became aware that his right hand was moving, as if looking for something between the front seats, and then she heard a click. A second later, she felt the cold steel edge of a flick-knife blade against her throat, while his left hand grabbed her hair, pushing her head down, until she almost choked.

"Do it right, bitch, or you'll regret it," he said harshly, moving the blade down her neck, the sharp edge almost grazing her skin. He began to utter obscenities. Silvia was terrified but she soon realized that as his obscenities became grosser, his pressure on the knife lessened. She applied all her skill to make him come as fast as possible; he shuddered briefly, and his release was followed by a long grunt. She felt the salty taste in her mouth; normally she spat it out of the window, but she did not want to risk offending this weirdo, so she swallowed it.

"That was good," he said, zipping up his trousers but still holding the knife. She contrived an admiring look.

"You are better than most men I come across," she murmured, as if overcome by the experience.

He held the knife up.

"You like a bit of excitement, don't you?" he said, his eyes glistening in the dark. "I have some very exciting equipment at home. Maybe you should come and spend the night with me."

Silvia thought fast before replying. "In five minutes, there'll be a police car waiting for me at the *allée*." She smiled coquettishly. "You are not the only man who appreciates me, you know, and the *flics* don't like to be let down. They will start looking for me if I'm not there soon. Paulette, the girl you saw next to me, will tell them which car I was in. We girls remember that sort of thing."

He looked at her thoughtfully. "I'll drive you back. But I really would like to see you at my home. . . . I can pay you good money." Silvia didn't answer.

"You are a foreigner. Where are you from?" he asked abruptly.

"Why do you want to know?"

"Because if you have any problems with your papers, we could come to a deal. I can alter any document; that's how I make a living. We could have some fun, and then I can do whatever you need." They had reached the *allée,* and he stopped the car. He wrote something in his notebook, and gave the sheet of paper to Silvia.

"Here's my number. My name is Pierre. Call me if you need me."

Silvia got out of the car without looking at him. She waited until the taillights had faded into the night, and only then began walking in the same direction. She crumpled the piece of paper in her hand and dropped it in the gutter, but then stooped down and picked it up. *You never know,* she thought.

ARIANNE and Silvia were having breakfast. Arianne was now two weeks overdue, and Nana had gone to do the daily shopping. It was the first time they had been on their own since Arianne had become housebound.

"In which hospital will you have the baby, in case I have to take you there?" Silvia asked, buttering a piece of *baguette.*

"You won't have to take me anywhere, because I'm going to have the baby right here," replied Arianne.

Silvia was surprised. "Why?" she asked. "It's safer if there are doctors around."

"Balls," replied Arianne, looking cross.

"It's not fair to the baby, you know," Silvia added.

"Mind your own business," Arianne said tartly, but then she patted her friend's hand.

"I'm sorry; I'm a pain in the ass at the moment. I know you're worried, but there is a reason why I don't want to have my baby in the hospital. They will start asking questions, and as soon as they find out that I am on my own, earning my living as a *putain,* they will take my baby away and give it up for adoption. People like you and me live outside the fence, and we should stay outside. If once you go inside they'll kill you."

Silvia was not so sure, but she did not argue.

"Don't worry," Arianne went on, "Nana knows everything about these things, and she'll be in charge. I'll just scream and shout, and you two will have to get on with it."

Arianne stood with difficulty and walked toward the kitchen, but she stopped suddenly, letting out a shout of pain. Water gushed down her legs, soaking her skirt and forming a pool on the floor. She rested one hand on the nearest chair, while she rubbed her lower back with the other hand.

"Here we go, honey," she said to Silvia. "That was a nice big pain."

Silvia rushed to her and helped Arianne to her bedroom, where she lay on the bed. Arianne turned on the radio.

"*. . . que c'est triste Venise . . .*" The mournful voice of Charles Aznavour filled the room. Arianne switched stations.

"I'm going to be the only one moaning here today, *merde,*" she said. She changed the station, and rested her head on the pillow.

Silvia began talking about her clients, in an attempt to take Arianne's mind off the pain. Arianne listened for a while, then suddenly her face contorted.

"Another one," she said. They heard Nana coming in, and Silvia rushed to meet her.

"Nana, thank God you're here. Arianne is in bed; her water broke."

"I can see that," Nana replied, looking at the puddle in the middle of the room. Silvia went into the kitchen, and came back with a bucket and a cloth. She mopped up while Nana left her shopping bag on the table and went to Arianne.

Once she finished clearing up the mess, Silvia washed the breakfast things and then returned to the bedroom. Nana was sitting next to Arianne, holding her hand. Silvia sat at the end of the bed. Nana's face was serious, almost solemn. Silvia had never seen her look so concentrated on anything; it was as if her life suddenly made sense to her.

The day passed slowly, or so it seemed to Silvia. It was nearly seven o'clock, the sun was setting, and Arianne's contractions were now very frequent. Instinctively, she began to push and bend up her knees, but Nana told her to wait. Nana had piled up all the pillows and cushions in the apartment behind Arianne's back. She now helped Arianne move forward, so that she could stand at the end of the bed and help with the delivery.

"I can feel it coming, Nana . . . ," Arianne groaned, her brow and upper lip moist with sweat. She squeezed Nana's hand. "Nana, I feel as if the baby is pushing in my ass. Please, let me push," she screamed, as her eyes filled with tears.

"I'm splitting, Nana, I can't stand it. Please let me, Nana, please!"

"It won't be long now, love, I can see the head. Push now! Push hard!" Nana said. Silvia moved on tiptoe behind Nana, eager to see. The crown of the baby's head was visible, the hair matted and wet. Slowly, very slowly, the head pushed out until the little face could be seen, eyes closed. Silvia felt a lump in her throat when she saw the tiny face, covered in a lardlike substance and streaked with blood.

Nana swiftly picked up some gauze from the little table she had set up by the bed, and wiped the eyes, nose, and mouth. She then seemed to kiss the baby's mouth and nose, and Silvia realized that she was sucking them.

Once the head was out, one shoulder soon followed, then the other. Silvia watched as the tiny hands appeared, followed by the skinny torso. Nana lifted the baby's head and shoulders up, and Arianne was able to see it between her raised knees. Her face lit up, and she stretched her hands toward her newborn child. "My baby . . . my baby . . . ," she repeated again and again.

Nana held the baby up, tears streaming down her cheeks. "It's a girl, my darling, an adorable little girl." Silvia was also crying, gripped by the urge to protect a being both so helpless and so wonderful.

The little girl's face seemed to show anger. Nana held her upside down, and sucked the tiny mouth and nose again. The baby began to cry, and Silvia saw her skin tone change from dark blue to healthy pink. Nana laid the baby on a folded towel on the bed, tied the cord in two places, and cut it with the pair of scissors she had sterilized earlier. She quickly knotted the cord, then wrapped the baby in a terry-cloth diaper. The little girl was crying loudly, and her skin was bright pink. With a smile, Nana presented her to Arianne.

"Here's your daughter," she said, handing the small bundle to its mother.

Silvia stood next to Arianne, and looked at the baby gripping her mother's little finger.

"What will you call her?" she asked.

"Gloria," Arianne replied. "She's the most wonderful thing that ever happened to me."

ARIANNE was washing Gloria's diapers, when she suddenly raised her eyes and looked out of the window.

"It's a beautiful night. Why don't we go out for a beer before work?" she asked Silvia. "I've been stuck here for three weeks, and I want to celebrate my last moments of freedom."

Silvia dropped the copy of the gossip magazine she was reading. She had become addicted to it because it gave her an insight into a fairytale world of aristocrats and castles.

"I'll be ready in a minute," she said.

The night before, Arianne had announced during dinner that she would go back to work the next day. "I can't afford to keep on doing nothing. I'll feed Gloria at midnight, and then we can go together to the Bois. I'm sure you'll hear her, Nana. Give her sugared water if she cries, but I don't think she'll wake up. She sleeps like a log."

"Don't worry, I know what to do about babies. It's all I really know," Nana had said.

Now Silvia noticed that Arianne had made herself up with particular care for her first night back at work. "Some guy is going to be very lucky tonight," she said. "You look very good."

"I don't give a shit about the guys, but I wanted to look nice. I've looked like a monkey for the last two months." As they left the building, Arianne glanced at the sky.

"We're lucky with the weather," she said. "It's very warm. Let's walk to Pigalle and have our beer there."

They walked along the Boulevard Barbès, and stopped briefly at a kiosk to glance at the covers of the women's magazines, all about the recent haute couture shows.

"That's lovely," said Arianne, pointing at a blue satin evening coat on the cover of *Jours de France*. The bold caption across the picture read, "Balenciaga — Autumn-Winter '68."

"Imagine thinking about winter clothes now; those people are crazy. Come on, let's go." Arianne took Silvia by the arm and led her away.

They turned into the Boulevard Rochechouart. As they approached Place Pigalle, the sidewalks became more and more crowded, and soon they were weaving their way through a throng of people, mostly men, drawn by the local fleshpots.

"In a year's time, I'm going to be out of this business," said Arianne. "It stinks. Look at these men; they are like dogs panting for food."

Silvia didn't look. She had seen the scene too many times. She saw it every day and sometimes at night, in her dreams. She also wanted out, and the thought of Pierre flashed through her mind. Maybe he could get her new papers, a chance of escape.

"What will you do?" she asked Arianne.

"I want to save as much money as possible, and then try to rent a small café by the sea, somewhere in the Bay of Biscay. I've never been there, but that's where Nana grew up, and I know she would like to go back. Gloria would be happy in a place like that, playing on the beach and making sand castles. Maybe you could come with us."

"I'd love to," said Silvia. For a moment she imagined herself with Arianne, Nana, and Gloria, happily working together in a little café by the sea, their own masters at last, but the improbability of the dream was horribly clear to her. Sooner or later she knew she would be thrown out of France. Even if Pierre were to get her new papers, she would have no guarantee that they would stand up to inspection.

Arianne pointed at the café across the boulevard.

"Let's cross the street. It's less crowded over there, and we can sit outside." As she stepped from the curb, a man approached her from behind and pinched her bottom, grinning at his mates on the pavement.

Arianne turned around, rage on her face. "You motherfucker," she screamed, looking at the man's face, at his self-satisfied grin. She stepped back farther into the street, to get some distance so she could kick him in the balls, but the black car with the dipped lights, driving too fast along the boulevard, didn't give her a chance. It sent her flying in the air like a rag doll. She hit the ground head first, hard against the granite curb. Her neck was broken before she could comprehend what had happened, even before she could scream. Silvia rushed to her, and gathered her limp body in her arms. Tears rolled down her cheeks as she embraced the best friend she had ever had.

She cried first in anguish, and then in rage at the stupidity of Arianne's being killed because of some lout showing off to his friends. Her anger overwhelmed her. She stood up, and started hitting the boy, insulting him, screaming out her hatred. The crowd around them enjoyed the scene at first, but then someone shouted, "Call the police," followed by a "Yes, yes, call the police" chorus of approval from the bystanders.

Silvia heard the word *police,* and her heart froze in panic. "People like you and me live outside the fence, and we should stay outside. If you go inside, they'll kill you." Arianne had said. The police would be there soon. They would take her to the station to make a statement, and they would ask for her papers. It would be just a matter of time before she ended up in the nightmare of a Brazilian jail.

There was no time to lose. She stood up, wrenching herself away from the inert body. She was swamped with guilt: she was betraying the person who had helped her most, but she had no choice. She pushed her way through the crowd, muttering, "I must get to a phone," and rushed into the café at the corner. She walked rapidly across the café and out again into the Rue des Martyrs. She ran as fast as she could along the Circus Medrano, until she reached the Avenue Trudaine. She could hear the police and ambulance sirens in the distance, but looking over her shoulder, she was relieved to see that nobody was following her.

As she relaxed, her grief took over. She walked back automatically, her face ravaged by sorrow and tears. Only when she reached home did she realize that she would have to break the terrible news to Nana. She thought of Gloria, left without a mother, in the hands of a grandmother who could not face the outside world. She was the only one who could look after them. As she began to climb the stairs, Silvia knew that these two helpless people were to be both her burden and her salvation.

She had regained her composure by the time she reached the top. She let herself in, and went to Nana's room. She knocked at the door, and then walked in without waiting for an answer.

Nana was sitting on her narrow iron bed, still dressed. Her prayer book was open on her lap, and she was holding her rosary beads. She raised her eyes.

"You have bad news," she said.

"Yes," Silvia replied, gathering her strength. "Nana, something terrible has happened." She told her about the accident, making an effort not to cry.

"I couldn't stay, Nana, but I assure you that Arianne was dead. You know that I have problems with my papers. If the police find me, they will throw me out of France, and I can't go back to my country." Nana did not ask why; there was only one thing she wanted to find out.

"Do you know where they took her? I want to see her." Nana stood up, as if ready to go. Silvia took a deep breath. She knew what she had to say, and she knew that it was the only solution for all of them. But it did not make saying it any easier.

"Nana, listen to me. Arianne was your daughter, and I know how you feel. You have lost the person you loved most in the world. But we have to think about the future. We have to think about Gloria. That's what Arianne would have wanted us to do."

She paused for a moment. Nana seemed about to ask something, but then she lowered her eyes, and Silvia continued.

"I know you want to see Arianne, and you want to bury her. It's your right as her mother to grieve for her. But I don't know where they took her. The only way to find out is to call the police. At the moment, Arianne is simply an unidentified body; as soon as they know who she is, they will find you, and then they will find me."

Silvia closed her eyes for a moment, and bit her lip. She couldn't stop now; she dug her nails into her palm, and went on, her eyes fixed on Nana's.

"Once I'm gone, there'll be no one to support you and little Gloria. It will be only a matter of time before you'll have to either give her up for adoption or worse. If you are prepared to leave things as they are, and Arianne is never identified, I swear to God that I'll take care of you and Gloria for as long as I live. I love Gloria as if she were my own daughter, and I'll look after you as if you were my own mother. I promise you that you'll never want for anything."

She was about to continue, when she noticed the anguish in Nana's face.

"You are asking me to give up my daughter," Nana said in a strangled voice. "It's too much."

"No, Nana," Silvia replied, "I wouldn't dare do that. I'm asking you to give up her body, for the sake of your granddaughter. And for your own sake as well as mine."

Nana walked around the room in silence for a moment, and stood in front of an old photograph of her husband, her back to Silvia.

"I'll have to think about what you said. I'll talk to you tomorrow morning." She didn't turn around. She just stood there, silently waiting for Silvia to leave the room. Nana already knew what her answer would be. She had lost Arianne. She would not lose her granddaughter.

As soon as she left Nana's room, Silvia rushed to Arianne's bedroom. She stopped for a moment to look at the sleeping baby. The sight brought tears to her eyes. She touched Gloria's cheek, then turned abruptly and began to look in the drawers of the battered old chest opposite the bed. She knew what she was looking for, and it took her just a moment to find it.

Silvia walked into her own room and slipped the dog-eared card inside one of the magazines. She emptied the contents of her bag on the bed, and picked up a crumpled piece of paper and her keys. She listened outside Nana's door for a moment, but she could hear no noise. Gloria was safely asleep. In any case, she would be back home in a moment. The café was just fifty yards away, and the phone call was going to be very brief.

THE magnificent dome of the Pantheon, shining silver in the moonlight, was visible at the end of the Rue des Carmes, but Silvia did not notice. As she turned into the Rue Lanneau, her thoughts were concentrated on her imminent meeting with Pierre.

She had been to see him ten days ago, soon after her phone call on the night of Arianne's death. She had given him the card, and explained what she wanted. He inspected the dog-eared *carte d'identité*, then raised his eyes.

"I assume that this person is not going to complain about the change. Otherwise, I can do what you ask without any trouble, but it will cost more money than you can pay."

"How do you know how much money I have?" Silvia had asked contemptuously.

"I don't, but my price will always be more money than you can afford." He fondled her buttocks. "Alternatively, you can pay me by spending the night here, and doing everything I ask you to do." He stared at her, a repellent leer in his cold eyes.

Silvia thought for a moment, but realized that she had little choice.

"I accept your deal. I don't know what you have in mind, but make sure that I get home the following morning. I'll leave a note for my mother saying that I spent the night at this address."

Pierre laughed.

"You are unnecessarily careful, but I respect that. We professionals have to look after ourselves." His face suddenly changed, a no-nonsense business look replacing his lascivious expression.

"I have to take some pictures of you," he said, beginning to set up a white photographic backdrop. He disappeared behind a closet at the end of the room, and came back with a set of lights and a camera on a tripod. Once the lights and camera were carefully set up, he sat Silvia on a stool. He checked the viewfinder and adjusted the height of the stool, and shot several pictures of her in quick succession.

"Come back in ten days, at the same time," he said. "It will be ready by then."

Now she had come to pick up the key to her new life. After walking a few yards down the Rue Lanneau, she came to his building. His studio was at the back of the courtyard. She knocked at the door, and waited.

He opened it with a smile, and let her in. It was a warm evening, but she noticed that all the windows were closed, and the white canvas blinds were rolled down.

The room was very large, and fashionably simple. The walls and the tiled floor were white, and light wooden beams spanned the ceiling, a few spotlights fixed to them here and there. At the opposite end of the room, a huge futon rested against a white curtain covering the wall from end to end.

Pierre led her by the arm to the table, and offered her a seat. He went to the kitchen and came back with a bottle of wine and two glasses.

"I'm very pleased with the results of my work, and I am sure that you will be too. Let's celebrate."

"I don't want anything," Silvia said. "Where are my papers?"

His eyes hardened. "Don't make it more difficult than it needs to be. Have some wine, and at least pretend to enjoy yourself. I'm sure you can do that very well."

Pierre poured the wine, then picked up an envelope from the table. He opened it, and handed an identity card to Silvia.

Her heart jumped. It was her face on the photograph, the stamp over it, as good as any other French *carte d'identité*. She read the name, so famliar and yet so odd juxtaposed with her own face. She would have to get used to it.

Pierre raised his glass.

"*Santé,* Arianne Delors," he toasted her, and took a sip of his wine. Silvia left her glass untouched.

"There's only one problem," Pierre said. "How are you going to explain your accent? Someone born in Arlanc wouldn't speak that way. I thought of changing the birthplace to Argel or Casablanca, but you would have trouble, sooner or later, if you had to produce the card together with your birth certificate. You'd better think of some explanation."

"I already have," replied Silvia. "My parents took me to Brazil when I was little, and I grew up there. They died in an accident, and I only learned French when I came back here, not long ago."

"Not bad," Pierre said admiringly. He took her hand and led her to the other end of the room, toward the bed.

"We've done enough talking. You stand here, and take your

clothes off. *Very* slowly. We have plenty of time." He lay on the bed, his arms behind his head.

She did as she was told, thinking only about the following morning, and her life from then on.

At last, she was naked. He stared at her admiringly and grinned, then stood up and pulled the curtain cord. The curtain behind him opened, revealing old stone masonry. A collection of whips was neatly lined up on a specially made rack.

"Now we are going to have a really good time," he said, unbuttoning his shirt.

IT was mid-September, and autumn was already in the air. Soon the leaves on the huge plane trees lining the avenue would begin to drop.

Silvia looked forward to the change of season. She wanted to plan for the future. A different season underlined the passage of time. What had happened in the spring was becoming the past.

Silvia had had no trouble adapting to a completely new set of circumstances. In no time at all she had convinced herself that her name was Arianne, and that she had a small daughter called Gloria. It went beyond conviction, because mere beliefs can be disproved or abandoned. In Silvia's mind, they became facts beyond dispute.

She just wished that Nana had at least some of her strength. Silvia had explained to her that she would be able to pass herself off as a French citizen only by saying that she had been brought up in Brazil. If Nana pretended to be her mother, sooner or later her lack of knowledge about that country would reveal the lie; therefore she would never be free to admit that she was Gloria's grandmother. Silvia had also insisted that they move out of the apartment immediately, to a place she had found in the Rue Beaunier, at the other end of Paris, where nobody knew them.

Nana had accepted the arrangement and its conditions, but it was obvious that she had not come to terms with it. She had given up calling her Silvia, and remained impassive when she introduced herself as Arianne, but Nana never called her by that name. She didn't call her anything at all. If unavoidable, she addressed her as "child." Silvia found the habit annoying, but she preferred not to raise the issue. She hoped that in time it would go away.

Money was the priority now. She was tired of living in squalor: it had been the nightmare of her own childhood, and she would not tolerate it for her daughter.

The day after Pierre gave her her new papers, she rushed downstairs to buy *Le Figaro* as soon as she woke up, ignoring her aches, and eagerly began to search through the employment ads. She was prepared to do anything: clean houses, be a waitress; any job that would take her out of the Bois would do. But she came up against the same word again and again: *references*. That night she was back in the Bois, as usual.

She found comfort in the thought that, even there, she now had alternatives. Until then the Bois had been her only option, a place where outcasts like her knew the police would leave them alone. But she was no longer an outcast; she was a French citizen. Arianne had mentioned the Avenue Foch. Maybe she should give it a try. But she needed much better clothes for that, and good clothes cost money. She would have to work extra hours.

Her thoughts were interrupted by the lights of a car approaching her. She moved to the curb and stood there, her legs slightly apart, her body visible through the wide mesh of her crocheted microdress. The car looked expensive, and she decided to up her rates.

The car stopped, and Silvia smiled invitingly, her eyes on the driver. Only then could she really see him: the man had dyed blond hair, eye makeup, gold bracelets, and a white shawl draped around his shoulders. She could not understand why such a raving queen would bother with her.

The driver got out of the car and walked up to her. He was smiling broadly.

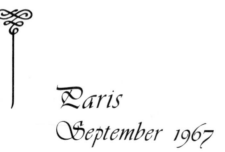

11

Paris
September 1967

CRISTOBAL Balenciaga was a master in his field. His whole life had been a search for perfection: the perfect fabric, the perfect cut, the perfect shape and, above all, the perfect woman to wear his masterpieces.

Now he was getting old and tired, and his world was coming to an end. His purpose had been to create dreams for swans. But suddenly there were no more swans, only common girls in miniskirts and tight sweaters, and they did not want the aggravation of endless fittings; an off-the-rack crotch-skimming shift in a drip-dry polyester was all they needed. An air of death hung over his gilded salons, and he sensed that he was working on his last collections. One, maybe two further shows, no more.

Because he felt it was his last year at the Maison, he was determined to make it the best ever, his farewell to a vocation he had followed with the intensity of a religious belief. At last, he had polished his *cabine* to perfection. Twelve models, twelve goddesses, each of them reflecting one aspect of his vision.

The showing of his winter collection in June had been as frenetic and exhausting as usual, but he had begun working on the next one the day after. As was his custom, he had locked himself in his inner sanctum with the model who most fired his inspiration. Only by draping the fabric on the chosen one could his vision become real. Once the concept had been perfected, the rest of the collection would follow, but only then.

That season, the model who was the essence of his vision was Ilona, the icy Hungarian beauty whose flight from behind the Iron Curtain had captured the public's imagination. They had worked together for nearly two weeks, day and night, until Ilona had insisted on a break and had left for a brief holiday on the Côte d'Azur. The framework of his dream was nearly complete, but more work was necessary. It would have to wait until his muse was back.

Disaster struck suddenly. Ilona's lover, an Italian industrialist, walked out on her after a row which had disastrous consequences for the furnishings of the Royal Suite at the Négresco. It was too much for the poor girl. Her inert body was found by a maid the following morning, two empty bottles of sleeping pills by the side of the bed. As soon as Ilona's coffin had been lowered into her grave, the other mannequins had tried on her dresses, the pearls of his next collection. It was no good. None of them had Ilona's special magic, her presence, her cool arrogance.

It was early September now, and somewhere in the world there was the woman he needed. If the collection was to be ready on time, the Maestro had to find her before the end of the month.

JACQUES Villette was fed up, really and truly fed up. He had been a makeup artist for many years, and he had done the couture shows for nearly ten seasons. He had worked for Dior and Chanel. Both of them were exacting masters, but nothing compared to what he had experienced today, trying to interpret the wishes of Monsieur Balenciaga.

He had been called at short notice, after the usual makeup artist employed by the Maison had left in hysterics, exhausted by the Maestro's requests. Balenciaga was interviewing new models to replace Ilona, and he wanted them made up to resemble his dead star. Jacques had tried everything, used every trick, but nothing seemed to please the Maestro. Two of the girls were in tears by the end of the afternoon, and one stormed out of the room, swearing loudly. Jacques was tempted to give up too.

"Maestro, we have tried everything on these girls. Perhaps if you were to describe the face to me, the vision that you have in mind, perhaps then I will understand." Balenciaga expressed his thoughts in his usual laconic manner, and Jacques listened very carefully.

Suddenly, something in the description struck a chord in Jacques's memory.

Jacques Villette never forgot a face. Faces were his business, his passion. He knew that somewhere, some time ago, he had seen a face which coincided with the vision of the great couturier. He sat at home, relaxing over a glass of whisky, and tried to remember where. After a while, he decided to think about something else, to take his mind off the problem. He needed some distraction, a bit of easy relaxation. He stood in front of the mirror and fluffed up his dyed blond hair, draped the white silk scarf over his shoulders, got into his car, and drove toward the Bois de Boulogne.

It was as he steered toward the Avenue de Saint Cloud and its collection of readily available studs that he remembered. A few months ago, driving down the same route, he had seen a whore in the road, trying to interest him. She had been naked, or nearly naked. Her body was long and graceful, but there was about her none of the exhausted air common to mannequins. She had seemed as serenely elegant in her whorish underwear as most models in evening dresses.

Jacques Villette didn't give a damn about women's bodies. Her face, though, was something else. He had not seen a face as perfect as that for a long, long time. For a moment Jacques thought of stopping the car and asking her to come to his place the following day for a test session, but these whores were like alley cats. He wanted to get to the avenue as soon as possible anyway, and he soon forgot about the encounter.

But now he remembered. He knew that girl was what the Maestro was looking for. If only he could find her. There were hundreds of tarts in the Bois. Still, he would give it a try.

He had driven only a couple of hundred yards into the Bois when he saw her, standing in his path in the full glare of his headlights, and his heart jumped. Not even the atrocious cheap dress, the exaggerated makeup, could conceal her uniqueness. As he got closer, her eyes shone like topaz in the dark. He stopped the car.

THE alarm clock went off at eight as usual, and Silvia woke up. She had been sleeping in this room for over a week now, but every morning, before getting up, she went through the same ritual. She looked around her, and hoped that one day she would have a bedroom as lovely as this.

The training had been exhausting, but Jacques seemed pleased with her progress. She had moved into his place the morning after their conversation in the Bois; he had wanted her to come with him that night, but she had insisted that she would make her own way the following morning. She wanted to see Gloria before going away, and to explain to Nana that she would stay somewhere else for a few days. Silvia gave Jacques's phone number to Nana and asked her to call her every day from the café, when she took Gloria out for a walk.

Silvia had been stunned by Jacques's apartment, at the bottom end of the Rue Henri Barbusse, near Montparnasse. Her only experience with comfortable living had been the apartment in Rio, but this was a new dimension. There was a large sitting room, with floor-to-ceiling windows on one side, overlooking a beautiful chestnut tree in the courtyard. Jacques had put her up in his bedroom, and he slept in the spare bed in the gallery overlooking the sitting room.

Jacques had coached her in every aspect of modeling: her posture, her walk, her makeup. He had borrowed clothes from friends, and explained to her how to show each type of garment to its best advantage. Every moment of the day was a lesson: how to eat, how to turn her head, how to sit gracefully. Jacques had also told her, again and again, never to smile. "Monsieur Balenciaga believes that truly elegant women have a disagreeable air," he explained.

After Nana's first phone call, Silvia had begun to explain to Jacques that she had a small daughter who was being looked after by an old friend, but Jacques wasn't interested. "We all have stories, darling," he had said. "I don't want to know about yours any more than you want to know about mine. Now let's try walking with a really big hat on" — and he had dropped the subject.

Silvia stretched her arms. Time to get up. She had a quick shower, and then got dressed in the borrowed clothes that Jacques had given her the night before. "Put this on tomorrow morning," he had said.

She walked out of her bedroom, and found Jacques in the sitting room having breakfast. She sat down opposite him. She poured coffee into her cup, adding three lumps of sugar. She then buttered her croissant, and spread a lavish amount of blackberry jam on it.

"I'm amazed that you can eat like a horse, and have a figure like yours. It's so annoying," said Jacques, toying with his box of saccharine tablets. He lit an extra-long Kent, and blew several smoke rings.

Silvia stretched her hand toward the cigarette pack, but Jacques moved them away.

"Not tonight, Joséphine. I wanted you to sleep well and look wonderful this morning, so I didn't tell you last night that we are seeing Monsieur Balenciaga at eleven o'clock. He hates women who smoke, and you won't get the job if you stink of cigarettes."

"If I get the job, I will not smoke. Ever again," Silvia promised.

She felt a mixture of excitement and fear. In two hours, her life could change dramatically. If she was accepted, she would leave the squalor of the past behind her forever; if not, she would be back in the Bois that night, pinned to a car seat by the body weight of some man. It was very simple: she could not afford to fail.

"Time to work now," he said, leading her toward the bedroom. He pointed at the dressing table, and she sat down in front of it.

Jacques picked up a brush and comb from the table. A handful of hairpins in his mouth, he skillfully pulled her dark hair back into a severe knot. "You don't need hair with a face like yours." He gently pushed her chin up, and looked at her in the full light of the huge window.

"You are perfect," he said after a moment. "Let's make you even more perfect." Brush in hand, he leaned forward, and she closed her eyes. For the next half-hour he remained in complete silence; the only sounds she could hear were his breathing next to her face and the rattling and shaking of bottles as he picked them up one by one, followed by the caress of sable brushes on her skin. Wide brushes, narrow brushes, some wet, some dry: they went over very inch of her face, until she finally heard him drop them on the glass-topped table.

"Now look at yourself," he said. She could hear the pride in his voice.

She opened her eyes, and her heart jumped. He had showed her the possibilities of her face before, but this morning he had worked a transformation. She stood up and kissed him on the cheek.

"Careful with your lipstick!" he said, immediately retouching her mouth with a small brush.

As their taxi drove onto the Pont de la Concorde, the magnificence of the scene in the morning sun struck Silvia as a good omen. It was as if a golden future were here, waiting for her.

They turned into the Avenue George V, and stopped outside an imposing stone building. "Balenciaga," read the elegant lettering on the cornice at both sides of the huge oak door, repeated on the smart white awnings over the eight windows along the street, and matched in gold embroidery on the uniformed doorman's cap. Suddenly she was terrified.

Jacques paid the driver, and got out of the car.

"Come on, you have nothing to worry about," he said, opening her door and holding out his hand to help her. Silvia squeezed his hand.

"I'm scared," she whispered.

"I can feel it, my dear; you are about to break my fingers," Jacques said. He embraced her. "Darling, compared to some of the things you must have done in the Bois, this is child's play." It was his first reference to her past since they had been together, and her face made him look away in embarrassment. After a moment, he patted her shoulder. "If it weren't for the makeup, I would give you a big kiss." He held her arm, and led her to the side door.

They found their way to the elevator among the bolts of fabric lining the tiled corridor, but Silvia was not particularly aware of the surroundings. Her eyes were staring ahead with extraordinary intensity, and she followed Jacques, oblivious to anything other than the back of his head.

The elevator stopped, and Jacques held the gate open.

"This is our floor," he said. She heard him only faintly, as if he were far, far away. She got out of the elevator and walked behind him, until he stopped in front of a padded double door.

"I'll go in now. I'll call you when he is ready to see you," Jacques said, and disappeared through the door.

Silvia began to shake violently. In a moment, it would all be over.

"Pull yourself together, you idiot," she said to herself. Suddenly, she remembered Gloria's little face, and her fear vanished. She took a deep breath and opened her eyes, just in time to see Jacques smile at her, holding the huge door open.

"Come on. Monsieur Balenciaga is waiting," he said.

Head high, shoulders thrown back, hips slightly forward. She remembered all of Jacques's instructions, and sailed into the huge room as if she owned it. Her eyes were fixed on the Spanish-looking elderly man sitting on a high stool at the other end of the room. He was wearing a white smock, as were the eleven exquisite models lined up behind him. She approached him, her eyes focused on his forehead, somewhere between the thick framed glasses and the roots of his slicked-back hair, as Jacques had told her to do.

"Maestro, this is Arianne, the girl I mentioned to you a while ago. I thought you might find her suitable."

Balenciaga stepped down, and walked toward her. It wasn't his expression that told her that she had won; it was the hatred on the girls' faces behind him.

"I am very pleased to meet you, Arianne," he said, holding out his hand. "Welcome to my Maison."

Part Three

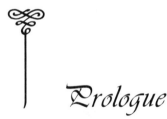

Prologue

HATRED is a great forger of character: it shaped Simón de la Force into the man he was. It had also determined the fate of the first de la Force to settle in Argentina, two hundred years before Simón's birth.

In 1707, at the time of the War of the Spanish Succession, Louis Delaforce, a young French surgeon from the Nantes region, was drafted into the medical staff of the King's Cavalry and sent to the front. He was wounded in the battle of Almanza and given up for dead, but he was picked up by monks from the nearby convent and, after nearly a year of convalescence, he recovered his health.

He did not, however, regain his love for his country. He felt betrayed by his compatriots who had left him behind like a discarded carcass; war-ravaged Spain was not to his liking either, and he decided to try the New World. He boarded a ship in Cádiz and sailed for Buenos Aires, the first leg of his long journey to Lima, the center of power in Spanish America, where he had been told that his skills would be in demand.

He had a very vague notion of the distances involved. After nearly two thousand miles of traveling by coach, horse, mule, and foot, on miserable roads, he reached the area of Northwestern Argentina now known as the province of Salta, which was then an empty land dotted with a few villages and towns in the valleys.

He was struck by the beauty of the mountainous landscape, the hillsides striped by the layering of gold, burnt siena, and red soils, their colors sharpened by the bluest sky he had ever seen. After the inferno of the central Argentine plain during the summer months, the dry climate was a blessing, and when he reached the village of San Simón he decided to rest there for a few days.

As soon as word got around that a doctor was staying at the inn, his services were eagerly sought out by the Spanish and Creole families who had settled in the area, and soon after his arrival he shared his bed with María Tupac, one of the Indian girls working at the inn. After so many months of penury and abstinence, both events contributed to his sudden feeling of well-being, and a few days later Louis's mind was made up.

He settled in a small adobe house rented from one of his patients. The Indian girl moved in with him, to the horror of the locals, particularly the pious matrons who occupied the front pews of the church, but the nearest reliable doctor was seventy miles away, and they needed him, so the arrangement was tolerated. In time, a baby arrived, then a second, and Monsieur Delaforce, or Don Luis, as he was now known, became an integral part of village life.

In 1719 Don Gaspar Céspedes del Campo, Marqués del Alcorcón, fourteenth Viceroy of Peru, decided to inspect the lands he governed on behalf of His Most Catholic Majesty. After months of slow progress through the various regions of the viceroyalty, the marquis and his interminable retinue of attendants and courtiers reached the Valle de Oro, near San Simón. It was here, in the middle of the huge plain, that fever struck. Soon the viceroy was delirious, and fear for his life spread among his courtiers. The viceroy's physician, affected by altitude sickness, had been sent back to Lima a few days before. Soldiers on horseback were dispatched to the nearest towns to try to find a doctor, while priests knelt around the stricken grandee and prayed around the clock to the Holy Mother for his recovery.

Louis Delaforce was the first doctor the soldiers found, and he was immediately taken to the viceroy's bedside. He realized that he must either cure the nobleman, or risk losing his own life. He tried everything. The viceroy was bled, purged, bathed in cold water, and wrapped in hot blankets, while Indian herbal potions prepared by María were forced between his almost white lips.

Some part of the treatment must have worked. After two days Don Gaspar was able to sit up in bed, and by the third day he was back on his feet. His gratitude was unbounded: the Valle del Oro was given to Don Luis and his descendants, consent was granted his marriage to María, and their children were recognized as legiti mate. It was at that time that the family name was formally changed to de la Force.

The viceroy also ordered that a church to the Holy Mother be built on the campsite, at the top of the Yanbi hill. One twentieth of that year's production of the Potosi silver mine was to be used for this purpose, and the six largest emeralds in the treasury in Lima were set into a gold necklace to adorn the image of the Virgin at the high altar. The custody of the church was granted in perpetuity to the de la Force family. Having thus expressed his gratitude, the viceroy returned to his capital. He never went back to Valle del Oro to see either the church or the solid-silver image of the Virgin with the six green stones around its neck.

The lavish shrine became an incongruity in the middle of a dry, empty plain, soon forgotten by anyone other than the local population. The vastness of the Valley of Gold ensured a modestly comfortable livelihood for Don Luis and his family, but its name owed more to the optimism of the first settlers than to the nature of its soil. No gold was ever found, and the lack of water made agriculture on any significant scale impossible. The valley was surrounded by the Sierras del Santo, a mountainous range that stopped all rain coming from the Pacific. The Rio Dulce flowed on the other side of the mountains, boxed in by a lower range of hills, its waters cut off from the fertile but parched soil in the valley.

In time, the de la Forces became one of the traditional families of the province. The males prudently married rich girls as a matter of principle, bringing into the family valuable farming land in other areas, either vineyards or tobacco plantations, but by the early part of the twentieth century, the family name was at risk of extinction.

Pedro de la Force, the last male of the line, had four daughters, and his wife died soon after the birth of the youngest girl. Don Pedro never remarried, but in his old age he took as his mistress one of the young Indian maids of the house. The girl became pregnant, to the shock of his married daughters. Then, to the horror of their husbands, Don Pedro promised marriage to the girl if the baby was a boy, with obvious implications for the daughters' eventual share of his estate.

The young mother delivered a healthy baby boy, christened Simón, and Don Pedro's joy was unrestrained. As soon as she had recovered, a discreet wedding ceremony took place, but the unleashed emotions took their toll. That evening, while sitting in his rocking chair in the gallery, listening to the splashing of the fountain in the courtyard and to the gurgling of his baby boy held by a servant girl, Don Pedro felt at peace with himself. He had secured the survival of his family name. He was enjoying this thought when his head dropped, and he suddenly stopped breathing the jasmine-scented air. A heart attack had killed him instantly.

His sons-in-law used their connections, and the apportionment of the de la Force estate took place in accordance with the letter of Argentine law. The daughters received the much smaller but fertile estates in various areas of the province, while Simón, the newborn son, became sole heir to the useless immensity of Valle del Oro, tens of thousands of hectares graced by the occasional cactus and over-valued for the purpose of probate to make them comparable to the daughters' share. No one was there to look after Simón's rights: his mother was an ignorant peasant overwhelmed by events, and his sisters had no desire to protect a half-Indian bastard at their own expense.

Simón grew up hating everyone around him: his mother for being an Indian peasant, his family for rejecting him, their friends for scorning him as a half-caste, the ludicrous carrier of a once fine name. Revenge was Simón's driving motivation; he would prove that he was better than any of them, he would make them beg for his condescension, let alone his forgiveness. But to achieve that he needed money or power, preferably both, and he had neither.

His mother struggled to raise him. Money was always desperately short. The contents of the house went piece by piece, but she under-stood only one thing: the house itself and the valley were untouch-able. Don Pedro had left them to his son, and Simón would receive them when he came of age. Her firmness of purpose was helped by the fact that it would have been impossible to find a buyer for the dusty valley, by then nearly empty. The young moved on to decent jobs in the new industrial belts around the big cities; only the old stayed there, to die.

In 1940, when President Castillo, himself a man from the North-west of Argentina, came to power, someone at Government House in the provincial capital dusted off the project for a huge hydro-electrical dam on the Rio Dulce. The Castillo government was over-thrown in 1943, however, and the interests of the Northwest once again receded into the background. But something much bigger began to rise in the political horizon: Colonel Perón.

Simón de la Force recognized the turning of the tide, and soon joined the new political movement, adding to the scorn of his well-off relations, all active in the Conservative Party. Perón and his followers were the scum of the earth to them, which made the new movement all the more attractive to Simón.

In the course of the presidential campaign at the end of 1945, when Juan Perón and his young wife, the popular actress Eva Duarte, visited the party headquarters in Salta, Simón de la Force was among those in the front line of the reception committee. He had the honor of a brief conversation with Señora Perón. It took only a few moments for them to recognize each other as kindred souls, and Eva suggested that if there was anything she could do for him, she would be only too pleased. Simón de la Force bowed in gratitude while the *señora* gave him a dazzling smile. A photographer recorded the charming moment, one of many on such a happy occasion.

Perón was elected president on February 12, 1946. On February 13, Eva started the frenzy of activity that would turn her into the most powerful woman of her time. That same night, Simón de la Force undid the padlock of the abandoned sanctuary at Yanbi, in the middle of his empty valley, and walked into the church for the first time since his childhood. Torch in hand, he climbed the altar and removed the necklace from the Madonna's neck.

As he was about to leave the church, the jewels in his pocket, he noticed that the high windows were rattling. He opened the door and realized that a violent windstorm had suddenly descended upon the valley, a sporadic phenomenon in the area. He took off his shirt and tied it over his horse's head. His left arm raised to protect his eyes from the clouds of dust, spurring on the terrified horse until its flanks bled, Simón de la Force rode through the valley, the storm raging around him. The next morning he went to the bank and emptied his small savings account. That night he was on the train to Buenos Aires.

He had never been to the big city, and he had not realized that life in the capital came to a standstill in January, when the summer heat softened the asphalt on the streets. The summer break lasted until March, and Simón was forced to spend a significant part of his money staying in a modest hotel in the Avenida de Mayo until then, waiting for the best jewelry shops to reopen. In the meantime he took one of the emeralds from the Madonna's necklace to the Banco Municipal, the city's official pawnbrokers, for evaluation. He could scarcely believe the figure they quoted.

He asked at the hotel for the name of the best jewelry shops in Buenos Aires, and went to look at them. He chose Ricciardi because they were the biggest. Simón put on his best suit, walked into Ricciardi, and asked for the manager. The salesman took one look at this half-Indian peasant wearing abominable clothes and felt tempted to show him the door, but there was something about Simón's presence that commanded attention, and he led him instead to the owner's office.

Before saying anything, Simón took five huge stones wrapped in tissue paper out of his pocket, and laid them on the black velvet tray on the man's desk. The jeweler was astonished by the finest set of emeralds he had seen in his life. The cut was very old-fashioned but they were nearly flawless. He was about to ask for their provenance when Simón put the photograph of his meeting with Eva Perón on the desk.

"These," he said, pointing at the stones, "are a present from the people of Valle del Oro to the *señora,* and you are going to turn them into the most beautiful necklace in Argentina for her. I know nothing about necklaces, but I know about pleasing the *señora.* If she's not pleased, you and I are going to be in trouble, and I wouldn't like that at all." The jeweler looked into Simón's eyes. The man's expertise in stones was second only to his knowledge of people.

"You will not be displeased, Señor . . ." — the man hesitated.

". . . de la Force," Simón said.

"Señor de la Force, we can make the most beautiful necklace in Argentina, and the *señora* will be delighted. However, as I am sure you know, such masterpieces are costly . . ." Simón put his hand in his pocket, and placed the sixth emerald in front of the jeweler.

"This one is in payment for your expenses. I know how much the stones are worth, and I will have the necklace valued at the Banco Municipal. It would be unwise to double-cross me. Your profit will be the *señora*'s appreciation of your superior craftsmanship."

The necklace was finished in two months, a spray of diamond

flowers with a huge emerald at the center of each blossom. As soon as he was notified that it was ready, Simón asked for an audience with Eva Perón.

The meeting took place at the presidential residence. He sat in the marble hall with dozens of other supplicants, but his name was called after he had waited for only an hour, a clear indication of Eva's recollection of their encounter.

"What do you want, Simón?" was her greeting to him. Whether plenipotentiary ambassadors or humble petitioners, Eva addressed everybody with coarse familiarity.

Simón took the folder from under his arm and placed it in front of her, on top of a huge blotter.

"Señora, these are the plans for a dam on the Rio Dulce. If the people of Valle del Oro don't get this dam, the valley will die. I look forward to the day when you will come to inaugurate the Eva Perón Dam, and save us from ruin."

Eva flicked through the dossier. "And what is that?" she asked, pointing at the large velvet box that Simón had placed on the blotter immediately after his explanation.

"The expression of our gratitude, Señora."

The dam was built in record time, and inaugurated by Eva Perón on November 20, 1948. By then, the Peronist government's grip on the financial system of the country was complete, and bank credits were available only to those whom the government wanted to encourage.

It paid to be a friend of the ruling party, and Simón de la Force was a very good friend indeed. Water from the dam and cheap bank credits gushed into the valley: irrigation and drainage systems were laid, roads and a railway system built. At last, the ground was ready, and millions of cane cuttings were planted. Fourteen months later the first crop was ripe for harvesting, the huge mills were waiting to process it into sugar, and the government was ready to buy it at a preferential price. The profits went into further investment into the factories that, using the cheap electricity from the dam, would turn the fibrous residue into paper, cardboard, and fiberboard, and into the distilleries that converted the molasses into industrial alcohol. The residues from molasses went into animal feeds, the filter mud from sugar juice clarification went into fertilizer production. Every leaf, every stem in the huge valley was profitable, and very soon Simón de la Force was the richest man in the Northwest.

But he did not stop there. The prices fixed by the government for beef and grain production were kept at absurdly low levels, unlike the price of sugar, and the value of prime land in the Pampas dropped dramatically. Simón became the main buyer of land during the Peronist years, until he was the largest landowner in the Buenos Aires province. He expanded his business into steel, textiles, banking, not only in Argentina, but in postwar France and Spain as well.

By 1955 Simón de la Force was the richest man in Argentina. The fall of the Peronist government cast a temporary shadow over his activities, but by then he was too big, too powerful to be affected by any change of government. He settled in Buenos Aires and became a leader of the Establishment, a member of the Jockey Club and the Círculo de Armas. He had long forgotten his grudge against his relations in Salta; they were too insignificant to deserve his hatred anymore. He had ruined them easily enough by choking bank credit to their businesses through his Party contacts, but now he felt magnanimous toward his sisters. When in Salta, he would send his chauffeur to distribute checks to them. The sums were not very large, because he did not wish to offend them.

In 1960, after fourteen years of thinking only about making money, his private life reduced to call girls brought in by his chauffeur to his office at short notice between business meetings, Simón de la Force decided that the time had come to secure his dynasty. He was forty-six years old. He had not married when he was young because no woman he would have wished to marry would have even glanced at him, but now he could have anyone he wanted.

The most beautiful girl in Buenos Aires society at the time was Dolores de Anzorena. After a brief engagement, the wedding of the year took place at the Santísimo Sacramento Church on October 20. Dolores looked exquisite. Simón's gifts to his bride included the best set of jewels in each precious stone at Ricciardi's shop, and a great house in the Avenida Alvear, the most elegant street in Buenos Aires, originally built by the bride's grandfather.

After a lavish honeymoon in Europe, the couple settled down to married life in Buenos Aires. Simón wanted a son as soon as possible. He wanted it more than anything in the world.

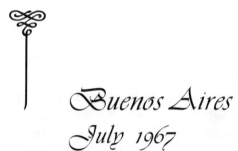

12

Buenos Aires
July 1967

... AND the future of our great nation, gentlemen, depends on you. I have no doubt that, like your predecessors, you will win that battle. The Argentine Revolution in 1966, under the tutelage of our armed forces, opened a glorious new chapter in our history. Now, only one year later, we can begin to see the benefits of order and discipline in our society, but much needs to be done to correct the damage of years of weak government. May God guide us in our struggle."

The Minister of Agriculture folded his notes and removed his glasses, confirming that his speech had come to an end. Eager applause followed from every corner of the restaurant in the exhibition grounds of the Sociedad Rural, the traditional society grouping Argentina's large farmers. Today, only the most successful among them had gathered for lunch.

It was the Society's Annual Show, the Exposición Rural, the main event for farmers in a country where farming is both the peak of the social order and the main source of exports. Today was *the* day: the parade of livestock would soon begin and the juries would choose the Great Champion bull in every breed, a moment of glory for its owner, worth years of work as well as vast expenditure. Nobody in that room had spent more money to achieve that glory than Simón de la Force.

As he approached the restaurant's exit on his way to the parade ground, he saw Dolores waiting for him near the door. By now, Simón didn't give a damn for his wife. She had failed to produce an heir, and she was as vacuous in conversation as she was wooden in bed. Still, after three miscarriages she was pregnant again. She looked very chic in her maternity panther coat, and she was flanked by María Carretas and Malena Hamilton, the two other reigning queens of the Buenos Aires social world.

Simón felt a surge of proprietorial pride; he slipped his vicuña overcoat over his shoulders, took a deep puff on his cigar and, wrapped in a mist of cigar smoke and Lanvin eau de toilette, he advanced toward the elegant trio, occasionally acknowledging somebody's greeting, more often simply ignoring them. He was, after all, Simón de la Force.

Dolores said good-bye to her friends, and held onto Simón's arm. "Simón, darling, I want to show you something. I've got a surprise for you."

Simón glanced at his watch and frowned.

"Where the hell do you want to take me now? We ought to go in," he said.

"It won't take a minute," she said, steering him toward the pavilion where the Shorthorn bulls were being groomed for the parade.

As soon as they walked in, the unmistakable smell of urine-soaked straw hit their nostrils. Dolores raised her collar and breathed in the Miss Dior scent on her lapel. They turned into the first of the three aisles where the Shorthorn bulls from "San Simón" were kept in individual pens.

"Look, Simón! Doesn't he look divine?" Dolores said proudly, pointing toward the magnificent white bull in the second pen on the righthand side.

San Simón Field Marshal 28, number 35297 in the *Argentine Herd Book,* was Simón de la Force's best Shorthorn bull that year, and a sure candidate for the Great Championship. His noble head stared impassively ahead, while the tip of his tail was being whipped into candy floss by the ministrations of Hubert, the star hairdresser of Buenos Aires, whose fame rested on the early patronage of Dolores de la Force. He appeared as resigned to his current circumstances as the bull, and impervious to the hatred in the eyes of the two gauchos whose job it was to look after the animal, and who were venomously staring at the hairdresser from a corner, chain-smoking Particulares.

"I thought I should do my bit to help you win, my darling," said Dolores, beaming at Simón.

He sighed, and took her arm. "Let's go," he mumbled before he virtually frog-marched her toward the grandstand.

It was Simón de la Force's afternoon. By four o'clock he had picked up the Great Champion prizes in the Shorthorn, Hereford, and Aberdeen Angus breeds, his bulls festooned in medals and rosettes. The Aberdeen Angus award, the prize among prizes, was presented by the Minister himself, and Simón and Dolores made their way to the ground amid the cheering and congratulations of all the lesser cattle barons around them.

As soon as they left the stand and walked into the arena, they were blinded by the photographers' flashbulbs. At last it was time for the grand finale, the slow march of the bulls on their way out of the ring, led by their owners. Prince Rupert of Valle del Oro, the Aberdeen Angus champion, was waiting for his master, barely able to see through the rosettes decorating his head.

Simón gallantly offered the bridle to Dolores. The band burst into the "Triumphal March" from *Aida* and the parade began. The spectators clapped as the procession unfolded in front of the stands.

It did not go far. Halfway to the exit, Dolores suddenly stumbled. She held her stomach with both hands, her shrill scream piercing the air as she collapsed to the ground, her New York furs smeared with dung.

"A doctor! Get a doctor quickly!" The word spread. The country's top veterinarians were on the grounds. They rushed to help, but Simón would not allow them to touch his wife. An ambulance was called, and twenty minutes later Dolores arrived at the Pequeña Compañía de María, the clinic run by nuns which was the usual choice of Buenos Aires' smart set.

The top gynecological specialists in Argentina had seen Dolores within two hours, and the following day a specially chartered jet brought Professor Lino von Kesti from Zurich. All medical opinions coincided: nothing could have prevented the miscarriage, and Dolores de la Force would never have children.

Simón de la Force had a problem. He could breed the best bulls in the world, but he could not have a son. At least not with his wife.

13

Paris
May 1968

EVERY morning, Arianne looked forward to her walk to work. It was the one part of her day when she could be alone with her thoughts. Her time at home, never enough, was either dedicated to Gloria, or to sorting out domestic matters with Nana, who had become her factotum as far as the running of the household was concerned. Arianne liked to be back early to be able to bathe Gloria, or at least put her to bed, but this was seldom possible. The Maestro's capacity for work was prodigious. He could inspect one hundred and eighty dresses in one day, tearing apart a sleeve here, changing the line of a collar there, his attention never waning. These fittings could go on well into the night, and it was impossible for any of the *cabine* models to leave before the Maestro had decided that he was, at last, satisfied.

After the January Collection, Arianne had become a star. Everybody had been dazzled by her beauty, her chic, and her aloofness, and the invitations had poured in: to grand balls, opening nights, elegant parties.

A different type of invitation had also been showered on her. Rich men, important men, dashing men — they all wanted at least to be seen with her, and most of them wanted more than just that. They wanted to go to bed with the most beautiful model in Paris, if only to be able to tell their friends.

Arianne invariably rejected these invitations. Sex had meant something to her with Ruben, but then it had become only a tool for

survival. Now that she no longer needed men, she was neither repelled nor attracted by them. She just wanted to be on her own.

Her reputation as a *femme de glace* grew, but it did her no harm.
Men redoubled their attentions, eager to be the first one to succeed
where others had failed. A very persistent German millionaire even
sent her a heavy gold bracelet, with an invitation to dinner at Maxim's. Before returning it, she showed it to her friend Cameline, a
beautiful English model at Balenciaga who was leaving soon to
marry a dashing Italian, the Principe di Sarteano.

"What an extraordinary idea," said Cameline. "Why would you
want to offend the poor man by returning it? It's just a present.
Look at it as though he had given you a box of chocolates. I would
keep it if I were you. And there is no reason why you shouldn't
accept the invitation. Just have dinner, and say 'thank you' afterward." Arianne went out to dinner and kept the bracelet, but felt
uncomfortable about it and never wore it.

The changes in every aspect of her life over the last few months
had been immense. Her greatest pride was that she had given Gloria
a proper home. She had taken a small apartment in the smart Rue
Bonaparte, near the Place Saint-Sulpice. Nana was able to take Gloria to the Luxembourg Gardens in the mornings, and Arianne enjoyed her daily walks up the Rue Bonaparte to the Quai, and then
along the river to the Pont de l'Alma.

But over the last two weeks her walks had become less pleasant.
Groups of students stood in the streets, around the Ecole des Beaux-
Arts and the École de Médécine at first, but over the last few days
they had mushroomed all over the Quarter. She had heard on the
radio that morning that thirty thousand people had marched from
the Gare de Lyon to the Place de la Bastille the night before, and
the police had been able to control them only after a tear-gas
bombardment. A group of demonstrators bearing axes, pick handles, and steel bars had broken into the Stock Exchange and set it
on fire.

As Arianne reached the Boulevard Saint Germain, she realized that
something had gone seriously wrong during the night. The scarring
of Molotov cocktails was visible on the front of several buildings,
and hundreds of police were patrolling the area. They had even said
on the radio that the president had left Paris.

Arianne found all this disturbing. She prayed to God that the showing of the collection would not have to be postponed.

"*NUMERO 243, 'Melodie,'* evening dress in blue taffeta." As soon as the announcement began, Arianne swept onto the catwalk, looking left and right. She paused at the center, did a quick turn, and continued to the end of the platform, where she let the huge shawl around her shoulders slide to the ground. Her fingers languidly held on to one end of the shawl, and she dragged it along with studied carelessness as she retraced her steps on her way out. As soon as she was back inside the *cabine,* she flung it to her *habilleuse,* and sat at her dressing table. The hairdresser quickly restyled her chignon, while Jacques Villette retouched her makeup and attended to the loose end of one of her fake eyelashes.

"Don't overdo the brown above the eyelid, please," Arianne said, keeping careful watch on his brushwork.

"You forget who created your face, *chérie,* but I suppose that oblivion is the reward of true artists," he said. "Off you go, the final lap," he added.

As Arianne came onto the catwalk, the applause was deafening. She was immediately joined by the eleven other mannequins. The clapping became frenetic, until finally Balenciaga himself joined his models. The faithful were astonished. His reserve was well known and, unlike other designers, he had always refused to take the customary ovation at the end of the show. But now, surrounded by his girls, he nodded to his audience, then raised one hand and asked for silence. A sense of foreboding descended upon the gilded crowd.

"I must announce, with great regret, that you have watched my last collection. I have decided to retire. The shows will continue for another month, and the Maison will meet all orders placed until then, but we will close at the end of July. I wish to thank everybody in the house, and all my clients, for their constant support. . . ." Visibly moved but maintaining his impeccable demeanor, Monsieur Balenciaga stopped his speech. He took off his glasses, and wiped his left eye with his immaculate handkerchief.

"Thank you very much," he concluded, and left the stage abruptly. The audience's concern was articulated by the young Duchesse de Brie-Montval, who whispered to her companion in a strangled voice: "First the riots and now this; *mon Dieu,* what is the world coming to?"

Unlike the duchesse, Arianne was not concerned about the world in general, but anxiety about her own little world began to gnaw at her confidence as soon as she heard the Maestro's words. Their meaning was clear: she was out of a job.

Her face showed nothing as she walked toward the exit. She stopped before the velvet curtain, turned around and, facing the audience, she sank into a deep curtsy. Her white silk skirts rose behind her, framing her head like a peacock's tail. She looked out at the audience and, for the first and last time, she smiled at them. After all, it was likely to be her farewell as a model, her last collection.

She rushed into the *cabine.* Madame Florette was there, embracing the other girls, her eyes full of tears. Arianne stood still in front of her dressing table while her *habilleuse* unzipped her dress.

Jacques stood behind her. He looked thoughtful.

"*Merde,* we need another job," she said to him, their eyes meeting in the mirror.

"*I* need another job. If I were you, *chérie,* I would find myself a millionaire while the going is good." He kissed the back of her neck, and Arianne glared at his reflection.

"*You* find yourself a millionaire; I don't need anyone to keep me now. I know what I'm going to do." Her anger subsided as she carefully explained her plans to Jacques. He shook his head, but he admitted it was a good idea. He had seen many good ideas in the fashion world come to nothing, but her determination was different.

"*AU revoir, chéri,*" said the stunning-looking girl, leaning down to kiss Simón on the lips, her pearl-and-gilt chains scratching his chest. She walked toward the door, and stopped by the seat near the window to pick up her quilted leather bag, its color an exact match to her beige Chanel suit. Before leaving the room she glanced at Simón lying naked on the wide bed, and smiled. Her shoulder-length blond hair, cut straight across, followed her every movement like a curtain of heavy silk thread. Simón took one last look at her, confirming that her legs were sensational. She made most of Dolores's friends seem coarse, and she fucked like a goddess. These Madame Claude girls were real value for the money.

They had been in Paris for nearly a week now, and he had screwed a different girl every afternoon, while Dolores went to see the fashion collections. Compared to what Dolores was spending, his pastime was a bargain and, after four weeks with her on the Riviera and the Côte d'Azur, he needed to recover his sanity.

Their doctor in Buenos Aires had advised Simón to take Dolores on a long holiday to cure the frequent bouts of depression she had suffered since the last miscarriage. Simón found it far easier to live with Dolores when she was silent for long periods of time, and he had postponed the trip for nearly a year. But the doctor had finally put his foot down, and they had left Buenos Aires early in May.

The trip seemed to have worked wonders for Dolores, and she had launched into her usual frenzy of social activity. Today she had arranged lunch at Maxim's with Zou-Zou Lobos and other Argentine friends, which meant that Simón would have the day more or less to himself. He had been on the phone to his office for nearly an hour in the morning, and then he had half-watched a Western on TV while reading the *Wall Street Journal*. The masseur came to the suite at eleven o'clock, and then he had had a quick lunch at the Relais du Plaza Athenée. Simón had been back at the suite by two o'clock for his appointment with Ingrid, or whatever her name was.

It was nearly four now. They had been asked to tea with the Ganays. It would take them some time to drive there, particularly with these damned revolutionaries all over the place, and he did not want to be too late. He had stressed to Dolores that she ought to be waiting for him outside Balenciaga at half-past four.

He had a quick shower before getting dressed. A good fuck and a clean shirt always made you feel like a new man, he decided as he picked up his cuff links from the bedside table. Before he left he called room service and told them to come and change the sheets.

Inside his rented limousine, Simón relaxed and lit one of his cigars. Dolores hated them, and she always made a fuss when he tried to light one. It was easier to present her with the fait accompli of a smoke-filled car.

They drove to the bottom of Avenue George V, and the driver

pulled up in front of the Balenciaga building. Dolores was not there. Simón looked at his watch; it was four thirty-one. He rolled down the window and shouted at the uniformed doorman: "Is Madame de la Force waiting inside? Tell her to come out immediately!"

The doorman bowed, and touched his cap. "I'm sorry, Monsieur, but there is nobody waiting in the foyer. Madame is probably still upstairs. The show started slightly later than usual."

"Then go upstairs and tell her to come out, damn it! I can't wait here forever!"

"I apologize, Monsieur, but we have strict instructions from Monsieur Balenciaga not to interrupt a show in any way. I'm sure that Madame will be here in no time at all."

It was not what Simón had expected this operetta figure to say. Nobody told Simón de la Force to wait, let alone a miserable doorman. His anger boiled over. Chomping his cigar between his teeth, he jumped out of the car, pushed the doorman aside, and rushed inside the building, a raging bull charging into the world's most exclusive *salon de couture*.

Simón stormed past the delicate vitrines along the entrance walls displaying antique folio illustrations, and he did not take any notice of the life-size pair of antique bronze deer flanking the elevator door. He pushed aside an elegant-looking woman, and got in.

"Take me upstairs, you asshole," he barked at the operator. Even inside the lavishly padded elevator, all buttoned-leather and red velvet, his voice was deafening.

The operator let him out at the second floor, and he found himself facing the immaculately chic *directrice* of the salon, whose job depended on her skill at assessing a client's mood. She sensed immediately that this man would be a problem. She approached Simón with a smooth smile.

"Anything I can do for you, Monsieur?" she asked, her manicured fingers toying with her long string of pearls. Simón's arm sent her flying across the room onto one of the Louis XV sofas, and he headed toward the majestic white and gilt double doors facing him.

It was the wrong choice. Three pairs of double doors led from the foyer into the enormous salon where the shows took place, but the central pair was permanently locked, because the models' catwalk ended in a circular platform just in front of them. The clientele entered the salon through the side doors, but Simon was not aware of such details. He tried the ornate door handle, but the door did not give. He did not hesitate for one second: he walked backward a few steps and then rushed forward, kicking the door with tremendous strength.

Inside the chandeliered salon, the astonished clientele saw the doors burst open, splinters flying in the scented air. Shocked whispers ran through the room as Simón, eyes glaring, his tie askew, stumbled in. Dolores's face went crimson. Sitting next to her, Zou-Zou Lobos squeezed Dolores's hand in silent commiseration.

Dolores knew what would follow: a string of "*carajo*," "*gran puta*," and other appalling obscenities, shouted at the top of his voice. Her only hope was that none of the audience would understand Spanish, although his tone would make Simón's meaning obvious enough.

But Simón did not utter a word. One yard away from him, standing on the circular podium, was a woman so beautiful, so exquisitely perfect, that he could never have even imagined her. Simón stared at this vision looking down on him, her bare shoulders emerging from a froth of white feathers. There was an amused glint in her honey-colored eyes, but otherwise her face was icily impassive.

Simón's life had been about wanting, and eventually owning, everything. First he had wanted money, then power, and finally status, and he had got it all. But he had never wanted a woman. They were easy to have, and even easier to buy. Now he wanted *this* woman. He wanted her desperately, and he knew that he was going to have her, regardless of what it entailed.

She towered above him like an idol on an altar, and he could not take his eyes off her. "You are going to be my wife," he muttered finally.

Her hands on her hips, head held high, Arianne flicked aside the stiff petticoats of her magnificent evening gown with her satin-shod foot and, without a word, she turned her back on him and walked toward the velvet curtain at the end of the catwalk. Her face was stony; after the last show, Monsieur Balenciaga had reminded her not to smile. And she didn't. Not once.

14

Portofino
July 1968

IT was a glorious day, and the view from the pool-side of the Albergo Splendido was almost unreal in its perfection: a small castle at the top of the hill across the bay, the pink and ocher houses around the harbor, and the white yachts bobbing gently at their moorings, their size reduced to that of a child's bath toy when seen from this height. Cameline and Arianne were lying by the pool on two yellow and white lounge chairs, languidly catching the morning sun.

"One of the few good things about the old man retiring is that we can sunbathe now," said Cameline. "He would raise hell if you appeared after your holiday not looking like a vampire." She stretched her arms, and yawned. "But I'm not used to this. Let's have a drink." She waved her hand at one of the waiters.

"Two Punt e Mès, please," she ordered.

They had arrived in Portofino the night before. Cameline had come to meet the old Principessa, her future mother-in-law, at her palace in Genoa. Their meeting would take place at Sunday lunch, when she would also be introduced to other members of the Sarteano family. "Bruno told me that it would be better if we don't sleep under his mother's roof until we are married," Cameline had told Arianne when she had asked her to spend the weekend with her. "Please come along," Cameline had begged her. "You Latins have some curious ideas, but I suppose I'll have to get used to them. I am sure that the old bag expects me to be chaperoned." Arianne had been glad to have an excuse to get away. She could ill afford the trip, but she needed a break after her frantic work over the last few weeks.

Soon after she became a model she had begun to take an interest in high-fashion jewelry. She noticed that the craftsmanship of the imitations she wore was almost as exquisite as the real pieces she coveted whenever she walked past the Place Vendôme. But she also noticed that, no matter how successful the setting, the fake gems still looked like colored glass.

Fashion was changing. After the last few years of geometrics, plastic, and pseudospace outfits, she sensed a return to romanticism. A new mood required a different type of jewelry. It was then that she remembered the enormous variety of quartz used in Brazil for cheap trinkets sold to tourists at street corners, the beauty of the inexpensive stones ruined by coarse wire mountings. She realized that the combination of Brazilian stones and Paris mountings would create the most ravishing pieces, and she knew the time was right for her idea.

This was the plan she had explained to Jacques some weeks ago, and she had immediately set to work on it. Through the Trade section of the Brazilian embassy she had been able to trace a French importer of cheap Brazilian stones, sold in the Paris markets as hippie beads.

Once in possession of the stones, she had obtained the addresses of the few specialist firms supplying jewelry to the couture houses. They were all in the Marais, and she had spent her days rushing from one corner of the old Paris quarter to the next, from atelier to atelier, testing different alloys of copper and brass until the antique gold effect she wanted was finally achieved by Refoubeille. She would never forget her joy when the final sample was at last produced, the alloy poured into the mold from the furnace, the old room reeking of acid and acrid fumes.

She had worked at home for two weeks, producing her designs at night after her work at the Maison, in the shape of the orchids and butterflies she remembered from her childhood. Once her sketches were ready, she had gone back to Refoubeille, where the *maquettiste* had painstakingly produced the delicate molds in fine clay for the metal casts, which were then given to the mounters. Just before her departure she had been able to see some of the finished samples.

As she had gazed at the necklaces, pins, and bracelets on a green velvet cloth spread on one of the huge wooden tables by the window, the pastel-hued stones and the mellow gold glowing in the soft Paris light, she had had an overwhelming sense of achievement. She had been right. The effect was almost Byzantine in splendor, and she had created the most beautiful fashion jewelry she had ever seen.

It hadn't come cheap, though. She had not been able to save any money from her salary, and the cost of the trial-and-error process and the manufacture of the prototypes had added up to thousands of francs. Wearing a scarf and her biggest sunglasses, she had taken the gold bracelet from the German admirer to the pawnshop near her old home in Pigalle. After bargaining in her most seductive manner with the pawnbroker, she still got less than she had thought she would, but at least she had been able to meet Refoubeille's first bills.

Jacques had introduced her to Monsieur Yves Osmu, his accountant, who had made plain to her that she needed seed capital to produce the line and meet the launching costs; nothing in high fashion could be done on the cheap. She had rented a room at the Crillon Hotel for the launch on September 20; it would be a waste of time to do it before the end of the summer break. She had also rented the most elegant glass display cases she could find for the occasion, and ordered engraved invitations, which she had already sent to the buyers of all the couture houses.

The overall cost was horrific, and she had to meet her living expenses in the meantime. Monsieur Osmu had suggested she secure a bank loan before going any further, so she had made an appointment to see her branch manager next week. She refused to consider the possibility of failure, and what that would entail for Nana and Gloria.

Troubled by the uncertainty of her future, she decided to enjoy the sunshine with Cameline. It was costing her virtually all the money she had left from the bracelet, but it might be a long time before she would have another opportunity for a break.

The waiter came back with their drinks.

"Mademoiselle Delors?" he asked Arianne. She nodded. "The

gentleman asked me to deliver this to you." He pointed toward a man in a sailor's uniform waiting on the upper terrace. Arianne noticed the small salver on the waiter's tray, holding a rolled piece of paper threaded through a ring.

Arianne picked up the note, exposing the ring's stone to the bright light. It was a heart-shaped ruby, the largest she had ever seen, and she was momentarily entranced by the depth of its color. She unrolled the message.

"I would be the happiest man in the world if you would have dinner with me tonight on my yacht. The one with the blue and white pennants. 8:30 P.M." The note was signed "Simón de la Force," and the letterhead read "Fortuna — Monte Carlo."

Arianne looked out toward the harbor. The biggest boat, at least twice the size of any of the others, was bedecked in blue and white bunting.

"Well, well, well," said Cameline, leaning toward Arianne and picking up the ring. She inspected it carefully, then read the note. She raised an eyebrow.

"Isn't this the guy who kicked his way into the show? Apparently his wife was so embarrassed that she bought the whole collection. Isn't that sweet of her? Monsieur B. was livid, and sent him the repair bills anyway."

"I don't care if he is the Shah of Iran," Arianne replied. "I am not going anywhere, and I'll send the ring back right now." She began to raise her arm to call the waiter, but Cameline stopped her.

"Oh, come on, you are taking this too seriously. If you send the ring back, it will probably get 'lost' in transit. He will never believe that you tried to return it. At least give it back in person." She gave Arianne a mischievous look. "Bruno is coming to the hotel for dinner tonight. If you go off for a long, relaxed evening, it will be possible for me to have a few moments of privacy with him, away from his awful mother."

"I don't want to go through some unpleasant scene with that man," protested Arianne.

Cameline turned her head toward Arianne, and lowered her sunglasses just a fraction to peer at her friend over the top.

"I have the feeling that you must have a pretty good idea how to

handle a guy if he gets difficult." She lay back on the lounge chair and sipped her drink.

Arianne remained silent.

"Listen," Cameline went on, "you told me about your financial problems. What you need is chicken feed for a guy like that." She paused for a moment. "I can see from your face that the idea doesn't appeal to you, but I'm not suggesting the casting couch, just a business proposition after a good dinner."

Cameline had a point. Arianne was living in the hope that the bank manager would agree to a loan, but if he refused, she would not be able to meet the household bills in ten days' time. Because she had been the star at Balenciaga, no couture house would employ her because they each wanted their own star, not somebody else's. Worse, she had been told that her face was too refined for advertising work. There were no available job options, and this man could be an alternative source of financing for her business.

"Make an appointment with the hairdresser now. You have nothing to lose, and you want to knock the guy flat tonight," murmured Cameline, indicating the yellow awning and the glass door near the pool.

Something made Arianne wish this man had not appeared in her life, but she was very aware that her bills would not go away. She was briefly torn between reality and an uneasy sense of premonition, until she suddenly stood up and walked toward the hairdresser's salon.

"I'M so glad that you could come," said Simón, standing by the top of the gangway and holding Arianne's hand as she stepped on board.

"Please come this way." He held her arm, leading her toward the stern. As they reached the aft deck, she sensed the throb of the engines under her feet, and the yacht began to move out of the harbor. Noticing Arianne's surprise, Simón smiled, and offered her a seat on the huge semicircular bench that followed the shape of the stern. He sat next to her.

"I thought that you would enjoy the view of Portofino from the sea, and we would also be free from snoopers. It is tiresome to be stared at by every tourist in the harbor." He fixed his eyes on her body, clearly outlined by her Pucci shift.

"It may get too cold for you, but I'm sure I can do something about that." His look was unmistakable.

"I can always borrow one of your wife's shawls," Arianne replied, as she watched the lights of the Albergo Splendido fade farther and farther away. She mentally cursed Cameline for persuading her to change her mind about the invitation.

"My wife is not on board. In fact, she's gone back to Argentina. I stayed behind to attend to . . . some business matters." A white-jacketed steward appeared with a drinks trolley. He stood in front of Simón, and bowed.

"Champagne, Pepe," Simón barked. The man opened a bottle of Dom Pérignon, poured two glasses, placed them on a silver tray, and presented it to Arianne.

"I don't feel like champagne, thank you," Arianne said to the waiter with a smile.

"I'm sorry, I should have asked you. What would you like?" Simón inquired solicitously.

"Now that you *ask,* I would love a glass of champagne," she replied, picking it up from the tray offered by the steward. Simón snapped his fingers, and Pepe swiftly pushed the trolley away, disappearing from sight. Simón raised his glass.

"To our future," he toasted, looking into Arianne's eyes.

"I don't think we have one, Monsieur, at least not in common."

He moved closer. "You can call me Simón."

She pulled the ring out of her bag. "The main reason for my being here is to return this safely to you. I'm sure it's very valuable, and I wouldn't want it to get lost." She placed the ring on the cushion between them. The stone glowed like an ember in the half-light.

He stared at her. An almost evil aura emanated from his deeply hooded eyes, but it was impossible to ignore their hypnotic appeal. He was several inches shorter than she was, and under the Lacoste shirt and the white linen trousers his body was clearly barrel-like, yet the glow of power around him was overwhelming. She found him physically repulsive, yet she knew that for the first time in her life she had come across a man whose every whim could instantly become reality. A man like that could solve all problems, make life a Garden of Eden. But he was repellent, the snake in his own Garden. Anyway, she had had enough of men.

"You are making a mistake in not taking me seriously," he told her. "I have never wanted anything or anyone as much as I want you, and I always get everything I want, whatever it takes to get it, no matter how long I have to wait." He paused for a moment, then raised his glass.

"To our future," he repeated, taking a long sip.

Under his spell for a moment, Arianne followed his example without thinking, but the taste of the cold champagne brought her back to her senses. She was annoyed with herself for having involuntarily shared his toast, and she decided to shift the conversation to less personal matters.

"This is a lovely yacht," she said. "Have you had it for a long time?"

"I chartered it yesterday evening, when I heard that you were in Portofino. I've been told that it is for sale. If you want it, please tell me."

"How did you know that I was here?" she asked.

"I have my ways," he said with a smile. He pulled a sheet of paper out of his trouser pocket, unfolded it, and began to read it.

"Monday. Eleven: Hair appointment at Alexandre. One o'clock: Lunch with fashion editor of *Elle,* Brasserie Lipp. Half past three: takes daughter to Jardin du Luxembourg..." He raised his eyes. "Do you want me to read you the rest of your week's activities?"

Arianne was outraged.

"Are you having me followed? You must stop it immediately!" She stood up, glaring at him.

The soft fabric of her long shift clung to her body in the breeze, her hair shone like a halo around her perfect face, and her nipples, hardened by the cool wind, were just noticeable under the multicolored silk. He leaned forward and looked up at her. His face was inches away from her body.

He was almost overwhelmed by the urge to make love to her. It would take one second to rip the flimsy dress apart. He had killed pumas in the Salta mountains with just his bare hands and a hunter's knife, and he knew that he could force himself on her. But he also knew that he wanted her beyond mere physical possession, and he wanted her more than once.

"I'll do whatever you ask me. I'm sorry if I upset you, but you must understand that I wanted to know you." Simón picked up the ring from the cushion.

"Shall we go in?" he asked. "It's getting cold. I don't know about you, but I'm hungry, very hungry." He led her toward the door.

Arianne remained silent until they were inside the dining room. A small round table had been set for two in one corner of the room, by the huge window framing the distant view of Santa Margherita, the city lights shining on the sea.

"It *is* getting cold," she agreed. Simón pulled out her chair, and helped her to her seat.

Arianne unfolded her napkin. A pair of diamond and ruby earrings, the stones even bigger than the one in the ring, slid out of the napkin and clinked against her plate. He pulled out the ring from his pocket an laid it next to the earrings.

"There is a saying in Spanish that you can't have two without a third. It usually applies to calamities, but I thought that it could have a positive side as well." Arianne looked at her plate, at the gift that could solve her financial problems for the rest of her life, until she was suddenly aware of the steward waiting by her side, ready to serve her, and she quickly put the jewels aside. The steward placed in front of her a crystal bowl of Beluga caviar resting on a bed of crushed ice, and a small pile of blinis in a silver dish. Beside her plate was a small bowl of sour cream, a dish of sliced lemon, and another of finely chopped raw onions.

Simón waited until the steward had poured iced vodka into small tumblers, then asked: "Do you like the earrings? Otherwise I will exchange them when we are both back in Paris. Maybe you could come with me to Van Cleef and choose something you would like better."

Arianne pretended to be transfixed by the jewels, waiting for Simón to pick up whatever was required from the endless array of cutlery at the side of their plates.

"I don't know if I like them or not," she answered. "Whenever I wear something like this, I have to return it after the show. It's foolish to like what you cannot have."

"You can have whatever you want from now on," he said, his mouth full. She followed his example and used the small horn spoon to scoop some caviar onto a blini, then some sour cream, but she did not touch the onions. She took a sip of vodka.

"I hear that you are Brazilian," he said, changing the subject.

"I'm not. I was born in France, but I was brought up in Brazil."

"I love the way you talk. Brazilian women always sound as if they are making love," Simón said, helping himself to more caviar.

"I wouldn't know; I don't make love to women," Arianne retorted.

Simón laughed. "You are difficult, but I like that." He drank his vodka in one gulp. "Maybe it's just that, like most Brazilians, you don't like Argentinians."

"I've told you that I'm French, and you are the only Argentinian I have ever met. But I don't like people who kick their way into rooms or into other people's lives."

"I wouldn't be able to give you rubies if I didn't." She noticed the instant rage in his eyes, and felt a flash of fear. Perhaps it was better not to anger him unnecessarily.

"I told you that I'm not used to presents like these," she murmured coyly. Their eyes met for a second, then Arianne lowered hers. "I didn't mean to offend you," she finished. She put on the ring and then the earrings. "I'll wear them during dinner, and I will give them back to you later."

Simón leaned across the table, and patted her hand.

"You can never offend me," he said soothingly, ringing the bell to call the steward. He wanted to finish dinner as soon as possible.

ARIANNE felt more relaxed. She did not like the man, but he had tried his best to be charming, asking questions about her work while clearly enjoying the flamboyant main course, lobseter à l'américaine. She told him about her business, and her plans for the launch.

"How are you financing your business?" he had asked point-blank. It was the opening she had wanted, but now she wasn't sure.

"Through a bank loan. I have no finance problems whatsoever," she replied smoothly. She could always approach him later if necessary.

"Do you have a date for the launch?" he asked, pouring more wine in her glass.

"September twentieth," she said. "At the Crillon," she added proudly.

"Presumably you'll only know what your commitments are, once you start taking orders," he said.

She stared at him.

"I thought this was a dinner party, not a business meeting."

He laughed. "You're right; it's just that I like talking about business. But I know nothing about fashion; we ought to change the subject." From then on, he carried the conversation, mostly about his recent travels.

Dinner over, they moved to the saloon. Simon took her arm, and led her toward one of the sofas.

"Would you like a brandy, or a liqueur?" he asked, snapping his fingers at the steward.

"No, thank you; I don't want anything else. It was a delicious dinner," she replied, sitting at one end of the long sofa. The steward brought Simón a large brandy. Simón sat down next to her, their legs almost touching. She noticed that the yacht was rolling gently.

"I hope that the boat doesn't move too much," she said. "I'm a very bad sailor."

"You have nothing to worry about," said Simón, resting his hand on her thigh. "The sea is quite calm."

Arianne stood up and walked toward the wall to inspect a portrait of a young woman.

"What a beautiful painting," she said, her back to Simón. "Is she your wife?"

"No, she is not. I don't know who the hell she is. I told you it's not my yacht. I wouldn't hang a portrait of my wife, anyway. She is one of the few mistakes I have made in my life." He took a sip of his brandy. "I hear that you have a lovely daughter. How old is she?"

"She was one year old last week," replied Arianne, without turning around.

"Who is her father?"

Arianne did not move.

"Not you," she replied calmly.

Her rebuke hit home. This woman had to be put in her place. He gulped his drink. The brandy was burning in his stomach, and he wanted her now. He stood up and walked toward her.

He embraced her from behind, his arms crossed over her stomach, his hands on her breasts. He turned her around and pressed his lips on hers.

She offered no resistance. On the contrary, her body went soft, and her arms encircled his waist as her legs almost gave. The warmth of her body pressed against his was unbearable. Simón began to undo the buttons at the back of her dress while forcing her lips open with his tongue.

Her sudden burp sent a gulp of her breath, redolent of semidigested lobster, down Simón's throat. Arianne pulled away, ran across the room, opened the door to the deck and leaned over the railings, retching violently. He ran after her and helped her to stand up. He could see the saliva trickling down her chin, and there were tears in her eyes.

"I'm so sorry," she murmured, as he helped her back into the room, his arm around her waist. "I told you that I am a very bad sailor."

"Please relax. Come over here and lie down on the sofa," he said. He slipped a cushion under her head, then stood up and bellowed: "Pepe! Giovanni! Come here, everybody!"

The stewards rushed into the room.

"Bring a glass of water to Mademoiselle immediately, and get some Dramamine. Tell the captain to go back to harbor as fast as he can, and put out a radio call for a doctor to be waiting at the dock. Get out now!"

Arianne, her eyes closed, moaned softly. Simón sat by her side, holding her hand and squeezing it every now and then. None of his previous seductions had ended quite like this. Arianne opened her eyes at intervals, only to close them immediately, as if exhausted by the effort.

The lights of Portofino harbor were soon visible through the windows, and the rolling stopped. After a few minutes, the boat came to a standstill.

Simón put his arm behind Arianne's head, and helped her to sit up. "Come on, we have arrived. The doctor will see you in a minute. I'll help you to the dock." He struggled to the door, carrying her almost dead weight with both arms around her waist. As they climbed down the gangway, he noticed an ambulance and a medical team waiting nearby.

As soon as her feet were on the ground, Arianne pulled herself away from Simón, and faced him.

"Thank you for dinner," she said firmly, swiftly taking off the earrings and removing the ring. "If you are so desperate for a fuck, try screwing the rubies." She pulled at the waistband of his trousers, dropped the jewels into the gap, and walked away. Her long-forgotten ability as a child to burp at will had been useful, and she smiled with glee. It was dark, and it was a long walk uphill to the hotel, but she didn't mind.

THE bank manager looked at the papers in front of him, Arianne's account statements and the business projections prepared by her accountant.

"How much money do you need?" he asked at last.

"I need three thousand francs for my expenses, and ten thousand to produce the collection." Arianne kept her eyes on him as she spoke.

The bank manager shifted his eyes away, his hands capping and uncapping the pen in front of him.

"I can see no problem in lending you three thousand francs; I can do that on the basis of your account. But I would not be able to lend you the rest. It is not our policy to grant unsecured loans."

Arianne concealed her disappointment, but at least she would be able to live until the launch. She had already thought Jacques might be a possible backer if the bank turned her down.

"That will be very helpful," she said. "I would have preferred not to, but I can raise the rest of the money from . . . other sources." She sensed the manager's relief; he obviously had expected her to plead her case, but they both knew it would be a waste of time.

I'm delighted to be of help," he said unctuously. "If you see Monsieur Raspard now, he will complete the paperwork for you and the money will be credited to your account tomorrow." The manager stood up, holding out his hand. Arianne did not move.

"There's something else I want to discuss with you." The man sat down.

"I know the business will work in the long term," she said, "but I will have a cash flow problem once I start taking orders. I cannot count on advance payments for first orders. It is unusual in the trade, and it wouldn't meet the production costs anyway. If, as I expect, I get substantial orders, I will have to finance part of the production cost until delivery." Arianne knew that she would have to finance the whole cost of first orders, but there was no point in making the situation sound worse than necessary. She had agreed with Refoubeille that they would not invoice her for her sample collection until September, but any money coming in from the orders would have to go into settling that debt. And Refoubeille would not produce anything until she paid for the samples.

"What sort of figure are we talking about?" the manager asked. Arianne paused for a moment before replying.

"I have calculated between twenty and thirty thousand francs," she said as if it were a small matter. The man wrung his hands.

"We have already discussed the problem of unsecured loans, Mademoiselle Delors."

Arianne smiled.

"But I will have firm orders from reputable couture houses by then. The loan would no longer be unsecured," she said briskly. The man thought for a moment.

"As a matter of practice, I would have to refer the request to my superiors. If the orders justify it, I can't foresee any problems, but the decision would not be up to me," he said.

"It all depends on the orders, then?" she asked.

"Yes."

She had no doubts about the orders. It was her turn to stand up and hold out her hand.

"Then I'll come to see you in September," she said. "Where do I find Monsieur Raspard?"

The manager gave her directions as he walked with her to the door, and told her that he would phone Monsieur Raspard immediately to tell him that she was on her way. But her thoughts were not on Monsieur Raspard. She would phone Jacques from the nearest public phone as soon as she left the bank.

JACQUES rolled his eyes. They were sitting outside Les Deux Magots, under one of its red awnings facing the church of Saint Germain des Près. Arianne crossed her fingers under the table and raised her eyes toward the church spire.

"The things I have to do for you . . . ," he sighed. "Ten thousand francs is all the money I've got in the bank. I saw the most divine pair of Art Nouveau lamps the other day. They were going to be my birthday treat, but now I'll have to live without them, I suppose."

Arianne felt her tension fade away as she heard him. She leaned across the table and kissed him.

"One day I'll buy you any damned lamp you want," she murmured. He smiled.

"You are ruining your eye makeup, *chérie;* there is no point in getting emotional in front of the tourists." He took her hand. "But you'd better make sure it works. I won't be able to bail you out next time."

She wiped away her tears.

"There won't be a next time, Jacques; I know it. I'll never look back," she said. "I never do."

"I hope you're right." Jacques called the waiter and asked for the bill.

15

Paris
September 1968

ARIANNE stood in front of the huge window overlooking the Rue Royale. It was already dark, and the traffic lights shone on the street, varnished by the autumn rain. She turned toward the room, lit only by the small spotlights inside the glass display cases, their glow dimly picked up by the gold edges of the paneled walls behind. Inside the boxes was the jewelry, *her* jewelry. She had reason to feel proud of herself.

It had been worth every borrowed franc. After a hectic day she had firm orders from four houses, for a total of seventy thousand francs, and she had managed to negotiate partial payment in advance with two of them, amounting to five thousand francs. She had been able to pay Refoubeille with Jacques's money, and she had used two thousand francs to pay for the renting of the room and other launch costs. She had two and a half thousand francs left to live on until early December, when she had arranged to deliver the jewelry to her customers, in exchange for full payment.

She went back to the desk in the middle of the room and picked up the signed orders. She would have no problem now in getting the twenty-five thousand francs she needed from the bank.

It was nearly seven. If she hurried, she would be home in time to put Gloria to bed. She had hardly seen her in all the rush over the last few weeks.

*   *   *

THE bank manager smiled broadly.

"Please accept my congratulations, Mademoiselle Delors. Your business is obviously a great success." Arianne nodded her head to acknowledge his compliment, but she was not there to exchange pleasantries. She didn't need to. It had not gone unnoticed by her that he had not led her to the chair facing his desk, as on their previous conversation. He had shown her instead to the sofa on one side of the room, and was sitting beside her.

"Do you see any problems in raising the thirty thousand francs I need?" she asked abruptly.

"As I told you before, it's not my decision. I have to send these" — he waved the orders in the air — "to the head office with your loan application, but I can't imagine that there will be a problem."

"Please let me know as soon as the money is available," she said, picking up her bag and gloves from the side table. Taking her cue, the man stood up.

"Rest assured," he said with a broad grin.

SIMON de la Force glanced at his diary. Today's date, September 20, was circled in red; he did not need any reminder of why he had marked it two months ago. He reached for the telephone and asked his secretary to place calls to Edouard Golbins and Céline de Merteuil in Paris. After a moment the girl called back: there was an hour delay on international calls, she told him.

Simón picked up a report on his desk, and forced himself to read it. Even he could do nothing about the exasperating Buenos Aires telephone system.

EDOUARD Golbins was a very successful investment banker. His success was based on simple principles: always stay one step ahead of the markets, dress impeccably, and do whatever a client requires, as long as it is within the law, or else untraceable. Simón de la Force had been one of his most important clients for many years; if necessary, Edouard would have climbed mountains to keep him happy. As he put down the telephone, he knew it would take far less than that to comply with Simón's latest request: just a few phone calls to trace the bank holding the girl's account and the owners of the building, most likely an insurance company, then a call to the right man to ask for a favor. Edouard was owed many favors by most people in the financial world.

"YOUR bank manager phoned while you were out," Nana told Arianne as soon as she came into the apartment. Arianne was already on her way to Gloria's room, where she could hear her daughter talking to one of her dolls, but she stopped halfway down the corridor and returned to the sitting room. She looked up the number in her address book and picked up the phone. "The manager, please." She stood still for a moment, then sat on the chair by the small table.

Nana didn't pay attention to the conversation until she noticed that Arianne had remained silent for an unusually long time. She turned around and noticed that Arianne was biting her lip. She seemed upset.

"No, I understand. I'll come to see you now to get my papers." She hung up and sat for a while, saying nothing.

"Everything all right?" asked Nana.

"Yes, everything's fine," Arianne replied. She picked up her coat and bag and rushed out of the apartment.

CELINE de Merteuil had one of the oldest titles in France. The family's financial difficulties were more recent, dating back only to the French Revolution, but several generations of making ends meet had sharpened into a fine art the skill of earning a living without seeming to work. To her, work was a pastime for vulgarians; if unavoidable, then it should be as invisible as possible.

Her income came from the discreet services and social introductions she performed for the parvenus and the nouveaux riches who could afford her fees. Simón's call at first surprised her. However, she guessed the reason behind his instructions, and by the time she put the phone down, a wry smile came to her lips. *A love intrigue. How refreshing,* she thought.

Her address book was next to her on the bedside table. She opened it to C, and ran her finger down the page until she found the numbers under "Couture."

She dialed the first number and asked for the *directrice,* an old friend with a title almost as good as hers. After two or three minutes of pleasantries and gossip, she came to the point.

"*Ma chère,* I believe you know Arianne Delors, that ex-Balenciaga girl; I hear she's gone into the *bijouterie* business. Are you by any chance buying from her? . . . You're not . . ." She managed to finish the conversation soon after that, without in any way giving the impression of cutting it short. When required, Céline de Merteuil's skill on the telephone was comparable to a bullfighter's use of his cape. The conversation ended in a mutual deluge of good wishes, and Madame de Merteuil cast a weary eye back over her address book. Christian Dior was next.

She was unlucky with the next two calls, but succeeded with the third.

". . . You are? Then I have something to ask of you, *ma chère,* but first let me tell you that Madame Sudharno is here next week. I am helping her with her wardrobe, and she spends like crazy. Of course I will take her to see your collection, Nicole. You must show her lots of furs as well; you know how she *adores* them. Now, Arianne Delors . . ." She explained what she wanted, then listened.

"Don't worry for a second, my dear. Your costs will be met, and any other expense you may incur. Just send me the bill. You know I'm good for my word, and I assure you that it will be settled without any delay. Yes, I appreciate how difficult this is for you, and I'm truly grateful. . . . Ah! Nicole, I nearly forgot to tell you that in two week's time my Saudi friend will be here, the one who bought so much from Givenchy last year. I will bring her to you this year, of course. . . ." By the end of the morning Céline de Merteuil had spoken to each of Arianne's clients.

ARIANNE came out of the bank and paused for a moment before joining the throng in the Boulevard Saint Germain. She pulled her dark glasses out of her bag and put them on. Head down, she began to walk away. She did not care in which direction; she just needed time to think.

The bank had turned down her loan application. The manager was at a loss to explain the reason, or at least he claimed to be. "Head office, Mademoiselle. It's a head office decision, as I warned you," he repeated again and again. She sensed that there was more to come, and she was right.

Having considered the matter, the head office had also decided that her personal loan should be called in under the circumstances. The manager had been instructed to deduct the outstanding balance from her personal account. There were not enough funds to cover it, and she now owed the bank six hundred and forty-three francs. It did not worry her unduly, not when she already owed Jacques ten thousand, and she had to pay twenty-five thousand to Madame Refoubeille within two weeks. But she had an even more immediate problem: the daily food bill for Nana and Gloria.

She couldn't ask Jacques for more money. He had already told her he didn't have any. For a moment she thought of asking Cameline, but she had overheard enough conversations between rich women at Balenciaga to know that while their husbands were quite happy to settle any bill sent to their office, they balked at requests for cash other than pocket money. Cameline's wedding was to take place next month, and she was working hard at winning over Bruno's impossible family. She would hardly want to ask Bruno for money now.

Arianne looked around her at the passersby. They all seemed so happy, wealthy and secure, wrapped in their silk scarves and fur coats. Poverty had been her nightmare. She had learned to live with it once. She could learn to again, but this was much worse than poverty. Not only did she not have any money, she owed far more than she could reasonably expect to earn within two weeks. Unless . . . unless she went tonight to the Avenue Foch. She could ask five hundred francs a time. If she worked long hours, in two weeks she could save enough to meet Refoubeille's bill.

She raised her head and saw her reflection in a shop window. She almost struck the glass in anger, sick at the thought of a man touching her again, hating her sudden vulnerability.

She had allowed herself to react like the old Arianne, when she had been cornered by a world she could not handle. But now she could, and she would. The obvious thing to do was to phone her customers, try to bring forward the delivery dates, and ask for immediate payment. As for the household bills, she would have to talk to the local shopkeepers and try to open accounts with them.

She turned and began to walk home. She had found a way out. It would be difficult, but she would make it work. She felt almost cheerful. Tomorrow morning she would phone her customers. Now she was going to take Gloria for a walk.

NANA laid Arianne's breakfast on the table, then placed next to Arianne's coffee cup the morning's mail she had collected from downstairs a short while ago. A moment later Arianne appeared in the sitting room. Her skillful makeup concealed any evidence of her sleepless night, and she was ready to phone her clients.

"Good morning, Nana," she said cheerfully, picking up her mail. She frowned at the first envelope; it was the telephone bill, and she set it aside. Then she glanced at the rest, surprised to see that, other than an envelope from some insurance company, they were all from her clients. She opened the first, placed the enclosed check on the table, and read the letter. Her face went white.

She tore open all the envelopes. There was another check with a covering note, and two letters which suggested treating the down payment as a suitable cancellation fee. Numbed by shock, she picked up the letter from the insurance company, then she walked to the telephone.

"Jacques! I need to see you," she said as soon as she heard his somnolent voice at the other end. "Yes, now. I'll be with you in twenty minutes."

She hung up and, without once looking at Nana, went to her room to pick up her coat. The bell rang as she was about to open the front door. It was a delivery man, almost invisible behind an enormous basket of white roses.

"Mademoiselle Delors?" he asked, holding out his pad for her signature. She scribbled at the bottom, picked up the envelope in her name attached to the pad, put it in her coat pocket and left the apartment.

"Just leave them inside; the lady will tell you where to put them," she told him before closing the elevator gate behind her.

"SOMEONE must be after you, *chérie*," said Jacques, sipping his coffee. They were sitting at the table by the huge window in his

apartment, and Arianne remembered her last breakfast there, before going to Balenciaga. For a second, the memory made her nostalgic for that time of hope.

"Don't get paranoid, Jacques; it's just a run of bad luck," she said.

Jacques shook his head.

"Your bank turns down a valid application for a loan, your clients cancel their orders for no apparent reason, your landlord tells you that they have run a routine check of your banking references and feel obliged to invoke the eviction clause of your contract all in the same day, and you think it is just bad luck? Next you'll tell me that you believe in the tooth fairy."

"What am I going to do?" she cried.

"Fight them. Go to court and fight them," he replied.

She couldn't. It was one thing to go about everyday life with a false identity, but she couldn't take the risk of legal action and a possible investigation of her past. She shook her head.

"I don't even have money to pay for our food. I can't afford a lawyer, I can't afford the rent, and I can't afford any trouble, Jacques. I don't have a past in the Sacred Heart Convent." She knew that she would break down if she continued talking, and she stopped. Jacques squeezed her hand, then stood up and walked over to a chair nearby. His jacket was draped over the back. He pulled out his wallet from the inside pocket, took a five-hundred-franc note from it and placed it in front of her.

"You already have my Art Nouveau lamps, so you might as well have my Saint Laurent suit," he said with a smile. She began to cry.

"Please stop it, *chérie*, or I'll start crying too," he told her. "Let's be practical. How much do you owe?"

"Twenty-five thousand francs to Refoubeille, ten thousand to you, and six hundred to the bank. The rent is due in a week's time, and the telephone bill arrived today." She folded the note and put it in her pocket. "And I owe you this as well. I can't tell you what it means to me."

"Don't say it then. How much money did you get for the canceled orders?"

"Five thousand francs," she replied.

"So you owe about thirty-two thousand francs. Have you tried to find other customers?"

Arianne shook her head. "The jewelry is too expensive for anyone other than couture houses, and they've all seen it. The ones who did not want it at first surely don't want it now that it has been turned down around town. You know the scene, Jacques; everyone will know about this by lunchtime."

Jacques poured more coffee.

"Something will turn up," he said. "In the meantime, blow your nose and dry your eyes. You will think better if you don't let your sinuses get all blocked up."

She put her hand in her pocket, and felt the envelope inside. She pulled it out.

"What's that?" Jacques asked.

"Someone sent me flowers today. They arrived as I was leaving, I didn't even look at the card." She handed the envelope to Jacques. "You read it while I deal with my eye makeup."

He pulled out the stiff white card, then he whistled softly.

"You *do* have style, my darling. I don't know of anyone else who gets asked to the best lunch in Paris when they are seriously broke." He read the card aloud, in a mockingly solemn tone.

" 'I hope you have forgiven my atrocious manners. I will be in Paris tomorrow, and I would be delighted if you would join me for lunch at La Tour d'Argent on Thursday, at one o'clock. Simón de la Force.'

"Who is this charming man?" Jacques asked. Arianne told him about her Portofino fiasco.

"If he put a detective on you, I wouldn't be surprised if he is behind all this. A guy like that can pull a lot of strings. I said to you at the show that you needed a millionaire. You seem to have found one."

"I don't want to go to bed with him, Jacques. The man is repulsive."

"I don't remember Alain Delon calling for you at the Bois, *chérie*, and the guys there don't walk around with huge rubies in their pockets so far as I know," he said acidly.

Arianne was stung, and he noticed it. He leaned forward and patted her cheek.

"I'm sorry; sometimes I'm a bitchy old queen. I didn't mean that, but perhaps you ought to remember that beggars can't be choosers. Go and have a great lunch, hear what he has to say, be very nice and don't promise anything. Just get him to lend you the money. And next time, keep the rocks."

"I NEVER cease to be amazed by how lovely you are," said Simón. "You make me forget the view."

Arianne turned her head toward the picture window behind her, framing the spires of Notre Dame across the river.

"I can't compete with a thousand-year-old church, but I'm flattered," she replied with a smile.

After the constant fear and worry of the last few days, she could not help feeling relaxed in the warm, plush atmosphere of the restaurant. The luxurious room floating high above Paris gave her the illusion of a great liner, and she felt as if she were sailing away from her problems, if only for a couple of hours. She was glad to have followed Jacques's advice. Simón had been good company, and she couldn't help being absorbed by his anecdotes about his extraordinary life. She could understand his willful fight against adversity. Not once had he talked about his feelings for her, but she knew that there was a purpose to this meeting. Certainly for her, and she decided to tackle the issue.

"You told me in Portofino that you would be prepared to help me with my business," she said suddenly. He seemed surprised.

"Did I? I can't remember . . ."

"You did, but let's not argue about it. The point is that I need financial support to make it work. Would you be prepared to become my backer? The business has done very well here," she said, keeping an impassive face, "but I have realized that Paris is too small a market. I want to relaunch my line either in New York or Germany. I need capital to do that," she said evenly, putting off the thought that all the money she had left in the world would not even pay for this lunch.

He shook his head, and sighed.

"I would love to help you, but I don't lend money. Not to friends, anyway; I learned long ago that one shouldn't mix business and friendship. And I want to be your friend." The polite refusal was clear enough, and his face left her in no doubt that she could expect nothing from him. But she had to keep on trying. Maybe if she sounded meek rather than self-assured . . .

"Please, I beg you . . . ," she began, but he raised his hand to stop her.

"Don't force me to say no. What I can say is that, as long as we are friends, you'll never have a problem. Are you free after lunch?" he asked thoughtfully, warming the brandy glass in his hand.

She fought the urge to stand up and leave. She hated him for making her feel cheap, for taking her for granted for the price of a lunch.

"I thought you said you would try to avoid further mistakes," she replied angrily.

"I've apologized for my unforgivable behavior, and I assure you that I am not trying to repeat it. It is not in my interest to upset you. But there is something I would like to show you. It is only five minutes away, and I promise you that you will be free in half an hour."

"I have to be home by three o'clock," she told him brusquely.

He gulped his brandy, and waved at the waiter.

"No problem; my chauffeur will get you there in time."

He signed the check and they left, Simón slipping ten-franc notes into the hands of any member of the staff who greeted him on their way out.

The limousine was waiting just outside the entrance. They drove along the river until they pulled in at the Quai Anatole France, in front of an elegant stone building. The chauffeur opened Arianne's door and Simón, who had leaped out of the car as soon as it had stopped, guided her by the arm toward the huge front door. He opened it and let her in.

The foyer reminded Arianne of some couture houses: the marble floor, the stone pillars, the curving staircase with a wrought iron and brass balustrade, all the features of eighteenth-century Paris at its most gracious.

Simón opened the elevator gate and followed Arianne into the gilded cabin.

"Where are you taking me?" asked Arianne as the elevator creaked its way up.

"You will see in just a moment," he answered, opening the door and letting Arianne out into a small hall. He pulled a key out of his pocket and opened the tall cream and gilt double doors leading off the lobby.

He stepped aside, and Arianne walked into a black and gray marble-floored circular foyer, leading on one side to a drawing room with three large windows overlooking the river and the Jardin des Tuileries on the Right Bank.

She walked into the room, taking in the lofty ceiling, the cream and gilt paneling, the superb furniture and paintings. She glimpsed a large dining room beyond the doors at one end of the salon, the rock-crystal chandelier sparkling in the sunlight pouring in from the windows.

"You ought to see the rest," Simón called from the foyer. She went back, and he opened another double door, which led onto a long corridor. He opened door after door, into bedrooms, dressing rooms, a library, everything as opulent as the reception rooms. Through the windows framed by silk curtains Arianne could see a large garden at the back, the smooth lawn emphasizing the whiteness of the marble statues and urns there.

They returned to the drawing room, and Simón leaned against the marble and bronze fireplace.

"Do you like it?" he asked.

Arianne did not reply. "Who owns it?" she asked.

"Someone I know who has moved to Switzerland. I am planning to rent it for a year, and I can sign the lease this afternoon, if you like it."

"What difference would it make if I like it or not?" she asked, already guessing his answer.

"Because I would like you to live here."

Arianne picked up her bag from the stool next to her chair.

"I thought we had agreed that I will not sleep with you, under any circumstances." She stood up. "I have to be home in ten minutes and I would like to go now."

"Please listen to me." The urgency in his tone stopped her. "I know that you still don't like me, but you misunderstand me. You are the most exceptional woman I have ever met, and I wish that I had married you. But I wouldn't have reached my position if I were not able to accept that it is better to have part of a good deal rather than no deal at all. I can't stand my wife, but there is no divorce in my country, and I cannot live without the company of a woman I love. I want you to become my companion when I am here in Paris, which is not often. We will go out together and, if you wish, we can travel together, but I will not live here, I will not force my presence upon you, and we will never have a physical relationship unless you change your mind about it. In exchange I will pay for this apartment and all your living expenses, no matter how extravagant, and any debts you may have. I hope you will say 'yes'; I will be the happiest man in the world if you do." He was so taken by his own speech that he almost believed it.

"There are only two conditions," he added. "First, you will not see other men, or have a lover. I am a proud man, and I could not tolerate it. Second, you must not work. I'm a very busy man, I can't say when I will be able to see you, and I need you to be free at all times."

Arianne had expected an offer that she could turn down flat, but not this. Even his restriction on men suited her. She did not want a lover.

Work was a different matter, though: it had meant her freedom at last. But she looked around the room, at the luxury surrounding her, and thought about the forty-three francs in her purse. What had she gained by her freedom? Her work had turned into a fiasco, pushing her into unaffordable debt, and she would be out on the street with Nana and Gloria in no time at all.

Her thoughts about debt reminded her that Simón had specifically offered to settle them. How could he know about them, unless he was behind her current predicament? She walked up to him and faced him squarely.

"Did you have anything to do with . . ." She realized there was no point in asking the question. He would lie to her. Maybe it was better not to know.

She walked to the window, staring down at the river for a few moments, and then turned around toward Simón.

"I need to think about it," she said.

"I'm going back to Buenos Aires tomorrow. Call me at the George V this evening, no later than half past seven. I'm having dinner with the Pompidous," he said, unable to keep the boastfulness from his voice.

They walked out of the building in silence. As Arianne was about to get into the car, Simón pulled out a square black velvet box from his pocket and gave it to her.

"I hope you will not push them down my trousers this time," he said. Arianne took the box and put it in her bag. She knew what it contained. Maybe the rubies were the answer to her dilemma. She could get a lot of money by selling them, and she would not have to put up with Simón de la Force ever again.

"If you don't like them, we can exchange them," he said. "Don't try to sell them, though; they are registered as a company asset, and you may find it troublesome to dispose of them," he added, as if reading her mind.

Arianne got into the car, and Simón leaned down to talk to her. "If you accept my offer you will receive the keys to the apartment tomorrow, with a letter giving you the address of my banker here. He will deal with all your bills." He closed the door. "Take Mademoiselle wherever she wants to go. I could do with a walk," he said to the chauffeur, and moved away without looking back.

"PITY that he wouldn't fancy *me*." Jacques's voice chuckled over the phone.

"Please, Jacques, this is not a joke. I can't see how I can turn him down, but there has to be a catch somewhere," Arianne said impatiently.

"Maybe, but it is probably nicer than being broke and without a roof over your head. I don't know why you are wasting time, *chérie*, it's already quarter past seven. *Please* say yes, then phone me back. I'm dying to see that gorgeous place. Good-bye."

She put the phone down, deep in thought. Perhaps Jacques was right. Here was her chance to have everything she could possibly want, without having to give anything, or very little, in return. Yet there was a warning signal somewhere in her mind. If only she could attribute her misgivings to something more tangible than fear and intuition. If only she were not crippled by debts. If only . . .

She glanced at her dressing table, at the photograph of the family group in Rio de Janeiro, so long ago. The picture brought back her memories of the *favela,* and she instantly made up her mind. She picked up the phone.

"*Le George V, bonsoir,*" said the operator at the other end, almost singing her greeting.

"Monsieur de la Force, please." There was silence on the line, and then she heard his voice.

"Yes." She could hardly bring herself to say the word.

"I am very happy. You will not regret it," he replied.

She slammed down the phone. She was not so sure.

16

Paris
November 1968

THE triple mirror reflected Arianne from all angles, allowing her to check every detail of the cream tweed suit. She turned round and looked at the back.

"The braid on the edge of the jacket isn't quite right," she said to the *première d'atelier* standing by her side. "It should be just a bit higher on the left."

"It is a pleasure to help a client as knowledgeable as you, Mademoiselle Delors," said the *vendeuse*. "So many of our clients simply don't understand clothes."

"Thank you, Yvette," said Arianne, as the assistant carried out the alteration. "I think that the buttons should be different. I would like the same buttons as on the blue coat you made for me last month. Not the fitted one, the straight one."

"Of course, Mademoiselle." Yvette made a rapid note on her pad.

Arianne cast her eye on the rack standing on one side of the fitting room. There were four other suits to try. She glanced at her platinum watch.

"I think I just have time to try on the yellow one," she told Yvette. "I'm meeting a friend for lunch at the Ritz, and I don't like being late." She instantly regretted the remark. It did not matter anymore if she was late. It was somebody else's problem, not hers. There was always something to remind her that she was not yet entirely used to her new life.

Simón had not been back since they struck their bargain. He

phoned every ten days or so, always announcing his imminent arrival, but then postponing it for some reason or other. She was free to do as she pleased.

Her debts had been settled the day after she agreed to his proposal. She was looked after by two maids and a cook, and there was a chauffeured car constantly at her disposal. Every day began with the arrival of a bouquet of white roses with a card saying "I love you," identical to the card attached to the black velvet box from either Cartier, Van Cleef & Arpels, or Harry Winston delivered every Monday. When she received the keys to the apartment there had been a separate envelope with the key to the safe in her bedroom, and a note from Simón asking her to be specially careful with it, because there was no duplicate. The need for a safe did not appear obvious at first, although it was useful to have a secure place accessible only to her, but by now it was nearly full of jewelry. And the presents kept arriving.

She was dressed by Chanel, Givenchy, and Saint Laurent, and there was hardly any shop on the Place Vendôme or the Rue du Faubourg Saint Honoré where she had not been. The day she moved into the apartment she purchased the Art Nouveau lamps Jacques wanted, and five Saint Laurent suits in his size. She gave him the presents that evening, when he came to inspect her new home.

She had expected Nana to share in her delight at their new opulence, but instead Nana had become even more withdrawn. If a particularly extravagant toy was delivered from Le Nain Bleau, or another avalanche of boxes arrived from Baby Dior, full of the most exquisite clothes for Gloria, she would just mutter, "It's too much," and shake her head in disapproval. At first, Arianne had tried to explain that it was all free, but she had given up by now. Obviously nothing could dispel Nana's fear of life.

The fitting over, she changed into her clothes and left the room, escorted by Yvette. At the top of the stairs they were joined by the *directrice,* who apologized on behalf of Mademoiselle Chanel, who was away at the time, otherwise she would have been delighted to see such a special customer as Mademoiselle Delors again. On her way out, Arianne cast her eyes over the vitrines displaying the bags and accessories typical of the Maison, but there was nothing new, and she already had them all.

She walked into the Rue Cambon, and turned toward the Ritz entrance. She was looking forward to meeting Cameline again, now the Principessa di Sarteano and on her first shopping expedition to Paris since the wedding. They had arranged to have lunch, and then to go and see the Balmain collection. She wondered how Cameline would fit into her new life, and how long it would last, but then realized that the same could be asked about her, and she dismissed the thought immediately. She gave the doorman just the hint of a "thank you" smile and walked into the hotel.

SIMON de la Force glanced at the Christmas cards lined up on the mantelpiece, leaned back in his thronelike leather chair, and chuckled. He had just spoken on the phone to Edouard Golbins, who had confirmed that Arianne's expenditure was doubling from month to month. Good. Simón loved that English saying about giving people enough rope to hang themselves.

He looked around his office. The mahogany paneling, the desk almost the size of a billiard table, everything in the lofty room confirmed that this was the workplace of the most powerful man in Argentina, and maybe in South America. His eyes lingered for a moment on the portrait of Coronel de la Force, an early nineteenth-century ancestor who had had the misfortune of being captured by rebellious Indians. His balls had ended up as the main ornament on an Indian chief's necklace, but he had gained a place in Argentine history. Simón fully identified with his martial counterpart: he was also planning a campaign, and he had won the early skirmishes. But the main battle was still ahead.

Simón trusted his nose for human weaknesses, and he had sensed during their conversation on the yacht that there was something in Arianne's past that made her vulnerable to him. It was just a matter of finding out what it was. But there was no police record of Arianne Delors in France, only the registration of her birth, and the detectives in Brazil had drawn a blank.

He had stayed away from Arianne to make her feel at ease in her new life, to become so used to it that she could not contemplate giving it up. Only then would he start turning the screws, but he could not rely on anyone else for what would now be required. He would have to go to Paris himself, and he was waiting for his call to Arianne to come through. He had to fly to Madrid in two days to deal with his developments in Torremolinos anyway, and he would tell Arianne that he was going to be in Paris within ten days.

The phone nearest him rang, and he picked it up immediately.

"I have Mrs. de la Force on the line, sir, and she says that it is most urgent."

"Put her through."

"Simón!" Her shrill, idiotic voice was enough to set his nerves on edge. "I have just spoken to Jacqueline, and she told me that there is a girl who is the talk of Paris, living like a queen. Her name is Arianne something, and the gossip is that you are keeping her. I will not — " She was not allowed to finish the sentence.

"Shut up, you stupid cow!" he roared. "I don't know why you listen to gossip. If I were to keep anyone other than you living like a queen, I would have to own Fort Knox. I have just seen some of your latest bills."

"Well, don't take it like that, Simón. I was just asking! Don't forget that we are having dinner with Miguel and Teresa tonight, and don't be late."

He put the receiver down with a sneer. She'd better enjoy it while it lasted.

"HELLO, my love, I've just checked into the George V. I'm so happy to hear your voice and know that we are in the same city."

"Thank you. Did you have a good flight?" Arianne knew that she ought to say that she was so glad, too, but she couldn't bring herself to do it.

"Very good; I slept most of the time." Stretched on the bed, his shoes on the silk bedspread, Simón noticed the clock: the girl from Madame Claude would be there in five minutes. Better keep the conversation short. "Listen, darling, I am very tired, but perhaps we could have lunch tomorrow, if you are free. I thought that we could go to the Grand Vefour, and do whatever you want afterward."

"Would you like to go to the cinema?" asked Arianne. That would take care of conversation, she thought.

"I don't like to sit next to unknown people," he replied. "If there is anything you want to see, I will ask my office to arrange a private screening." He looked at the clock again: three minutes left. "I was thinking on the plane that I have never met Gloria. I saw in the paper that the Budapest Circus is in town, and I thought she might like to see it."

"Gloria is only one-and-a-half years old, and you just said that you didn't like sitting next to strangers," protested Arianne.

"I was thinking of taking over the circus one afternoon and your nanny could ask other children to come if you like. It would be like Gloria's own party."

Arianne began to explain why she thought that the idea was not a good one, when Simón heard a discreet knock at the door, and interrupted her.

"I'm sorry, my darling, but they are knocking at the door. I asked for something to eat. We can discuss this tomorrow. Good night, my darling."

Simón stood up and quickly slipped the envelope from Edouard Golbins with the address of the detective agency and the duplicate keys into his bedside table's drawer. He began to undo his shirt as he walked toward the door. Soon he would not need any more Claude girls, but in the meantime he had to remember to tip that helpful, discreet man at the reception desk. The hotel management would not be very pleased to find out about Simón's pastime. Like so much else about Simón's life, it was better to keep it quiet.

THE box, specially built for the day, stood next to the circus ring. It was draped in pink velvet, and candy-colored chocolates spelt out "Gloria" across its front. On their arrival, Simón, Arianne, Nana, and Gloria, followed by a few bewildered children, their nannies, and the whole of Arianne's domestic staff, were escorted to the box by a troupe of somersaulting clowns and acrobats.

Simón had been at his most convincing over lunch a week before, and Arianne's reservations about the preposterous idea had melted away. "I have always wanted to have children, and I long to give the nicest possible party for a child I love," he had said. He had insisted that her staff should come: "It will be like a family party." Arianne suddenly relished the thought of her little girl having the most wonderful party in the world. To enter into the spirit of the occasion, she was wearing her new fitted hussar coat in red wool, delivered from Saint Laurent the day before.

As she sat down and looked at Gloria's face, her eyes shining with excitement, Arianne turned toward Simón and briefly touched his hand.

"Thank you," she said gratefully. "This is the best present you have given me so far." She was genuinely moved by his thoughtfulness. The emeralds, rubies, and diamonds piling up in her safe were props to his vanity as well as bribes to her, but this was different. She found that, for the first time since his arrival, she was warming to him.

"You have nothing to be thankful for, my darling," he said. "This party means as much to me as it does to Gloria."

The band burst into a fanfare of trumpets, and the clowns walked into the arena pushing enormous red and yellow balls. One of the clowns, helped by the others, climbed laboriously on top of a ball. The rest of the troupe began to push the ball slowly around the ring while the clown stumbled backward and forward, trying to maintain his balance.

It was at about this time that a black Simca pulled in fifty yards away from the building on the Quai Anatole France, and the driver got out. He walked to the front door of the building, and looked at his watch.

At the circus, the older children in the box noisily celebrated the attempts of a second clown to climb onto the ball. He succeeded at last and, pulling a water pistol from his pocket, squirted the first clown in the face.

The concierge at the Quai Anatole France building was reading *Le Figaro* when the telephone rang in his room, at the other end of the hall. He grumbled at being disturbed, and left his desk to take the call. The man outside quickly walked in, silently ran up the stairs to the first floor and pulled out a key from his coat pocket. By the time the concierge returned to his desk, annoyed by having to deal with a wrong number, the man had let himself into Arianne's empty apartment.

At the circus, the merriment reached a higher pitch when a troupe of white horses came into the ring. The clowns on foot jumped on the horses running around the ring, weaving their way around the balls scattered on the arena. The two clowns on the ball held on to each other in mock terror, until they lost their balance and fell noisily, raising clouds of sawdust as they hit the ground. They immediately stood up, and jumped onto the two horses at the end of the line.

In the apartment, the man unfolded a small plan, and found his way to Arianne's bedroom. He quickly identified the particular picture hinged to the wall, and pulled it toward him with his gloved hand. He slipped the duplicate key into the lock, and opened the safe without any trouble.

The riding clowns now pulled out rolls of ribbon from their pockets and flung them to the rider across the ring while holding to the end of each streamer, forming the multicolored spikes of a swirling wheel. A second fanfare of trumpets was heard; the clowns jumped off the horses in unison, and bowed to the rapturous applause of their little audience. The ringmaster announced the next act: from Budapest, the fabled Toncnogy Brothers, masters of the trapeze.

In the meantime, the man in the apartment surveyed the contents of the safe before touching anything: he had been told that there must be no evidence whatsoever of his visit. He quickly began to open the boxes. His instructions were to disregard the jewelry and concentrate on any papers or documents he might find, but he found none on the top shelf.

The circus lights changed color, the drums rolled, and three tall, athletic men ran into the ring, their swirling satin cloaks embroidered with their names, which were shouted out by the ringmaster as they came in: György, Albert, and Henrik. They swiftly climbed to the high-level platforms at both ends of the ring, and unfastened their cloaks, letting them fall to the ground. One by one, they climbed onto the trapezes, and began their act. As the Toncnogy Brothers flew over the ring in a dazzling display of physical skill, the audience was spellbound by their prowess.

The search of the middle shelf of Arianne's safe was also unsuccessful, but the man was not disheartened. He began to check the bottom shelf, and soon found what he had been looking for: a Brazilian passport was hidden behind one of the piles of jewelry boxes. He pulled out a powerful light and a camera from his leather holdall, plugged the light into a socket nearby, and placed the passport on the dressing table.

A single beam of light shone on the climax of the Toncnogy

Brothers' act, the triple somersault and the Loop of Death, flawlessly performed, while in the apartment the man aimed his light at the open passport, photographed every page of the document and returned it to the safe. The Brothers bowed to the audience while at the other end of Paris the man made sure that there were no further documents or papers to photograph, and then closed the safe.

It took the man no longer than the first half of the performance of Géza the Fire-Eater to check the contents of the drawers in the bedroom dressing table and the desk in the library. There was nothing there of any consequence. While Géza proceeded to swallow an enormous sword, to the amazement of his public, the man phoned his office from the library phone, to remind them to make the second phone call in precisely one minute. He immediately left, closing the door behind him without a sound, and waited in the second-floor hallway.

He could hear the phone ringing downstairs, and the mutterings of the concierge as he left his desk to take another call. As soon as he heard the door closing behind the concierge, the man rushed downstairs. He was out of the building long before the old concierge returned to his desk, cursing the dialer of yet another wrong number.

By the time Xenia and the African Lions came into the ring, the man was driving away in his car, along the Quai Anatole France. He hoped that the monsieur with the Indian face and the funny name (the man had stopped believing in his clients' names a long time ago) would be pleased with his work.

As the man joined the traffic on the Pont de la Concorde, Simón de la Force was leading his guests out of the box, holding Gloria in his arms. Arianne couldn't help being delighted by the sight of them together, Gloria struggling to pinch Simón's nose.

17

Paris
December 1968

"WASN'T it a lovely Christmas, Nana?" asked Arianne.

They were crossing the Pont de Solférino, on their way to the Jardin des Tuileries. Arianne did not like taking Gloria out in the cold, but Nana made it a point that Gloria should go to the park every morning, regardless of the weather. Arianne found it difficult to disagree with Nana on matters concerning Gloria: she was her granddaughter and, above all, Nana *knew*. Not the whole of Arianne's story, but enough to bring their world crashing down around them if she chose to. Better to humor the old woman, or at least not to contradict her unnecessarily. Driven out of the kitchen by the cook and kept away from other domestic chores by the Portuguese maids, who spoke little or no French, Gloria had become Nana's sole occupation. The little girl was her obsession.

"Yes, it was," answered Nana, steering Gloria's buggy to avoid a small hole in the pavement.

Gloria was wearing the cheap blue coat from Prisunic that Nana had given her for Christmas. Row after row of expensive clothes hung in Gloria's closets, and the meaning of the present was not lost on Arianne. She could not understand Nana's disapproval of their life now since she knew very well how Arianne had earned her living until she became a model.

It had been their second Christmas together. Outwardly, it had been magnificent. The enormous tree glowed at one end of the drawing room, logs burned in all the fireplaces, and Arianne had bought an exquisite Nativity scene from one of Céline de Merteuil's antique dealer friends. Gloria had become particularly fond of one of the Three Wise Men and had played endlessly with the plaster figurine, bearing its gift of gold.

Arianne had given her staff the night off. The food had been delivered from Fauchon early in the evening, and they had kept busy making everything ready for dinner. At last, the preparations completed, the three of them sat at the lavishly appointed table.

It was only then that the grandeur of their surroundings underlined the absurdity of the situation, the loneliness of two women with little to say to each other sitting in a dining room for eighteen people. Gloria, kept awake much later than her usual bedtime, became impossibly fractious by eleven o'clock. Nana took her to bed, and the two women then finished their dinner in silence. Afterward, as they sat by the drawing-room fire, the conversation limped along until the time came to open the presents, and they were at last free to go to bed.

Simón had phoned from Buenos Aires to say that he would be able to come to Paris for New Year's Eve, and that he had arranged a most special evening for the two of them to toast the New Year. No, he would not tell her what it was; it was a surprise. Simón had also said that he would not send her a Christmas present, because he wanted to deliver it in person.

But Christmas was behind them now, and it was a beautiful morning. Although it was bitterly cold, the sun shone on the roofs and spires of Paris, crisply outlined against the blue sky. As they crossed the road toward the park Arianne raised the collar of her fur-lined coat, pulled the edge of Gloria's knitted hat down over the child's ears, and smiled. She looked forward to a better year.

AS was often the case, Simón de la Force was pleased with himself. Surrounded by his usual retinue of acolytes and fawning airline staff in the VIP lounge, he was waiting at Buenos Aires airport to board the flight to Paris. It was probably his last commercial flight: his new Learjet was due to arrive from America early in the New Year.

After a week in Punta del Este with Dolores and her family, he was more than glad to escape from them. As arranged, Edouard

Golbins had phoned him two days after Christmas to say that it was imperative that Simón come to Paris immediately for an urgent meeting at the bank. Dolores had made the customary protests, but Simón was sure that she was as glad to see him leave as he was to go.

An airline employee approached him, and gave him his passport. "You don't need to go through passport control, Señor de la Force. You can board the plane now. Have a good flight."

Simón put the passport in his pocket and walked to the exit from the lounge onto the tarmac. One of his minions noticed that the edge of the passport was still visible and promptly mentioned it to Simón. As he tried to push the passport further in, he realized that it was resting on top of the small leather box at the bottom of his pocket. He moved the passport to his inside pocket.

The leather box was another reason to be pleased. Simón was glad that the gift would be more than just Arianne's Christmas present. Even Golbins had been surprised by Arianne's relentless extravagance, and it was nice to be able to save some money.

As he climbed the steps toward the smiling stewardess, he thought that, nonetheless, it was all money well spent. He was not in love. Love was an emotion that, as far as he could judge from his observation of other people in such a predicament, he had never experienced. But he wanted Arianne more than he had ever wanted any other woman. Now, at last, he was going to have her.

He had married Dolores to prove to Buenos Aires society that he could buy any of them, but he knew now that, ultimately, he had merely acknowledged their superiority to him. Although his money was the only reason for Dolores to stand out among her peers, she felt above him, almost as if she had condescended to marry him. It would not be like that with Arianne. He now knew enough about her to keep her under his thumb for the rest of his life.

He fastened his safety belt, closed his eyes, and relaxed in his seat. He was going to enjoy this trip.

18

Paris
December 31, 1968

"WE are nearly there, Mademoiselle."

The chauffeur's voice could be heard through the dark glass screen between the front and rear seats, but Arianne was not able to see him. She was unable to see the outside either; all the windows at the back of the car had been papered over. When she had been picked up at her apartment, the driver had explained that the windows had been obscured at the request of Monsieur de la Force.

This had been enough for Arianne to try to open her window as soon as the car pulled away, but after pressing the switch several times, she realized that the driver must have disconnected the power to the electric windows at the back. At first she was annoyed, but then she entered into the spirit of the occasion and became amused by the idea of being driven around like an Oriental princess, invisible to all. She switched on the radio above the drinks cabinet, sat back in the velvet seat, and listened to the music.

She was not wearing her watch, but she guessed that she had left home nearly an hour ago when the car slowed down, then turned sharply and came to a standstill. The door by her side was opened, and she saw Simón, standing a few feet away, wearing his dinner jacket. The door was held by a footman in court uniform and powdered wig, who helped her out of the car.

"You are looking gorgeous, as usual," said Simón admiringly, kissing her on the cheek. Distracted by the physical contact, she pretended to rearrange the folds of her full-length coat, matching the crystal-and-gold-beaded white satin sheath she was wearing beneath it.

"That is some outfit. What sort of bill am I going to get this time?" he continued in the same tone. The remark hinted at a proprietorial role, and it put Arianne on guard.

"I hope you are not complaining," she said frostily.

"I could never complain about you, not tonight anyway," he said, guiding her toward the floodlit building in the background. The red carpet muffled the sound of their steps on the white gravel.

"But this is the Petit Trianon!" Arianne exclaimed, as she stopped in front of the building. "What are we doing here?"

"Having dinner first, and then toasting the New Year. I thought it would amuse you," replied Simon, stepping aside as they reached the entrance.

"How could you possibly rent this place?" she asked.

"I heard through friends that there is a major restoration program going on at Versailles, and they need money. One of my companies in France has agreed to foot the bill for the restoration of one of the state rooms in the palace in exchange for this small favor."

Arianne was overwhelmed. Nothing, absolutely nothing seemed beyond the reach of this man. Simón noticed her expression, read her thoughts, and relished the moment.

"I am sure you know that it was built by Louis the Fifteenth for Madame de Pompadour, as her private retreat. I thought that made it quite suitable for us," he boasted.

"I came here during the summer, for a picnic with Nana and Gloria, and the guide who showed us around said that the last owner was Marie Antoinette. I am not sure I like that thought," Arianne retorted.

Simón smiled, and patted her shoulder.

"Don't worry; I haven't brought my guillotine along."

THE bewigged waiter offered Arianne more coffee.

"No, thank you," she said. He poured Simón another cup. "Is there anything else that Monsieur requires?" he asked.

Simón glanced at the corner, to check that an unopened bottle of champagne stood in the ice bucket on a side table.

"Leave the wine on the table, and that will be all for now. We don't want to be disturbed," he answered. The waiter left the room.

Arianne relaxed in her chair. In a night of surprises, dinner had been a delightful one. They had dined in the small boudoir off the music room, its oak paneling carved with the delicacy of lace. The round table in the middle, just big enough for two, was covered in pink damask, and scented candles burned in gold candlesticks. The food had been as light as Simón's conversation, which had been mostly about beautiful areas of Argentina, where he seemed to own an estate in every corner of the country, and how he hoped Arianne would see it all one day. She had listened to his inconsequential small talk, and was actually beginning to enjoy herself. But his last remark to the waiter had aroused her suspicions.

Simón looked at his watch.

"Its a half-hour to midnight," he said, pulling out a small leather box from his pocket. He leaned across the table and placed it in front of Arianne. "Just enough time for what I have to tell you." She knew from his tone that she was not going to like what he was about to say.

She opened the box and gasped. She was staring at a square diamond the size of a large postage stamp.

"Isn't it a bit too much for a Christmas present?" she asked.

"Perhaps," he answered. "But it is just adequate as my future wife's engagement ring."

Arianne put the box aside. "I thought we had a deal," she said.

"I learned a long time ago that deals can always be reviewed, if the circumstances change," he replied.

Arianne stood up and walked toward the door.

"I wouldn't be in such a hurry to leave, Florinda. We have a few things to discuss," he replied calmly. He could afford to be calm: he held all the trump cards.

Arianne froze at the mention of her sister's name. It was what she had called herself on the Bois, on the rare occasions when a man had asked her name. After more than a year, the men were as faceless to her as she hoped she was to them. Most of them had been respectable bourgeois, terrified of being found out in the Bois. If any of them had seen a photograph of her as a model, recognized her, and decided to make money from his knowledge, he would have discreetly approached her first. If one of the whores had found out, she would probably have gone to any of the scandal sheets with the story, not to Simón. There were only four people in Paris aware of her connection to Simón. Neither Edouard Golbins nor Céline de Merteuil would risk Simón's wrath by embarrassing him with the revelation of her past. She cringed at the thought of Jacques betraying her, but he only knew her as Arianne. No, it couldn't be Jacques. And it couldn't be Nana. It had to be that shit at the Rue Lanneau, the forger. She waited for a moment until she had regained her composure, then turned around and returned to her chair.

"I don't know who you are talking about," she said, looking straight at Simón. She knew it was useless to pretend, but she had to gain time. There had to be a way out of what was to follow, and she needed to find it.

"I admire your aplomb. It is one of the many reasons why I think you are worthy of becoming my wife," he said, unable to conceal his amusement. "We could play cat and mouse if you wish," he continued, "but it might be quicker to review a few facts. I have been told that the police in Rio would very much like to talk to a girl called Florinda Souza. She is wanted in connection with some murder or other. Her photograph looks very familiar. I will not say more. We are within earshot of at least twelve servants, and blackmail can be a very profitable line of business."

She understood at last. He didn't know about the Bois. Simón must have traced her passport, Florinda's passport, made inquiries in Brazil, and now he believed her to be her own sister.

She briefly considered explaining the truth to Simón, but realized there would be no point. It would make no difference to her predicament if he decided to bring in the Brazilian police: she was equally guilty of Ruben's murder in their eyes. Somehow the remaining confusion reassured her: it was as if her real self were still safely out of Simón's reach.

At least she was no longer fighting in the dark, and she was relieved by his mention of blackmail. He seemed as concerned about exposure as she.

"I wouldn't know; it's not *my* line of business," she said pointedly.

His eyes flashed. "I'm sure you understand your position, but I will spell it out just in case. Unless you agree to my new terms, I will reveal your name and whereabouts to the police. I haven't spent all this time and money on you to end up with nothing."

He poured himself another glass of Château Yquem and held the glass to the candlelight, admiring its pale glow before continuing.

"Don't imagine that your past makes any difference to my feelings for you. I don't put any moral value on what people need to do in order to survive, or simply to get something they want. But I don't believe that Brazilian prisons provide haute-couture uniforms for their guests, and I don't imagine that you want to change your current life-style."

He stood up, undid his bowtie, and began to unbutton his shirt.

"We can continue this conversation next door. There is a beautiful bedroom and the fire is lit. We have wasted enough time." He walked around the table and stood behind her, leaning down to kiss her neck. The feel of his wet lips on her flesh made her shiver. He encircled her waist with his arm and tried to lift her from her seat, tearing the fragile beadwork of her bodice.

She stood. She had been cornered before, but she had always managed to get away. She turned to face him.

"I'm not going to sleep with you," she said calmly. She continued before he could react. "I know that you want me, and you know enough about me to think that you can force me to go to bed with you. But I don't know if you love me. I know that you are obsessed with me, but there is a great difference. If we sleep together, you could get tired of me as quickly as you have become infatuated with me. Not only would I become a nuisance to you, but I could cost you a lot of money if your wife learns about me and uses me as an excuse to divorce you then. It would be cheaper for you to send me to jail. No, we are not going to sleep together. Your desire for me is my only safeguard."

"That's your problem, not mine," he retorted. He came closer and gripped her in his arms, his hands fumbling at her zipper. Her reaction was immediate. Her hand on his groin, she squeezed his balls as hard as she could, and he screamed in pain. Gasping for air, he let her go, and she ran to the sideboard. She picked up the champagne bottle with her left hand, and the ivory-handled carving knife with her right.

"If you move, this one goes into the Fragonard" — she waved the bottle toward the painting facing her — "and the knife goes right between your ribs. You can try to rape me if you wish, but I wouldn't recommend it."

Simón stared at her for a moment, then slowly began to do up his shirt. He reknotted his tie and sat down. He wasn't particularly worried about the knife; he could deal with that. But the prospect of a fracas here, and the headlines that would follow any damage to one of France's historic monuments, was a different matter. He had expected fear and submission from her, not a fight. There was no point in enraging her further.

"I admire your spirit," he said in a soothing tone. "I apologize again for my obtuseness. However, you are wrong. Sit down, and I'll explain why."

Still holding the knife, Arianne went back to her chair, relieved to have regained some control of the situation.

"You are right that I want you, but I'm not interested in you just as my mistress. You are exceptionally beautiful, and you are very intelligent. You have also shown that you can take care of yourself. I told you before that I want you as my wife, and I say it again now."

"You flatter me," Arianne replied, "but what guarantee would I have that you wouldn't get tired of me as your wife in the same way that you could become tired of me as your mistress? Now you know who I really am, you can always get rid of me by sending me to jail. I can't see what difference it would make, from my point of view, whether we are married or not."

She took a sip of water, then went on.

"Having reached this point, the only sensible thing is to part now. I'll give all your presents back to you, and you will keep silent about what you know. It's the fairest arrangement for both of us."

He sighed. "You still don't understand me. The main reason I want to marry you is that I desperately want a son. My wife can't have children."

For the first time since she had met him, Arianne heard an emotion other than pride or arrogance in his voice. He leaned across the table and took her hand.

"You have a child, so you probably can't imagine how desperately I want one. I have created an enormous business from nothing and

I have no one to continue it, to keep my memory alive once I'm gone. I've reached a point in my life when I can no longer take tomorrow for granted. I want a son, I want him as soon as possible, and I want you to be his mother. You already have a lovely daughter, and you are going to give me a lovely son. As many as God will send us, in fact." He tightened his grip on her hand. "I wouldn't want to send the mother of my children to jail, would I? Our children will be your safeguard." His eyes locked on hers. "Your future depends on me, and my future depends on you. I can't imagine a better basis for a marriage. I will not let you down." His voice dropped a fraction, and there was sudden, distinct menace in it. "And I am sure that you will not let *me* down."

Arianne recoiled. She was now in a far worse predicament than she had thought possible. She could not tell him about her sterility. Not now. He had come here this evening expecting total victory. If she were to tell him that all his efforts, all his expectations, had been for nothing, his rage would be uncontrollable, and he would turn her over to the police out of spite and humiliation. She knew him well enough by now to understand that. Still, she had to play for time, if only to delay the inevitable.

"Could I have more wine, please?"

"Of course," he replied, getting up and filling her glass. "Shall we drink a toast?" He pulled the ring from the box, and offered it to her.

"Not yet," she said. "It's not quite midnight." She sipped her wine slowly.

"You told me that there is no divorce in your country," she said after a while.

"What difference would that make? I can get a divorce anywhere else, and then marry you."

"It would make a lot of difference to me. Our children would not be legitimate in Argentina, and I would not be your wife under the law there. It wouldn't matter while you are alive, but it could matter to our children once you are dead. You are much older than I am."

He laughed.

"You are excessively cautious. Half of Argentina is married for a second time, and there are ways of ensuring the future of the second wife and her children."

"Maybe, but I have been an outcast for most of my life, and I have no wish to remain one. You must understand that feeling. If you want me to be your wife, you must get a Vatican annulment; that's the only thing that would make our marriage valid in your country."

She knew from gossip that it took years to arrange. In the meantime, she could get another set of forged papers and disappear with her jewelry, somewhere out of this bastard's reach.

Simón chuckled to himself. If that was all she wanted, his own plans were certainly faster and cheaper than appealing to the Sacra Rota in Rome.

"If what you are saying is that you will only marry me when our marriage would be fully valid in Argentina, then I will drink to that with pleasure." He raised his glass.

"And no sex until we are legally married," she added.

"I very much dislike that condition, but I'll go along with it. No sex until then," he replied. It would take rather less time than she thought. Better to humor her now that he had almost won.

The clock struck twelve. Simon stood up and began to open the champagne bottle.

"Please go to the window. You will see my last surprise of the evening."

It was a dark night, but the outline of the trees was just visible. The loud pop of the champagne cork coincided with the first flash of bright white against the sky, followed by another and then another, until the park was lit by the dazzle of giant fireworks.

Simón stood behind her, and handed her a glass of champagne.

"Happy New Year, my love," he said, kissing her shoulder softly and slipping the large ring on her finger. A new wave of fireworks covered the sky in intertwined *A*'s and *S*'s in brilliant red and blue.

Her eyes fixed on them, Arianne clenched her fist, her nails digging into her palm. The ring felt far, far heavier than she would have ever guessed.

19

Salta, Argentina
March 1969

CARLOS Gardes owed everything to Simón de la Force. He had been born in the valley thirty years ago. He grew up in the local orphanage until, at the age of fourteen, he was considered old enough to earn his living. He found a job on the then booming Valle del Oro estate. Four years later, encouraged by his success as a tango singer at the estate's barbecues for the staff, he decided to go to Buenos Aires to try his luck.

He soon found out that while his voice might have earned him the applause of sugar-cane harvesters in Salta, it took a greater voice and a greater stage presence than his to succeed as a tango singer in the capital. However, his Salta background did not go unnoticed by the owner of one of the many seedy cafés where he tried to launch his career, and Carlos eventually drifted into work as a courier for the profitable cocaine trade between Bolivia and Argentina. Salta was a key stage on the route.

During one of his trips to Salta, disaster struck. He was receiving a delivery at the Bolivian border when the *gendarmería* appeared. The other courier resisted, and was shot on the spot; Carlos was taken to jail in the city of Salta to await trial.

While in his cell, Carlos had a stroke of inspiration and wrote to Simón de la Force, explaining his connection with the Valle del Oro estate. In his letter he claimed he had been sent to collect the parcel without being told what it contained, the same alibi he had used during his questioning by the police. His letter also included a detailed account of his unhappy childhood.

Simón relished his role as a feudal lord, and his secretaries had strict instructions to pass on letters asking for help from anyone connected with his estate. Something in Carlos's letter pierced his armor, and Simón arranged for the young man to be brought to his office under police custody. This was technically in breach of the law, but Simón made his own laws in the province.

During the interview Simón sensed in Carlos the same quality noticed by the café owner in Buenos Aires. Maybe because of his circumstances, or simply because of his nature, Carlos was one of those men who would do anything, if the order came from someone he recognized as his boss. Moral considerations were his superior's problem, not his.

A man like that could be very useful to Simón. He arranged for Carlos to be released for lack of evidence, the cocaine parcel having mysteriously disappeared from police headquarters, and he offered the young man a vaguely defined job within the company. He had no specific use for him, but Simón was sure that one would be found eventually.

It soon became clear that Carlos had an uncanny instinct for tracking and trapping animals of any kind. He became responsible for the success of many of Simón's hunts, which were held for Simón's friends or business contacts from Buenos Aires or abroad. This was the respectable side of Carlos's job for Simón. There had been other tasks, better left unmentioned, but none that could compare to Simón's latest orders.

DOLORES de la Force hated Salta. The heat was impossible during the day, and the nearest neighbor worth talking to was one hundred miles away. One couldn't even put together a decent canasta table in such a place.

She had longed to stay in Punta del Este until the end of summer, but early in March Simón had insisted that she go to Valle del Oro to ensure that the household was running smoothly by the time he arrived with some friends he was expecting from Spain.

She had been there for ten days now, and she was desperately bored. She loathed the house, Simón's palacelike interpretation of a colonial hacienda. It had been nearly two years since her last visit, but now she had decided that the place needed drastic redecoration.

As soon as she was back in Buenos Aires she would phone Diego, her favorite interior designer. He would understand exactly what she had in mind.

She finished breakfast, and then thought about what she was going to do with the rest of her day. Suddenly she remembered that Carlos had mentioned he had noticed some very unusual orchids growing on the rocks at the other end of the park, where the water from the artificial lake was pumped out to form a waterfall on the side of the hill. It was a very isolated area and she seldom went there, but flowers were one of her very few passions. The blossoms must have been unusual indeed for someone as experienced in the region as Carlos not to have seen them before; perhaps she could send a few divisions to her greenhouses in Buenos Aires. It would take her at least half an hour to walk to the lake, a good way to kill time and to get some exercise before lunch.

She dressed quickly, putting on a white pleated skirt and a lovely pink shirt she had bought in Capri. She usually would not have worn such clothes in the country, but after a week in Salta she longed for civilized living, and she could not bear the thought of trousers, jodhpurs, or anything that would stick to her legs in this atrocious heat. But she would have to wear boots for the walk; she put on a pair of long cotton socks and some flat-heeled walking shoes in the meantime.

She left the house by the side door and turned left, along the guest wing, toward the kitchen courtyard. As she approached the gun room she noticed Zenón, the handyman, fixing the door lock. He stood up as soon as he saw her, and took off his beret.

"*Buen día, Señora Dolores,*" he said respectfully.

"*Buen día, Zenón.* What's wrong with the door?"

"Someone broke into the gun room two nights ago, Señora. I had to wait for the new lock to arrive from the city."

"Nobody told me about it! Was anything stolen?" she asked, as if she cared.

"All the boots, Señora, but nothing else. Perhaps Pancho did not want to bother the Señora about something so insignificant. It is very odd, because they left all the guns. Must be some *loquito.*"

Dolores sighed. Yes, only a madman would steal the boots and leave everything else, but it was a damn nuisance. She would have to go back to see if there was a spare pair in the dressing room, or send some maid for it. She did not fancy the idea of walking all the way back, and she knew that she could wait forever for one of the Indian girls to try to find something unless she was told precisely where to look for it. She decided that her walking shoes would have to do. The need for boots was probably an old wives' tale anyway. These Indians loved to frighten intruders from Buenos Aires.

"I hope that the break-in has been reported to the police. I'll have a word with Pancho," she said, and walked away. She wouldn't put it past the majordomo to be behind the robbery himself.

As she left the house behind her and walked farther into the park, she almost reconciled herself to her surroundings. The harsh contrast of arid rock mountains and fertile valleys, of an impossibly blue sky against the ocher of the hills was very beautiful in its own strange way. If only the damn heat would go away.

But she didn't think about the landscape for long. As so often these days, her thoughts turned to the state of her marriage.

Dolores had been brought up to marry well, and Simón was the best catch in Argentina. She knew that Simón had been unfaithful to her from the beginning: some of her friends had taken good care to make her aware of his peccadillos, but it had not mattered then. She was Señora de la Force, and that was enough for Dolores. In her circle, mistresses came and went, but wives remained.

Her miscarriages, and the eventual confirmation that she was barren, had opened the first cracks. Simón's sporadic visits to her bedroom had stopped as soon as it became clear that there was no hope of a child.

This did not bother Dolores. Sex did not concern her very much. But it had hurt her pride, and she worried about her future. She knew how much Simón wanted an heir, and sooner or later he would find another woman who could give him one.

The gossip from Paris had rung further warning bells, and she became concerned about the possible implications for her position. As usual when really serious matters troubled her, she decided to consult her father.

His wisdom had reassured her. "He cannot divorce you, anyway. He can only ask for a legal separation. Any good lawyer, and I know a few very good ones, would make it so expensive for him that he could not seriously consider the option. He will probably end up having a baby with some maid; it runs in that family. You can then adopt the child. I wouldn't lose any sleep over it, darling." Her father had then taken her for a comforting lunch at the Jockey Club, and she had stopped worrying for a while.

Simón's sudden departure from Punta del Este after Christmas had rekindled her fears, but he had returned soon after, and he had spent the rest of the summer with her, other than short trips to Buenos Aires for business reasons. Perhaps her father had been right after all, and she worried too much.

Relieved, Dolores decided to concentrate on more pleasant thoughts, and turned to the redecoration of the main house. She had to plan every room to be able to tell Diego what she wanted.

The house should look cozy, that was the word, like an English country home. By the time she reached the lake, she had decided that the chintz curtains in the dining room should match the wall coverings rather than contrast with them. She had seen it in Chiquita's London dining room, and she found it lovely. As she approached the waterfall, Dolores realized that Carlos had been wrong. There was nothing unusual about the orchids there, at least from a distance. She decided to have a closer look.

Carlos was hiding behind the rocks. He had already spent the previous afternoon there, waiting for her to appear. He had returned before dawn to avoid being seen, and was beginning to doubt whether she would turn up at all when he saw her walking along the lake, toward the waterfall.

Dolores stood in front of the blossoms climbing up the rocks, her back to him. Carlos unfolded a thick canvas bag, and waited until she moved farther to one side, where the large boulders made her invisible to anyone walking in the park, although it was unlikely that anyone would be there at this time of the day.

He approached her as silently as he would have had she been a wild animal. He swiftly slipped the bag over her head and shoulders until it reached her hips, then he tightened the bindings before she could react. He held her with both arms and found it quite easy to lift her in spite of her resistance. He carried her to a large wicker basket he had hidden behind a rock, kicked the lid open, and placed Dolores standing inside.

It had taken Carlos two days to track a large *cascabel* snake, and he had kept it in the basket for a further ten days, to ensure that its poison sacs were full. Tormented by hunger and disturbed by Dolores, the snake struck immediately; her cotton sock offered no resistance to its needle-sharp fangs. In her blind, terrified struggle, Dolores suddenly felt a sharp pain in her left leg, followed by a burning sensation.

As soon as he saw the snake strike, Carlos pulled Dolores out of the basket, kicked the lid shut, and waited. It would not take long now. He was not worried by Dolores's screams. They would be silenced by the roar of the waterfall next to them, and she soon would be too weak to cry out.

He could feel her frantic movements slowing down until she went limp in his arms, but he waited for a while before removing the canvas bag. He had seen people dying from *cascabel* bites; there would be a lot of internal bleeding oozing out of the mouth, nose, and ears, and he had to be careful not to stain his clothes. Don Simón had been very insistent about that.

After a while he laid Dolores on the ground. He pulled his cigarettes and lighter from his shirt pocket, and searched in his bag until he found his transistor radio. He connected the earphone, and looked at his watch. It was time for *The Tango Show,* one of his favorite programs. Carlos was so absorbed by the music that he did not notice the last spasmodic convulsions of Dolores's agony inside the bag as the poison finally destroyed her nervous system.

Carlos did not much care for female tango singers but he had to admit that Suzy Leiva was nearly as good as a man. The lack of movement in the bag when he finally turned the radio off confirmed what he expected: it would be safe to remove it now. He undid the bindings and uncovered Dolores's body, but he closed his eyes. He did not want to see the poor *señora*'s face.

He left her body lying on the ground and tipped the basket open; the snake slipped away and quickly disappeared into a crevice in the rocks. He would have liked to have killed the creature, but it would mean taking unnecessary risks to walk away from the scene with the dead snake, and he couldn't leave it there. Better to let it go, as Don Simón had said.

Carlos picked up his cigarette stubs and dropped them in the basket with the canvas bag. He erased his tracks with his poncho, and then began the long walk back to the house. Along the way he stopped at the incinerator building, and flung the basket into one of the roaring furnaces.

Carlos realized that he was very tired, but it didn't matter. He had done a good job, and he hoped that Don Simón would be pleased.

THE Recoleta has been Buenos Aires' smartest cemetery for over a hundred years. Most of the country's heroes, as well as most of the country's rich, are buried there, the regular setting for splendid funerals. But few could compare with the burial of Dolores de la Force.

Simón led the cortège along the narrow lanes between the marble pavilions. He was flanked by Dolores's family, the primate cardinal of Buenos Aires, and the archbishops of Salta, Jujuy, and Tucumán, the sugar provinces of Argentina. Half the government, the best of society, and more or less the whole of Argentina's business establishment followed him, rubbing their elbows against the wreaths and floral tributes piled up against the front of the tombs on both sides of the procession route from the cemetery gates to the Anzorena family vault, a few hundred yards away. The warm air was heavy with the scent of carnations.

Dolores's mother had insisted that her daughter be buried in Buenos Aires, in their vault. Simón had put up some token resistance, but the de la Force family tomb in Salta was rather modest, and it would have been impossible for the people who mattered to attend a funeral a thousand miles away from the capital. He soon agreed to her request.

Simón glanced at Dolores's mother, shaken by sobs under her thick black veil, and felt some sympathy for the woman. It must be hard to lose a daughter in such a tragic accident. But it was equally hard to lose one's beloved wife, and his face immediately regained the stern composure he had adopted when leaving his house to attend the requiem mass at the Pilar Church next to the cemetery.

Simón was beginning to feel the effect of the previous night's vigil. He had to stand for hours next to Dolores's coffin, laid out in the library. He had listened to an endless stream of "Poor Simón," "Poor Dolores, so young," "Such a terrible accident," and similar

20

Paris
April 1969

ARIANNE had just finished getting dressed when her maid announced through the half-open door to the dressing room that the car was waiting for her downstairs.

"Thank you, Rosinha," said Arianne. She took one last look at herself in the full-length mirror, and decided to change out of the plain navy blue dress she had just put on: it wasn't somber enough for her mood. She went back to her closets, and finally chose a severe black suit and a black silk shirt. She knew she was late for her appointment with Simón, but she did not care. Let him wait.

Ever since receiving Simón's cable informing her of Dolores's sudden death, she had wished that time would stand still. All her plans, her delaying tactics, had crumbled as soon as she had opened the envelope and read his message.

Simón had phoned her the following day to expand on his brief description of what had happened, and to announce that he would come to Paris in April to make plans for their future. No matter how credible his explanation, how viable the accident, Arianne knew that Simón had killed his wife. She also knew that there was no way out for her now.

If she disclosed the full facts to him, he would send her to jail out of spite, and Gloria would become an orphan. If she waited until they were married, he probably would not send her to jail. He could not tolerate the consequent embarrassment. But neither would he put up with a woman who had tricked him into marriage, thwarting platitudes until the early hours. At first he had replied to the effect that "we are all in the hands of God," alternated with "I can't forgive myself for not having stressed enough the dangers of walking without boots in that area." But by two o'clock most people other than Dolores's family or his business associates had left, and he did not need to bother much about them.

Still, he could not just leave and go to bed, much as he wanted to, and he had drunk endless cups of black coffee to stay awake, with the occasional Scotch to counteract his boredom. The undertakers had arrived early in the morning to seal the coffin and load it on the hearse, and at last he had been able to leave the house.

The procession reached the vault. Simón and the family, their heads bent, stood at both sides of the ebony and silver coffin, while the cardinal gave his last blessing and prayed for Dolores's soul. The family and the archbishops joined in the prayers, but their voices could not muffle the instructions shouted by the undertakers from the second basement of the vault, advising their colleagues at the top as to how to maneuver the ropes for the coffin to negotiate the narrow openings on each floor until it reached its final resting place on one of the stone shelves, alongside several generations of Anzorenas. At last the undertakers left the tomb, the bronze gates of the vault were closed, and Dolores de la Force was left to rest in peace.

Simón had to stand at the cemetery's colonnaded portico for at least another hour to receive the mourners' condolences, but he enjoyed this part of the ceremony in spite of his tiredness. The caliber of the mourners was an homage to him, not to his wife. The end of the long line was at last visible, and soon afterward he was free to go. He stiffly embraced his in-laws and walked to the car, maintaining his sad countenance until the limousine pulled away and the onlookers were left behind.

As soon as the car joined the traffic in the Avenida Alvear for the short ride home, he loosened his tie and undid his collar button, sat back and gave free rein to his thoughts. Not about Dolores, and not about Arianne either. He thought about what he would like to have for lunch. He was very hungry.

his obsession to found a dynasty at the same time. No, he would not send her to jail. Dolores's death was as much a confirmation of Arianne's early suspicions as an indication of her own eventual fate. He would kill her.

Simón had arrived in Paris the night before and phoned her from the hotel. He had said that he would move into the apartment the following day, but Arianne mentioned the need to maintain at least some appearances until their wedding was announced. He had reluctantly agreed, and suggested that they meet the following morning at Cartier, to choose a present to celebrate their forthcoming wedding. "We don't need to hide now. I want the whole world to see us together," he had said.

She checked the time: he had been waiting for half an hour, and it would take at least ten minutes for the car to reach the Rue de la Paix. She picked up her bag and left the room without bothering to glance in the mirror. How she looked had suddenly ceased to matter to her.

"PERHAPS Mademoiselle would care for sapphires?" asked the jeweler, presenting yet another velvet tray to Arianne.

"These are truly exceptional stones," he continued in a silky voice. "They belonged to the Maharanee of Baroda, but we have recut them and set them in a much more flattering style. Mademoiselle should try the necklace," he said, picking up the sparkling piece of jewelry with both hands and holding it in front of Arianne. She barely glanced at the giant stones.

"I don't wear sapphires," she replied, her tone as dismissive as the wave of her hand. "They don't suit the color of my eyes."

"Of course," said the jeweler, promptly passing the tray to his assistant nearby, who laid the sapphire parure next to the numerous trays already rejected.

"Is there *anything* you like?" asked Simón, unable to conceal his exasperation.

He had started the morning in a radiant mood, his joy at the prospect of seeing Arianne doubled by the early morning call from his office to confirm that the discreet disposal of Dolores's jewelry through his Geneva contacts had been arranged. The price virtually covered the cost of the jewels Simón had so far given to Arianne and, since saving money came second only to the pleasure of making and spending it, he had walked into Cartier in a glow of self-contentment.

But they had been there for an hour. They had been shown endless sets of breathtaking jewels, but nothing seemed to please Arianne. First she was nearly an hour late, and now she seemed to be in an impossible mood.

The jeweler was as puzzled as Simón by Arianne's lack of interest, but decades of experience with awkward clients ensured that none of his annoyance was apparent. It was his rule to do the utmost to clinch a sale. He whispered some instruction to the attendant and, always smiling, he turned to Arianne.

"Perhaps the answer is for Mademoiselle to have something specially made for her, with stones equal in quality to any of the jewels I have shown you so far, but to a more personal design. I have asked my assistant to bring some of the pieces we have in stock for resetting. He won't be a moment."

The assistant returned with further velvet trays, and the jeweler picked up the top one.

"The history of this jewel would perhaps interest you, Monsieur de la Force. We recently accepted it in partial payment for another necklace from one of our American clients. The gems are magnificent, but the design, alas, is not fashionable now. We understand that it was made in Buenos Aires for Madame Perón, probably in the late forties. Our client bought it at the auction of her jewelry in 1956."

Simón recoiled at the sight of the necklace as if the tray held the bloody entrails of an animal.

"I would never buy anything that belonged to that thief!" he bellowed. "She ruined our country, and I was a fierce opponent of their despicable government from the beginning." Years of practice gave a convincing intonation to his outburst.

"Take it away immediately," he continued in a slightly quieter voice, "or I shall become very upset indeed."

"Wait a minute," said Arianne, placing her hand on the tray. "It's really exquisite." She examined the huge emeralds shining in the center of diamond flowers. She did not know why the jewel upset

Simón so much, but she did not care; it was enough that it annoyed him.

She tried on the necklace and looked at herself in the small mirror standing on the table. It was one of the most vulgar things she had ever seen.

"It's lovely, truly lovely," she said. "I will wear it at our wedding. Thank you, darling." She leaned toward Simón and kissed him on the lips. The jeweler rose to the occasion and launched into an incantation about Mademoiselle's unerring eye, her superb taste, her knowledgeable disdain for conventional style. Simón took in Arianne's determined expression and knew that he was defeated.

"At least have it reset," he protested.

"Absolutely not; I adore it just as it is." Arianne's tone made it clear that the matter was closed. "Let's go," she said. She walked toward the exit, without waiting for Simón. She smiled for the first time that morning, but by the time Simón was beside her in the car she looked as impassive as usual.

IT was mid-June, and Arianne noticed that the chestnut trees in the Jardin des Tuileries were in blossom. She also realized that it was probably the last time she would see them. She gazed at her drawing room, the furniture shrouded by dust sheets laid by the moving men who had come that morning to take their luggage away. Seventeen Louis Vuitton trunks, God knows how many suitcases, and the enormous crate from Saint Laurent holding her wedding dress.

When they had discussed the wedding plans four weeks ago she had insisted that she wanted a totally private ceremony, only witnessed by Nana. Simón had agreed, and told her that the wedding would take place at Our Lady of Yanbi, the colonial church on his Salta estate, far away from Buenos Aires and the social crowd. However, he had asked her to wear a white wedding dress for the occasion. "I am very sentimental, and I am entitled to a bride wearing a proper dress," he had said cheerfully. Arianne found Simón in a good mood even more grating than his usual dictatorial persona.

Futile as it was, her only means of evening the score with him was to spend his money, and this she had done over the last weeks with a vengeance. Apart from her wedding dress, suitable for a royal marriage, she had ordered seventy-five couture outfits. She had stopped only when she realized that the fittings would prove more exhausting for her than the bills were for Simón. She hadn't bothered to have the second fitting for many of the clothes, or even to pick up those that were ready.

Arianne had come to terms with her predicament, but she could not bear to think about what would become of Gloria and Nana because of it. She had had dinner with Jacques the night before. She had said nothing to him about what was troubling her, but at the end of the evening, when she kissed Jacques good-bye, she had given him a shoebox holding her best jewels and a letter asking him to use the money from the sale of the jewelry to support Gloria and Nana. Arianne had never mentioned her friendship with Jacques to Simón, and she hoped Simón would not be able to trace him, at least for a while.

"I want you to hold this," she had said. "If anything were to happen to me, please open the box and read the letter inside, but only once Gloria and Nana are back in Paris. I've given Nana two open tickets, in her name and Gloria's. I have asked Nana to contact you."

Jacques took the box.

"The wax seals are unnecessary, darling. I would not look into your box any more than I want to look into your past, but I will do what you ask me." His eyes had shifted away. "Better go now. I'm not as good as you are about not getting emotional," he had said, gently pushing her out of his apartment.

That morning she had been to the Argentine consulate to go through the formalities of the civil marriage by proxy that would enable them to marry in church in Argentina as soon as she arrived. Edouard Golbins had stood in for Simón. Officially, she was now Mrs. Simón de la Force.

It was nearly dark. Nana had already retired to her bedroom, after helping Arianne to put Gloria to bed. Ever since Arianne had mentioned to her that she was going to marry Simón, Nana's attitude had changed and her tacit disapproval had vanished, as if she had sensed Arianne's difficulties. Nana was incapable of expressing her feelings, but Arianne had learned to gauge them, and she knew that in her curious, irrational way, Nana understood what was going on.

She walked into her bedroom. Everything other than her beauty case and the clothes she would wear tomorrow for the trip had been packed away. She looked at the fireplace, at the pile of ashes that had been Florinda Souza's Brazilian passport. The room reeked of Chanel No. 5 and burned paper. She had poured a large bottle of scent on the passport to fuel the flames.

After the ceremony at the consulate, Edouard Golbins had handed her a letter from Simón, which she had read in the car. He had arranged for an Argentine passport in Arianne's married name to be delivered to her the next morning. "The plane may have to make an emergency stop in Brazil, and I wouldn't want you to run into immigration problems. They can be very tiresome," the letter said. He did not need to say more; they understood each other. "The passport will be handed to you by the chauffeur just before you go through passport control in Paris. I want to make sure that you board the right flight," he had added. Arianne picked up the poker from the side of the fireplace, and crumbled the ashes until they blended into the dusty pile in the grate.

She sat at her desk, switched the desk light on, and picked up a few sheets of her pale blue writing paper from the stationery tray next to her. She stared at the blank sheet for a while, and then began to write, page after page. It was easier than she thought.

Her letter finished at last, she put it in an envelope, wrote "Simón" on it, and put it away in the silk pouch inside her beauty case. She walked into her bathroom and ran her bath, but she did not linger in it. She wanted to go to sleep as soon as possible. Before getting into bed she returned to her beauty case for a bottle of Seconal, and took two pills. She rattled the bottle before putting it away, and was relieved to notice that there were still many pills left.

21

Salta, Argentina
June 1969

$\mathcal{T}$HE afternoon sun shone on the hilltop, outlining the whitewashed building of Our Lady of Yanbi against the cobalt blue sky. As they began to climb toward the church, Arianne noticed Simón's car parked outside it, in the shadow of a cluster of giant cacti. The solitary car accentuated the emptiness of the landscape.

They had been driving for nearly an hour, across endless fields of sugar cane at first, and then through the stony plateau that surrounded the isolated hill. Arianne sat in the back seat, almost drowning in the froth of her wedding dress.

Arianne, Nana, and Gloria had arrived in Salta the night before, exhausted by the twenty-hour flight to Buenos Aires. At Ezeiza airport they had boarded Simón's jet for the last leg of the journey. They had landed at midnight, and they had been driven to one of the guest houses in the park, far away from the main house, where Arianne found an enormous basket of white orchids. "I'm not supposed to see you until the wedding, and we can't sleep under the same roof, since it brings bad luck. I love you," read the unsigned card. Arianne crumpled it in her hand. Bad omens would not have made any difference to her now, but she was relieved not to have to see Simón. A maid showed them to their rooms, and Arianne fell asleep almost immediately, her tension defeated by her tiredness.

She woke up close to midday, to find that Nana and Gloria had been taken for a buggy ride in the park. By the time they came back, escorted by gauchos in leather chaps and a French-speaking nanny in uniform, lunch was being served in the dining room. Arianne was unable to eat anything. After lunch, the nanny took Gloria to her room for a rest, and the butler suggested that the ladies retire to their rooms to get ready for the ceremony. They should leave for the church at five o'clock. The ceremony was scheduled for six o'clock, and Don Simón hated delays.

At four o'clock the maid had knocked at Arianne's door and announced that the hairdresser from Buenos Aires was ready for the *señora*. Arianne found Spanish surprisingly easy to understand. The hairdresser was shown into the room and introduced himself as Hubert, the Frenchness of his name belied by his atrocious accent. Arianne immediately sensed his animosity, the reason for which became clear when he explained that he had been Dolores's hairdresser.

However, once he noticed Arianne's wedding dress on a dummy in the corner of the room, he launched into an ecstatic praise of Paris couture. Arianne sensed an opening and told him about her life as a Balenciaga model. His enmity receded, and his passion for gossip exorcised Dolores's ghost. Even now, when time had nearly run out and everything mattered so little, Arianne was not prepared to be under anyone's shadow.

Her hair done, Hubert waited while Rosinha helped Arianne into her wedding dress, and quickly made her up. Only then did he pin the immense veil, sprinkled with hundreds of silk orange blossoms, to her chignon. Arianne asked Rosinha to bring her the black silk box on her dressing table, and she fastened the emerald necklace around her neck, throwing Hubert into further spasms of admiration.

She left her bedroom and was joined by Nana, dressed in her usual black. For once, she thought, Nana was the most appropriately attired person for the occasion. Gloria was holding Nana's hand, the nanny standing behind them. As Arianne appeared, Gloria ran to her.

"Where are you going, Mummy?" she asked, trying to pick at the orange blossoms on Arianne's dress.

How could she explain to Gloria where she was going? What could she say to her two-year-old child? Arianne just stroked Gloria's head, and waited for the lump in her throat to subside.

"I'm going to a party, my darling. A very big party. I'll see you later." Arianne pulled her veil down and turned toward the nanny. She did not want anyone to see her face now. "Please take her away," Arianne whispered. Gloria's light footsteps echoed on the tiled floor, until Arianne finally heard the door close behind her daughter.

They walked out of the house. The car was already waiting by the entrance. Arianne turned toward her maid, who had begun to gather the long train of her dress. "Rosinha, please don't forget to take my beauty case to the main house after we have left, and leave it in my . . . our bedroom, on the bed."

"Don't worry, Mademoiselle, I haven't forgotten your instructions," the maid replied, as she carefully laid the train on the seat next to Arianne. Nana and the driver got into the car, and the butler closed the doors. The clunk of the locks sounded like prison gates.

THE *warden pushed Florinda inside the cell, and slammed the steel door shut behind her. Florinda stumbled, then fell on the narrow bed, the dirty cotton cover soaking in her tears, new stains over the old ones. It had all been Santos's fault. She had been an idiot to fall for him, under the spell of his slow eyes and his hard fists.*

If only she knew what had gone wrong at the last job. She had left the villa during the early hours, when she knew the security guard would be asleep. Either the man or the woman must have awakened while she was crossing the park, noticed the jewelry missing from the dressing table and rung the alarm. The park lights went on and the security man came out of his hut, gun in hand, just before she reached the gates. She pushed him aside and ran to the street. Santos, damned Santos, should have been there, waiting for her in a stolen car, but he wasn't, and she heard the bullet whistle past her ear. She didn't have a chance; she dropped her bag on the sidewalk and held her arms up in surrender.

The police soon matched her fingerprints to those found on the gun at the scene of Ruben's murder, and she was found guilty at the trial. She would spend the next twenty-five years in jail because of Santos. Hatred was all she had left.

But Santos was not the only one responsible for this. She would have got two, at worst three, years for the robbery. If she was going to be in jail for as long as she had been alive it was because of her sister. She had ended up paying for Silvia's crime. No, she didn't hate Santos most. She hated Silvia, and she hated her more than even she would have thought possible. Prison wasn't bad enough for Silvia: she ought to be dead.

ARIANNE walked into the cool shadow of the church entrance, and stood still as Nana arranged her train behind her and straightened her veil. She could not help noticing the unadorned wooden doors in front of her, leading into the church, and the modesty of the architecture, the plain whitewashed walls, the terra-cotta tiles on the floor. She was surprised that Simón's vanity could be satisfied by such a humble venue for their wedding.

The music filtering through the doors was vaguely familiar. It was not organ music. The sounds were much fuller, much richer than any church music she had ever heard. But she *had* heard it before, this passionate crescendo of strings, the bass accents a foreboding of something portentous yet to come.

The crescendo of strings came to an end, leading to the melancholy sound of the horns punctuated by a solitary violin, a moment of calm before what she now knew would follow. The doors slowly opened in front of her, the melody as haunting as the fear that suddenly gripped her, and the splendor of Our Lady of Yanbi was revealed to her eyes.

"Go, just go," Nana whispered behind her, gently pushing her forward.

As Arianne stepped into the nave, the National Symphonic Orchestra and the hundred and twenty singers in the choir burst into the magnificence of Beethoven's "Ode to Joy." The waves of sound crashed against the silver-covered walls, rising to the vault, where silver cherubs sat on silver clouds against a golden sky. The light of hundreds of candles sparkled against silver pillars, shining on the petals of the white lilies banking Arianne's path.

The music rang in her ears during her slow progress down the aisle. She walked, barely able to see the high altar through her tears, which refracted the candlelight into a thousand stars.

Whoever has created
An abiding friendship,
Or has won
A true and loving wife,
All who can call at least one soul theirs,
Join in our song of praise;
But any who cannot must creep tearfully
Away from our circle,

sang the choir as Simón de la Force surveyed the scene from the altar, waiting for his bride by the silver balustrade. He did not understand the words, but it did not matter. The rapturous sounds echoed his feelings.

Of all his many hours of triumph, this was the one that he savored most. The power of the music, the silver of the viceroy, the silks of Saint Laurent, Arianne's beauty: they all fused into a perfect monument to *his* might and *his* glory. He cast a contemptuous glance at the silver Madonna in her niche above the altar, her jewels now adorning Arianne's throat; there was no limit to what he could achieve. As he offered his arm to Arianne, he enjoyed the significance of the gesture, and felt a flutter in his heart.

The archbishop of Salta, in full attire, began the ceremony. As he asked the incongruous gathering of hundreds of musicians and one old woman for any reasons why this marriage should not take place, Arianne's mind went blank, oblivious to anything other than her anguish, the archbishop's voice blending with the music into a distant din. Finally she realized the archbishop was addressing her, waiting for her answer. The moment had come.

"I do," she murmured.

Simón raised her veil and kissed her on the mouth, but she felt nothing. Her lips were numb. In despair, she raised her eyes to the Madonna. She had never been truly religious, but she needed to believe that there was still hope. Her eyes fixed on the naive face carved by an Indian centuries ago, she asked Our Lady of Yanbi for her help, and she made her vow.

The archbishop gave his final blessing to the couple, the orchestra burst into Mendelssohn's "Wedding March," and the wedding was over. Simón shook hands with the archbishop and turned to Arianne. He offered her his arm, but she did not pay any attention to him. She addressed the prelate instead.

"I want to give you this, to help the poor people in this parish. It is a vow I have made," she said, unfastening her emerald necklace and handing it to the archbishop. It had been a long time since he had had to deal with requests of this nature, and he did not even know who handled such matters in this diocese, but he betrayed none of his momentary confusion and blessed Arianne for her generosity. Simón remembered the Cartier bill and cursed her silently, but he felt too elated to really mind. *Trust a woman to get carried away by her emotions,* he thought as they left the church.

A Cadillac convertible was waiting outside, its top down. They climbed in, and the car slowly pulled away. Arianne looked back, and saw Nana being led to a second car. She could not bring herself to talk to Simón, but she knew she had to say something, anything to break the isolation of her silence. She noticed a plane flying over them. A moment later, she noticed another one, and then a third, far away on the horizon.

"Why are there so many planes?" she asked. "This place can't be on the route to anywhere."

"It is on the route to our wedding party. I chartered ten planes to bring the guests from Buenos Aires," he replied, an amused smile on his lips.

"You promised we would have a private wedding," she said quietly. She couldn't even be bothered to be angry, and it didn't make much of a difference. A party might even serve her purpose.

"We had a private wedding, but I never said anything about the reception." As the car slowed down, Simón turned to Arianne.

"Stand up," he said. "We are about to join the main road to the house."

On both sides of the road men dressed in bright red ponchos with a broad black stripe along the edges lined up into the horizon, waving sugar cane stems as the car moved slowly past. Simón was already on his feet, waving to his peasants. Ahead of them, the road was white and glittering in the setting sun, as if covered with snow.

"I thought sugar would be the best possible carpet for us." Simón pointed at the men. "Stand up; they want to see you." She obeyed, waving at the cheering crowd.

She had always disliked Simón, but now she hated him. He had ruined her business, denying her the opportunity to have her own life. She had justified her decision at the time with the excuse that she didn't want Gloria and Nana to face poverty, but it hadn't been the ultimate reason; poverty would have been preferable to what she now had to face. The truth was that she had been tempted by what Simón had offered her, at no apparent cost, and she had taken it. She hated him for manipulating her, and she hated herself for having allowed it.

"You are mad, completely mad. I hate you." She said it again and again, shaken by her own sobs. Simón paid no attention. He was engrossed in receiving the homage of his people.

AS Simón had planned, everybody who counted was at the party. Or nearly everybody. The president had had to cancel at the last minute because of the recent troubles in Córdoba, where rioters had torched the center of Argentina's second largest city, causing tension in several parts of the country. And Simón still rankled at the polite refusals received from the Borns, the Fortabats, and a few others like them, too rich to feel the need to humor his whim. Some of Dolores's relations had also declined, but by and large all the people who mattered were present.

They were trying their best to be festive, but the conversations seemed to turn, again and again, to the increasing uncertainty and the escalation of political unrest in the nation. The country's leading trade union leader had been assassinated the previous day, there were rumblings in the army, and the days of General Onganía as president seemed numbered. The guests all conveyed their good wishes to Simón, particularly when he said again and again that he looked forward to Arianne having a baby as soon as possible, but Argentina's uncertain future loomed over the reception.

Such matters may have concerned his guests, but not Simón. One general would be followed by another general; he could deal with any of them. He had sensed the crisis coming long before anyone else, and over the last three years he had concentrated on expanding his business abroad. Thanks to Bob Chalmers's advice, he was now worth even more money in the United States than he was in Argentina, and that did not take into account his vast interests in Europe.

Simón made a mental note to have a few words with Bob, who was somewhere in the party. He knew that it paid to be nice to really useful people. He picked up a glass of champagne from the tray offered by a waiter, and moved on to talk with the Chilean ambassador.

While discussing the future of the mining industry in Chile, a matter in which Simón had more than a passing interest, he noticed Arianne coming toward him. Even from a distance, he could see that she was deathly pale.

"Excuse me," he told the ambassador, and walked to her.

"I'm about to faint," she whispered. "I need to lie down for a while. I have very low blood pressure, and I will pass out unless I rest."

Simón was annoyed. He could not possibly leave the party now. It was another hour and a half to the announced end of the reception, when the planes would take his guests back to Buenos Aires, and there were twenty-odd ambassadors in the house. He had not talked to half of them.

"Why don't you sit down?" he said.

"It would make no difference; it's the crowd that affects me. I will go to our bedroom now. Please make my excuses." She walked away without waiting for his answer.

She made her way through the crowd and walked upstairs. Rosinha was waiting for her there.

"This way, Madame," the maid said, leading her down one of the corridors. Rosinha opened one of the doors leading off it.

"In here, Madame."

As she entered the room, Arianne's first thought was that this had been Dolores's bedroom. She could see the marks on the walls where pictures had recently been removed. She was relieved to notice her beauty case standing on the table by the side of the enormous four-poster bed.

"Please help me undress, Rosinha."

"Already, Madame?" The maid was surprised.

"Yes, now," Arianne replied impatiently. Without further questions, Rosinha unpinned the veil, unzipped her dress, and helped her out of it. Arianne took off her underwear, and put on the satin and lace nightdress laid out on the bed.

"Don't bother to put the dress away, Rosinha; you can do that tomorrow. Leave it on the chair."

"Would Madame want me to brush her hair?"

"No, that will be all for now." She wanted Rosinha out of the room as soon as possible. She knew what she had to do, and she couldn't wait any longer.

"Good night, Madame." The door closed behind the maid, and Arianne was alone at last.

She opened her beauty case and searched for the letter to Simón, which she laid on the pillows on the other side of the bed. She then took out Gloria's picture, kissed it, and put it back in the case. Before closing it, she removed the Seconal bottle and placed it on the bedside table, next to the water carafe.

She sat on the bed, poured a glass of water, opened the bottle and swallowed the pills one by one. There were twenty-two tablets, but she did not count them. She knew there were enough.

THE last guests boarded the coach and Simón waved good-bye until the taillights disappeared in the direction of the airstrip. At last. He ran into the house, and climbed the steps in twos, pulling at his wing collar and his silver gray cravat. His pearl tiepin dropped to the ground, but he didn't care. He did not have time to stop for something so insignificant. He wanted Arianne, and he wanted her now.

He burst into their bedroom, his face beaming. Arianne was asleep on the bed. He noticed the soft silk satin clinging to the curves of her breasts and her belly, the folds gathered between her legs. He tore off his clothes as he walked to the bed, ready to wake her.

When he came closer to Arianne, he realized there was something unnatural about her sleep, and he noticed the letter on his pillow. He leaned over her, picked up the envelope, ripped it open, and began to read.

Rage and frustration burst inside him, and his animal roar echoed in the silent house. This cow, this whore, this . . . this . . . this *woman* had tricked him. He had spent millions to get her, murdered his wife to marry her, and she had tricked him. His dream, to which he had devoted so much of his energy, had been shattered in a second: she could not have his child. She was right! He would kill her. But before that he was going to have her. For the first and last time he was going to screw her as he had never screwed any woman before.

He tried to wake her but he could not, even when he slapped and then punched her. It scarcely mattered. He did not need her to be awake.

He ripped her nightgown to shreds and spread her on the bed. Holding her thighs apart with his hands, he plunged into her, his fury increasing his pleasure. He had never hated anyone so much. His hands encircled her neck, and his urge became unrestrainable. He began to tighten his grip, increasing the pressure in unison with each thrust.

Simón sensed his climax approaching as his thumbs dug into Arianne's soft flesh. He felt the rush in his balls, and squeezed her neck harder. "Die, bitch, die," he shouted as he pushed deeply into her.

He never felt his orgasm. What he felt was a ball of fire in his chest, an agony so great that it obscured everything else. Simón gasped for air, but he could not breathe. His eyes were open, but he could not see. He did not even realize that his hands were no longer grasping Arianne's neck, that he had raised his arms in a mortal spasm of pleasure and pain.

His sperm and his life left his body simultaneously. As he slumped forward his hand caught the bell cord by the bed, his fingers gripping it in an unconscious reflex. His face contorted by his agony, he collapsed on top of Arianne. At long last, he had made her his wife in the eyes of God and man.

Part Four

22

*New York
May 1987*

PANDORA had been in the library for hours, and she was tired. She squinted at the bright screen, her hand slowly moving the lever across the microfiche on the plate.

She had begun her search by looking up Arianne's entry in *Who's Who*: she was not listed. She then moved on to the *International Who's Who*. Again she found nothing. She tried several editions of *Who Was Who*, until she found Simón de la Force listed in the 1970 volume, giving some general information and the date of his death. There was nothing on his marriages other than "*m* 1st 1957, Dolores de Anzorena (*d* 1969), 2nd 1969, Arianne." Just the first name, nothing else.

Then Pandora went to the microfilm library and checked for any Argentine newspapers. The only one was the international edition of *La Nación*. With the date of his death as a reference, she quickly traced Simón's obituary, which took up half a page. Even with her little knowledge of Spanish she was able to understand that the obituary mostly consisted of platitudes about his great significance. It mentioned the sad fact that his wedding had preceded his death only by a few hours, but Arianne was barely mentioned and only as Mrs. de la Force. Again, no other name. Pandora carefully checked the ensuing issues through to the end of the year, but she only came across a very occasional mention of Arianne de la Force on the business pages.

By then her right arm and her legs were numb from remaining in the same position at the microfiche and she began to hurry her research, feeding cards from the box at random and scanning the first three pages of each issue only, until she reached 1975. She found a number of reports of guerrilla incidents, but none concerning Arianne. At last Pandora concluded that the library route was a dead end. If it had just been a matter of finding facts from old newspapers, some other journalist would have picked up the story long ago. If there was one.

But she was then annoyed by her own doubts. The next step was to talk to Geraldine. She would have to go to Argentina, even Brazil, and spend some time doing research there. The prospect suddenly filled her with excitement.

"DARLING, how nice to see you! I gather you are doing *wonderful* things with your section," Geraldine said, leading Pandora toward the sofa with the usual clanking of bracelets. Having waited for nearly a week for her appointment with Geraldine, Pandora did not want to waste time on small talk.

"Thank you, but there is something more important I want to discuss with you," she said as soon as they sat down. "I've been doing some research on Arianne de la Force."

"How clever of you! Did you find anything worthwhile?"

Pandora was chafed by Geraldine's patronizing sympathy, but ignored it.

"Yes, I found out that I am wasting my time in the library. Women like Arianne don't talk to journalists about their secrets."

Geraldine sighed.

"You shouldn't dismiss research. You'll find out in time that it's the basis of all good journalism."

"I'm not dismissing it, not at all. I'm simply saying I've been doing it in the wrong place. If I'm really going to find out anything about Arianne, I have to go to Argentina, and perhaps to Brazil as well."

Geraldine looked away. She regretted having started this charade. She had encouraged Pandora while it momentarily suited her, but she was not prepared to waste time and money on stale social gossip. If she were to put people on the trail of every lurid tale about rich women's pasts casually dropped in party conversations, the magazine would come to a standstill. If the story was really worth it, she would put an experienced journalist onto it, not a novice. More to the point, if Pandora went off chasing nonexistent leads, she would have to find somebody else able to put two words together and willing to spend her time visiting shops. It didn't make sense to waste another staff member's time for Pandora's sake. She turned toward her friend with her usual dazzling smile.

"What a wonderful idea! Why didn't I think of that? We must arrange it at once. Have you met Stephen? He's our 'Features' editor, he will make the arrangements for you. I'll call him right now."

Geraldine walked briskly to her desk and picked up the phone, humming loudly as her immaculately manicured nail ran along the staff directory. Pandora was slightly surprised by her enthusiastic agreement. She had expected Geraldine at least to ask what she had done so far, but it was in Geraldine's nature to be supportive, and she felt grateful to her friend. Geraldine dialed a number, paused, then put the phone down.

"I've suddenly remembered something," she said, looking pensive. "I have a friend at *The Sunday Times* who wanted to go to Argentina, and it took simply ages to get his visa. They can be quite awkward about visas for British journalists, you know. Those godforsaken islands, I suppose . . ." Geraldine's voice trailed away. "I wonder if it would be safe for you to go there, after all."

For a second, Pandora was slightly suspicious. Concern about personal risk, her own or anyone else's, was unlike Geraldine. But she had no reason to doubt Geraldine's sincerity, and she dismissed the thought.

"I wouldn't walk around with the Union Jack, and I have an American passport as well. I wouldn't have any problems if I use it instead of my British one."

Geraldine sighed with relief.

"Of course, silly me. Then it's full steam ahead. Leave it with me, darling; I will talk to Stephen as soon as I can. His number seems to be engaged all the time these days." She wrung her hands. "Goodness, I'd *love* you to stay for a chat, but I must throw you out. I'm *so* behind with my work." Once Pandora had left, Geraldine made a quick note in her diary to ring her in three days. Then she picked up the phone and gave Vanessa a list of calls she wanted to make. By the time she put the phone down, her mind was on a million other things.

"I LIKE this," Tony Andreotti said after checking Pandora's feature on wedding parties for the forthcoming issue.

"I'm glad to hear you say so. I have an idea I want to discuss with you," she told him. It was her third piece for the magazine and she had tried to do what was expected of her, but now she wanted to do more. Her feature on Arianne de la Force had come to a sudden end that morning, after Geraldine's brief phone call.

"Darling, it was *so* stupid of me not to have thought about it, but we are already doing a profile on Mrs. Gonçalves in two months' time, and it would be too much exotica to have two features on South American women one after the other. Let's leave your wonderful project until the new year, shall we? You are so busy anyway. . . . Talk to you soon. Bye-bye." Geraldine had hung up before Pandora could open her mouth. She thought of phoning back, but she knew it would be a waste of time. She could not give Geraldine any reason to continue the project other than her own boredom and her determination to follow up on Arianne's story; that would not be enough to counter Geraldine's plausible excuse about editorial scheduling. Perhaps it would be more sensible to grind her teeth, be patient, and find something else she would like to do in the meantime. This morning's newspaper had given her a possible idea. If nothing else, it had helped her deal with her disappointment after Geraldine's call.

"I was just reading in *The New York Times* about the hole in the ozone layer," she said to Andreotti. "Everybody is getting concerned about the environment. I thought we could do a feature on environmentally safe products." The subject had begun to interest her in England a few months ago, and now she felt she could do something about it.

Andreotti shook his head. These girls were all the same. He gave them something to do, and they immediately began to have their own ideas about something completely different. This one wanted to rewrite *The Fate of the Earth*.

"We are not the *Village Voice*, honey. You just find me nice things in nice shops. That's what our readers want, that's how we get the ads, and that's what you're paid to do. You shouldn't worry your pretty head about the world's problems."

That self-satisfied prick. Pandora stood up.

"I'm glad you acknowledge I've got a head at least. We've made some progress. I'll let you have the copy soon. Don't worry in the slightest if you find it ghastly; it would just even the score vis-à-vis your compliments." She left his office before he could reply.

She stormed along the corridor and slammed her office door behind her. She was wasting her time here. She had to find something worthwhile to do, and all the ideas that excited her seemed to leave her colleagues cold.

She didn't fit in here. She had come to New York to give herself a break, to leave her old problems behind her. But a change of scene was not enough. Her job was almost routine now, and other than Geraldine and her superficial warmth, there was no one she really cared about here. Loneliness had been behind her decision to come here as well, and now she felt lonelier than ever.

But she didn't want a man in her life, not yet. She had heard friends going through a love fiasco complain that all men were the same, and she had smiled indulgently. Now she found herself sharing their view. She had thought that Johnny was different when they met, years ago.

She met him at a dinner party, just after he had started work in the City. A few months later, Pandora moved in with him, and their engagement was announced in *The Times* soon afterward.

The thrill of finding their new home, the shared work during weekends spent wallpapering the rooms and moving the furniture from here to there, the joys of new love and equally new ownership — it all added up to the happiest months in Pandora's life. After the honeymoon in the Caribbean, real life began. Fed up with her private clients, she borrowed money from her father to open a small shop instead, at the cheaper end of the Fulham Road, selling her furniture designs and a small line of furnishing fabrics printed to her patterns. She would never forget the excitement of those days, the hours spent working out a prototype chair or sofa, her relentless pestering of suppliers until the right weave or the right shade was achieved, then going back home in the evenings and telling Johnny about it.

The shop had been a small success at first, but once the novelty wore off the occasional passerby was not enough to carry the cost of producing one-offs or small runs. After two years she had to accept that the shop had been an ill-conceived dream. Eventually she got an offer for the shop's lease, and in the meantime Johnny had moved to another job with great prospects.

Once or twice she mentioned to Johnny that she would like to take up her private work again, but he had laughed at the suggestion. "What you did wasn't real work," he had said. "Why don't you think of something else?" She couldn't think of anything else she really wanted to do. It was at that time that Johnny's interest in her began to wane.

The cooling of their physical relationship brought to the fore a new, fundamental difference between them. They had both been brought up in the belief that the acquisition of money was distasteful as an obvious priority in one's life; it had to be overshadowed by at least a token display of compassion toward those less fortunate than oneself. But the crises of the seventies and Mrs. Thatcher had challenged the old values. The changed climate in the City was pivotal to this new world, and Johnny became first a convert, then a preacher of the new ideals. At the time she thought that perhaps all men weren't the same at the start, but they became the same as time went by.

She shook her head, annoyed by her reminiscences. It was silly to dwell on the past. She had to look forward. She glanced at the clock, and was about to leave her office for lunch when the phone rang.

"Hi, remember me? I'm the man who owes you lunch." She recognized Tom Cansino's voice.

"Oh, hello, how are you?" She was trying to sound noncommittal.

"I'm fine, but I have the sneaky feeling that you may not like me anymore," he said quite cheerfully.

"I haven't considered whether I like you or not," she replied crisply.

"You *don't* like me; I knew it. That's the problem with us divorced men, we put the nice girls off. We just can't help it; Mother has warned you about us too many times."

Pandora remembered her mother's endless admonitions about the dangers of getting close to a divorced man, and smiled.

"Maybe you're right. Listen, I'm very sorry, but I have to rush. Could you phone me another time?"

He laughed. "It's better than 'Don't call me; I'll call you,' but you still haven't told me if you are free for lunch."

"Unfortunately, I'm not."

"Well, then, how about a movie tonight? I hope you didn't see *My Beautiful Laundrette* in London. If you're free, we could have dinner afterward. Please say yes," he pleaded. "It may not be mutual yet, but I really enjoy being with you."

Pandora was flattered in spite of herself. She had not been out with a man for months; she suddenly looked forward to the prospect, but she was not going to sound too eager.

"Thank you very much for the thought, but I'm busy tonight too," she lied.

"Is that the British way of giving me the brush-off?" he asked.

"No, I was going to add that I'm free the day after tomorrow, if you hadn't interrupted me."

"I hope you heard my sigh of relief. OK, we can meet at the movie. It's the Quad on West Thirteenth." She quickly wrote down the address and the time of the show.

"See you then," she said before hanging up.

"THE check, please," Tom said to the waiter. "Would you like another coffee?" he asked Pandora.

"I would love one." She wouldn't really, but she was reluctant to end the evening so soon. Although she had felt slightly uncomfortable during the film, its acid view of get-rich-quick Britain during recent years showing the down-market side of the process she had seen in Johnny. She had enjoyed being with Tom. Sometime during the film she had noticed his arm next to hers on the armrest, but his conversation afterward, both during the short walk to the restaurant and at dinner, had been friendly and not at all flirtatious.

"I've been meaning to ask you where you got your tan," she told

Tom after the waiter poured more coffee and moved off, leaving them alone.

Tom smiled. "Why do you ask?"

"Goodness, I didn't expect to be cross-examined over dinner conversation. Out of curiosity, I suppose."

"What a pity! I hoped it would be out of interest. I've just been to the Seychelles. I stayed at a wonderful place, some bird sanctuary. There's an old plantation house there where they take a few boarders. It's run by a very nice guy, a compatriot of yours who's crazy about tropical birds; I think he's writing a book about them. The house is beautiful, with bare floorboards and large verandas. You can have your evening drink watching the sun set over the sea."

"Sounds like a dream," she said.

"Do you have tropical fantasies?"

She smiled, and shook her head.

"No, my fantasies at the moment are slightly more practical than that. I just want to concentrate on my work, and enjoy it." She told him about her latest project for the "Lifestyle" section.

"I don't think that Tony will make anyone's fantasies come true, but I wish you luck," he said, briefly squeezing her hand and releasing it before she had time to react.

"I hope you haven't been bored tonight," he said as he slipped his credit card inside the folded check and handed it to the waiter.

"Not at all, and I hope I haven't given you the impression that I was. I've really enjoyed myself," she replied. Tom settled the check and they walked toward the exit, where he picked up her coat from the girl by the door. They began to walk along Fourteenth Street and Tom looked at his watch.

"It's not too late," he said. "Would you like to come to my place for a drink? It's quite near here, and since you told me you were an interior decorator, I would love to have your professional opinion."

Although she had half-expected it, his invitation jolted her. She did not want the evening to come to an end, but neither did she wish to encourage him. To accept might lead to awkwardness later on, but to turn him down would be acting like a frightened fifteen-year-old.

"I can't stay for long. I have some things to do at home," she said at last.

"I'm just a minute away," he told her, and she thought that proximity to his home might have been the reason behind his choice of restaurant.

They turned on Seventh Avenue, then into a side street, and he stopped outside a run-down building, its front criss-crossed by metal fire stairs. Tom opened the door and let her into the lobby, harshly lit by a bare fluorescent tube.

"Not the kind of place Geraldine would take you to," he said. "And don't look for the elevator either," he added, pointing at the stairs.

"Having seen the outside, I wasn't expecting one. As long as you have running water and electricity I'm not complaining," she told him.

"Are you planning to move in, then?"

She laughed.

"No, I just wanted to make sure you can make a cup of coffee."

When they reached his floor, Tom took out a fistful of keys and began to undo a succession of locks, until the door finally opened and he let her in. It was the first loft she had seen, and she looked around while Tom hung their coats on a steel hook near the entrance. The setting was similar to the interiors used for beer commercials in London, but here it was real. She immediately began to think how she would rearrange the furniture to maximize the impact of this wonderful space.

"Your chairs are too tall, the table is not big enough, and you need a longer sofa," she said.

"The problem is that my wallet is too thin," he shouted from the other end. She could hear the hiss of the espresso machine.

She walked around while Tom was busy in the kitchen, then absentmindedly glanced at the pictures lined on a long shelf along one wall, until her eye caught a series of framed prints. She recognized them, her vivid reminiscence catching her by surprise. Her memory telescoped over the years, to a particular moment during her father's last visit to England.

It had been a glorious summer evening at Glyndebourne. They had their picnic in the park among the other operagoers, the scene framed by the mellow brick and stone house behind them. She remembered looking at her father, with whom she had made her peace after so many years of bitterness, and then at Johnny, the setting sun reflected on their faces. She had wished the perfect moment would never fade away, and now she remembered every detail: the food in the hamper she had prepared, the pink champagne Johnny had bought, the new dress she had bought from that nice girl in Fulham before she became unaffordable. Her father had asked her and Johnny to come with him to see *The Magic Flute,* and she had particularly admired the sets designed by David Hockney. Now she found herself, years later, in a New York loft, in front of framed prints of the sketches for those very sets.

It was a stark, unexpected reminder of what she had lost, and she moved quickly away. Tom found her sitting on the sofa when he came back.

"Why are you so pensive?" he asked, sitting next to her.

She shook her head. "I'm sorry. I was . . ." She stopped. There was no point in brooding. "Maybe I'm just tired. Black coffee for me, please," she said, anxious to change the subject. "Have you ever been to South America?" she asked.

"I might go there soon, to follow the old Inca trail from Peru to Northern Argentina. Are you planning to go?"

She smiled.

"I was," she replied. "I wanted Geraldine to send me to Argentina to research a piece on Mrs. de la Force, a very glamorous lady I met here and who seems to have endless money, but Geraldine turned me down. In the nicest possible way."

Tom chuckled.

"You should know that your friend does not like spending money if she is not sure about the result. Sometimes she makes the wrong judgment, but it's difficult to prove it unless you can write the piece and it comes off. The old problem of chicken and eggs."

Pandora sipped her coffee. "She certainly doesn't think I'll lay the golden egg."

"And what do *you* think?" he asked.

Pandora raised her eyes.

"I would have phrased it differently if I didn't believe I could," she said sharply.

"It's her loss, then, and please put your gun back in your holster." He leaned back against the cushions, and she could feel the warmth of his arm through her silk shirt. She did not move. After a while she glanced at him, noticing for the first time the golden flecks in his brown eyes, and then she moved forward to place her cup on the coffee table, ending the brief physical contact between them. He got up and walked toward the corner, searching through a pile of compact discs. After a moment, the sound of Nat "King" Cole filled the room.

The slow music put her instantly on her guard. He returned to his seat next to her. She stood up.

"I'm sorry," she said, "but I really should go." He followed her toward the door, and helped her put her coat on. Then he turned her toward him, his hands on her shoulders. She kept her eyes on the open collar of his shirt, on the skin of his neck only inches away from her face.

"I hope I'll see you again," she heard him say. She pulled herself away and opened the door.

"I'd like that. I'll call you," she replied without stopping. The door closed behind her.

She rushed down the stairs, glad to find herself free at last. It had all been too sudden, and she needed time. She liked him, but there was no need to rush things. She forced herself to think about what she had to do at work tomorrow. She rapidly walked away from the building and scanned the street for a taxi. As she waited at the corner, her thoughts went back to Tom.

She had felt uneasy in his loft, but now she was angry with herself. She felt trapped by her memories, the memories triggered by the prints on the wall, and she had behaved as if it were possible to go back to that time. Her reaction had been her way of preserving the illusion that nothing had changed, that there was no room for anyone else in her life. The empty street was a reminder of her true situation. She was here now, not in London. Johnny had left her and her father was dead. She turned back and began to walk fast.

"It's me," she said when he answered the entry phone. She pushed the door open without any hesitation.

New York
May 1987

"G OOD morning, Miss Gloria."

The uniformed maid rested the tray covered by a pink linen napkin on the table next to Gloria de la Force's bed. She walked to the window, drew open the silk curtains, and returned to the bedside. Gloria leaned forward, and the maid plumped up the huge pillows behind her.

The girl placed the breakfast tray in front of her mistress, and uncovered it. "Thank you, Corazón," Gloria said. The maid bowed her head, the morning sun briefly shining on her blue-black hair, set off by the starched white piqué toque.

"Do you want me to run your bath now, Miss Gloria?" Corazón asked, while her mistress opened her mail.

"Yes, Corazón, but run it very hot because I have to do my exercises after breakfast. I wouldn't want to have to ask you to run it again if it gets cold." Early in life Gloria had been taught that it is important to be considerate to servants. She spread marmalade on her croissant, brought fresh by messenger from Pâtisserie Claude on West Fourth Street, and looked at her mail: invitations to the Gigli and Versace shows in Milan next month, the weddings of two school friends, one in Geneva and the other in Caracas, and the Wyndham-Stewarts' dance at Highbury Castle just before Ascot. She sighed deeply; she just didn't have the energy to do so much.

She took a sip of black coffee, picked up her pen from the bedside table, and wrote "No" on the Caracas invitation; there was no way she could go there at that time of the year. She was fond of the Geneva friend, so she wrote "Yes" on that one. She hesitated for a moment about the English dance. It was during Ascot week. She could wear one of those wonderful Lacroix things, for instance. She would drop Christian a line, and ask him to make her something really special. On the other hand, the Royal Enclosure seemed to be full of rather dreadful people these days. She wrote "Maybe" on the English card, and turned to the Milan invitations.

She found Italian designers amusing for everyday wear but Milan in summer was so hot; it would be easier to see the clothes here. She wrote "No" on the Italian cards, piled her mail on the tray, and rang the bell. A minute later there was a knock at the door, and Corazón came in.

"Corazón, please take this to Kayzie. I'll phone her in a moment to tell her what I want," she said.

Corazón picked up the tray. "I'll leave it on her desk, Miss Gloria, but François told me that she phoned early to say that she was ill."

"Did she say when she will be back?" asked Gloria, her impatience showing in her voice. "I can't wait forever to have my mail dealt with."

"I don't know, Miss Gloria. I can ask François if you want me to," Corazón replied.

"No, just leave it; I'll talk to her tomorrow." Gloria waved her hand toward the door, dismissing her.

Gloria raised her eyes toward the window, which framed a perfect view of Central Park, its trees covered with a blanket of new leaves. She adored New York at this time of the year, and she adored it even more when her mother wasn't around. Anywhere in the world could be adorable if her mother wasn't there. Sometimes she felt guilty about the feeling, but it was very hard to be the daughter of a woman like Arianne, someone who seemed to have been born with an invisible spotlight on her. Her mother's money would have been enough to guarantee her the world's attention, and her beauty was at least as remarkable as her fortune. Gloria guessed that anyone meeting her would automatically compare her with Arianne, and she knew what the outcome of such comparisons was likely to be.

Gloria had not inherited her mother's looks, although someday she would inherit her money. She was a de la Force only because the change of name had been arranged after Simón's death. Her claim to his fortune was as indirect as her right to his name. She had pressed her mother again and again for her real name, until one day she told her that it was de Souza, a Portuguese name common enough to be untraceable. Her mother had been even more vague about her father. According to her, he had just walked out one day, and she had never heard from him again. As Gloria grew up, she began to ask more and more questions, and eventually she asked for a photograph of her father.

At first her mother had said that she had none, because they had all been destroyed in a fire at their home in Brazil before she had moved to Paris. Then one day her mother appeared with the photograph of a dark-haired man, neither handsome nor ugly. She told her that she had found it among some old papers, but Gloria was sure that it had been obtained from some casting agency. She tried to believe in the picture and put it in a silver frame, but it took only one look at Nana's face when Gloria showed it to her to realize that the man had nothing to do with her at all. The photograph ended up in a drawer, and her mother never asked after its whereabouts.

Gloria set aside her breakfast tray. She stretched her arms languidly and snuggled up for a moment under her feather-filled comforter, covered in the same apricot silk as the walls, enjoying the warmth of her bed, the smooth freshness of the linen sheets rubbing against her bare skin. Her body was many things to Gloria: a prop to her vanity, a tool for her pleasure, and a weapon to use against her mother. Through sheer dedication she had turned an indifferent figure into a superbly fit machine. It took endless time and money to achieve it, but Gloria had both.

Long before her body had become a source of pride, Gloria had discovered the unique, spine-tingling delights of a good fuck, particularly with an older man. A further frisson was added when she found that her mother was hurt by the voracity of her precocious sexuality, and further mortified when it involved the staff, as Gloria realized at the age of fourteen, when Nana found her in the pool house at "La Encantada" straddling the hips of one of the gardeners. It was the first in a long list of similar episodes, leading to an equally long list of staff dismissals and angry recriminations from her mother.

It was at that time, five years ago, that she had begun to sense Nana's rejection; it had hurt her more than any of Arianne's terse admonitions. Nana had been with her for as long as Gloria could remember, the first one to come to her when she cried in bed at night, long after her mother had kissed her goodnight before going out, a fleeting vision as incandescent as her diamonds. The old woman would stay with Gloria until she went back to sleep. Her mother had never been there; nannies, Mademoiselles, Fräuleins, a whole collection of them, studded the early years of Gloria's life, but only Nana had been a constant presence.

She remembered an episode a long time ago, when she must have been only four or five years old. Her mother was away, and Gloria had remained in Buenos Aires, in the enormous house on the Avenida Alvear. It must have been late in the spring, in November, because the jacaranda trees in the garden were covered in lilac blossoms, forming a deep carpet on the lawn. It was early in the afternoon, and the house was under the usual blanket of silence at that time of the day. The staff were either resting in their rooms or doing work in the kitchen area, far away from the family quarters.

After lunch Gloria had been taken to her room for her usual nap, but she couldn't sleep. She left the nursery, and nervously ran along the length of the gallery overlooking the main hall. The nursery was at the back of the house, facing the garden, while her mother's rooms looked out to the Avenida Alvear. She was not allowed there. She tried the double door, the curlicued door handle almost too big for her tiny hand, but she managed to open it, and she found herself in a long pillared corridor. The white double doors between the marble pillars had overpanels painted with fruits and exotic birds.

She opened the door facing her, and walked into the shoe room. Three shelves formed by paired brass rails ran along the walls holding her mother's shoes, padded-silk shoe trees inside every pair. They were grouped by color and aligned by tone, from light to dark, the evening shoes on the bottom shelf. Farther up the walls, a triple row of pigeonholes in polished mahogany held the handbags, matching or corresponding with the shoes below.

Gloria was fascinated by the room. She began to inspect the shoes, picking them up and then dropping them on the carpeted floor. An arched opening led to the next room, where dozens of evening gowns were stored, each on a wide shelf of scented cedar wood. A pair of enormous floor-to-ceiling mirrors faced each other across the room; Gloria stood in front of one of them, admiring her infinite reflections, making faces until she got tired of the game and moved on.

Two further dressing rooms followed, clothes hanging on all sides, with large shelf units in the middle. Gloria found these rooms less interesting than the shoe room, and opened yet another door.

At last, she found herself in her mother's bedroom. Gloria walked across the vast chamber and reached the four-poster bed, slowly running her hand over the embroidered bedspread. The photograph on her mother's bedside table caught her eye, a young woman with two children, and she picked it up. It was then that a side door opened, and Nana came in.

She rushed across the room, took the photograph away from Gloria, and began to admonish her in a harsh voice. Frightened by her tone, and overwhelmed by the shame of having been found, Gloria burst into tears, and the old woman's face changed. She hugged the little girl, patting her head and saying, "It's all right, my baby, your Nana will always be here." Gloria was carried back to her room, and nothing more was said. Much later, when she was allowed to move freely around the house, and she was able to walk into her mother's bedroom any time she wanted, she noticed that the photograph was gone.

But as Gloria grew up, Nana had become increasingly distant. Occasionally, Gloria had tried to ask questions about the past, but Nana's invariable answer was to say that she did not remember, or know about, such things. If further pressed, she would claim some urgent task and leave the room. Nana's increasing introspection eventually turned her into a virtual recluse, until she refused to leave "La Encantada." Gloria saw her only during January or February, and even then Nana endeavored to make herself invisible, her only concern to keep the tower inaccessible to anyone other than Arianne and herself. Gloria felt sorry for the dotty old woman obsessed with her little kingdom in the tower, but she seemed content enough. It had been a long time since Gloria had felt really close to Nana. . . . She looked at the clock. Shit, Milka was coming to wax her legs in an hour's time. She jumped out of bed, slipped into her dressing gown, and walked to the gym, at the other end of the apartment.

As she came into the room she noticed that Charles was already there, working out his arms and pectorals on one of the Nautilus machines. He stopped and smiled at her, his arms pushed back by the padded flaps, the damp T-shirt clinging to his broad chest. "Good morning," he said cheerfully.

"You shouldn't do exercises if you are not feeling well," said Gloria, ignoring his greeting.

"What makes you think I'm ill?" Charles asked. He was surprised at her concern, but it pleased his vanity and suited his plans.

"It's so unusual for you to get up early that you must be ill," she answered, her back to him. He grinned and said nothing. Gloria took off her bathrobe and threw it on the floor. She was wearing only her panties, almost as small as a G-string, and she sensed Charles's eyes on her body.

"Don't get excited; you've seen it before," she said as she stepped onto the treadmill. She turned the control knob and began to run. Charles moved to the bench next to her. He set his digital timer at twelve-second intervals, and interlaced his fingers behind his neck. He counted "one" aloud, raising his head and shoulders off the bench, then counted "two," and lifted both feet. He was able to look at Gloria in the mirrored wall facing them.

"Gloria, I want to apologize for our little fight." The timer bell rang. He stopped talking and, mentally counting to four, returned to the starting position while breathing in, and then repeated the start of the exercise.

"I hope you understand that there was nothing I could do, I . . ." The bell rang again, and he went through the second half of the exercise. "I would have had trouble with your mother otherwise," he continued.

Gloria turned up the speed knob. The machine's humming became noticeably louder.

"I can't hear you," she shouted.

Charles stopped talking and completed his fifty-exercise cycle, while Gloria began her warm-up schedule. They remained silent, absentmindedly listening to the tape of the Allegro ma non troppo from Elgar's Cello Concerto, which was playing over the sound system.

The first part of her routine completed, Gloria put on her ballet shoes, then moved to the barre on the opposite wall. One hand loosely placed on the barre, her arm almost straight, she pulled her stomach in and stretched her neck upward. As Gloria started her pliés and demi-pliés, Charles left the bench and moved toward a large ball on the floor, a couple of yards behind her. He began to jump sideways over the ball, raising his arms when he was up in the air.

"You must understand my position," he gasped between jumps, watching her in the mirror all the time.

"The only position someone like you understands is the missionary one," she retorted, sliding her foot backward and forward in a battement tendu movement.

Charles managed to contrive a sad face, and stopped jumping.

"You really hurt me, Gloria. We have known each other for twelve years. I know you don't think much of me but I love you, and I wish we could be friends." He really couldn't delay the cooldown sequence any longer; he stopped talking, and began his sidebends.

Gloria stopped halfway through a grand battement. Charles's conciliatory manner was a surprise to her; there had to be a reason for it. It might be useful to humor him, and find out what he was up to. She waited until he had finished with his bends, and then came over to him.

"I'm glad to hear that, Charles. It's no good to fight. After all, we are almost family." She leaned against the mirror, her arms slightly spread, hands on the barre. "I *would* like to be friends with you," she said, looking into his eyes. She couldn't believe that this shit was so desperate for a screw that he would risk it with her. But it would be an excellent way of getting rid of him. Once and for all.

"Then we are friends," Charles said. He returned her gaze for a second, then looked down. No need to rush anything, and he'd better be careful. "Great. I'm going to have a sauna now," Charles took off his T-shirt, and walked to the shower cubicle behind a marble screen. Taking off his shorts, he stood for a while under the high-pressure jets, then walked out, picked up a towel from the pile on the marble shelf, and opened the heavy wooden door into the sauna cabin at the opposite end of the shower area.

Gloria was already there, stretched along the bench on one side, her panties carelessly dropped on the wooden floor. She slowly moved her leg on the inner side of the bench, bending it slightly at the knee. Her body was in full view, and her position emphasized the flatness of her stomach and the firmness of her breasts. She smiled at Charles.

"The sauna's a really good idea," she said.

He moved his eyes over her body, taking in the gentle sloping of the belly, the softness of her inner thighs, the silky skin glowing under a dew of fresh sweat. He removed the towel from around his waist, spread it on the seat opposite her, then turned and faced her.

"I'm glad you did. It really does wonders for the system," he said, before sitting down and closing his eyes.

Gloria suddenly understood why he had kept her mother under his spell for twelve years: his prick was sensational. *It would be nice to play with that toy for a while before letting Mummy know,* she thought. *Then bye-bye, Charles.*

"Charles, would you mind giving me an oil rub?" she asked in a languid voice, her hand waving toward the tray on a side table, covered by a damp cloth.

"It would be a pleasure. Which oil would you like?" he asked.

She rolled onto her stomach and let her arm drop down, her hand languorously resting on the floor, palm up.

"Jasmin de Chypre is my favorite, but I really like them all," she murmured.

"Jasmin de Chypre it will be," he replied, holding up the bottles to the light until he found it. He stood next to Gloria, close enough to feel her breath on his leg. He pulled out the stopper and leaned down, his broad chest overshadowing her body. He tilted the bottle and let a trickle of oil drip onto Gloria's shoulders and back, the scent of jasmine rising in the hot dry air. She turned her face away from his legs, and closed her eyes.

He laid his hands flat on her shoulder blades, his palms pressed against her skin, and rubbed in a circular motion, very gently at first, then applying just a fraction of pressure, a hint of the weight of his body on hers. Every now and then he would move his fingers and, for a second, the edge of his nails would glide over her skin.

He rubbed gently downward until he reached the hollow in her lower back, where he could feel her vertebrae under the thin layer of firm flesh. He pressed both his thumbs on the bony ridge, and pushed hard. Her bones cracked, and Gloria moaned softly. He paused for a moment.

"Did I hurt you?" he asked solicitously, his hands still on her.

Gloria raised her head from the bench and looked up toward him. The massive head of his penis was just inches away from her eyes, dangling above her like forbidden fruit. Nothing was more exciting to Gloria than what she should not have.

"No, not at all, I like it," she said, clearly scanning his body. "It's hot in here," she moaned. Gasping for air, she aimed her breath straight at his balls. Her eyes were fixed on his prick, waiting for any stirring of his flesh, but there was none.

"We can make it cooler." He paused for a moment, his hand sliding down her back. "Or we can make it even hotter." He dripped some oil onto her buttocks, and then let a thin trickle drip between them, the oil slowly slipping between her legs. "What would you prefer?" he asked in a low voice.

She let her head rest on the bench. "How could you make it hotter?" she murmured, spreading her legs just a fraction.

"Easy," he answered, picking up the wooden pail by the heating coil, and pouring some water on the stones at the top. The water sizzled on the hot rocks, and a cloud of eucalyptus-scented steam enveloped them. "But one has to be careful with these things; sometimes one can get badly burned." He had just begun to rub her buttocks, cupping them in his hands, when the extension phone on the wall next to him rang. He continued rubbing her bottom with his left hand, his thumb gently digging into the crack between her cheeks as he answered.

"Hello, darling!" he said, moving his hand to the upper thigh, his thumb sliding between Gloria's legs. "How are things there? I miss you!"

"Gloria? She's here in the gym, doing her exercises." As he said this, Gloria let her arm slide down the wooden side of the bench until her hand rested on the top of his thighs, her wrist touching his smooth foreskin. Charles did not move.

"Yes, I got up early," he continued. He looked at his watch. "The time here is nearly ten now . . ."

Gloria jumped up, and rushed out of the sauna. She had completely forgotten about her leg-waxing, and she still had to have her bath. Milka did not like to be kept waiting, and she was much in demand. After all, she was the best in New York.

"I HAVE to go to the airport now. I'll be there tonight. Good-bye." Arianne put the receiver down, took one last look at her favorite room, and then left.

On the landing, she caught sight of the sun shining on the still waters of the Laguna del Sauce in the distance, through the narrow window in the thick stone wall. She did not want to think of this trip as a farewell journey, but in many ways it was.

Gloria, once the most important thing in the world to her, had become a time bomb. In another year she would be of age under Argentine law, the sole heiress to her mother's estate in Argentina. She would not be hampered by guardians, trustees, delayed access to the estate, or any other legal arrangements available elsewhere to protect the property of rich parents from their offspring's mistakes. Arianne knew Gloria. She also knew the way Charles's mind worked, what his reaction would be to her refusal to marry him. She had no illusions as to how far Gloria would go in order to hurt her.

She had to remain in total control, and the first step was the disposal of the Argentine part of the de la Force estate, denying Gloria any automatic rights to a significant portion of the fortune. It had taken her over three weeks of round-the-clock negotiations, but at last terms had been agreed for the sale of San Simón, the holding company for all the de la Force agricultural business in Argentina other than the sugar company.

It had not been easy to find a buyer at short notice for nearly a million acres of prime farming land scattered among thirty-seven estates, plus the innumerable assets of an enormous agricultural company. Her options had been further restricted by her wish to sell for a token sum in Argentina; most of the price had to be paid abroad, outside the stiff restrictions on foreign currency transfers imposed by the Argentine government.

Over the years there had been approaches from a number of prospective buyers. Once her mind was made up to sell, Arianne had quickly sounded them out. The choice had finally come down to two: the Yakimura Gami Group, a Japanese company with vast interests in South America, and the Benvenutti interests, an Italo-Argentine concern.

Negotiations with the Japanese had been ultimately unsuccessful. The Italians had offered less money, but discussions had proceeded rapidly. Forty-five million dollars were to be paid in Argentina, and three hundred and twenty-seven million transferred into a front company incorporated in Liechtenstein by a subsidiary of the Italian group registered in Campione d'Italia, the transfer to take place through an agreed third party in the Cayman Islands. Arianne's ownership of the Liechtenstein business was as untraceable as the transfer of funds itself. San Simón owed the Argentine government twenty-three million dollars in taxes, creative accounting showed a loss for the year of approximately twenty million, and lawyers and accountants' fees would take care of the last two million. The balance on the transaction that would be accessible to Gloria in the event of Arianne's death was precisely nil.

Her plan, however, was pointless unless she sold Valle del Oro as well. She could justify her hesitation on financial grounds, but it was not the main reason. She had come to see the valley as a symbol of her triumph, her ability to rise to Simón's challenge and beat him at his own game, against the odds. To sell it now could forestall Charles's plans, or what she imagined his plans to be. But it also implied giving up what she valued most, to acknowledge unequivocally that Gloria had become her enemy. Perhaps it was wiser not to rush into a decision just yet.

Nana was waiting for her at the bottom of the stairs, dressed in black as usual, a crocheted shawl around her shoulders. Arianne embraced the old woman. "Take care of yourself, Nana. I'll try to come back soon."

"May God be with you," replied Nana. She walked away from Arianne, who turned around and slipped into her coat, held by a waiting maid. Arianne was suddenly struck by the foreboding that it was the last time they would see each other, but she quickly dismissed the idea, the maudlin thought undoubtedly triggered by her own feelings in the wake of her visit to Buenos Aires.

She briskly walked to the waiting car and got in without looking back. As they drove down the hill, she wasn't thinking about Nana anymore. In a few hours she would be in New York, facing Gloria. And Charles.

New York
June 1987

$\mathcal{O}$F course I can do something for your nephew, Rodney. I'm delighted to hear he wants to become a journalist, and I'm offended by you even considering the possibility that I wouldn't help him. There's nothing I wouldn't do for you, darling." The ensuing exchange of gratitude and compliments brought the conversation to an end, and Geraldine put the phone down. She had a problem.

Rodney Gibson was chairman of one of the largest cosmetics corporations in America, and they took forty pages of advertising in the magazine every year. It would be foolish to upset him. It would be equally foolish to ignore the fact that Connie van Naalt sat on the same ballet committee as Mrs. Greene, the owner of *Chic*. Like all rich people, Mrs. Greene had pet obsessions, and the slightest indication of overstaffing was one of them. She would not blink at the magazine's spending tens of thousands of dollars on a party, but she regularly checked the personnel list and asked probing questions about each employee. Connie would love nothing better than being able to go to Mrs. Greene with evidence of Geraldine's recklessness in that respect. Geraldine was not prepared to waste one minute of her time explaining the reasons, and it usually took longer than a minute to convince Mrs. Greene. But she had to please Rodney.

PANDORA struggled for a moment with the unfamiliar locks, until she managed to let herself into the loft. Tom had gone to Vermont with the children for a few days, and he had asked her to keep an eye on the place and water the plants. Although saddened by the thought of his temporary absence, she had jumped at the offer. She preferred not to admit it, but she was growing fonder of him every day. They were still at the stage of keeping each other at some distance for the sake of self-protection, but she had begun to face the possibility of loving Tom. What had started as her acceptance of the fact that she did not want to be alone had almost become the certainty that she wanted him.

She went slowly around the empty space, checking that everything was switched off. It was unnecessary, she had already done it during her first visit, but it pleased her to have a reason to play a proprietorial role. She moved to the kitchen and put away the few dishes she had left in the drainer, Tom's breakfast things, which she had washed up after he was gone. She filled a jug, making sure that the water was not too cold, and watered the small pots along the window sills, leaving the biggest task for last. Then she refilled the jug, walked across the room and emptied it into the huge planter holding a thriving ficus tree under the skylight. Tom was very proud of the tree. He had told her that he had bought it four years ago. "It was *this* size," he had said, his hand in line with his waist. Its foliage now brushed against the soot-smeared skylight; she would suggest to Tom that they climb to the roof and wash the glass next weekend. The soil was almost dry, and she had to pour three further jugfuls of water into it. The watering finished, she thought of leaving but decided to stay for a while. She liked it here.

She moved to the bed at the opposite end of the loft and stretched herself along Tom's side, her head on his pillow. She brushed her cheek against it, the faint trace of his after-shave confirming how much she missed him. She remained still for a moment, her eyes closed. *Enough of this, time to go,* she decided. He would be back soon.

She sat up and absentmindedly glanced at the bedside table, her eye caught by a blinking pair of red lights. Probably she wouldn't have noticed the pinpoint flashes if it had been still light, but it wasn't, and she had not turned on the lamp. Without thinking, she pressed the "Play" key.

The unknown woman's voice sounded as angry as Pandora would feel in a few moments, demanding to know where Tom was. The next message was from another woman, giving a loving description of what she would do to Tom's body next time they were together. Pandora stood up and switched off the answering machine. She was too numb to move, and tried not to cry. All his apparent caring, everything had been a lie. She had been cherishing the possibility of loving him while he had been seeing other women, and she had probably slept in the very same sheets as they had.

Suddenly she was filled with a rage more intense than any she had ever experienced. She had been betrayed by Johnny, but at least she had had years of growing awareness prior to the definitive confirmation, and she had had few illusions left by the time it happened. Tom's duplicity was unexpected, grit rubbed into a not yet healed wound, and she wanted to hurt him as much as he had hurt her. She looked around through her tears at the place where she thought she had been happy until a minute ago. Then she ran to the kitchen, picked up a bottle of bleach and dashed toward the ficus tree. She was about to empty the contents into the pot, but she couldn't. She thought for a moment, then walked toward the closet and opened it. Very slowly she sprinkled the bleach over Tom's clothes. Then she flung the empty bottle away from her and rushed out of the loft.

"WOULD you like some scrambled eggs?" asked Geraldine, nodding at the butler standing by the Regency sideboard. Compton immediately uncovered the silver chafing dish.

"No, thank you," replied Pandora. Compton replaced the lid, and returned to his post.

"I don't know why we have scrambled eggs at breakfast," Geraldine continued, sipping her coffee. "I don't eat them because they're fattening, Solly doesn't eat them because he is terrified about cholesterol, none of the staff eat them because they're cold by the time they get back to the kitchen, and the dog doesn't like eggs. Must be my nostalgia for England." Geraldine laughed. "And it's very like us to worry about wasted food. Why should I care? I don't even pay for the damned eggs."

It was obvious to Pandora that Geraldine was making small talk before tackling whatever was on her mind. Pandora had been surprised to be asked for breakfast at her house, but Geraldine had explained that they had not talked for a while, and her daily schedule was simply impossible. "Breakfast tomorrow morning is the only time I have to see you until the end of the month. You can come to the office in the car with me. Don't worry about Solly; he's gone to Madrid until Saturday, and we'll be free to talk."

Geraldine glanced at her watch and then spread sugar-free jam on her toast.

"Darling, I must ask you this, and please believe me that I do it only because I want you to be happy. Are you planning to stay in New York?"

Pandora was startled. It was the last question she had expected, and she could not guess the reason behind it.

"I appreciate your concern. The answer is I don't know. Why do you ask?"

Geraldine peered at Pandora over her glasses.

"As Elton John would say, it seems to me that you live your life like a candle in the wind. I will be here when the rain sets in, but it might be wiser if you buy yourself an umbrella in the meantime."

"What do you mean?" Pandora felt uncomfortable, and she was in no mood for lectures.

Geraldine leaned back in her chair, and crossed her arms.

"Darling, I worry about you. If you don't grab the bull by the horns, nobody is going to do it for you. You married that idiot Johnny, and you thought that all you wanted to be was a nice wife. Then the roof caved in and now, rather than try to make the most of your work at the magazine, you get yourself entangled with Tom Cansino, a good-looking jerk who lays every girl in the building for a maximum of two weeks each. I could staff another magazine with the girls who have left in tears because of him."

Pandora was irritated by Geraldine's well-meaning intrusiveness. What she did with her life outside the magazine was not her friend's concern.

"What are you trying to tell me?" Pandora asked angrily. For once, Geraldine was not taking the trouble to blunt her knife.

"We are not in England, sweetheart. I'm not trying, I'm telling you that what you ought to do is concentrate on doing what *you* want to do, what would help *you*, rather than trying to find another miracle man to solve your problems. I fear that you may be wasting your time here. You can write, but I wonder if that's what you really like to do. You were an interior decorator once; maybe you should try that again. But you need contacts for that, and probably London would be a better place to start again."

"Everything you say is perfectly reasonable, and I've been thinking about going back to London. But there is one thing I would like to know before we go any further. Are you firing me? If so, I want to know why." At least now she had some grasp on Geraldine's motives, and she felt more at ease.

"Darling, how can you even think that! Of course not, I only want to help you. But I think you ought to seriously consider if New York is the best place for you. I don't want you to waste your time."

"That's very kind of you, and I wouldn't want you to waste yours, either. If you want me to leave my job, just say so."

Geraldine looked at her pensively.

"I'm so sorry that you misunderstand me. I just want you to do what you really want. I would be terribly sad if you decide to leave, but I can't force you to stay against your will. It's you who mentioned the possibility of your leaving, not I. The decision is yours, and that's what I think you have to do: make decisions. But don't rush anything." She turned toward Compton. "Let's have another coffee, and then we should go to the office. It's getting late."

Geraldine fluffed her hair with her hand and smiled at Pandora endearingly, as if nothing had been said other than warm chitchat between old friends.

"Guess who I saw last night at the Mortons? Arianne de la Force! She is just back from Argentina, and she looks ravishing, as usual. Have you heard from her?" she asked, as if Pandora and Arianne were inseparable. Pandora waited until Compton had finished serving them.

"Amazingly enough, her secretary called me some time ago to ask me to lunch tomorrow, on Arianne's behalf, then she called again two nights ago. Arianne was still abroad and apparently the cook is ill, so the lunch has been changed from her apartment to La Côte Basque. I have no idea why she asked me any more than I know why you asked me here today, but I hope I'll enjoy seeing her as much as I always enjoy seeing *you*," she said pointedly, but she got no reaction from her friend. Geraldine finished her coffee and stood up, Pandora following her.

"I love La Côte Basque," Geraldine said as they crossed the entrance hall. "Give my love to Arianne. It's such a shame you won't be doing her profile now, but I must confess that I never thought Arianne was a good subject."

Pandora was tempted to remind Geraldine that a few minutes ago she was supposedly waiting for Pandora's decision, but decided not to. She was still uncertain about Geraldine's motives, but the conversation had helped her crystallize the thoughts she had been having ever since she had left Tom's loft, and she was beyond needling — or needing — Geraldine now.

Compton held the door open, and they left the house. As they reached the waiting limousine, Pandora stopped.

"Do you mind if I don't come with you? I feel like walking," she said.

"Of course I don't mind," Geraldine replied, brushing her cheek against Pandora's before getting into the car. Pandora waved as the car pulled away, but Geraldine had opened her briefcase and was already studying her papers.

Pandora began to walk toward Park Avenue. Puzzled as she still was by the conversation, it had touched on an issue she could not postpone any further. When Geraldine had appeared in London, Pandora was adrift after a shipwreck, and she had climbed onto the first boat she could find. A few months ago, she would have followed wherever Geraldine led. Now she wanted to make her own choices.

She had come here partly to try to live by her father's values in his world. But it wasn't her world, and she did not want to become like Geraldine. She had hoped that her choices would somehow sort themselves out for her. New York had been, in essence, her way of leaving her old world behind her, of running away. It was a negative reason. If she really wanted to change her life, it was possible anywhere; if she didn't, then no place would do it for her. Tom was the evidence of that. She had seen him as a new beginning, but only her unconscious wish to fall back into the old pattern, her hope of finding another man as the center of her life, could justify her reaction. He had never promised her anything, and she had expected too much.

Upset by her thoughts, she glanced at the store window on her left. It was a small, art-gallery-like decoration shop, a few pieces of furniture elegantly displayed against the white walls and skillfully lit. She could not help admiring the simple beauty of the furniture, and her eye was caught by a discreet notice next to the entrance: "The Shaker Style." A week ago she would have gone in, because this was good material for her section. It no longer mattered now, and she kept on walking.

But she was glad to have come to New York. She had seen a different world, and learned more about her own. She was not going to be a candle in the wind. Not any longer. It was probably one of the few true things Geraldine had said over breakfast, and it had hit home. She had to find her own way, and she would.

As she walked past the newspaper stand near the office, she noticed the cigarette ad on it, showing a beautiful girl confidently walking ahead. "You've come a long way, Baby" was boldly printed across the white background. No, not yet, Pandora smiled to herself, but at least she was at the starting gate.

CHARLES removed his earphones and switched off the cassette deck. He had listened to the tape early in the morning, but he wanted to check the facts before talking to Gloria. He congratulated himself on his wisdom in tapping Arianne's phone while she was away. It was nearly one o'clock. Arianne would have left for her lunch party at La Côte Basque by now. He had checked Kayzie's diary an hour ago, and Gloria was having lunch with her friend Paola Santa Coloma at Condotti at 1:30. Knowing Gloria, he realized that she was unlikely to leave before then, but he would take no chances. He went to the library and left the door open. He sat in the armchair closest to the door, giving him full view of the entrance gallery. He opened *The New York Times,* and waited.

Half an hour later, he heard Gloria's footsteps on the marble floor. He dropped his newspaper, and walked toward her.

"Gloria, have you got a moment?" he called.

She stopped by the front door and faced him.

"Not now, Charles; I'm in a hurry."

"I'm sorry, but it is important, something vital to your interests."

Gloria was perplexed for a moment, then dropped her bag on the marble console by the door, its chain straps clinking against the stone.

"What is it? Please be quick. I'm late."

"Let's talk in the library. What I have to tell you is highly confidential," he said, leading her by the arm.

Gloria sat by the fireplace, and Charles stood next to her.

"Before I say anything, I want your assurance that you will never mention me as the source of your information. It would put me in an impossible position with regard to your mother, which you may not mind, but it would mean that you would never be able to find out anything else about what is going on from me. I am only taking this risk because you know that I always have your best interests at heart," he said.

"Fine, I promise not to mention you. What is it?" she asked impatiently.

He told her. He described Arianne's phone conversation with Bob Chalmers, almost word-for-word. He had a very good memory.

". . . which means that, very soon, there will be no de la Force property in Argentina. If your mother dies, under Argentine law you would be entitled to her estate, but if there is no estate in Argentina, then you will only receive what she leaves you in her will. She is disowning you, Gloria." He quickly glanced at the mirror above the fireplace, to check if his expression was suitably aghast at the pain of what he had just disclosed.

Gloria stood up. Her face was white, and she was shaking. Charles embraced her, holding her tightly against him, and kissed her forehead.

"I know how painful this is for you, my darling, but you know that you have a friend. I'm on your side," he murmured. He felt her arms tighten around his waist. For a second, he considered whether to kiss her on the lips, but decided against it.

After a moment, he let her go. She ran away, slamming the apartment door behind her.

Charles paused for a moment, then went to Gloria's bedroom. He walked in without bothering to check if the room was empty. The maids would be having lunch now. He searched Gloria's bedside table drawers and then moved to the medicine cabinet in the bathroom, concealed behind one of the mirrors, where he found what he was looking for. He took one of the many pill boxes piled on a shelf, put it in his pocket, and went to his room to make a phone call.

Gloria left the building and walked into the waiting limousine, the doorman holding the door open for her. She must have told the driver where she was going, because he took her to the restaurant, but it did not register, nor did Paola's kiss after she was shown to her table by the maître d'. Paola's voice was a million miles away, as blurred as the writing on the menu in front of her eyes.

She said "Yes, fine" to the waiter's first suggestion, without hearing it. Neither did she hear Paola's attempts at conversation, soon turned into a monologue. "Gstaad . . . the Goulandrises . . . black taffeta . . . Mustique . . . screwed him . . . my analyst . . . Jean-Paul Gaultier . . . Do you like my hair? . . . coke . . ." Every now and then words from Paola's drone would briefly pierce the fog around her, but they did not register. She was only aware of her rage at her mother's betrayal. She had always lived in her mother's shadow, and now her mother was making sure that there would never be any light for her. Choked by her despair, she knew that she could not wait a moment longer.

She suddenly stood up, her chair crashing to the ground, and ran away from the table, not looking at Paola's startled face, not even bothering to pick up her bag.

". . . AND she told her husband that she wanted to go to Rio to stay with Elizinha. What she did not tell him was that she wanted to have *everything* lifted by Ivo. He did her face, the tits, every bit between her hairline and her toes. The husband was at home in Geneva, and he became quite restless because he thought that she'd found a toy-boy. He started sending her ultimatums. She got really worried when she got a 'come back, or else' wire. Ivo warned her she was in no condition to fly but she paid no attention, and discharged herself. By the time she landed in Geneva, the poor darling looked like a Halloween pumpkin! She was in the hospital for a few weeks, but I saw her not long ago and she's fine now."

Arianne caught a waiter's eye and nodded toward the silver wine cooler. The waiter refilled their glasses while her guests laughed at her amusing tale.

Desserts were offered and declined by all but Pandora, who asked for a Grand Marnier soufflé with raspberry sauce.

"That sounds delicious. I think I'll keep you company," said Bob Chalmers, sitting on Pandora's left. Arianne confirmed the orders to the waiter, and asked for coffee.

"I'm very glad to see you again," said Bob. "I've been meaning to call you and ask you out for lunch ever since I met you with Geraldine, but I could not face the embarrassment of you not remembering me."

"Of course I remember you. You were interested in my work, which is unusual. Most men can only talk about theirs," she replied.

He laughed and raised his glass to her.

"I really enjoy your company. I would be delighted if you enjoyed mine," he added smoothly, after a brief pause.

Pandora now understood why she had been asked to the lunch, and she decided to stop his interest from going any further. A few weeks ago it might have been amusing, but now it was tiresome.

"Thank you, but I won't be able to have lunch with you. I'm going back to London soon." The Principessa di Sarteano had finished talking to the man on her left, some up-and-coming New York fashion designer, and Pandora addressed her across the table.

"I gather from what you said earlier that Arianne and you worked together as models in Paris. Do you ever miss your work?"

Cameline raised her hand to her throat and toyed with her multiple strands of pearls.

"My dear, that was so long ago that it's almost embarrassing to remember it. We both have grown-up children . . ." Cameline never finished her sentence, because the door of the restaurant burst open and Gloria stormed in, her eyes blazing.

She stared at her mother at the head of the table. Here, everywhere, her mother was the center of attention, her beauty and her money guaranteeing her the spotlight. Now she was scheming to deny Gloria her only chance of recognition. Her rancor, accumulated over the years, burst forth.

"You shit! You bitch! You are stealing my money! I hate you!" she screamed.

Arianne stood up. Her face was very pale.

"Gloria! I don't know what's come over you. I have no idea what you are talking about, but whatever it is we will discuss it at home. I'll be there soon. Please apologize to my guests and leave now," she said. All conversation in the restaurant had stopped, and everybody's eyes were fixed on Arianne's table. The maître d' hovered in the vicinity, anxious for an opportunity to bring the ghastly scene to an end.

"You are the one who ought to apologize. I know that you are trying to cut me out of my inheritance. This is what you deserve!" Gloria shouted. She picked up Pandora's dessert from the table and flung it at Arianne, but she was so shaken by her own sobs that the soufflé landed on the bosom of a woman sitting at a table nearby, splashing the jacket of her white suit. It was Maria Dimitrescu, who had been unsuccessfully trying to catch Arianne's attention all through lunch. She shrieked as the raspberry sauce stained her couture outfit, and the maître d' rushed to her, napkin in hand. He uttered apologies in French as he tried to pacify his hysterical customer and her escort, who was threatening to sue him.

Bob Chalmers stood up, put his arm around Gloria's shoulder, and firmly led her away. She was overcome with emotion and went with him without resistance.

"I'll take Gloria home, and I will call you later today. Thank you very much for a wonderful lunch," he said to Arianne over his shoulder as he led Gloria toward the door. The fashion designer muttered some excuses about an urgent engagement, and left immediately behind Bob Chalmers. Cameline conspicuously looked at her watch while Arianne apologized to Maria, who regained her composure only when Arianne asked her to send the bill for a new outfit to her secretary.

"Dear me, it is terribly late. We must go, Bruno." Cameline stood up, followed by her husband, and kissed Arianne.

"Darling, it's been lovely to see you. It was the most marvelous lunch, but we have to go. Please call us next time you are in Rome." Bruno kissed Arianne and followed his wife toward the door.

Arianne smiled at Pandora, but her sorrow showed in her eyes and her voice.

"You are the only one left. I'm very sorry for all this trouble. Gloria seems to be at her very best whenever I see you."

"Please don't apologize; it wasn't your fault." Pandora moved up the table and sat next to Arianne. She didn't know what else to say, but Arianne was obviously distressed, and she thought it would be unkind to leave in a hurry like everyone else.

"It *is* my fault, but maybe not in the way you mean. Let's go, anyway. I think that I have provided the audience with enough entertainment for one day." She nodded at the waiter, and smiled gratefully at Pandora. "Thank you for staying. I wouldn't have liked to be seen leaving on my own." The waiter returned with the check, and Arianne signed it. She briefly made her excuses to the maître d' before leaving the restaurant. Her car was waiting outside, and the driver opened the door. Arianne paused for a moment.

"I was thinking of going for a walk in the park before going back home. Would you like to come with me?"

Pandora hesitated. Three weeks ago she would have seen it as a God-sent opportunity to probe into Arianne's life, to find out as much as possible. Even yesterday, it would have boosted her ego to be able to puncture Geraldine's condescension by casually referring to her budding friendship with one of New York's richest women. All that was behind her now, yet she sensed that, for some reason, Arianne did not want to be left on her own. She could understand the fear, and felt sympathy for her. She had never imagined she could feel sorry for Arianne de la Force.

"Thank you. I'd love to come with you." The driver held the door open for her and she climbed into the car, Arianne following her. As soon as the car pulled away, Arianne turned toward her.

"I'm ashamed to have to ask you this, but I hope you will not write anything about what you just witnessed. It would hurt me to see what Gloria said in print," Arianne said, in a very low voice.

Pandora was astonished.

"It would not cross my mind to write about something like this. I may be a journalist, but I'm not a muckraker." Arianne's request annoyed her. As usual, she had misjudged motives. The reason for Arianne's invitation had not been her wish for company but simply her fear of scandal.

"You shouldn't worry, in any case," Pandora added coolly. "I'm no longer a journalist. I resigned yesterday, and I'm going back to London next week. Even if I wanted to, which I don't, there is no longer any reason for me to write about anything at all. Certainly not your life."

"I'm sorry. What I've just said is unforgivable. Anyone else would have sold the story of what happened at my apartment to the tabloids, but you didn't." Arianne looked at Pandora thoughtfully. "You are very unusual," she added.

"I always thought my problem was that I am so very ordinary," Pandora replied.

"Not in my circle," said Arianne. "I'm beginning to realize that you may be that rarest of creatures, a normal human being."

"Maybe it's just that I haven't had the opportunity to be anything but normal."

"You devalue yourself. What we make of our lives has less to do with the opportunities we have than how we use them," Arianne said, her face turned toward the window. "Few people have had Gloria's opportunities in life, and yet she's a mess. I blame myself for that. I was too busy being Mrs. de la Force."

"I've been busy over the last eight years being Mrs. Lyons, and I have achieved nothing. At least you have something to show for it," Pandora said.

Arianne seemed surprised.

"Is money what you want? I wanted it desperately because I thought it would take me away from what I wanted to leave behind. It has helped me, but I wish that Gloria would set herself a higher aim than just being my daughter."

"No, money is not all that I want, and I would guess that neither do you, since you have all the money you can possibly need, and yet you still work. I want to do something I care about, and not as a dilettante. One of the few things I've learned is that being somebody's daughter, or somebody's wife, or somebody's anything, for that matter, is not the answer."

Hearing Pandora's words, Arianne couldn't help thinking about Gloria again. Arianne's power only allowed her to alter the course of future events. It could not undo the last fifteen years, or place Gloria where Arianne would have liked her to be, making decisions about her own life, like Pandora. There was something about this girl that touched her.

The car drove into the park and slowed down as they reached the

Mall. Arianne tapped on the glass screen, and the driver stopped the car. "Please wait for us here, Mike," she told him.

The driver opened Arianne's door and they got out, Arianne briskly climbing the stone steps toward the fountain, Pandora following her until they reached the balustrade overlooking the lake. Arianne pointed at the view across the water. "I love coming here; it reminds me of an English park," she said. Pandora glanced at the scene, and she felt homesick for a second.

"When are you leaving New York?" Arianne asked. They began to walk along the path bordering the lake, joggers rushing past as they talked.

"Next Saturday. I used to be an interior decorator. I want to start again, but on a completely different basis. I had my own business for a while, and I'd like to take that up again. But times have changed, and I need to do some thinking about it, about the right approach."

"I had my own business in Paris, a long time ago. I was a costume jewelry designer very briefly after I gave up modeling." There was a wistful edge to her voice.

"Why did you give it up?"

"Because . . . I got married," Arianne replied. "Why did you give up your business?"

Pandora laughed. "Same reason. But at least your husband gave you a chance to prove yourself later."

"Maybe, but I wouldn't advise you to marry a man like my husband." There was bitterness now in Arianne's voice.

"I'm not planning to marry anyone, don't worry," Pandora said jokingly, trying to dispel the sudden mood. "I've just had an . . . unfortunate experience, and I think it's put me off men for a while."

"That's wrong; don't let it happen," Arianne murmured.

Pandora was nonplussed by her comment. Perhaps Charles meant more to Arianne than she had thought.

"I know, I suppose I'm just convalescing. Probably I'll marry again. I'm almost thirty now and I know I want children."

"I also wanted children. Perhaps my real problem is that Gloria is not . . ." Arianne suddenly heard her own words and stopped in midsentence. She had almost been carried away by her introspection, but she was not going to give hostages to fortune. She knew nothing about this girl, and making her party to her problems would only add to them. She was not going to throw away the defenses painstakingly built over twenty years of her life in one second of weakness. ". . . my favorite person at the moment," she finished, staring at Pandora to gauge her reaction.

Pandora was momentarily thunderstruck. It could not be that Arianne had tried to tell her that Gloria was not her daughter. It would explain what Pandora had seen of their relationship, but there were less farfetched explanations for a daughter's hostility toward her mother. In any case, she did not want to know. She had come here spurred by sudden companionship, not to dissect Arianne's life.

"But she is your daughter, and you can't change that," she said. "Sometimes it is better to start from a different relationship. I used to think that I was just like my mother, only to find out that we had very little in common at all." She glanced at her watch. "I'm very sorry, but it's getting late for me." Arianne did not seem to hear her last words.

"You have begun to find your way, Pandora. Gloria hasn't got a clue. After what you have seen, you can understand that I blame myself for it." She shook her head. "But enough of Gloria. You're right, we ought to go back." They turned and began walking toward the car, Arianne's eyes fixed on their long shadows ahead of them.

"What have you done with your painting?" Pandora asked after a while, to break the uncomfortable silence.

Arianne raised her head, and Pandora noticed that once again she seemed her usual, confident self.

"You may see this as another indication of my terminal extravagance, but it is in storage. I've been thinking where I would like to hang it, but I haven't made up my mind yet. Too many choices, perhaps. At least now you know one of my secrets." Their eyes met and they smiled, their faces warmed by the dappled sunlight filtering through the leaves.

25

New York
June 1987

PANDORA walked into her office. It was her last day, but she had finished her work yesterday. The only thing left was to see Geraldine. By now she was in no doubt about Geraldine's motives for the breakfast invitation. Pandora had bumped into Tony yesterday, and he had told her during the short elevator ride that her replacement had already been hired. "He's the nephew of one of our big advertisers. You need a rich uncle, honey." The comment had been meant to hurt her, but it didn't. On the contrary, it ended any lingering doubts she might have had about leaving. But she still had to say good-bye to Geraldine, if only for old times' sake. It was too early to call her; Geraldine was probably looking at her mail, and Vanessa would not disturb her on Pandora's behalf. She decided to get herself a cup of coffee and read the paper to kill time. She was about to leave the office when the phone rang. She didn't bother to pick it up, and went to the coffee dispenser at the end of the corridor. The phone was still ringing when she came back. It was Vanessa.

"Pandora, Miss Freeman would like to see you right now, if you have a moment." Obviously Geraldine was as concerned as she to keep up appearances, and she told Vanessa that she would come to see Miss Freeman now. She left the weak brew in the plastic cup on her desk without much regret. She would go home right after seeing Geraldine, and have a decent cup of coffee on her way.

Vanessa showed her into Geraldine's office. In spite of what had happened, Pandora realized she still held some affection for the place, if only for the sake of her earlier illusions. Geraldine walked toward her with both hands stretched out, as if she were holding an invisible hank of wool.

"Darling, I'm *so* glad to see you! I was worried that I wouldn't be able to find you. We must talk, right now."

"I wouldn't have left without saying good-bye," Pandora said tersely.

Geraldine waved her hand in a dismissive gesture, her wrist clanking with gold bangles in the shape of crocodiles.

"I'm sorry I didn't phone you as soon as I got your note, but you know what my life is like. I simply haven't the time to do what I really want anymore, it's *ghastly*. But we must talk about this nonsense. I can't believe that you could have misunderstood me so dreadfully! Would you like some tea or coffee?" she asked as they sat down.

"No, thank you." She did not want to prolong the conversation a moment longer than necessary. Whatever Geraldine could say would make no difference to her decision, but she was mystified by her tone. It made no sense to reopen the issue once it had been settled to everyone's satisfaction. Geraldine toyed with her bracelets for a moment.

"Darling, I know how hard it is for you now after your disappointment with that Cansino creep, but life goes on and you must think about work."

Pandora knew that she had not been summoned to discuss her personal life. She waited.

"I believe that you have come across a wonderful opportunity."

"What do you mean?" asked Pandora.

"I heard at dinner yesterday that there was the most spectacular row between Arianne de la Force and her daughter at Côte Basque. You were there. You can write your profile of Arianne around the incident. Here is your chance at a feature article at last." Geraldine's voice was full of excitement.

Pandora almost expressed her disbelief, but then thought better of it. It wasn't outrageous; it was just amusing. It could be *very* amusing, in fact.

"But you told me you were running another feature on a high-powered South American woman. I already agreed that my piece would clash with your editorial policy, and I have to bow to your experience," she said sweetly.

"Forget about other boring pieces; this is *really* exciting." Geraldine's enthusiasm was plain to see. Pandora pretended to think for a moment.

"You're right. After lunch I spent some time with Arianne, and she told me the most *fas-cinating* things about her life. It's really incredible!" Pandora replied, mimicking Geraldine's excitement.

"Then write about it, darling! We could knock the pants off *Vanity Fair*. You will be famous!" Geraldine clapped her hands in glee. Pandora looked at her. She found Geraldine absurd, and she had had enough of this charade. She stood up.

"I can't do that," she said quietly. "I gave Arianne my word that I would not write about what happened."

"Did you put it in writing?" Geraldine asked, clearly perplexed.

"No, of course not, but I said that I wouldn't, and that's that."

Geraldine sighed.

"Darling, please listen to me. We are no longer at school, and there is no house-mistress here to make you a prefect because of your impeccable behavior. This is the real world, where you told me you wanted to be. Honor is admirable, but it doesn't get you very far. Don't waste your big opportunity! I might even say don't waste your life."

"I don't intend to, and that's why I'm going back. I'm sorry, but I have no intention of writing anything else," Pandora said. It was clear from her voice that she meant it.

Geraldine's face hardened for a moment, then she realized that she had lost and flashed her best smile at Pandora.

"I think you are hopelessly wrong, but I wouldn't dream of forcing you to do anything, my darling." Pandora returned her smile.

"I'm not wrong, and I'm sure you wouldn't force me to do what I don't want to, aside from the fact that you cannot. I'm leaving for London the day after tomorrow." She began to walk toward the door, then stopped and turned back to face her oldest friend.

"Thank you for everything. I really mean it."

Geraldine came to Pandora and threw her arms around her. "I only wish you'll find your own way. I'm sure you will."

"I hope so," Pandora said. She kissed Geraldine on the cheek and left.

ARIANNE looked at herself in the elevator mirror. She removed her heavy diamond earrings, put them in the evening bag, and rubbed her aching earlobes. François was waiting for her in the vestibule. He opened the elevator door, and followed her into the apartment.

"Would Madame require anything else tonight?" the butler asked.

"No, François, thank you. Tell Rosinha that I will not need her tonight either. She can put my clothes away tomorrow morning," she replied, walking toward the far end of the entrance gallery.

Alone in her bedroom, she took off her evening dress and flung it on the nearest chair. She kicked off her pumps and put on her dressing gown. The touch of the cool silk felt pleasant to her skin; it was a warm evening, and she was glad to be leaving for the yacht the following day. She was cheered by the thought of being on her own, lazily cruising around the Aegean.

Gloria had gone to stay with Paola in Cap Ferrat. She had left yesterday afternoon, soon after their row. With hindsight, it might have been preferable to have kept quiet after the fracas at La Côte Basque, but she couldn't. The memory of the scene that followed when she returned to the apartment would live with her for a long time.

Gloria had poured out her venom as only Gloria could. She had accused Arianne of denying her a father, of lying to her about him, and then she had launched into a tirade about Arianne's new machinations to deprive her of her money. "You want it all yourself. You want me to have nothing so there can be no other Mrs. de la Force, only you, the legend, the one and only *you!*"

Other than the accusations about the money, Arianne had heard it all before. Many, many times. But like cliffs continually beaten by the sea, her resistance had begun to crumble. For a second she thought of telling Gloria the truth about herself and her past, but she recoiled from it, for her own sake as well as for Gloria's.

At the time she wondered how Gloria could have found out about the sale of San Simón. Arianne was sure that it had not been through Bob. It had to be Charles, but how did he know? After a while, it dawned on her that Charles must have tapped her telephone. He had left yesterday evening, saying that he was going to Capri for the rest of the summer. She had the apartment checked by an expert sent by Bob, but the man could not find anything.

She had been relieved to see Charles go, although she guessed that he was following Gloria. His allowance enabled him to travel as he pleased, and she was glad to be rid of him, if only temporarily. Her dearest wish was to get him out of her life for good, but she knew the price for that. Her money.

Her money, her money, her money. It all came down to that. Aladdin's lamp had become Damocles' sword. Gloria wanted it, and Charles wanted it too. Through Gloria, she assumed.

Her money had given her power and everything she had wanted. It had been the ruling element during all these years. Whom she saw, what she did, where she went, it had always been determined by that one priority, her money. She had lost sight of many things in the process, Gloria foremost among them. She had the best jewels, the best sables, the best pictures. She had palaces and yachts. She had everything. She had too much, in fact, but it was not enough.

Her thoughts drifted to her conversation in the park with Pandora Doyle. Maybe it was just her fantasy, but she had sensed in Pandora qualities she would have liked Gloria to have, a determination to find her way concealed by her quiet manner. A sudden impulse overtook her, and she went to Kayzie's office. She looked up "Doyle" in the card index, and dialed the number.

SEAT belt fastened, Pandora was ready for imminent landing. She looked out of the window at the lights of London, and suddenly recognized the unmistakable roof of the Albert Hall. A few moments later the plane began its final descent into Heathrow Airport. She stretched her legs. She had not been able to sleep on the plane but she was not tired. She was too excited for that. She was about to begin the next stage of her life.

Her thoughts went back to the conversation with Arianne the day before. Pandora had been packing her bags when Arianne phoned her. She had been tempted to decline Arianne's invitation, but then thought better of it. Their unlikely acquaintance had turned out to be one of the pleasant surprises of her stay in New York. For whatever reason, she enjoyed Arianne's company, and the thought of seeing her again suddenly cheered her up. If nothing else, it would break the solitude of her last day in New York.

It had not been a long conversation. Arianne was leaving for the Turkish coast the following morning, and Pandora noticed through the open doors that the furniture in the enormous drawing room was already shrouded in white dust sheets, and an assortment of expensive trunks stood in the entrance gallery. "I'm sending a few things to Venice, I always go there in September," Arianne had said as she welcomed Pandora. Pandora remembered the first time she had been to the apartment, not long ago. Then she had been both overwhelmed by Arianne's grandeur and aware of her condescension. It felt different now. At first she put it down to the piles of luggage somehow breaking the formality of the place, but she realized as soon as they moved into the immaculate library that it was something else. The inexplicable rapport established at the park had not faded away. Arianne prepared the drinks herself and made small talk about her imminent trip. Then, suddenly, she changed the subject.

"I have been thinking about what you said yesterday about going back to London to set up your own business. I know that what I'm about to say is perhaps easier for me than for you, but I would advise you not to start small, if the business can carry it. I don't know how you are planning to finance your company, but I know from experience that it can hinge on being able to convince a bank to lend you the money. If so, it takes the same effort to convince most bankers about the viability of any loan, irrespective of size, and you will be less vulnerable if you are a bigger customer. I learned that many years ago."

A discussion with Arianne about financial vulnerability would have seemed unlikely to Pandora until that moment.

"Thank you for the advice. I learned from my first business about the problems of being small, and it's one of the things I told you I was planning to study in more detail in London. I have to see what the options are," she replied rather vaguely.

"Please let me know if you have any problems with your bank about raising the money. I can put you in touch with other bankers."

Pandora smiled. "One of the few advantages from my marriage

is that I met quite a number of bankers. If I decide to start on a larger scale I'll approach them, otherwise I can just finance myself, but I'm grateful for your concern." However much she warmed to Arianne, she didn't want to be beholden to her — or to anyone.

"I just want to let you know that if you have any trouble, I'm prepared to help you if I can." Arianne was as surprised as Pandora when she heard herself make the offer. She decided to put it down to her earlier feeling of gratitude, but Pandora did not quite know what to make of it. She thought for a moment.

"It would be disingenuous to say anything other than that I'm astonished by your generosity. Thank you very much for your offer, but I can't accept it. We hardly know each other, and I don't know yet if I will need help or not. It may sound foolish to you, but our conversation yesterday meant more to me than you think. We were just two people talking without ulterior motives. I hope we will become friends, but to accept your offer would probably make that very difficult." She kept her eyes down as she spoke, suddenly embarrassed by the personal turn of the conversation, as unexpected to her as Arianne's offer had been a moment ago.

Arianne was deep in thought for a while.

"I was going to say that it is unwise to question somebody's offer of help if you need it, but you are right. I have my reasons, but they don't concern you. Also, I remembered while listening to you that I once accepted an apparently irresistible offer without much thought about it. I've regretted it ever since. I understand what you are saying; I can only add that I enjoyed our conversation yesterday as much as you did. I'll be away until September. Let's talk then; I'll make a note of your London number." She walked to her desk and picked up her address book, then opened a drawer and pulled out a stiff white card edged in gold before returning to her seat.

"I hope you are free in September," Arianne said as she handed the card to Pandora. "I give a big party every year, and I am giving a costume ball in my palazzo in Venice this time. I would love you to come. It's on September fourteenth."

Pandora smiled gratefully.

"My calendar is far less busy than yours. I'm sure I'm free, and I would be delighted to come to your party." She gave Arianne her London phone number.

"Don't forget you are a businesswoman now," Arianne said cheerfully. "You may find that you are too busy by then."

"Even if I become wildly successful, I hope that I'll still have time for my friends," Pandora said.

Arianne looked at her affectionately. "I truly hope to see you in Venice," she murmured as she kissed Pandora good-bye.

On her way home, Pandora tried to find an explanation for Arianne's unaccountable kindness toward her. The last thing she had expected as she was about to leave New York was this extraordinary, unlikely . . . well, friendship. Perhaps there was no need to look for reasons; in any case, she had an invitation to Venice, and it sounded wonderful. New York had made her feel like Cinderella sometimes; now she would be going to the ball. But there was work to do first.

Part Five

26

Buenos Aires
June 1969

ARIANNE felt extremely weak. She looked around at the unfamiliar room, wondering where she was, glad to find her curiosity returning. She had been conscious for a little while but indifferent to anything, even to the doctor's visit. Until this moment, she had just felt like closing her eyes and going back to sleep, but now she struggled to stay awake.

There was a knock at the door, and the nurse came in.

"You have a visitor, Señora," she announced. "A Señor Chalmers."

The name meant nothing to Arianne. "Show him in," she said. She probably looked ghastly, but she didn't care. After a moment, a man walked in, and the nurse left the room.

"I'm very glad to see you," the man said in French. He had an American accent. "I came as soon as the doctor told me your condition was no longer critical. I am not allowed to stay for long, though," he added.

"Who are you?" Arianne asked, horrified at the weakness of her own voice.

The man smiled.

"I'm sorry; I should have started by introducing myself. We met at your wedding, but I wouldn't expect you to remember. My name is Bob Chalmers. I advised Simón on his business. I am a director of the de la Force holding company."

Arianne wondered why he was here, but there were more pressing questions on her mind.

"Where is my daughter?" she asked anxiously.

"She is at the house here, with her governess. Don't worry; they are perfectly fine."

Arianne was at first confused by the reference to the governess, then realized that he meant Nana.

"Where am I?" she asked.

"At the Pequeña Companía clinic in Buenos Aires," he replied.

"Who brought me here?" Now that her strength was returning a little, she found she wanted answers to a string of questions.

"I arranged for an ambulance plane to bring you from Salta to Buenos Aires. I thought it would be unwise for you to stay in a critical condition in a local hospital. The de la Force family must have many doctor friends there," the man said.

She was thoroughly puzzled now. "Please tell me what happened," she said weakly. "I can't remember."

"May I sit down?" he asked.

"Of course." She tried to indicate the armchair in the corner, but couldn't find the strength to raise her hand.

"Simón had asked me to stay at the house after the party. I don't like going to bed early, so I stayed in the library doing some work after you all went to bed. Suddenly I heard this great commotion, and I noticed the staff running around like headless chickens. Someone had gone to your bedroom to answer a bell, and found you unconscious. You were immediately taken to the hospital in Salta, and I arranged for your transfer here." He tactfully avoided any reference to the doctors' pumping her stomach in Salta. Until then he had never come across a woman who had attempted suicide on her wedding night. He had expected some neurotic wreck, but other than her pallor she seemed perfectly normal and calm.

"Where is Simón?" Arianne forced herself to ask the question. She had tried to push him out of her mind since regaining consciousness.

Bob's face showed his surprise.

"Haven't the doctors said anything to you?"

"No," she replied.

He left the armchair and stood near her. She became anxious at his obvious hesitation.

"I'm very sorry to have to tell you this," he said at last, "but Simón died that evening. His family immediately asked for an autopsy. It showed that he died from a massive coronary." He did not tell Arianne that they had also asked for evidence that the marriage had been consummated, in a desperate attempt to find some reason to have it declared null so they could claim his inheritance. The doctors had confirmed to them that the evidence was there.

Arianne leaned against her pillows, tears running down her cheeks.

"It is very hard for me to have to disclose such bad news to you. I didn't know they hadn't told you yet. Simón was buried in Salta yesterday," Bob said.

Arianne remained silent. She could not tell him that her tears were tears of joy. Her nightmare was over. She would soon be back in Paris, with Gloria and Nana. She would sell her jewelry, and get on with her life as she wished.

"When will I be able to leave Buenos Aires?" she asked.

"In accordance with Argentine law, you will inherit the whole of Simón's estate. He may have made provisions in his will for other beneficiaries, although I think it is unlikely, but he can only dispose of one fifth of his estate. The rest will be yours in any case. You will have to stay here at least until the estate is settled."

Her reaction was immediate.

"I don't want it," she said.

Bob stared at her in surprise. She looked as if she meant it.

"The night before your wedding, Simón gave me a letter for you which I was to take back to New York for safekeeping, and only give to you after his death. Nobody could have guessed that it would become relevant so soon. I don't know its contents," he said, pulling an envelope out of his inside pocket. "It might be better if you read it before making any decision." He handed the envelope to Arianne.

She tore it open and unfolded the letter. It was in Simón's unmistakable jagged handwriting. Her face became even paler as she read it.

Valle del Oro, 15th June 1969

Dear Arianne,

In accordance with the provisions of my will, you are to be the beneficiary of my estate. If we have children, the estate will be apportioned in equal shares between you and them, and you will be their trustee until they are of age. If we do not have children, you will then be the sole beneficiary.

I do not wish the estate dispersed or disposed of in any way until my children can take control of it. To ensure this, I have left a sealed envelope with a lawyer, holding the photocopy of your Brazilian passport and an explanation addressed to the Brazilian police with regard to your identity. His instructions are to refer the envelope to the Brazilian Embassy as soon as he is aware of any significant disposal of the estate by you, or any evidence that you are not willing to take control of my business.

This restriction applies for a period of ten years after my death or until the children are of age, whichever is the sooner. Once these conditions are met, the lawyer has instructions to return the sealed envelope to you. If I were to die childless, I have set the ten-year limit in the knowledge that, once you have become used to running the business, you would find it very difficult to relinquish control. I have also made it a condition that you do not remarry during that time. I am sure that after ten years of absolute power you would not wish to share it, and thus put my estate at risk.

I have taken this action because I trust my judgment of people, and I know that you are up to the responsibility. I am only seeking to ensure your willingness to execute it. My estate is my monument, and my family its keeper. I wish to ensure its survival in my name after I'm gone.

Simón

She slowly folded the letter, stunned by Simón's machinations to trap her even after his death. Ten years. It was difficult for her to encompass the implications. Ten years ago she had been living in the slums, with Florinda and their mother. Ten years from now . . . it was futile to think about it: she had no choice.

She sat up in bed and turned toward Chalmers.

"Simón's letter explains what he expected of me. I will take over the business," she said firmly.

"I'm very glad to hear that, Mrs. de la Force. There is a board meeting scheduled for next week, and key decisions have to be made."

"No, it's not going to be like that. If I'm in control, then I set the rules. I don't know anything about the business, and I will not approve anything until I do. And please call me Arianne." There had to be a reason behind his concern for her. "Why are you here, anyway? I'm sure this is not just a courtesy visit."

He smiled.

"Not entirely," he answered. "I just wanted to let you know that I hope I can be of assistance in these difficult times. It could be in your interest as well as mine," he added.

Arianne liked his frankness. She knew he hadn't come to see her out of kindheartedness only. He needed an ally, and so did she. Her instinct told her that she could trust him.

"How much did Simón pay you?" she asked point-blank.

He hesitated for a moment.

"I'm on a percentage fee. I don't think it is the time to discuss it," he said.

"You are wrong. I will double it for this year. I'm going to check out of here tonight. You will find me the best language teacher in Buenos Aires, and I want him in the house tomorrow morning at nine o'clock. He has to teach me Spanish in two weeks, mornings only. In the afternoons, you will explain the business to me. The board meeting will take place only when I know both the language and the rules."

"But . . ."

"No 'buts.' That's the way it's going to be from now on. There will be no decisions on *anything* other than day-to-day matters until I know what I'm doing. I'm tired now. I will see you tomorrow at the house." She didn't know where the house was, not even the phone number. "Please leave me the number where I can phone my daughter," she added. Bob wrote it on the notepad on her bedside table, said good-bye, and left.

As he walked down the corridor toward the elevator he thought about his conversation with this woman who had been nearly dead three days ago. Simón had obviously met his match when he had chosen her as his wife. But she was in the hospital while the board was planning to get rid of her. Bob hoped that he had made the right choice.

THE car turned into the Avenida Alvear, and Arianne noticed the enormous gum tree, its top overshadowing the corner like a giant's umbrella. Her eye caught the name of the side street in white letters on the blue enamel plate fixed to the ornate railings of a big house at the corner, lit by the white glass streetlight at the top of a gilded steel column. Everything, even the street names, was alien to her, but the French-style mansions along the avenue reminded her of Paris. It was like Paris with tropical trees.

The car slowed down and turned right, stopping in front of a pair of massive wrought-iron and brass gates. The gates were opened by a uniformed porter, and Arianne looked at the house through the car window as they drove toward it.

The house front was at least two hundred feet long. It was built of pale gray stone, an obvious copy of the facades of the Place de la Concorde. The car drove slowly up the wide gravel pathway and stopped under a massive stone portico. The driver opened Arianne's door, and she got out of the car. She paused for a moment in front of the huge glass and iron doors. A liveried footman opened them for her. Head high, she walked into her new home.

The staff were lined up on both sides of the wide stone stairs leading from the entrance to the foyer, the red carpet held in place by thick brass bars. Arianne went up, nodding her head to acknowledge the bows of the servants as she walked past them. When she reached the top, a short, plumpish woman dressed in black, her dark hair pulled into a roll at the back, came toward her.

"I am Nelly, the housekeeper, Señora. It is an honor to meet you," the woman said, almost curtsying.

"Thank you, Nelly," replied Arianne, walking into the large square room at the top of the stairs. The dark oak paneling carved with garlands of fruit reached the coved cornice, and a massive crystal chandelier hung from the ceiling, nearly fifteen feet above

Arianne's head. She noticed the huge painting hanging between the doors on one of the walls. It was a full-length portrait of a beautiful young woman in turn-of-the-century clothes, her strands of pearls reaching down to her waist.

"Where is my daughter?" Arianne asked.

"She was very tired, so she was put to bed at seven, Señora. Her governess is waiting for you upstairs."

She was eager to see Gloria and talk to Nana but realized that, as the new master, she had to go through the motions of this virtual handing-over of the keys. She walked up to the portrait and glanced at the small brass plate at the bottom of the ornate frame. "Josefina A. de Anzorena — Giovanni Boldini — Paris 1911," she read.

"Who is the lady in this portrait?" she asked.

"It is Mrs. de la Force's grandmother, Señora. I believe it is a family heirloom. It is by a famous painter," Nelly answered proudly.

Arianne cast an icy look at the housekeeper.

"I appreciate how sudden all this has been, Nelly, but I am Mrs. de la Force, and this lady is no relation of *mine*. Have the portrait taken down and returned to her family, please."

Nelly's face went crimson. She could sense the silent satisfaction of the staff behind her at the rebuke.

"Of course, Señora," Nelly said humbly. She would have to be careful with this one.

Arianne walked through the double doors on her left, and rapidly went through a succession of reception rooms, crammed with exquisite French furniture, until she reached a small oval salon. Nelly caught up with her at last, and opened the doors on one side.

"This is the dining room, Señora. It is a copy of one of the main rooms in a French palace." Arianne found her "helpful" comments grating, but decided to say nothing. She had to make some allowance for the housekeeper's pride. There was no point in making an unnecessary enemy.

Arianne walked into the vast chamber, her steps echoing on the Versailles parquet. There were fireplaces at both ends of the marble-lined room, with huge painted hunting scenes above them. A set of silver tureens had been placed in the middle of the polished mahogany table.

"I would like to see the silver and the china," Arianne said.

"There are seventeen sets of china, Señora. Would you like to see them all?"

"Show me the silver now. I'll look at the china another time," Arianne replied tersely.

Nelly went to the side door at the far end of the room, and opened it with one of the many keys hanging from her large key ring. They walked into a vast pantry lined with glass-fronted cabinets, the china stacked in neat piles on the shelves on one side of the room, crystal glasses on the other. She opened one of the many cutlery drawers at low level, the silver gleaming against the green baize lining the compartments. She then moved to another cabinet, and opened the top drawer.

"The silver-gilt is kept here, Señora," she said. Arianne picked up a fork from the first drawer, and inspected the monogram on the handle. "dlF" read the ornate cipher.

"If there is any silver with a monogram other than this, send it to the silversmith to be altered. If it cannot be changed, then I will sell it. The same applies to the linen and the china, Nelly. I'm tired now. I would like to see my bedroom."

The housekeeper closed the drawers, and locked the door behind them. She then walked across the dining room and opened the double doors leading into the main hall.

Arianne had been able to conceal her amazement at the grandeur of the house, but now she found it impossible. She stopped in her tracks, her breath caught in her throat, overwhelmed by the splendor of the room.

The Renaissance-style hall was sixty feet square and forty feet high. Five massive brass chandeliers hung from the carved oak ceiling, matched by the oak gallery at high level. Enormous tapestries hung on the stone walls, and medieval statues in wood and stone stood on the massive chests lined up against the wainscoting. The gold background of the Sienese religious paintings glittered in the half-light, matching the embers of the fire in the monumental hearth on one side of the room, between two cathedral-size windows with stone mullions.

Arianne regained her composure and rapidly walked across the hall, back into the foyer dominated by the rejected portrait. Nelly opened the wrought-iron gate near the staircase and followed Arianne into the elevator.

They came out and walked along the second-floor gallery in silence, until Nelly stopped in front of one of the many doors and opened it.

"Were these Señora Dolores's rooms?" Arianne asked before walking in.

"Yes, Señora. They are the best rooms on this floor," replied Nelly defensively.

"Please show me my husband's bedroom," Arianne said. "And show me the way to my daughter and her governess's rooms. I would like to see them. I want breakfast at seven-thirty. Black coffee, orange juice, and toast. That will be all for now, Nelly," she added.

The housekeeper did as she was told, made a short speech about how honored she was to have had the opportunity to meet the señora, wished her goodnight, and began to walk toward the stairs. Arianne called her back.

"I am most impressed by the superb job you have done in running this house, Nelly. I just wanted to thank you, and let you know that I will double your salary as from this month." From the expression on Nelly's face Arianne knew that she had achieved her aim. She did not care if she had the best-paid housekeeper in South America; she wanted her to be on her side.

Once she was alone, Arianne suddenly felt weak and sat on one of the thronelike chairs set at intervals along the wall. Still, she could feel the excitement rising inside her.

Until this day, she had been at the receiving end of Simón's largesse. He had bought her a life of inconceivable luxury, but now she realized that what she had had so far had been only the dividends. Before, she could buy anything in any shop. Now she could have anything in the world. Everything that Simón had owned she now owned, everything that Simón had been she now was. *She* held the power.

She stood up and went to Nana's room. She paused for a moment before knocking at the door, and smiled. Perhaps she was going to enjoy being Mrs. de la Force after all.

27

Buenos Aires
July 1969

BOB Chalmers held the massive door open.

"This way, please, Mrs. de la Force," he said. Arianne had noticed he had stopped calling her by her Christian name as soon as they had walked into the building. Tact was obviously one of his virtues.

The memory of a similar moment flashed in her mind. Less than two years ago, Jacques Villette had held a door open for her at Balenciaga. She had not failed then, and she was not going to fail now.

She walked into the large room, taking in the full-length portrait of Simón on the far wall facing the door. The twelve men sitting around the long table stood up as she entered. The man sitting at the head of the table, under the portrait, came toward her. She recognized his hawkish face and slicked-back black hair from the photographs she had studied at the house. He was Simón's vice chairman.

"I'm very pleased to meet you, Señor Massera," Arianne said, before he had time to introduce himself. He started to address her in heavily accented French, but Arianne interrupted him.

"It is very kind of you to speak to me in French, but it is unnecessary," she said in fluent Spanish. The man escorted her around the table, trying to introduce Arianne to the members of the board, but she addressed each of them by name, and Massera remained silent after his second attempt. The introductions completed, he then pulled out an empty chair in the middle of one side of the table.

"Please sit down, Señora," he said courteously. Arianne paid no attention and walked to the head of the table, sitting in his seat. Massera was startled and seemed about to say something, then thought better of it. He collected his papers, and returned to the seat he had just offered to Arianne. As soon as he sat down, she spoke to the table at large.

"Gentlemen, I'm truly pleased to meet you today. These have been very difficult times for all of us but I hope that, with your help, I will be able to make this transition period as short and as smooth as possible. My husband's sudden disappearance undoubtedly creates problems, and I understand your position at the moment." She rested her elbows on the table. "I'm sure that you understand mine," she added, her right hand toying with her enormous engagement ring in full view of her audience. She paused for a moment, her silence underlining her point.

"Now let's get down to business," she finished.

As soon as she ended her speech, Massera stood up.

"It is a great honor for us to welcome you today as a visitor, Señora, and were it not for the tragic loss we all share, it would be a joyful occasion. We were delighted to hear of your wish to come here, and we sincerely appreciate your interest in becoming acquainted with us. It is the duty of any board to take the shareholders' interests to heart, and we will endeavor to run Valle del Oro S.A. along the same path of growth and prosperity as during the days when Don Simón was our chairman. Please rest assured that we will keep you informed of our activities, even when you return to Europe. You are more than a shareholder, you are Don Simón's widow, and as such you are very dear to us all." He sat down, taking in the mute approval of his fellow directors for his tactful speech.

He now waited for Arianne's reply, hoping that it would be as short as his welcome. She surely had better things to do with her time than sit here. He hoped that he would not be forced to remind her that she really had no right to attend the board meeting at all. He had to admit that she was the most beautiful woman he had seen in his life, though. No wonder the old bastard had died trying to perform his marital duties.

Arianne looked around the table.

"I'm truly touched by your kind welcome, gentlemen. I appreciate your concern, Mr. Massera, but I would like to put your mind at ease on several scores. I will live in Argentina from now on, and it will not be necessary for you to keep me informed, since I will be party to all your decisions. In fact, I intend to make them myself."

A stony silence fell on the scene until Massera spoke again.

"Señora, I fully appreciate how distressing these times must be for you. It may also be that your relative inexperience of business matters has led you to several well-intentioned, but misguided, assumptions. One of the purposes of the board meeting later today is to confirm my appointment as chairman and chief executive officer of Valle de Oro S.A. Only members of the board can attend a board meeting." He smiled indulgently. The poor girl was obviously out of her depth, and he felt sorry for her inevitable embarrassment. He hoped that this nonsense would not go on for much longer.

Arianne returned his smile.

"You are one step ahead of me, Mr. Massera. I was not thinking of the board meeting yet. I came here to call an extraordinary shareholders' meeting, which it is my right to do. Since I hold one hundred percent of the shares, we have a full quorum. The purpose of the meeting is to dismiss the current board, and the motion has the shareholders' approval. The second item on the agenda is the eventual reappointment of the board, with myself as chairman and chief executive officer. Before casting my vote on this second motion, I would like to ask the ex-members of the board if they would have any objections to their reappointment under such conditions. Otherwise I will have to find suitable replacements."

She glanced around at the well-dressed, obviously affluent men, clearly dumbfounded by her speech. She was sure that they were quickly thinking about the implications of fighting a legal battle against her, the immediate loss of income, and the slim chance of success. She knew the likely outcome, but Massera spoke before any of them could open his mouth.

"Señora, it is my duty to warn you about the possible consequences of the course of action you seem to be considering. I have a contract ensuring my position as vice chairman of Valle de Oro S.A.," he thundered.

Arianne enjoyed the mounting tension in the room, which reminded her of a poker table when the stakes are impossibly high. She knew she held a royal flush.

"Mr. Massera," she said at last, very quietly, "I know about your contract. It was signed twelve years ago, and it is understandable that the small print may have slipped from your mind. However, there is a copy among my husband's papers, and I have read it. Your appointment is conditional on the shareholders' approval every year. I'm sure that my husband had no reason to revoke your appointment, but I'm the only shareholder now, and I take a different view. Your appointment has not yet been confirmed this year. There is a termination clause in your contract, and I assure you that it will be honored in full. Since you no longer have anything to do with this company, I would be grateful if you would leave us now so that the board can continue with its business."

Massera's face went crimson, and he held the edge of the table with both hands. He forcefully stood up, overturning his chair, and grabbed his papers.

"You will hear from my lawyers, you bitch!" he screamed.

"Good afternoon, Mr. Massera. Before leaving, please put your chair back in place. I don't like untidy rooms." The directors on both sides of Massera rushed to pick up his chair as soon as he left, slamming the door behind him.

"Now, gentlemen," Arianne said with a captivating smile, "let's continue with our meeting, shall we?"

"THANK you very much, Rosinha, that will be all."

"Good night, Madame." Carrying her mistress's evening gown and her opera cloak, the maid left the room. It was nearly two o'clock in the morning.

Arianne had been sleeping in this room for almost three months, ever since the decorators had finished removing every trace of Dolores's presence. It was her room now.

Not that she had been in it much. After a month of mourning which had been nothing but an alibi to keep people away until she was sure of her ground, she had begun to accept the inevitable invitations arising from her position, and she had immediately found herself at the center of the Buenos Aires social whirl. Everybody wanted to meet her, and it was useful for her to make contact with all the people who mattered.

But she found being the focus of so much attention disturbing.

For many years she had lived under the fear of being found out. She had begun to outgrow that feeling in Paris, when first her modeling career and then her life-style had brought her to the attention of a small circle of society. But now she was a focus of interest for the whole country, and it worried her. She half-convinced herself that her power was her shield. Even if someone were to find out about Silvia in Brazil or the Bois de Boulogne, she reasoned, no one would dare to follow up on the story, let alone divulge it, if the consequence would be the wrath of Arianne de la Force.

The fear nonetheless remained, but she had to learn to live with it if she were to survive because, as she soon realized, the public attention would be constant. Tonight, when she had appeared in her *avant-scène* box at the Teatro Colón for the gala performance of *Norma*, she knew that three thousand pairs of eyes were on her as soon as she took her seat. Everything about her was commented upon, as it had been from her earliest public appearance here.

It was unnerving, but by now Arianne relished it. Her position ensured admiration from everyone, even from those who were themselves in an enviable position, and she found it irresistible. Money no longer mattered to her; she had very quickly gotten over the brief thrill of possession, dulled by the knowledge that she could have anything she wanted. But there was no end to the excitement of undisputed ascendancy.

She was about to get into bed when she decided to look in on Gloria, asleep in her room. She hardly saw her daughter these days. Arianne left the house early, came back late in the evening to change her clothes, and her weekends were spent visiting the de la Force estates all over the country. She had taken Gloria with her on her first visits, but soon realized that the child was upset by the constant change of surroundings. There had been too many changes in Gloria's life recently, and it was better for her to stay at home with Nana.

She turned off the lights as she left the room, leaving only her reading light on. It was enough to make the diamond bracelets she had carelessly dropped on her bedside table sparkle, their glow picked up by the polished silver frame of the photograph of a woman and her two children in a Rio de Janeiro square, years ago.

28

Buenos Aires
November 1969

"WE are now flying over the *estancia*, Señora. We will be landing in ten minutes. Please fasten your seat belt," the captain's voice said over the loudspeaker. Arianne gathered her papers from the table in front of her, and looked out of the window as the steward folded the table away.

In preparation for her visit, she had read a brief history of the "San Simón" estate, which was located in the south of Buenos Aires Province. It had been settled in the 1840s, a land grant to General Anzorena from the Buenos Aires government in gratitude for his efficient elimination of the local Indian tribes. His successful campaign opened up the region, and the general's reward was half a million acres in the Tandil arena.

The estate was christened "El Fortín de Anzorena" and became the backbone of the family fortune, making the Anzorenas into an archetype of Argentina's landed families. But the relentless division of the estates among three or four generations of a large Catholic family had led to the decline of the family wealth. By the time Simón married Dolores, her father had just a small holding in the area. The *casco* of the original estate, the main house rebuilt in 1907 and the vast park around it, belonged to a relative, and Simón bought it from him soon after his marriage. It was still called by the original name of the estate then, but Simón immediately changed it — predictably — to "San Simón."

Within a few years, he bought more and more surrounding land until he had put together one hundred thousand acres of the original estate, making it once again the largest holding in the area, and turned it into the flagship of his agribusiness in the Pampas region. The house, an idiosyncratic reinterpretation of Scottish baronial style as understood by Dolores's grandfather, was returned to its original grandeur by her. The long-neglected park was restored, and an eighteen-hole golf course was added, a birthday present from Simón when Dolores briefly took up the sport. "San Simón" became one of the most visible props to Simón and Dolores's leading role in Buenos Aires society, a monument to both Simón's money and Dolores's lineage.

The estate's close association with Dolores had delayed Arianne's visit until she had felt ready for yet another confrontation with a ghost. She finally scheduled her trip for September, but the wave of labor unrest during that month, aggravated by the government's fierce repression of the strikers, meant that most of her time had to be spent in urgent meetings with management and trade union leaders to try to minimize losses in the de la Force factories.

There was a further, personal reason for her delay. Soon after taking control of the business she had made her first visit to a de la Force *estancia,* where the harvest of winter corn was taking place. She left her plane dressed in her severe suit and high heels, only to face the estate manager and a stableboy, both on horseback. The stableboy was holding a third horse by the bridle, a horse for the boss. It had been Simón's pride to ride across his land.

The boy was sent back to the house at great speed, and a car soon appeared, but Arianne was embarrassed by the episode. She did not need to imagine the sneering jokes after her departure about the foreigner, the woman, the city doll now playing at being the boss. It would not happen again.

As soon as she was back in Buenos Aires she arranged for daily riding lessons at the crack of dawn in the Hípico Club. After three months she felt confident enough in the saddle; no one would be able to say that the *patrona* could not ride. And she was not wearing Chanel but her riding breeches and boots now, sufficiently worn to look acceptable to a country man's eye, together with a white shirt and an old jacket.

The ostensible reason for her proprietorial visit was to inspect "San Simón's" recently completed silos and grain-drying facilities, the latest stage in a massive investment program. Storage capacity, drying temperatures, planted areas, size of trucks: all the figures were at her fingertips.

The Learjet began its descent to the airstrip, and Arianne lay back in her seat, closing her eyes. As she felt the wheels touch the ground, she quickly reviewed the résumé of the estate manager who would be waiting to meet her: Paul Liehr, thirty-six years old, graduated from the University of Kansas, employed at "San Simón" since his graduation.

The steward opened the door. Arianne picked up her briefcase and walked toward the exit, into a rectangle of light cast by the bright sunshine on the red carpet.

". . . AND I am very pleased with the results so far. I hope you are as well, Señora." Paul Liehr was referring to their inspection of crossbreeds between Charolais dams and Hereford and Aberdeen Angus bulls, a program under his direct control. She had been able to see for herself that morning that the results were indeed encouraging, both with regard to calves' weight at birth and when weaned. Their tour over, he had driven her back to the house and they were now standing outside the main entrance.

"If it suits your plans, Señora, I will be here at four o'clock to continue our inspection." Arianne would have liked to carry on immediately after lunch, but she had to make allowances for rural working hours. People woke up before sunrise, and the midday heat made work almost unbearable at this time of the year. To disregard the fact would make her unnecessarily unpopular among the staff, but she did not relish the prospect of a few hours in the house on her own. No matter how much she glossed over the fact, she still saw it as Dolores's territory. The answer came to her in a flash.

"Why don't you stay for lunch?" she asked. "Then we can talk about other aspects of your work," she added, uncertain about the justification. It was unnecessary, certainly on his behalf. He hesitated for a moment, obviously surprised by the invitation.

"Let's go inside; it will be cooler," she said, not waiting for his reply and walking up the steps toward the studded oak door. He rushed ahead and held the door open for her. They walked into the hall, and Arianne noticed the butler waiting for her nearby. "Mr. Liehr will be staying for lunch, Oscar." The butler nodded his head in a discreet bow, but not before Arianne noticed the fleeting disapproval reflected in his eyes. Neither Don Simón nor Señora Dolores would have invited any member of the staff, no matter how high his position, to lunch with them. But she was the boss now, whether the butler liked it or not.

ARIANNE was about to order more coffee when she noticed Paul surreptitiously glancing at his watch. It annoyed her at first, because she had found lunch in his company more enjoyable than she had imagined, and she was no longer used to people showing signs of anything other than enraptured interest toward her.

"Please let me know if I'm boring you," she said. He didn't notice the sharp edge in her voice, but she did.

"On the contrary, Señora. *I* was wondering if I hadn't taken too much of your time already." His embarrassment was genuine, and she felt sorry for him. He was telling the truth, and she had probably kept him past the time of his afternoon nap anyway.

"I've really enjoyed our conversation, but maybe we should take our siesta now." She was briefly amused by his possible misunderstanding of her remark, but decided not to look at his face just in case. She stood up, the butler immediately rushing to pull her chair out. Paul followed her to the hall, where they quickly made their good-byes at the foot of the stairs, and he confirmed that he would be back at four o'clock. She stared at him as he walked away, then turned around and swiftly climbed to the upper floor.

She wandered along the corridors for a while, opening door after door until she glimpsed a room larger than the others, with a four-poster bed covered with a lace bedspread. It probably was Dolores's bedroom, and she quickly shut the door. She walked to the other end of the corridor and opened another door. A tweed jacket still hung on the clothes stand by the mirror. It was Simón's bedroom, and she walked in.

To her surprise, she felt like an intruder at first. It had been different in the Buenos Aires house, perhaps because she had gone there under the desperate need to establish her position as Señora de la Force, pushing aside any other feeling. But the need was no longer pressing, allowing her to acknowledge her true feelings now, if only for a moment. She was tempted to leave the room, and for that reason she forced herself to stay. She began to glance at the pictures, without really taking them in, until her eye was caught by the silver-framed photograph on Simón's bedside table.

It was her own portrait, and she was strangely touched by the discovery. Simón must have placed it there when Dolores died. Maybe he had loved her, after all. She had always thought that he was unable to love, but finding her photograph where she had least expected it to be made her wonder.

She shook her head, and checked the time. It would be almost an hour before Paul came to meet her. She walked to the window and gazed at the park under the full glare of the afternoon sun, the sky almost white and the trees standing in pools of black shadow. After a moment, she turned away and sat in the leather armchair by the empty fireplace. She felt restless, without being able to focus on the reason.

Her thoughts went back to the earlier part of the day. By now she was familiar enough with most aspects of agribusiness, and her task had been made easier by the fact that Paul Liehr, unlike her other estate managers, had not made a point to impress her with his knowledge whenever the opportunity arose. He was obviously passionate about his work, and they had spoken about it for well over an hour, but at no point had he made her feel out of her depth.

Arianne had reassured him that she would maintain the current investment program in the estate, and he had obviously been pleased by his employer's support. She suddenly reproached herself for her rashness at the end of lunch. She had to be more thoughtful about the difference in their positions. The man was just a farmer in the middle of the country, not an ambassador at a dinner party in Buenos Aires.

The clock on the mantelpiece struck four. She rushed downstairs, surprised by her own enthusiasm.

Paul was already waiting for her outside, his Land Rover parked in the forecourt. As he greeted her, a stableboy approached them, leading two horses by the bridle, one of them a magnificent black Arab stallion. The silver trimmings and decorations on its saddle and reins glistened in the afternoon sun. The other horse, a bay, recognized its master, and nuzzled against Paul's shoulder.

"The horses are ready, Don Paul. I was told that you would need them at four o'clock," said the boy. Paul was visibly annoyed.

"I sent a message with Don Segundo that we will not need them," he said brusquely. The boy shuffled his feet, obviously uncomfortable.

"He didn't tell me anything, Don Paul," he mumbled, his eyes on the ground.

"I'd love to have a ride. I have been sitting all day," said Arianne, walking toward the Arabian.

"That is — " Paul was going to say "Don Simón's horse," but he stopped in midsentence. "Azucar is a very nervous animal, Señora. He doesn't like riders he doesn't know." Paul turned toward the boy. "That horse's tail is too long. I wonder what you've been doing over the last month. Not much, by the look of it," he admonished.

Arianne took the reins from the chastened stableboy and swiftly mounted the horse.

"Azucar will soon learn to know me. Let's go," she said with a smile.

AS Arianne and Paul approached the gate into the park, the gables and pinnacles of the house were visible in the distance, their brickwork almost orange in the setting sun. Their tour was over, and Arianne realized she might be home in time to see Gloria.

They were on their way back from the stud farm, which had been the last item on their schedule. Arianne's interest in horses did not go beyond turning herself into an accomplished rider for the sake of her image, and before coming to "San Simón" she had considered the possibility of closing down the stud farm as an unnecessary extravagance. But having listened attentively to Paul's explanations of the work in progress, she was not so sure. She wondered if he had guessed her thoughts, because time and again he stressed the fact that, although small in the context of the overall business, the stud farm was profitable.

Toward the end of the inspection she had kept her eyes on his face to appear attentive. The vivacity of his features in motion and the enthusiasm in his eyes made her realize that she found him good-looking. The thought briefly disconcerted her, and she decided to make an effort to concentrate on his talk. She had not come here to inspect *him*.

Intrigued by her silence, he suddenly interrupted his explanation and looked at her. Troubled by his likely awareness of her scrutiny, she quickly glanced at her watch.

"I ought to go back soon," she said. He apologized for taking so much of her time, and they left the stables. They had barely exchanged a word on the way back, and she thought it would be counterproductive to leave him with the impression that she had been less than pleased with his work.

"I am truly impressed by everything I've seen today. You are doing very good work here."

He smiled. "I am relieved, Señora. I have heard that you fire people on the spot otherwise, and I love what I do." She looked at him sharply for a moment, but she realized there was no malice in his words; he was just being honest. She smiled at him.

"Only when necessary, and you have nothing to worry about, Paul." It was the first time she had addressed him by his name, and she briefly wondered why she had not done so earlier. They stopped at the gate and Paul leaned down from the saddle to unhook the lock, pulling it open. Arianne steered her horse to the side, onto the grassy bank of the road and out of the gate's path until Paul had passed through, waiting for her on the other side. She spurred her horse on, unaware that a dry thistle on the ground had become entangled in the horse's long tail. As they went through the gate, the thistle pricked the horse's hind legs. Startled, the animal jumped toward Paul, who swiftly moved his mount to block the way. Stretching his arm, he encircled Arianne's waist and pulled her out of the saddle. He held her tight against his side, her legs in the air. Relieved of her weight, the horse ran around in confusion for a few seconds and then came to an abrupt halt nearby.

Her face pressed against his shoulder, Arianne automatically flung her arms around his neck to regain her balance. For a second she was only conscious of the feel of his shirt on her cheek, his heartbeat, and the smell of soap and warm leather. Paul jumped down, still holding her. As soon as they were on their feet he released her and walked calmly toward her horse, until he had hold of the reins. Very quietly, he moved along the horse's side. Its tail within his reach, Paul gently disentangled the thistle. He then led the horse back to Arianne.

"Are you all right, Señora? I told that boy the tail was too long. He's going to hear from me now," he muttered.

"Thank you very much for your help. I'm perfectly all right." She wasn't. Her legs were shaking, and she walked slowly toward her horse so he wouldn't notice. She climbed into the saddle, hoping Paul would not attempt to assist her. He didn't and a short while later they arrived back at the house.

THE lights of Buenos Aires spread in every direction beneath her, and Arianne was delighted that she would soon be home. The visit had jolted her. She told herself it was because of her surprising find in Simón's bedroom, but she did not allow herself the luxury of personal ruminations. Whatever Simón may or may not have felt toward her was in the past.

The plane landed smoothly, and her limousine was waiting for her on the tarmac. As she was driven away, she was pleased to notice that it was still early. She would indeed be home before Gloria went to bed.

The jacaranda trees lining the street were in blossom, huge puff-balls of lilac-colored blooms, carpeting the sidewalks with their bell-shaped flowers. It reminded her of the streets of Rio de Janeiro, a long time ago, which had also been covered in jacaranda blossoms at this time of year. But personal memories were as painful as personal feelings, and she endeavored to push them both out of her mind.

But her thoughts returned to Paul. She couldn't deny she found him attractive, but there was nothing inexplicable about it. He had the figure and glow of health of a man who spends his life in open-air pursuits, a change from the broad bottoms and pasty faces of most of her Buenos Aires managers, and he had the quiet authority of a country man with none of the arrogance of her city executives. Yes, he was attractive, but she was not going to do anything about it. She had had enough of men.

Ever since Ruben, she had seen men as nothing other than a tool for survival. They wanted her, she needed their money. Since she could not afford to respond to her emotions, she ignored them.

Before Simón appeared in her life, her looks were still her livelihood, but now she would be well paid just for being herself. No longer an inevitable imposition, sex became a cherished denial, to be able to refuse it as much a part of her vanity as the knowledge that she could trigger the need.

Perhaps Paul was the first attractive man she had come across since the roles had been reversed, since she was the one who could make things happen. Or maybe it was because *she* could now dictate the terms that she allowed herself to notice the attraction. It didn't matter, she thought as the car stopped outside the house. It was the one luxury the all-powerful Señora de la Force could not afford.

She ran upstairs and rushed into the nursery. Gloria was already in her nightgown, riding the enormous rocking horse Arianne had bought for her during her last visit to Geneva. Nana was sitting in a chair by her side, oblivious to the vitriolic glances from the uniformed nanny standing in the far corner of the room.

"Hello, my darling," she said, picking Gloria up and kissing her. As soon as she put her down, Gloria ran back to the wooden horse and climbed on it again. The nanny left her corner and came to Arianne.

"I'm giving my notice, Señora. I don't like any interference in my work. I have been offered a job by Señora de Lobos, and I have accepted it," she said disdainfully.

Arianne thought of placating her, but took one look at Nana and realized that it would be unwise.

"Fine," Arianne replied tersely. "Have a word with Nelly. You can settle all pending matters with her." The nanny left the room without a further word or a backward glance. Arianne did not like the woman, but her departure was a nuisance. She was the third nanny she had engaged since their arrival in Argentina, and Arianne was desperate to create a stable environment for her daughter. She knew that the reason behind their huffing and puffing and eventual departure was Nana, whose role in the house was impossible to explain to the staff, but equally impossible for Arianne to control. She knew that Nana wanted to be in charge of the child, as she had been in Paris, but Arianne wanted Gloria to learn Spanish and to grow up with other children, not isolated in her nursery with Nana and unable to talk to anyone else. At least Gloria had begun to speak the language; maybe it would be possible to humor Nana now.

"I want to look after Gloria," Nana said, as if she had read Arianne's thoughts. "I have that right."

Arianne was about to say something when Gloria fell off the rocking horse. Both women ran to the crying child.

"My darling, are you all right?" Arianne said, kneeling down and holding out her arms. Gloria stood up and ran straight to Nana, who took her up in her arms and rocked her gently. Arianne stood in silence for a while, then walked over to them, but Nana made no attempt to hand Gloria over to her. Arianne suddenly felt too tired, too distressed by the scene; there had been so many similar episodes recently. She leaned forward and kissed Gloria on the forehead.

"Good night, my darling. Nana will put you to bed. Sleep well," she said before turning and leaving. It was much easier to deal with business problems, she thought as she walked toward her rooms. She had some urgent papers to read tonight in preparation for tomorrow's Valle del Oro meeting. She went to her desk, turned on the reading light, and sat down. Five minutes later, she was completely absorbed by the problem of sugar export quotas to the United States and the rigidity of the Argentine market.

ARIANNE put down the phone, deep in thought. The problems, anticipated for a long time, were now reaching a crisis. She knew who she was dealing with, though, and it would have been foolish to expect anything other than a lukewarm response at first. The Russians were wily negotiators, and Madame Sherbatiev, the woman in charge of their sugar trade, was the wiliest of them all. But Edouard Golbins, whose network of contacts never ceased to amaze Arianne, had confirmed that Madame Sherbatiev would be in Paris tomorrow, ostensibly on an unexpected courtesy visit. Arianne decided to fly to Paris immediately.

Encouraged by the government's tax incentives fourteen months ago, Arianne, like most other producers in Argentina, had increased sugar planting to record levels, and conditions in the valley had ensured a bumper harvest. But, against the expected trend, domestic demand for sugar had remained static. Exports were her only hope, but Argentina was not usually an exporter, and its only market of any consequence was the U.S.A., rigidly controlled by long-agreed import quotas. She needed a substantial sale elsewhere, and she needed it immediately, but production costs in Argentina had remained above the spot market prices in London and New York for a long time.

In the tightly knit sugar market, word soon spreads about a possible supplier troubled by overproduction. She had been approached by London brokers a number of times, but she had turned down their loss-making offers, waiting for an improvement in market conditions. But the sugar was in her fields now, losing her money every day.

Hurricane Eliza was her chance. It had been expected, but it had changed course the day before, sparing other Caribbean islands but devastating Cuba. The implications for their sugar crop were obvious and, judging by their record grain purchases in America, the Russians were no longer prepared to accept the consequences of food shortages. They would have to come to the market soon. Or at least that was her guess. She would find out in Paris tomorrow.

"MADAME Sherbatiev doesn't want to see you" was Edouard Golbins's opening line to Arianne after they sat down on the sofa at one side of his large office, overlooking the Rond-Point des Champs Elysées. "I wouldn't take it personally, because she's not seeing anyone at the moment."

"I *have* to see her. Can she be persuaded?" Arianne asked.

He smiled.

"If you are suggesting sending her to Christian Dior at your expense, she is not the type. However, these Russians like to be entertained, and I spent a lot of time last night with some members of her entourage. It was exhausting, but useful," he said with a smile. Arianne noticed the dark rings under his eyes. She had some idea of the type of entertainment which would appeal to Russian negotiators abroad.

"The problem is that Argentina is not significant for them. They are looking for deals, but they can get them somewhere in the Caribbean, where they already have a large presence through Cuba, or in Africa. If the Russians were to consider a deal with you, it would only be because you offer them something you shouldn't, if you have any sense. I was told they are not interested in deals under two hundred thousand tons, they will only consider offers below the spot market price, and they want the price fixed now. A bad deal of that caliber will cost you a lot of money."

It would. Two hundred thousand tons was about double her surplus. She would not only lose on her own sugar, but she would lose much more in securing the additional tonage they required.

"Are you saying they are open to offers?" she asked.

"They haven't said that. But they haven't said they would not listen, either. I can contact them. I would say it's up to you to make an offer, but if you decide to go any further don't blame me for the consequences."

"I have a deal to offer that I don't think they will turn down." Arianne went to his desk, quickly wrote a few lines on a piece of paper, and gave it to him.

"You are mad!" Golbins said. "You're not only losing millions on the deal; you are compounding the loss."

"Maybe," she replied. "But I have a lot of sugar sitting at home, and I have to get rid of it. Sometimes one has to play Russian roulette. Phone them now."

SIX months later, twelve cargoes of sugar, amounting to three hundred thousand tons, were unloaded in Vladivostok. Scrupulous as ever in the observance of their contracts, the U.S.S.R. government immediately released payment under the unusual terms agreed. As expected, Arianne de la Force suffered a loss amounting to many millions of dollars in the transaction. As in everything else she did, she took it gracefully.

Three months after the deal was completed, OPEC's dramatic increase of the price of oil sent fear of inflation rippling through the world markets. The price of gold, depressed for years, began to climb beyond anyone's expectations, until it reached record levels at nearly three times its value nine months before. The Russian gold Arianne had received in payment for her sugar was stored in a Zurich vault; its swift disposal resulted in a net profit equal to four times her loss on the sugar deal. Madame de la Force was very pleased, but not surprised. The markets had simply behaved as she had expected.

Her marriage had made her known in business circles. Her Russian deal made her a legend.

FUCK the nun, fuck the nun, fuck the nun, Florinda repeated mentally with every stitch of bright thread into the stiff white cloth, the pattern of flowers she was embroidering at its edge slowly taking shape as the afternoon faded into evening. Soon it would be time to go back to her cell. A shadow fell on her work and she turned her head. Used as she was to it, she still found the old nun's ability to walk without making any noise unnerving. Maybe she had also been a thief before deciding to become a saint, she thought.

"That's very good work, Florinda," the nun said approvingly.

"Thank you ever so much, Sister Rosario," Florinda replied humbly, a smile of gratitude on her lips.

"You ought to put your things away until tomorrow. It's almost time now." It was Florinda's turn to sweep the room, and she rushed to the closet in the corner, picking up the broom and dustpan as if they were tools of pleasure. She meticulously swept every thread off the floor into the pan, giving a beaming smile to Sister Rosario in the process. She was careful not to include Palmira, the warden, in her smile: the ogress needed less encouragement than that to check whether a prisoner had washed properly. It was Florinda's good fortune to be small-breasted, making checks on her personal hygiene less interesting for Palmira, but she had endured a few with the same beautiful smile she now gave to Sister Rosario.

She thought of the years still ahead. Twenty-two years, or seventeen if she became eligible for parole because of good conduct. She had jumped at the chance when the pasty-faced nun had asked for volunteers. She was prepared to embroider every shitty tablecloth in Brazil for the sake of five years of her life.

Five years of what would be left of her life. By the time she got out of jail she would be forty-five, an old woman from her perspective. She would be finished. No man would want her then, not even her junk dealer. No money, no men, she would be ready for the junk pile herself. As she walked down the cheerless corridor, she kept her eyes on the back of the woman in front of her and closed her ears to the shouts of the warden. But she did not close her mind to the only thought that mattered to her: one day she was going to find her sister. Imagining what she would do to her then was the only source of joy left in Florinda's miserable life.

Part Six

29

London
July 1987

PANDORA piled up her suitcases in the entrance hall. During the cab ride from the airport into London she remembered the first time she had returned from New York, many years ago, and how small the buildings and roads had seemed by comparison. She wondered if the city would look any different to her now, but she soon realized it was as familiar, as reassuringly known, as when she had left. She was home.

She hesitated for a second before the door to her flat, then she turned the key, pushed the door open, and quickly walked across the hall into her sitting room. There, in the most personal of her environments, at its best in the morning sunlight, she was suddenly confronted with the evidence of how much she had changed.

She took in the pale yellow stippled walls, the chintz curtains in soft Vermeer blue with their pattern of cream magnolia blossoms tied back by silk ropes and tassels exactly matched to the dominant yellows and blues, the facing sofas upholstered in eau-de-nil chintz in a contrasting yet harmonious pattern with the curtains, the woodwork and the carved fireplace glazed to an ivory tint. She sat on a needlepoint stool, her eye caught for a second by the small medallion pattern of the carpet, and stared at the room for a while. She had been inordinately proud of it six months ago. Now she found it almost asphyxiating in its predictability.

She picked up her address book, and quickly flicked through it. Then she went to the telephone.

"Hello, Mr. Howard. I'm sorry to phone you at home. It's Pandora Doyle. . . . Yes, Mrs. Lyons, but I now work under my own name. . . . I wondered if you could send a couple of men to repaint my flat as soon as possible. . . . Yes, I know you did it only six months ago, but I want to change it. . . . Of course I appreciate that you're terribly busy, but I really need this done immediately. . . . "

THE girl switched off the hair dryer and put it aside, then held up a small mirror behind her customer's head. "It's *so* much more attractive; it really suits you."

Pandora raised her eyes to the mirrored wall in front of her. The short, brushed-back style brought out her high cheekbones, and the new streaks in a subtle shade of copper enhanced the blue-green of her eyes, complementing the makeup she had adopted in New York. She checked the back of her head in the girl's mirror: the haircut also flattered the long, graceful line of her neck, and she smiled her approval.

"I like it. You've done exactly what I wanted." She stood up, and the girl helped her out of her pink kimonolike robe, then began to brush Pandora's shoulders meticulously, but Pandora moved away, too impatient to wait for her to finish.

"Please don't bother; it's all right. Thank you very much for your help," she said as she opened her purse to tip the girl. She was eager to leave, and took her jacket from the closet before the girl had time to get it for her.

She had spent her first Sunday in London taking down curtains and packing away pictures and ornaments. A few pieces of furniture could be auctioned; the rest would go to a house-clearance dealer. Then she had gone through her wardrobe, weeding out her old outfits to make space for her New York clothes. It had been then, while briefly holding up her new clothes against her body in front of the mirror, that she decided she needed a new haircut *now*. That morning she had waited impatiently until 9:31 to phone her hairdresser for an appointment. After a long discussion with the receptionist about how booked they were, she had managed to cajole an appointment for ten o'clock. Now it was done, and she wanted to get on with the rest of her day.

A few yards away from the hairdresser, she was approached by a smiling young man holding a green box.

"It's for Friends of the Earth," he told her, and she stopped. During the flight from New York she had read a *Newsweek* cover story on the devastation of the Amazon rain forest. She had felt both concerned and powerless about it. This was her chance to do something. She pulled a ten-pound note from her purse and slipped it into the collection box.

"Thank you *very* much. Would you like to become a member?" the man asked.

She thought for a moment.

"Yes, I would. I admire what you do." He leaned down and rummaged through his satchel, propped against the wall behind him. He produced a clipboard, asked her for her name and address, and filled in a form, which she signed. It took less than a minute, and she was once again on her way, her head feeling light and free without the accustomed weight of her hair.

SITTING on her drawing-room floor, Pandora checked her notes. There were a few shops she hadn't covered during her wanderings around different areas of London over the last three days, and she would visit them tomorrow. But she was already able to form a picture of the interior design market.

The corollary was clear. There was a mainstream modern style, epitomized by designer mat-black, expensive fabrics, and Italian furniture at the top end of that market. Then there were endless variations on the Victorian period, from cheap to high-priced. Both styles were ready for retirement: they had been around for a decade. She had to find a new angle.

She glanced at her now empty sitting room, and realized there was an equally urgent, although less momentous, priority. She had to buy new furniture for her own home, at least a few basic pieces. She had seen in various shops a few modern pieces she would like to have, but there was a four-to-six-weeks' wait. Ironic as it was, old furniture was immediately available.

"I'LL take the kitchen table and that pair of Welsh chairs," Pandora told the lady at the antique shop. "Please arrange for delivery as early in the morning as possible. I live just around the corner."

The starkly simple furniture, its old wood stripped of any polish, had been the only items that had appealed to her. Not only did she like them, but also there was something pleasantly familiar about them. She wrote a check and left, glad that the whole operation had taken very little of her time. She was now ready to start her tour of the few remaining shops she had listed the night before.

It was when she reached the railings around the Kensington Church yard that she suddenly remembered why her choice of furniture had seemed so familiar. The old Welsh chairs and the plain table were very similar to the Shaker furniture she had glimpsed briefly in New York, on her way to the office from Geraldine's home after they had had breakfast together. She felt a rush of almost uncontrollable excitement. She had found *her* theme.

"FROM what you've said, I think I know someone in London who could be very useful to you. His name is Chris Outram, and the firm is Outram Cullinan. They are business and management consultants, and they advise me on certain aspects of my business in France. They are tops in their field. I'll phone him, and tell him to expect your call." Arianne's voice came very clear over the occasional satellite blip.

While going over her figures the day before, Pandora had decided to phone Arianne on impulse, partly in genuine need of advice, but also for some much-needed support after her latest conversations with her accountant, who was clearly worried about the possible risks of her plan. But she had been told that Mrs. de la Force was away on her yacht, and she had been relieved when she put the phone down. Her problems were her own concern, after all.

But Arianne returned her call, showing genuine interest in Pandora's ideas. It was wonderful to have somebody's support for a change.

"I'm really grateful for your help," Pandora said. "I need an objective view as to how viable my project might be. I'll call Chris Outram and mention your name." The conversation had reached its end and, warm as her response had been, Arianne had given no indication that she wanted to discuss anything else, but Pandora decided she ought to give her the opportunity to do so, if she wanted to.

"I hope everything's well with you," she said.

"Yes, thank you, the weather is glorious and I'm having a very relaxing time. You mentioned you're drafting a report on your proposal for your bankers. Please send me a copy as soon as you have it. I would like to read it. I'll see you in Venice, I hope."

Pandora took the cue.

"I will send you a copy, and of course I'm coming to Venice. I couldn't possibly miss it. It will be marvelous," she said.

"I look forward to seeing you. Please call me if you need anything else. Good-bye."

Pandora put the phone down, and inspected the figures in front of her once again. There was only one way to go, only one viable strategy. But it was better not to think too much about the consequences if it didn't work.

IT was a beautiful morning, the large plane trees filtering the sunshine into patterns of light and shade. The pale gray stonework of the twin towers of St. John Smith Square seemed almost white in the midday sun when Pandora left the building on the corner.

Chris Outram had asked her some piercing questions at first, but once she had explained her project to him, and he had realized that she knew what she was talking about, he had been extremely supportive, although carefully underlining the risks. After a while he had called in one of the firm's experts on the retailing sector and had made his excuses, leaving them to go through the proposal in detail. They had spent the whole morning discussing every aspect of it. Both her hopes and her fears had been confirmed.

After her moment of discovery four weeks ago, she had put together the designs for her Shaker-inspired furniture and fabrics. One morning, while working at home she received a thick envelope from Friends of the Earth. Inside she found holding literature on ecology and guides to environmentally safer products, as well as confirmation of her membership. She read it all, and it sparked a further refinement of her idea: she would use renewable resources and natural dyes as much as possible. It not only made sense to her because of her personal views, but it would also be a valuable marketing angle: *A gentle style for a gentler world,* she thought.

She then approached her old suppliers for manufacturing prices and color-test runs on the fabrics. It had meant several trips to the north of England and many hours in East End workshops. She had stressed the urgency of it, and she had begun to receive estimates during the last week.

As expected, the cost difference between large and small runs was staggering. Small-scale production meant opening a shop similar to her former one, and she already knew the dangers involved. The investment would not be beyond her means, but she could not afford another failure.

There was a further danger. While it would have been possible a few years ago to open a small shop on the strength of a fresh idea, and expand carefully on the basis of its eventual success, the retailing scene had become ferociously competitive. It did not take long these days for the established chains or large retailers to pirate any successful idea from the more adventurous small outlets, killing it off in no time with lower prices and market saturation. Her concept was her main weapon, and if she was to exploit it to the full, she had to appear on the market with a presence strong enough, and prices low enough, to overcome the inevitable copycat businesses. She had a new angle, she had the designs, and she sensed it would work. But at a price.

Several outlets, central locations, and sizable stocks were essential, apart from capable staff, a warehouse, vans for distribution, a large promotion campaign. She remembered Arianne's advice about the dangers of starting small. It was sensible, and easy from Arianne's perspective. It just meant money, lots of money, of which she had an endless supply, but Pandora did not.

She had spent most of her day yesterday on the phone to people she knew in the real estate business, making preliminary inquiries. The response was identical in all cases, accompanied by much sympathetic murmuring. It was very difficult to find suitable space in central London in the middle of the current retailing boom; where such space was available it commanded substantial key money, and landlords preferred to rent to established chains rather than unknown newcomers. She would have to pay significantly over the odds to be considered as a suitable tenant. She would need to pay no less than three quarters of a million per shop of the size she needed, before she even began to think about the refurbishment costs. It would require millions to go ahead.

She had phoned her broker to sell some of the stocks she had bought with the money from the sale of her house in Fulham, but she had already used the proceeds for the prototypes and trial runs she had commissioned. Even if she sold the whole lot in the currently buoyant market, she would raise only about two hundred thousand pounds. She could mortgage her flat for a further hundred and fifty thousand, and her father had left her money in trust which she could borrow against. She could sell the New York apartment. But even counting every penny she could lay her hands on, it was still a fraction of the total she needed. She would have to borrow the rest. It was not yet possible to quantify the precise figure, but her guess last night had been between five and six million.

At least one of her worries seemed to have been taken care of. She had mentioned the question of competent management to Chris Outram. "I can work seven days a week, but I can't do everything myself. I will need efficient managers, and it takes a long time to put a working team together. Ideally, I ought to find an existing team, and poach it."

"I know for a fact that Martha Bradley's management is very unhappy," Chris had told her, "and a few of them are looking for an opportunity like this. They are the best team around. We can arrange informal contacts for you." Martha Bradley had been one of the great success stories in the decorating world during the early seventies, but she had sold her company last year and had retired to Barbados. Pandora would definitely contact the Bradley team, but she needed a secretary now. She would phone some agencies once she was back at the flat.

The first massive hurdle was to raise the money, though. Nothing would be possible without it. Pandora remembered Arianne's offer, but decided she had been right to turn it down. She did not need a friend to do her a favor; she needed a banker willing to invest in a viable business.

*　　*　　*

"I did not have dinner in my room that day. Young man, I have not had dinner on my own for the last twenty years, and I find it intolerable that I should be presented with such a mistake at a hotel like La Reserve," the old woman said. She had been complaining about her bill for the last five minutes in the nasal tone peculiar to the French aristocracy. Charles Murdoch was tempted to interrupt her and ask the concierge for the key to his room, but he had recognized Céline de Merteuil. He had never asked why, but he knew that Arianne disliked her and, as with so many of Arianne's likes and dislikes, he had made it his own. He preferred to avoid her.

It had been an enjoyable holiday, or rather a most constructive use of his time. *Holiday* was a word that had long ceased to have any meaning for Charles, but the purpose of his visit here was accomplished, and he was now leaving for Saint-Tropez.

As soon as Gloria had left New York, he had found out from Kayzie that she had made last-minute arrangements to stay at Paola Santa Coloma's villa in Cap Ferrat, and he had immediately booked himself into La Reserve in Beaulieu. At the Nice airport he had briefly toyed with the idea of renting a small Renault, less noticeable than a bigger car, but he was not able to overcome his reluctance to squeeze his six-foot-three frame into it, and settled for a two-door Mercedes.

It had taken him three days of waiting outside the gates of Paola's villa before he was able to make contact with Gloria. The first day, he saw the two girls drive in Paola's Ferrari to one of the villas nearby, where they spent the day. On the second day he followed them to Monte Carlo harbor, where they boarded one of the big yachts moored there. His opportunity came on the evening of the third day, when the girls left the villa with a couple of young wimps dressed all in white, both with slicked-back dark hair.

He tailed their car until they stopped outside Les Hirondelles and went into the restaurant. Charles waited for a moment, then followed them.

He told the man at the door that he was joining some other people. He quickly scanned the room: Gloria and her friends were sitting on the terrace overlooking the harbor. He stepped outside and walked around the tables as if searching for someone. His eyes met Gloria's, and he approached her.

"Gloria! What on earth are you doing here? You're the last person I was expecting to see."

Gloria raised her eyebrows.

"What are *you* doing here?" she asked.

"Oh, I'm trying to have a few days of peace and quiet on my own. New York was a bit hectic," he said, his voice conveying the significance of the last sentence. "I'm at La Reserve. I bumped into the Cliffords earlier today, and they said that I could join their party for dinner, but I must have misheard the restaurant they mentioned."

He sensed Gloria's hesitation. If their conversation went on for much longer, she would have to introduce him to her friends or, even worse, she would have to explain to them who he was.

"I'd better go back to the hotel and have dinner there." He indicated his book. "I'm enjoying my solitude, but I would love to spend a little time with you. Give me your number, and I'll call you tomorrow." Gloria dithered for a moment, then asked Paola for the number. Charles wrote it down. He sensed Paola's eyes on him, but he did not return her look; he had to be careful now. He said goodbye to Gloria, smiled sweetly at the table at large, and sauntered out. He truly enjoyed his dinner at the hotel that evening, particularly the half-bottle of very fine Chablis suggested by the wine steward.

The rest had been easier than he had expected. He went to Paola's villa for a drink the following evening, and he was at his most charming. As he was leaving, he managed to take Gloria discreetly aside for a moment to tell her that he would like to have a quiet word with her as soon as possible, because he had something very important to tell her. He got up early the following morning, and notified the desk to transfer any calls for him to the poolside telephone. He only had time to improve the tan on the left side of his face before Gloria called.

She told him that she would be on her own in the house later that day, as Paola had arranged to sail with some people whom Gloria found unbearable. She suggested that he spend the morning with her by their pool. As he was let into the house the servant asked him to wait in the drawing room. He left Charles alone for a moment while he went to tell Gloria that her guest had arrived. Charles quickly returned to the hall and slipped the brown envelope he was carrying into the top drawer of a chest close to the staircase. By the time Gloria appeared he was standing in the drawing room, absorbed in the contemplation of Warhol's portrait of Paola's mother.

Although it was very hot, he did not follow Gloria into the pool. After a moment he announced that he was going inside to the bathroom, and walked briskly toward the house. He took the envelope from the drawer in the hall and rushed upstairs. Earlier, he had asked Gloria if her room had a view of the sea. She had pointed to her window, and he had no trouble now in finding her bedroom. He went into the bathroom, and locked the door. He saw Gloria's beauty case on the marble vanity. He opened it, and found what he wanted. It took him only a moment to make the swap. As he left the room he noticed a pile of discarded shopping bags by the door, soon to be removed by the maid. He put the brown envelope and the box he had removed from Gloria's case at the bottom of one of the bags, covered it with crumpled sheets of tissue paper, and ran downstairs again.

Gloria was still in the pool when he returned. Feeling on top of the world, Charles rushed down the broad staircase linking the terraces, flung his Lacoste shirt onto one of the chairs by the pool, and dove in, pausing just long enough at the edge to give Gloria a full view of his muscular body, his tan emphasized by his white swimming trunks.

He swam a few lengths and then stopped in the shallow end, waiting for Gloria to join him.

"Your breaststroke could be improved. You don't spread your arms wide enough," he said. "I'll show you; just swim toward me."

As she came close, he slipped his left arm under her belly, holding her weight. The tip of his fingers slid under the edge of her bikini top, barely touching her nipple. He held her hand with his right arm, their fingers intertwined, and gently guided her strokes.

"There, you see, a wider reach makes it much more powerful," he murmured. He repeated the motion a few times, his left arm thrust forward by her body movements, until her breast was cupped in his hand. A white-jacketed waiter appeared, carrying a tray. The man briefly surveyed the scene, left the tray on a table by their seats, and returned discreetly to the house. Charles sensed Gloria's confusion, and decided it was time to stop. The prize was within reach now, but a little more work was necessary.

"This is lovely, but I need to talk to you," he said, gently helping her to the pool steps. They went back to their chairs, and he poured two glasses of orange juice from the iced jug on the tray. He handed a glass to Gloria. His eyes on hers, he began his long-rehearsed speech.

"Gloria, this is very difficult for me to say . . ." He paused briefly, to underline the significance of the moment. "I have decided to leave your mother. All relationships run their course, and it would be foolish for me to pretend otherwise." As he expected, her face betrayed a mixture of suspicion and interest. He stood up and continued talking, his head down as if overwhelmed by the burden of what he was saying.

"I know what you are thinking, that I am a worthless gigolo, only interested in money. You are partly right, as far as the past is concerned. I was a carefree young man when Arianne and I met. Your mother's money overwhelmed me, as I know it has overwhelmed you in a different way." He hoped that the frank admission of guilt would pass for sincerity, and the reference to their shared predicament might stir Gloria's sympathy.

"But I am a different person now. I know that money is just a mirage. Other things are much more significant, at least on a personal level. I have changed, and I need the help of someone who believes in me to keep me honest." He knew from experience that few women would not respond to such an appeal from an attractive man. For someone so lacking in self-confidence as Gloria it would be irresistible.

"I have long accepted the fact that your mother does not love me. In fact, I think she would be glad to get rid of me. Our relationship has been just an arrangement for years." It was the first true statement he had made so far, and it helped to maintain the sincerity of his tone. "My pride stopped me from confronting it, but what has happened now, your mother's machinations against you, made me face the fact that you are the one that really matters to me."

He sat down and hid his face in his hands. He sighed deeply, then carried on.

"As you became a woman, I realized that you meant much more

to me than I wanted to admit. I knew that you did not like me, and I don't blame you for that. More to the point, I also knew that you could only see me as interested in your fortune, and even I had doubts in that respect. But your mother's duplicity toward you has made things much clearer for me. She might make you penniless, but I still want you. You are the only woman in the world to me." He stood up abruptly and walked away, as if his embarrassment at having bared his feelings was too much for him. As soon as he disappeared from Gloria's sight behind the pool house, he stopped and waited.

At last able to gather her thoughts, Gloria was puzzled. She had been tempted to stop him in the middle of his platitudes: she found it almost insulting that he could believe she would fall for such a pack of trite lies. But he was not a fool, and the only possible reason for him to make such an embarrassing speech was that somehow he meant it. She had noticed before that a man trying to be sincere about his feelings usually makes an ass of himself. He was not there because of her money; he was the only man in the world who knew her mother was disowning her.

She wanted him. She found him physically very attractive, and he could be useful as an ally. Her original plan had been to taste forbidden fruit, have a good time, and then embarrass her mother by revealing their affair, getting rid of him in the process. Now it would be more productive to join forces with him, at least for a while, and have a spy in her mother's camp.

Whatever his reasons he was there now, and the sun always stirred her appetite for good sex. It would be fun to humor him. She stood up, adopted her sweetest expression, and walked after him, hoping that the fool had not left the villa.

Behind the pool house, Charles heard her approaching steps and left his cover, walking toward her. One look at her face was enough. He opened his arms and drew her tightly against him.

"My darling, my darling," he murmured, stroking her hair. His hand under her chin, he gently raised her head and kissed her, softly at first, then his tongue pushed into her mouth.

He picked her up in his arms without breaking their kiss and walked into the pool house. He undid her bikini strings and laid her gently on the pile of sun mattresses, her golden skin shimmering in the blue half-light reflected from the pool. Staring at him, she yanked down his swimming trunks and pulled him on top of her.

His hand moved slowly down her body, his teeth gently gripping first one nipple, then the other, his fingers and his tongue making her longing for him unbearable. Guiding him with her hand, she moaned as he entered her, her nails clawing his back. She was overcome by her pleasure. She needed him now, and she would need him again.

"I love you, I love you," he said, in rhythm with his long, deep thrusts. After a while he mentally began to count them. Premature ejaculation was not one of his problems, but he needed to take his mind off what was going on. Even for him, what he was about to do required unusual control.

As he counted "forty," he suddenly pulled away from her, and stood up. "No," he cried, "no, this is not right! I'm forcing you to do what I want, without any consideration for your feelings." He picked up his clothes and quickly slipped on his trousers. He knelt by her side; her face was covered by the flush of her imminent, and now suddenly truncated, orgasm.

"I want you to come to me when you are sure of what you are doing, not before . . ." He kissed her deeply and walked away, then he stopped by the door and looked longingly back at her.

"I'm driving to Saint-Tropez now. I think that we both need to be alone for a couple of days. I'll be staying at Byblos. We have to think very seriously about this, my love," he said, then he turned and left. He ran to the gate, got into his car and drove away.

As soon as he was out of sight of the house he stopped the car, slapped his thigh, threw back his head, and roared with laughter. He knew that she would come to Saint-Tropez even if she had to walk on water to get there. But he needed to pick up some girl fast. His balls were aching and he felt randy as hell.

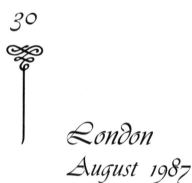

30

*London
August 1987*

PANDORA did not like the restaurant. The food was too rich, and the decor attempted to suggest elegance and class by piling up brass-framed hunting and racing prints on its Ultrasuede walls. She found it crass, although it probably worked for the clientele, mostly Far Eastern businessmen escorting expensive call girls with streaked blond manes, and a few local Mayfair men with exotic-looking young women. Pandora lost interest in the scene, and tried to concentrate on her companion.

He was not very interesting, either, but he could be useful. She hoped he would be. She had not seen Peter Wentworth-Briggs for years. He had married a girl who had been at school with Pandora, and she and Johnny had bumped into them a few times at cocktail parties or City functions.

Things had moved fast since her meeting with Chris Outram, and they had met a number of times to develop the business strategy. Pandora had developed her design concepts at the same time, discussed production and delivery schedules with suppliers, and had talks with her prospective management team. Her enthusiasm and drive were contagious, and soon she had the core of a first-class management group. They were ready to jump on board as soon as *she* was ready. But she still had to find the money.

She had phoned every friend, every relation with a banking connection. It was always the same story. A very interesting concept, the figures appeared good on paper, but they were either fully committed to their existing clients, or they were hesitant about increasing their exposure, or, or, or. One of her second cousins said charitably, after turning down her proposal with the utmost tact, that he hoped she would find another husband soon.

In the course of one of her many conversations in some City conference room or other, someone had mentioned to her that Peter Wentworth-Briggs was in charge of venture capital at Tomkins & Cruikshank, a long-established merchant bank. She phoned him the following morning.

It took him a moment to place her, but he sounded encouraging over the telephone. He was about to go on holiday, but he suggested she send him the papers. If he thought that her proposition made sense, he would call her. Pandora would have preferred to see him in person first, but she had no choice. She sent him the documents by courier as soon as she put the phone down.

He called her two days later. He was interested, but there were a few points he would like to discuss with her. He suggested dinner the following day, the only time he could see her before leaving for Nice in the morning to join his family. She agreed.

The situation was critical. A real estate agent informed her ten days ago that a small chain of retail outlets in Central London were for sale: four shops of the ideal size, located on the King's Road, Long Acre, Kensington Church Street, and Brook Street. They were excellent locations, and the agent told her that it would be a waste of time to offer anything under four million. It was almost impossible to find properties like these for sale in the current climate, and it was a unique chance to set up her London chain in one go. She could not miss it. But after inspection she realized the shops would need substantial alterations for her purposes, adding a further million to her costs. She would need five million *now*, without taking into account any other commitments.

Pandora had walked into the restaurant with the conviction of the desperate. She *had* to get the money. She put up with Peter's small talk while they had a drink, but as soon as he ordered, she pulled her papers out of her briefcase and spread them on the table.

Once she began to go through the proposal, she realized that Peter seemed to have forgotten most of the facts, and she carefully went over each item, point by point. Halfway through her explanation about her marketing strategy, she noticed that his eyes were wandering around the room.

"There you have someone who could solve your problem very quickly. He can't stop looking at you, and I can't blame him. You look gorgeous tonight," he said.

"Who are you talking about?" she asked, her annoyance just showing in her voice.

"Ted Carson," Peter replied. "His eye for women is obviously as good as his eye for business."

Like most people in England, Pandora knew who Ted Carson was. He had built a large conglomerate in Australia from nothing, and had now settled in Britain, where his audacious (some said buccaneer) approach to business kept him in the newspapers virtually every day. She would not have glanced in his direction, no matter how many breweries or newspapers he was trying to buy, had it not been for the fact that she remembered he was supposed to have been the underbidder for the painting on the night she first saw Arianne. She was curious to see what he looked like.

In fact he looked exactly as she would have imagined. He was big, not fat, the white hair at his temples emphasizing his leathery tan. He had just enough lines to give character to his face, but he was not old, probably in his mid-forties, and his casual clothes added to his youthful appearance. He was not handsome but he was attractive in a coarse way, and he smiled broadly as he caught her eye. Pandora immediately turned her face away, and carried on doggedly with her explanation to Peter.

He made occasional comments, but by the time Pandora reached the last page it was obvious that he was not really interested in anything she had been saying.

"... and the short of it, Peter, is that I need five million at least. As I've shown you, the market is there, and the return would be well above average retail profits. It will work, and you know it," she finished forcefully, in a last desperate attempt to capture his attention.

The waiter cleared their plates away.

"Would you like some coffee?" Peter asked.

"Yes, please," she replied impatiently. It was about time he committed himself either way.

"The bill, please," Peter said to the waiter. "We can have coffee at my place," Peter continued. "We can talk in peace and quiet there. Miranda is already in France with the children," he finished, giving Pandora a meaningful glance.

She felt outraged, but restrained herself from showing it.

"I can't imagine what we can discuss at your home that we can't discuss right now. Since we are already here, please ask the waiter to bring the coffee."

A quizzical expression briefly came to Peter's face, then he called the waiter back and ordered. As the waiter left, Peter leaned forward, his hand almost touching hers.

"I like your business proposition. I like it a lot. But as you can appreciate, I would have to convince my people about its merits. It would help my enthusiasm if *you* were as convincing as possible tonight."

"Are you saying that you would consider lending me five million pounds if I go to bed with you? In other circumstances it might be almost flattering, but certainly not now," she said point-blank. She felt enraged at his easy assumption about the eventual outcome of the evening.

"You are putting it rather crudely," he replied, clearly uncomfortable at her directness. "What I would say is that there are plenty of takers for five million pounds, all with viable propositions. You ought to be flattered that I might be prepared to consider yours. I told you that you are a very beautiful girl. I remembered you as soon as you phoned me," he said, touching her hand. Pandora began to gather her papers and put them in her briefcase, then she stood up. She noticed she was attracting attention to herself, but she didn't care.

"Why don't you buy yourself a calculator and strap it to your prick? It will make your approach to business meetings a great deal clearer to prospective clients." Impervious to the commotion around her, Pandora stormed toward the exit.

She did not even notice that Ted Carson's eyes were on her, like everybody else's. It would not have mattered if she did. The only thing on her mind was that she had to find five million pounds within three weeks.

*   *   *

LYING by the side of the hotel pool at the right angle to maximize his exposure to the sun, Charles waved his hand at the waiter nearby.

"Campari and soda, please," he ordered.

He had been in Saint-Tropez for ten days now, and he was bored. More than that, he was worried. He had expected Gloria to turn up the day after their meeting, but she hadn't.

After four days he rang Paola's villa. The butler told him that Mademoiselle de la Force had departed the day before.

He had no choice but to stay put and wait for Gloria to appear. He had scored with a couple of girls during his enforced stay, but casual pickups were no longer much fun. Both girls had insisted on safe sex.

The waiter returned with his drink. Charles sipped it slowly, watching the crowd around the pool. Most of the women were lean and fit, their gold jewelry and white bikinis showing off their tanned skin, but a few of them had slitlike navels, the unmistakable sign of a belly tuck, the surgeon's scalpel creating a navel where none used to be. He wondered if Arianne had had a few tucks here and there. She still was as beautiful as when they had first met, even more so. She was a bit of a wreck then, but even at her worst she had looked better than most women. Still, that had been twelve years ago, and the clock ticks for everyone.

It was perfectly possible that she had had a face-lift during one of her many trips on her own, but maybe she didn't need it; maybe money and power were her Elixir of Youth. People would say that she was gorgeous even if she used nitric acid to take off her makeup. She didn't need to worry about her looks, and not worrying about something was probably the best way to ensure that it would not become a problem.

Maybe he should listen to his own wisdom and stop worrying about Gloria, he thought. He *had* to believe that she would turn up, sooner or later.

It was past one o'clock. He didn't feel hungry, but he decided to have a light lunch. Anything to kill time. He walked to the poolside terrace, where the maître d' immediately showed him to one of the best tables in the shade. He had just finished ordering when he saw

Gloria. His heart jumped. He immediately stood up and walked toward her, an adoring smile on his face.

"My darling, you don't know how worried I've been for you. I called the villa, but they couldn't tell me where you'd gone," he said, taking her hand.

"Oh, I've been here and there," she replied rather curtly.

"Would you like to have lunch?" he asked as they sat down.

"No, thank you. I have to tell you something." She seemed distracted.

Shit, he thought. This was not what he had expected, and it didn't sound as if he would like whatever she had to say. His only chance was not to let her speak, not at least until he had had time to work on her.

The waiter returned and placed a lobster salad in front of Charles. It looked delicious, but he couldn't afford to sit here now and give her time to say whatever was on her mind.

"Take it back, I'm not hungry. Just put it on my bill," he told the waiter, handing him a hundred-franc tip. He immediately stood up.

"We can't talk here," he said, nodding toward the occupied tables nearby. "Let's go to my room. We'll have more privacy." He walked away before she had time to reply, but was relieved to notice that she was following him.

Once inside the elevator, he embraced her.

"You don't know how I've longed for this moment," he murmured between kisses. She seemed to respond, but guardedly. He was seriously worried now.

They walked into his room, his arm around her waist. He kicked the door shut, and kissed her again before she could say anything at all. He lifted her and carried her to the bed, his hands all over her body. She was wearing just a long T-shirt. He endeavored to roll it up without breaking their embrace.

"Not now," Gloria said twice, but her conviction was noticeably weaker the second time.

"I love you, I love you," he said again and again, kissing her constantly to shut her up. Occasionally she was still trying to speak, and he briefly thought soixante-neuf might be a solution. It would certainly silence her, but on the other hand it might be counterproductive if tried so soon. This was supposed to be romance, not fun. At last he heard her moan and decided that it was safe to take off his clothes, but as soon as he shifted his weight from her she sat bolt upright.

"I must tell you this now," she said, avoiding his eyes and clearly embarrassed. "I've got herpes. I had a flare-up at the villa, and I'm very contagious at this stage. That's why I didn't come to you immediately."

Charles was thunderstruck. He knew from friends that the condition is extremely painful and incurable, but he could not risk delaying making love to her any longer, giving her time to change her mind, and he couldn't wear a condom either. He had no guarantee she would stay with him; he needed to score a bull's-eye. He had no choice.

He managed to conceal his fear. He also managed to regain his excitement, momentarily deflated by Gloria's sudden revelation.

"My darling, it doesn't matter to me. There's nothing in this world I want more than you, and I want you now," he said, taking her in his arms.

"Do you really mean that?" she asked. He sensed hope in her voice.

"Making love to you, being with you, is all that matters to me," he reassured her.

He slowly pushed her down on the bed and, after a few moments, resigned to his possible fate, he gently parted her thighs.

The things one has to do for money, he thought.

31

*London
September 1987*

PANDORA held the check up for a few moments, staring at the figure in the box immediately above the dotted line. It was the largest check she had ever written, and now she had to sign it.

She looked at the stream of zeros, which reminded her of the jackpot of a TV game show. She could imagine the host, probably wearing some lurid tuxedo, holding his hand up and shouting to the audience: "Give me a four!" "FOUR!" they would roar. "Now give me a zero," the man would bellow, only to be dutifully obliged. "Now give me another zero," he would plead, the figures going up in lights behind him, one after the other. ". . . and another one . . ." At last, his silhouette outlined against the wall of lights, he would chant "Ladies and gentlemen, we have FOUR HUNDRED THOU-SAND POUNDS!" At the mention of the figure the audience would applaud wildly, the chorus girls would launch into a dance routine displaying their highest kicks, and the band would burst into . . . what? Pandora thought for a moment; maybe any of the disco versions of the Beatles' "Money" would do. She not only wanted it, she needed it desperately.

Since her fiasco with Peter Wentworth-Briggs at the restaurant she had tried every other possible source of venture capital. She was still waiting to hear from a couple of people she had seen two weeks before, but events had finally overtaken her. The offer for the chain of shops had to be submitted tomorrow, and a check for an amount equivalent to ten percent of the offered price had to be included as a deposit with the tender documents. It would take months, maybe years, to find similar properties, and she could not afford to lose her team or her suppliers, neither of which would accommodate an indefinite wait. Her only chance was to send in the tender documents with the check, commit every penny she had, and hope that the rest of the money would materialize from somewhere. She preferred not to think about the consequences if it didn't.

Having gone this far, she could not back down. It was not just that she couldn't tell anyone she wasn't able to raise the money. What she really and truly could not do was to face yet another personal failure.

She was starkly aware of her recklessness. She was about to sign a commitment to pay nearly half a million pounds, and a promise to pay a further three and a half million on completion, plus legal fees, plus . . . money, money, money. She had been advised to pay well over the odds to get the shops, and she was likely to succeed. If she found the money. The adjustment to the originally estimated starting cost had pushed the figure she really needed to six million pounds.

Well, it's only *money,* she thought. Either she would find it, or she would not. She picked up the pen, swiftly signed the check, and clipped it to the other documents. She carefully sealed the huge envelope, and left it on the other desk in the tiny temporary office she had rented a month ago. She had asked Sophie, her new secretary, to send the envelope by courier first thing in the morning.

She looked at the envelope for the last time, and left the room. She still had to pack. She had thought of canceling the trip at the last minute, but the invitation to Arianne's ball had arrived with a first-class plane ticket and a note that a room had already been booked at the Gritti. She would be in Venice only for the night, and she badly needed a break.

One last fling in Arianne's glamorous world, and then back to reality. Next week either she would get a phone call saying that the money was available, or all hell would break loose.

ALONE in her suite at the Hassler, lying on her bed, Gloria stared at the ceiling. The huge box from Tirelli holding her costume was in one corner of the room, next to the rest of her luggage, soon to be picked up by a porter. But she couldn't think about her costume, or anything else. Not since the phone call she had received about an hour ago.

During her last days in the South of France she had noticed that she was feeling nauseated in the morning. The smell of cooking fat in restaurants made her feel sick, and she had a metallic taste in her mouth. Just before she left for Rome, she had noticed that her breasts had become fuller, and sometimes she felt a tingling sensation around the nipples. If it weren't for the fact that she was on the Pill, she would have worried about being pregnant. The alternative was that she was ill, a thought which frightened her. She had asked Paola for the address of her doctor in Rome, and had made an appointment to see him the day she arrived there.

She now knew that she was pregnant. Charles's child, of all people's. Her first reaction was to curse her bad luck, then the damned, useless Pill. Next she thought of having an abortion, but after a while she realized that she could not do it. Her child was the first thing in her life to be truly her own, something which she did not owe to her mother in any way. She suddenly had a role, to be somebody's mother, and she did not give a damn about the implications or what other people would say. Some years ago she would have been terrified of Nana's reaction to the news, of her displeasure, but even Nana's feelings did not matter much to Gloria now. Nana had been the only person who had really loved her, but in the end she had been as unsympathetic to Gloria as everybody else.

Obviously she would have to tell her mother, and she would do it as soon as possible. But Arianne did not need to know who the father was. It was unlikely that, having kept Gloria's own father a secret for so long, she would have the nerve to press Gloria on the subject. As for Charles, it would suit him to keep the matter quiet. Disclosure would mean the end of his meal ticket.

The news had forced her to think about Charles and what she felt about him. It had all begun as a lark. But she had to admit that the sex had been great. It was hard to spend nearly a month having torrid sex with an attractive man who talked about love without somehow entering into the game oneself. She did not know what she felt for him, but whatever it was it no longer mattered. What mattered to her now was her baby.

She heard a discreet knock on the door. The porter was there; time to go. Gloria got up, picked up her bag from the dressing table, and walked to the drawing room to let the porter in. She was ready to go to Venice.

CHARLES liked his reflection in the mirror. The shaving lather brought out his deep tan, which in turn accentuated the luminous blue of his eyes. He smiled at himself, but quickly dropped his smile when he realized that the white foam made his teeth look yellow. He began to shave instead.

He was glad to be back in New York, temporarily out of Gloria's reach, although his time with her in the South of France had been better than expected. After a few days, the little vixen had owned up that the herpes story was a complete fabrication, her way of checking the sincerity of his feelings. He was greatly relieved to know that he was not at risk, and that his courage had paid off.

Gloria had been good company at times, and certainly enthusiastic about sex. They had been together for nearly six weeks, with sporadic breaks for Gloria to keep up with part of her schedule of invitations to yachts and villas. Charles dissuaded her from completely disappearing from sight, because it would trigger Arianne's concern. The last thing he wanted was some private detective on Gloria's trail.

Gloria could already be pregnant, but maybe not. There was always the possibility that he had been sold genuine birth control pills at the ludicrous price of fakes, but he preferred not to consider that possibility.

He had contacted Louis Morello in New York as soon as he found out what pill Gloria was taking. Although he had bargained hard on the strength of their long-past association, it had cost Charles three thousand dollars a box to have the duplicates made. It was an outrageous price for sugar pills, but a bargain in the context of what they would do for him. It was pointless to agonize about what might have gone wrong.

Before leaving the room, he stood in front of the full-length mirror for a final inspection. There was no doubt in his mind that he was a fine-looking man, but there was one thought that had been worrying him for a short while. He went closer to the mirror and smiled. He was immensely relieved to notice that, the shaving cream gone, his teeth were as white as usual: he would not need to make an appointment with the dental hygienist after all.

HER arms resting on the railings, her hair blowing in the lagoon's breeze, Arianne could see the distant outline of Santa Maria della Salute in the summer haze. The yacht had just dropped anchor, and the motorboat was being winched down to the sea to take her ashore.

Over the last ten years she had looked forward to her annual ball, but not now. It had started as a business tool, a way of building up her profile and strengthening her contacts. After a while, the original purpose became clouded by habit, and she simply enjoyed the pomp and glitter of the occasion. But now she had gone through the process many times, and the game had lost its edge.

Now that she sensed that she was about to lose Gloria, she wondered if it had been worth it. But her problem was not really Gloria; there had been troubles between them before. Her problem was Charles. It was true that he was able to hold her to ransom for his silence, but any ransom is payable in the end. She had thought a lot about Charles during that summer, and she had thought about herself.

She had agreed to Charles's terms originally because of fear, but once her fear had subsided, as time went by, she could have made him an offer he could not refuse, and see him off. If she had not made it, it was because the arrangement had suited her. Charles's presence by her side had been her shield against other men, the eventual risk of going yet again through the pain she had experienced twice in her life, and it had only taken money to keep Charles around. It would only take money to throw him out. She had plenty of it, but she was not going to settle on his terms. While in Argentina, she had heard that Inés de la Force, the last member of Simón's family, was seriously ill. Charles's threat could soon come to an end.

32

Venice
September 1987

"WHO is the father?" Arianne asked. She felt a mixture of love, rage, and pity. Her daughter's capacity to make a mess of her life would never cease to amaze her.

"It's none of your business," Gloria replied angrily. "It could well turn out to be my own father, for all I know about *him*. Frankly, I hadn't realized that fathers mattered in this family. Anyway I couldn't possibly guess. You know that I screw around," she added acidly.

"I can't do anything about your nymphomania, but I wish you had taken precautions, at least," Arianne retorted. She regretted her remark as soon as she had uttered it, but Gloria had a way of needling her until she was beyond control.

"I took the Pill, if you must know, which is more than you did when you had me. I'm sorry; I always forget that you were legally married, and all that. You can sue the Pill company, if you wish. You've always been very good at making money out of everything, haven't you, Mummy?"

Arianne decided not to explore any further the subject of the child's father. It opened up a scar that ran along the length of their years together, and it served no purpose. It was better to be practical about it. Cameline had told her she had a similar problem with one of her daughters last summer, and how she had dealt with it.

"I'm glad you are at the beginning of the pregnancy. The plane is here. We can fly to London tomorrow and you can have an abortion.

It can be arranged very quickly there." She realized from Gloria's face that she had made another mistake. She had tried to handle this as if it were a business decision, by assessing the problem and coming up with the speediest solution.

"Is that what you thought of doing when you were expecting me? It might have made your life easier, but not mine," Gloria said, nearly in tears. She stood up and walked to the door. "I don't know why I decided to tell you. I should have guessed what to expect. But there is one thing I do know: I'm going to have this baby, whether you like it or not. Even better if you don't," she shouted before slamming the door behind her.

Arianne went to the window. As usual, crowds of tourists were walking along the Riva on the other side. Some were staring at the marble facade of her palazzo, probably wondering who the lucky person was who lived there.

She was almost certain that Charles was the father, but Gloria had said that she was on the Pill. Gloria had told her that she was the first person to hear the news. Perhaps Charles had no reason to suspect what had happened, and didn't know yet. If so, there might still be time to make him an irresistible offer. She left her room and ran up the broad stairs to the next floor. Walking decisively down the central hall, she knocked at Charles's door. She waited for a while, then opened it. He wasn't there.

She was enraged by the thought that he could be with Gloria, and dashed to the stairs, on her way to her daughter's room, but she suddenly stopped in her tracks. If she were to find him there it would not help matters; it would only increase her fury. She paced up and down the hall; she felt humiliated by having to wait, but nonetheless she stayed.

The clock struck the hour. Her hairdresser would be here any moment now, she had to check the last details in the reception rooms below, and she still had to get ready for her party. Perhaps it was better to give herself some time. She needed to be calm to confront Charles.

STANDING in front of the mirror, Pandora adjusted her lace jabot, its ruffles spilling over the edges of her gold-braided satin jacket. She was dressed as a Louis XV courtier, and she was pleased to notice that the line of the outfit emphasized her slim figure. The powdered wig had startled her at first, but she got used to it after a while. She grimaced at the mirror, wrinkles forming on her forehead and around her eyes, trying to imagine what she would look like when she was old. Her hair was unlikely to be as white as this, and she would certainly wear it in a different style, but it gave her some idea of her future. She was comforted by the thought that white hair seemed to bring out the green in her eyes; perhaps it would be better not to dye it when the time came.

She wished it could be as easy to fathom the future of her business. She had phoned her secretary earlier: the envelope with the tender documents had been delivered that morning, and there were no messages. She felt a moment's panic: the check would probably be deposited on Monday.

If only time could stand still. She would soon be taken by gondola to the world's most glamorous party, and she enjoyed the feeling of anticipation. She had thought of herself as Cinderella when Arianne invited her. The comparison had turned out to be more apt than she had imagined. It would probably all turn to rags in the end, with no crystal slipper to bring about a happy ending.

Her thoughts were interrupted by a knock on the door. It was room service, bringing in her omelette. The ball did not start until ten-thirty, and supper would be served late. A rumbling stomach would not add to her temporary royal persona. She took off her jacket and sat down to her solitary meal.

"FERUCCIO told me that you wanted to see me," Charles said as he walked into Arianne's dressing room. She was standing in front of a gilt-framed mirror, and Rosinha was on her knees next to her, fluffing up the ruffles of her train.

"Please knock on the door before coming in. Yes, I wanted to see you," she added, adjusting some crystal beads on her huge head-dress. "It's all right, Rosinha, you can go now."

"You look gorgeous all in black. Who are you supposed to be?" asked Charles with a smile.

"The Queen of the Night," replied Arianne curtly. "And cut the crap. I don't need it, and we don't have much time. I have to go downstairs in a moment." She moved to her dressing table, and fastened her long ropes of pearls around her neck.

"You don't seem to be in a party mood," said Charles, crossing his arms and leaning against the damask-covered wall.

"I find it difficult to be in a party mood with you around, but that is not what I wanted to tell you." She turned and faced him.

"I have been thinking about our conversations in New York, and I have decided that it might be better if you and I part company," she said.

Charles raised an eyebrow.

"Have you thought about some suitable compensation?" he asked.

"Fifty million dollars," she said. "On two conditions: you keep your mouth shut, and you never appear in the same place where I am at the same time. The world is big enough, and you will be able to afford a lot of plane tickets."

He whistled softly, and then chuckled.

"You are a very good businesswoman. I appreciate your trying to get things as cheaply as possible, but you ought to know me better than that." He came close to her and took her hands. She tried to pull away, but he tightened his grip.

"I have already explained this to you, but I will try again. Fifty million would not even buy me that nice picture we bought together last May. I couldn't possibly face a future of commercial airlines when you've got me used to a private jet. You know you have to come up with a better offer than that."

"Eighty million," she said, her voice revealing her rage.

"Try again. You really disappoint me," he replied calmly.

"A hundred million!" she screamed, nearly out of control.

Charles was astonished. Nobody, probably not even she, knew her precise worth: hundreds of millions, perhaps billions. He could make her lose everything, and yet she kept coming up with these ridiculous offers. On the other hand, it was unlike Arianne to increase her offers so readily, even if it was almost petty cash for her.

He was about to tell her the sort of figure he would consider reasonable when he realized that, other than on their first night together many years ago, he had never seen her like this. She was out of control. It could not be because of confronting him, nor could the bargaining have that effect on her. He knew that she had learned long ago to live with her dislike for him, and bargaining was part of her life. No, it had to be something else, something that mattered much more to her. Could it be . . . ? His heart jumped at the possibility, but he had to make sure.

He flung his arm around her waist and pulled her against him.

"My darling, this is nonsense. You and I can't part like this," he murmured, trying to kiss her.

The feel of his body, the thought that those hands had touched Gloria not long ago, revolted her. She pulled away from him and slapped him hard across the face.

"Stay away from me, you bastard!" she screamed.

He didn't need to know any more. His suspicions had been accurate. There was no point in discussing his price any further. He wanted it all, he wanted it now, and he knew he was going to get it. He turned around and left the room.

PANDORA was helped out of her gondola by a liveried servant, one of many who were assisting guests onto the small pier outside the floodlit palazzo. There was a crowd waiting to go into the building, and the Grand Canal was almost completely covered with gondolas bringing in further guests, their lanterns bobbing like huge fireflies in the night.

She joined the crowd, moving with it until she found herself in the foyer. The scene was breathtaking. The huge double-height space was lit only by candles in massive candelabra, their glow reflected on the marble walls. The gothic pillars and arches were outlined by ropes of orchids, which were also banked at both sides of the huge staircase leading to the main floor. Arianne was standing on the landing at the top, greeting her guests.

"You look gorgeous!" "*Bellissima!*" "*Ravissante!*" The compliments showered on her like tropical rain, in many languages and in every possible accent. She greeted them all with a dazzling smile, her face the face of a ravishing woman without a care in the world.

"I'm delighted that you could come," she told Pandora as their cheeks briefly brushed against each other, the otherwise standard greeting accompanied by Arianne's hand affectionately squeezing

Pandora's for a second. Their eyes met briefly, and Pandora thought she saw a shadow in Arianne's, as there had been during their conversation in the park, but she was pushed forward by the crowd behind her before she could take a second look, and she went through an archway leading into the main salon.

It was at least eighty feet long, and the whole width of the building. Full-size *brunus* trees in full bloom stood in the corners, pale yellow silk ribbons threaded through their foliage, their pale blue blossoms glowing in the candlelight from the gilded chandeliers. The massive carved beams and coffers in the ceiling were also bordered by orchids, forming a thick floral grid high above the sparkling crowd. The din of hundreds of voices was muffled by the sound of an orchestra playing in the minstrels' gallery.

Pandora took a glass of champagne from the tray presented by a waiter, and walked aimlessly around the room. Everybody seemed to know each other but she didn't know anyone, or so she thought. She was startled to hear her name.

"Pandora!" said a familiar voice. She turned around and saw Geraldine, wearing a huge Spanish comb, a lace shawl, and yards of black ruffles. She had not expected to see Geraldine here. Now that she was facing her she realized that what had happened between them, awesome as it had seemed a few months ago, now mattered very little to her.

"Geraldine, how nice to see you! Who are you supposed to be?" Pandora asked as if she cared.

"Goya's 'Maja.' Can't you tell?" Geraldine asked with a giggle. "I thought of coming as the naked version. I would have stolen Arianne's thunder for sure, but I don't think that Solly would have approved."

"Where is Solly?" Pandora inquired.

"Oh, he's somewhere over there, talking to some very grand French woman. She is la Duchesse de Brie-Montval. I can't resist name-dropping, and Solly is trying to buy some land she owns near Paris. I probably won't see him until he's made her sign a contract on a napkin. How are you, anyway? I haven't seen you for *a-ges!*" It had been less than three months since they had parted company in New York, but anything over a couple of days counted as *a-ges* in Geraldine's calendar.

"I'm very well, thank you." After a moment, Pandora realized that she couldn't leave her answer at that, if only for old times' sake. "I'm setting up my own business," she added.

"Oh, I'm so glad to hear that. Are you still in New York?" Geraldine asked, scanning the room over Pandora's shoulder.

Pandora wondered if that was a barbed remark, but it was obvious that Geraldine was distracted by the crowd, her mind not focused on their conversation. Pandora felt tempted to say that she was living in Bangkok, but realized it would not register anyway.

"No, I'm back in Lon —" she began to say, when Geraldine interrupted her.

"I'm sorry, darling, but I've just noticed Paloma and Rafael over there. I simply must say hello to them. I'll see you later. I'm delighted to hear that you're doing so well." She grinned toothily at Pandora for a second before dashing away.

Pandora shook her head and smiled. She should have known better. She took a sip of champagne and continued her tour of the room until she reached the windows overlooking the Grand Canal. She leaned against the marble sill and surveyed the scene. It astonished her. She had been to many dances in England, some in houses as magnificent as this one, but she had never seen wealth so carelessly displayed. Her current difficulties came to mind, and she couldn't help thinking about how much it had all cost. Throwing in the clothes and the jewels, probably much more than she needed to start her business. Maybe it was better not to know the figure.

"Many millions." Pandora heard a man's voice next to her. It was Bob Chalmers, wearing a pirate's costume.

"Are you talking about your loot, or the cost of the party? If the latter, I'm amazed by your intuition. I'd better watch my thoughts if you can read them," she said.

"I always try to read the thoughts of attractive women," he replied, almost whispering in her ear.

"Then you are going to have a very disappointing evening if you stay with me for long. But how did you know what I was thinking about?"

"Whenever I find myself somewhere like this, I always think about how much it costs. But I'm a businessman; maybe you were just thinking about how beautiful it all is. I'm very glad to see you again." He leaned forward and kissed her on the cheek.

"I tried to phone you in New York after our lunch, but there was no reply," he said. A few months ago his attention would have been flattering, but now it simply amused her.

"I'm back in London. I'm setting up my own business," she said.

"Are you?" he asked, a new note of interest in his voice. "Please let me know if there is *anything* I can do for you. . . ."

Pandora had learned to recognize what that tone and that expression meant. His approach was more credible than Peter's, but only because he was a more intelligent man.

"Actually, there is something you can do for me. I'm having some problems financing my company. Do you think you could find me five million pounds? I would be truly grateful," she said, not a hint of guile in her voice.

His face froze.

"Are you serious?" he asked at last.

"I'm never anything but serious, particularly if I'm talking business," she replied with a deadpan face, enjoying his brief bewilderment. He thought for a moment.

"This is not the best place to discuss something like that. But we could have lunch at my hotel tomorrow. I'm staying at the Cipriani. My wife is having lunch with a friend here in Venice, and we would be able to talk in peace and quiet," he said.

"I would love to talk with you in peace and quiet," she agreed, giving him a Geraldine-like grin, "but I'm flying back to London first thing in the morning." She took in his disappointed face. "I wouldn't have thought about millions if you hadn't mentioned them. Don't blame me," she added before walking away from him, into the next reception room.

It was a smaller room and it was not so crowded. She noticed Gloria in a group at the center of the room, pointing toward the ceiling. Pandora looked up and saw the oval fresco, Tiepolo's famous *Triumph of Venus*. Gloria's dress was a copy of the goddess's. She also noticed a masked man dressed as Zorro approaching the group and exchanging a few words with Gloria. The tall, athletic figure seemed familiar, but she couldn't place him. After a moment she saw Gloria and the man leave the room together.

STANDING in the middle of the Great Gallery, glittering in the soft-hued light from the golden *torchères,* Arianne held court. She took compliments and returned them, her small talk polished to a mirror finish, glad that the incessant parade of guests gave her an excuse not to think about Gloria. She knew that she had made a mistake, but this was not the time for recriminations. She would talk to Gloria tomorrow.

Arianne realized that her attention was slipping, and instantly focused on the conversation around her, on the rumored marital difficulties between the Prince and Princess of Wales. Arianne turned to greet some newcomers to the group when she noticed Pandora Doyle in the distance, talking to Cameline Sarteano.

Arianne was briefly struck by the change in Pandora since she had last seen her in New York. There was an air of apparent confidence about her, and she remembered their recent phone conversation. She was about to make her excuses and break away from her group to join Pandora and Cameline, when Ferruccio, almost unrecognizable in his court uniform instead of his usual butler's outfit, came through the double doors in the middle of the gallery. He tapped his long silver and ebony stick loudly on the marble floor three times before making his announcement in a voice that silenced all conversation.

"Your Royal Highnesses, ladies and gentlemen, dinner is served," he boomed.

Arianne gathered her train and, on the arm of her dinner companion, Prince Wenceslas zu Liechtenstein, led the procession of her guests down the marble stairs. The orchids on the sides still looked as fresh as if they had just been cut.

THE shimmer of the crumpled silks on the floor was just visible in the moonlight, Zorro's black cloak lying next to Venus' shell-pink dress. Both naked, stretched across her bed in each other's arms, Charles and Gloria did not pay much attention to the muffled sound of music and conversation from below. At least Gloria didn't; she had no reason to take notice of anything other than her sudden peace of mind. Charles had given her a new certainty.

"We ought to get dressed and go downstairs. It's getting late," he murmured.

"Not yet," she replied, rolling on top of him. "Plenty of time for that."

He tightened his arms around her waist.

"Tonight you've made me . . . ," he began to say, but her kiss silenced him. Her hand slid down his body, and they did not hear the noise from below any longer. Not for a while, at least.

". . . AND I've heard from someone who knows her very well that she is the illegitimate daughter of a Brazilian plantation owner and one of his maids, and . . ." Pandora had listened attentively to the first part of her dinner companion's virtual monologue about the secrets in Arianne's life until she realized that it was all gossip, most of which she had already heard from Geraldine. The man was a bore, and she was relieved to notice that people were standing up at Arianne's table, at the far end of the enormous room.

"Excuse me, please," she said as she got up, then walked away. She wandered around the ground floor. There was a discothèque in one of the salons and it was already packed. In the laser-lit crowd she caught sight of Maria Dimitrescu and a few other faces she had seen at Geraldine's party in New York. Some man dressed as Othello asked her to dance. It was one of her favorite Pet Shop Boys songs, and she was pleased. She was a good dancer, and she enjoyed it.

We never calculate the currency we spend,
I love you, you pay my rent.

The crowd cheerfully chorused the key lines of the lyrics. Her partner suddenly leaned toward her and placed his hand on her forearm, slowly rubbing it up and down.

"Do you shoot?" he murmured close to her face. Pandora stared at him, hardly believing her ears at first. English was obviously not his first language, and she couldn't place his accent.

"Yes, oh yes, I love it," she humored him.

"Great. Let's find somewhere quiet. I have some heroin, and really good coke. What would you prefer?" he asked, his arm around her waist.

"Grouse, if you have it, but we would have to be very careful with

Arianne's ceilings," she said, pushing him away and moving on. After a while, she looked back and saw him busily talking to a Scandinavian-looking girl nearby, dressed in a few ounces of feathers. Some of Arianne's guests were more surprising than Pandora had expected.

She went back upstairs to the saloon now returned to its original use as a ballroom. The orchestra was playing Cole Porter music, a crescendo of songs leading up to "Anything Goes." Arianne was dancing with Bob Chalmers, and apparently having a good time. As Pandora continued her inspection, she was surprised to notice the man dressed as Zorro standing on the side of the orchestra balcony.

The music became faster and faster, until a blast of trumpets underlined the final line, and it came to a sudden end. The dancers paused, waiting for the music to start again, but the pause seemed longer than usual. Like many others in the crowd, Pandora raised her eyes to the minstrels' gallery and noticed that Zorro had come to the front. He had removed his mask.

It was Charles. He clapped his hands loudly three times, and all conversation stopped. Gloria suddenly appeared by his side.

"Ladies and gentlemen," his voice boomed across the expanse of the room, "tonight is the happiest night of my life, and I hope of Gloria's too. We just wanted to let all our friends know that we are going to get married." As he finished, he gave a signal to the conductor, and the orchestra launched into "I Get a Kick Out of You," drowning the astonished murmurs of the guests.

Gloria's expression was a terrifying mixture of triumph and hatred. She was staring at someone in the crowd. Pandora followed her gaze.

Gloria's eyes were fixed on Arianne, whose face reminded Pandora of the stone sphinxes in Uncle Harold's garden. It was impossible to read anything in it. She remained impassive for a few moments, then a smile came to her lips. It was not the joyful smile of a mother at the announcement of her daughter's happiness, nor the plastic smile of a polished social performer for the benefit of the audience. It was the calm smile of polite pleasure at an event which, pleasing as it may be, does not have much bearing on one's own life.

Arianne raised her hands slowly, and began to clap. She was followed by the crowd around her, hesitatingly at first, until the applause spread across the whole room, encouraged by her visible approval of the match.

"These South Americans are incredible," Pandora heard somebody say behind her. The extraordinary announcement had not broken the party mood. There would be plenty of time to dissect the news, to examine the implications over lunches and dinners. But that could be done tomorrow. Now they were having fun. As Charles and Gloria joined the crowd on the dance floor, the first wave of well-wishers burst forward, following Arianne's example. Her congratulatory kiss to her daughter was enchanting to see.

". . . WE are going to get married." As she heard Charles's words, Arianne's first instinct was to scream in rage and pain. She thought of bringing the party to a sudden end, to be left alone with Charles and Gloria, to say exactly what she thought and then to throw them out of her house forever.

But she couldn't. Not when she had God knows how many newspaper owners, magazine editors, and social columnists under her roof. The story would make the columns, there was no doubt about that, but as it stood now it would be today's wonder and tomorrow's old news. Any hint of a feud and it would run for weeks, encouraging the gossip columnists to probe, to become interested in her past, to find out more than they already knew. There was no way of guessing what Gloria would do if Arianne publicly humiliated her. She did not know enough to bring the house of cards down, but she knew just enough to put an eager newspaper hound on the right track. But Charles certainly knew enough. God knows what he might or might not have disclosed to Gloria to strengthen his hand.

There was a further danger to causing a fracas. If Arianne were to oppose them, it might encourage Charles to try to strike a deal with Simón's family before it was too late. She wondered if he knew his time was running out.

She needed to gain time. There were eight hundred people around her waiting for her shocked reaction. Gloria certainly was. Her face said it all when she stared at Arianne from the orchestra balcony. Arianne's pain was Gloria's victory, and she wanted her spoils. Well, she was not going to have them.

She was going to give them the last thing any of them was expecting: her public approval. As she raised her hands and began to clap, the diamond in her ring shone brightly in the candlelight.

". . . WE are going to get married." Staring at her mother as Charles, standing next to her, said the words, Gloria was overcome by joy and fear.

She had expected Charles to shy away from her once he heard about the baby, to take Arianne's view, to give her a speech about the most sensible course for all concerned. Meaning whatever would make life easier for him.

But he hadn't. He had been delighted at the news, and suggested that they marry immediately and move away together. "I have always wanted to live quietly in the country. I have saved some money, and we can manage on that. Just the two of us and our baby, far away from all this." Gloria would have her baby, a way out of her mother's grip, and her revenge on Arianne.

The reasons behind her fear were equally obvious to her. She was tying her fate to Charles. But Charles could not be marrying her in order to wait many years for her eventually to inherit whatever Arianne cared to leave her. There were plenty of rich, bored women around, and he could take his pick. Everyone, her mother most of all, had always seen her as a worthless, spoiled brat, and treated her accordingly. She knew differently; perhaps she ought to extend Charles the same credit she was granting herself.

As he put his arm around her waist, her fear seemed less and less justifiable, until it faded away in the warm applause that surrounded them.

AT three o'clock in the morning, the chimes of seventeen clocks around the reception rooms rang simultaneously. Hardly anyone heard them because the party was in full swing. Pandora was one of the very few who took notice. Less jaded, or maybe less indifferent, than most of the other guests, she had had her festive mood punctured by the scene in the ballroom two hours ago. In other circumstances, Pandora would have left soon afterward, but she knew that reality, her reality, was waiting outside Arianne's bronze gates, and she did not want to confront it. Bothered by the noise, she climbed a second flight of steps, leading to the top floor of the palazzo.

As on the floor below, the stairs led to a central hall, a row of Gothic-arched doorways at the far end opening onto a terrace. The moon cast the pattern of the marble clover-shaped lights above the doors onto the bare floor of the hall. One of the doors was open, and Pandora decided to look at the Grand Canal in peace. But someone else was already there, leaning on the balustrade. She recognized the remarkable headdress at once. It was Arianne.

The moon shone on her face as she smiled at Pandora. Although there were no tears, her distress was plain to see in the tension around her mouth and eyes. By the time Pandora greeted her, however, Arianne's perfect mask was back in place.

"I'm glad to see you. Please come and join me. The view is marvelous at this time of the night," she said calmly.

Pandora stood next to her. She could not take Arianne's cue and embark on a vapid discussion of the view to avoid the subject that was really on their minds.

"I shouldn't say this, but I'm really sorry. I hope you don't feel responsible for Gloria's actions. It's her mistake, not yours, although you might not see it that way."

Arianne looked at Pandora with a sad smile. It was the first honest thing anyone had said to her that evening.

"Maybe you're right, but let's not talk about Gloria. Not now. I've read the report and the proposal you sent me. I'm truly glad that things are going well for you in London. Tell me about it." Pandora doubted that Arianne could be really interested, but at least it would make their conversation easier, and she launched into her speech with the enthusiasm rehearsed time and time again for her London meetings.

"Things are going *really* well. I've finished all the designs, which will soon go into production, and I've found a chain of shops in perfect locations. I am in the process of negotiating the lease; in fact, I'll complete the deal as soon as I go back to London. I have every confidence . . ." By then she was talking as if on autopilot, and she could hear herself, uttering lies, or at least hopes rather than facts, as she had had to do in London so many times, of keeping up appearances for no reason. It was half past three, probably she would never see Arianne again, and she might as well go to bed.

"I'm sorry," she said, midsentence. "It's very late. I think I'd better go. Thank you for a marvelous party and a most generous invitation."

Arianne stretched her arm out and held Pandora's wrist for a second.

"I don't want you to go," she murmured. "Now just tell me the truth."

"What makes you think I'm lying?" Pandora asked, concealing her embarrassment under her best shade of quiet, polite indignation.

"I'm not saying that you *are* lying, but you are not telling me the truth. After twenty years of dealing with — let us say nontruths — one learns to recognize them. I'm sorry if I have offended you, but I'm genuinely interested." She wanted to take her mind off what happened earlier, and this girl was a window into something else, something different.

Pandora leaned on the balustrade. Maybe it would be better to say nothing and just go, but she couldn't. There was nothing ahead of her now other than her own problems. She had to speak to someone about them.

"I've made a mistake, a big mistake. You told me in New York that I ought to start my business on as big a scale as I could. When I went back to London I thought you were right, and you probably are. But I have run into serious difficulties raising the money, and I can't help questioning my motives. I wonder if I am just driven by the wish to prove to myself, and everyone else, that I'm not a failure. It seemed a good motivation but now I'm facing the biggest failure of my life."

"It's simply called ambition, and it's rather pointless to question your motives," Arianne interrupted her. "Are you unhappy about your decision?"

Pandora thought for a moment.

"No, I'm just doubting my motives, though I admit that if things had turned out differently, if I were all set, I wouldn't be. I thought that work would give me my own certainty, but maybe I was naive."

Absorbed by what she was saying, she did not notice that Arianne's eyes were also fixed on the middle distance.

Arianne was not looking at the churches and palaces on the other side of the canal; she was looking back over the years, to her conversation with Simón in the Paris apartment when they had gone there for the first time, when she had thought the same things as Pandora about her own work. Her doubts had pushed her into accepting Simón's offer. She had also had dreams then, the urge to prove to others, and to herself above all, who she was and what she could do, only to give it all up because the prospect of failure had seemed so intolerable. Her fears made it seem a difficult time, but it wasn't, not when compared with the present, when everything was possible but very little was true. When her own daughter cared more about hurting her than for her own happiness.

"Never doubt your motives if they lead you to something you want to do, something which is yours and yours alone. You may question the results, you may even give it up, but at least try as hard as you can to make it work first. You'll regret it forever otherwise."

Pandora thought for a moment. "Maybe you're right, but this conversation is becoming a self-indulgence, at least as far as I am concerned. I have no right to bore you with my troubles."

Arianne smiled.

"You are too British for your own good. All conversations on personal matters are ultimately self-centered, otherwise they would serve no purpose. You call it self-indulgence, but it isn't. It is a perfectly valid way to work out what you really want."

"But that's the problem. I'm no longer sure if I want what I want because *I* really want it, or because I want to prove myself to others. I took the easy option by marrying, I wasted those years, and now I'm trying to make up for lost time. Perhaps one can't."

"Of course one can! You can't afford to think otherwise." Pandora was surprised by the sudden urgency in Arianne's voice. "I think you're questioning the consequences, not your motives, and I think you're talking about fear of failure, nothing more. Nobody likes it. In any case, why do other people matter so much to you? They are not important."

Pandora stared at Arianne.

"You wouldn't have come out here on this terrace, alone, if Gloria didn't matter to you. She probably matters more than anything else to you, and rightly so. It doesn't matter in the end if 'others' are just one person or a hundred people."

"I thought we were talking about work. Now you are talking about love. It's a different subject." The strain in Arianne's voice showed that she was now as uncomfortable as Pandora had been during the early part of their conversation.

"Not really. Meaning something to other people is what we, or at least I, ultimately want from work *or* from love, and only because other people matter to me. If it's no longer a question of survival, one works because one loves the work, but also because it is a way of proving one's worth. I failed to get that out of my marriage, and now I'm trying to get it out of my work. It's probably going to cost me everything I have. When we began this conversation I thought that it was pointless, but now I wonder." She paused, and laughed softly. "Otherwise I should jump into the canal right now." Suddenly she felt less anguished. "And it's not true that the conversation has been pointless; far from it. You've taught me a few things. I've been talking like a spoiled brat, trying to justify the easy option and giving up."

Arianne was not listening. While Pandora spoke she had felt an indulgent benevolence toward her naïveté, the certainty of cynical knowledge facing guileless candor. But in the same way that the earlier reference to doubts had reminded her of her mistake in accepting Simón's offer out of fear, what Pandora had just said touched her more deeply. This girl, in her ultimate innocence, was right, and she had helped Arianne perceive something more important than anything they had discussed so far. Much, much more important. She turned toward Pandora.

"You haven't yet told me what the figure is that's causing you so much trouble," she said.

"Five million pounds at least. It's an awful lot of money," Pandora answered. Arianne leaned forward, her eyes on the water below, her pearls dangling over the balustrade.

"It *is* an awful lot of money," she agreed. "But it all depends on your viewpoint. It is everything to you, yet it would be far less than the cost of another painting on my walls for me."

"I'm not asking you for a loan, and I hope you are not taking this conversation as a request. We discussed this in New York. There is no reason why you should lend me any money, let alone a figure like that," Pandora said defensively.

"I don't lend money," Arianne replied, briefly taken aback by the realization that she was using the very same words Simón had used during their lunch in Paris. "I give it to charities, but I don't lend it. I do make investments. Sometimes in people, sometimes in businesses, although I'm not sure that there is much difference. Both turn either good or bad in the end, but perhaps people can let you down to a greater degree."

The implications of her last sentence hung over them and they lapsed into silence.

"In the end, it's all a matter of making a choice, of making the right decision," Arianne said at last. "You are trying to prove something for the sake of others as much as for your own sake. I can understand that; I just hope you are clear about *your* reasons. In any case, I intend to help you."

Pandora recoiled as she heard her. Her heart beat faster, her perplexity mixed with budding excitement. She could no longer afford to turn down Arianne's offer. She had no other options left, and the alternative was to give up. But she could not yet believe the offer was true.

"But why? It means everything to me, but why on earth would you do something like this?" she murmured, choked by her emotion. Arianne adopted a matter-of-fact expression.

"You're reading too much into it. I asked you to send me your proposal, and your business seems more than a viable proposition. Let's say that I want to invest in a good prospect. I know that you only succeed from a position of strength. You say that you need five million, which probably means that you need six. I'll back your company as an investor, but you will be in complete control of the business. I'll talk to my bankers in London tomorrow, and everything will be arranged on Monday. Now go back, give hell to the competition, and good luck."

Pandora was overwhelmed, her sudden relief almost bringing tears to her eyes. "You are making everything I want possible. I know it cannot just be a business decision. I don't know how I can thank you for this," she whispered.

Arianne smiled. "By making a success of it. I only hope that what you think you want is what you really need. And don't think that there is anything else to this other than a business decision. Please go now. I would like to stay here for a moment before going back downstairs."

As she walked away, Pandora felt a surge of energy. It was no longer very late, it was the morning of the best day of her life, and she ran down the stairs, toward the light and the music below.

Alone again, Arianne stared at the gondolas lined up by her pier, soon to take her guests away. Time would tell if she had made a wise investment. The risk was worth taking, but any business can go sour. Nonetheless, it had been worth it for tonight's sake. The girl had a purpose, as she herself had had once, a long time ago, and she had shown her something about herself which mattered more than money. Pandora's mention of belief in others took her back to her days in Rio, when her love for Florinda and Ruben had been the center of her concern. She had been happiest then, she realized, and she had never found such happiness again.

Pandora, so outwardly different from everything she had ever been, so transitory a presence in her life, had triggered something in her when they had first spoken in New York. She had thought then that it was simply that she saw in Pandora the girl she would have liked Gloria to be, but it was more than that. She had reacted unknowingly to Pandora's essential values, which had burrowed through Arianne's defenses because she had protected herself against an attack from the opposite direction. She had learned to deal with malice or calculation because they had become part of her everyday life. But she remained vulnerable to someone still willing to trust others. Once that kind of trust had also been the most important quality in Arianne's life, but she had been forced to shed it in order to survive. She had pushed honesty and trust out of her life a long time ago, until they seemed irrelevant, but something in her had withered in the process.

If she had failed with Gloria it was because she had refused to trust her with the truth. She had lied to Gloria, as she had lied to everybody else. But while lying to others had been inevitable, she had *chosen* to lie to her daughter. Her lies had secured her a fortune, everything she was, but they had caused her to lose the one person who was most important to her. She had not lied to Gloria to make Gloria's life easier, but to make *her* own life easier. She had feared that Gloria, if she knew the facts, would be a potential enemy, like everybody else. If Gloria now saw her as an enemy, it was her own fault.

Their rift had begun many years ago, when Charles had appeared in her life and she had sent Gloria away to boarding school. She had told herself then that it would be best for Gloria to stay away from a home which had become hell, and she genuinely wanted to keep Gloria away from her life with Charles, but her decision had been equally based on her fear of Gloria's incessant questions. Gloria was always trying to find out the truth about her, and truth could mean losing everything she had.

But love became impossible without truth. She had considered love as a Trojan horse, something which, if allowed into her life, would push her back to what she had wanted to leave behind. It wasn't. But love was a choice, and she had made hers long ago. Silvia had chosen to become Arianne, and now Arianne wanted what Silvia once had. It was ironic to discover it through Pandora, someone who, until moments ago, had been nothing more than a pleasant acquaintance. She had not been able to explain to herself why she had felt inclined to help her in New York; now she knew. She had not really invested in Pandora's business, she had invested in herself, in what she had once been.

The clock struck four. Breakfast would be served downstairs any minute now. Her ruby earrings felt heavy on her earlobes, and she removed them. They were Simón's gift to her in Portofino, the beginning of a long journey leading to this awful night.

She stared at the earrings. She had not liked them when she had first seen them, but she had changed her mind as time went by. Now she looked at them with eyes of twenty years ago. She weighed them in her hand for a short while, then raised her arm with slow deliberation and flung them out into the canal. They glowed like red fireflies flashing in the moonlight before disappearing into the murky water. A moment later she joined her guests.

Part Seven

33

London
December 1987

*H*ER hands in the pockets of her Barbour jacket, her green Wellington boots and thick cable-knit socks protecting her feet from the damp coldness of the Norfolk soil, Pandora started out across the wood, the shortcut between her mother's home and the hall, when she remembered that she would disturb the pheasants, the most frequent reason for Uncle Harold's scoldings during her childhood. Uncle Harold was senile now, and beyond such preoccupations, but she imagined it would trigger a similar reaction from Harry, her cousin and Uncle Harold's heir, now living on the estate with his wife and in charge of everything, including the shoot. She backtracked, and had begun the long walk across the fields, skirting the wood, when she heard a helicopter flying above her head. She caught sight of it briefly before it disappeared in the distance.

The success of Doyle during the first three weeks of December had been beyond anyone's wildest expectations. The general prosperity had created a new mood in the country. Spend, spend, spend, was the rule, and it kept Doyle's tills ringing in an incessant crescendo.

Her designs had also proved to be exactly right for the market. After a decade of designer black at one end, and chintz nostalgia at the other, her natural look reflected the new mood of the times, a style both distinctive and desirable at a price most people could afford. The environmentally friendly angle had been a further boost to the public's reaction. On the evidence of the sales figures it had been possible to raise the money for expansion almost immediately, and new shops were scheduled to open in the Greater London area within two months.

It was all thanks to Arianne. She had kept her word, and since Venice everything had become possible. Pandora had tried to phone her after her return to London, but she was told that Madame had left for Tokyo that morning. Then she tried to phone her in New York two weeks later, but Arianne's secretary told her that Mrs. de la Force was in Zurich. Then Pandora had written her a long thank-you letter, but she had received no reply. Geraldine had phoned Pandora three weeks ago, during one of her lightning visits to London, and told her that she had heard that Charles and Gloria had married, "very privately," and had disappeared from sight. "She's probably sent them to Mongolia. Can you imagine her position, poor thing? But she *is* admirable. She carries on as if nothing had happened," Geraldine said. At first Pandora had ascribed Arianne's silence to her ever-busy schedule, but after hearing Geraldine's information she thought that a combination of embarrassment and pain because of Gloria was the more likely cause for it. The only communication Pandora had received from Arianne had been an elegant Christmas card, with a handwritten seasonal greeting.

Partly because of pressure of work, and mainly because she found the prospect of three or four days of enforced coexistence with her mother daunting, Pandora had not decided to come to Norfolk until the last moment. When her mother had phoned earlier in the month to ask if Pandora would be coming home for Christmas, she had said she probably wouldn't be able to get away. But as the date approached, she found the option of being alone in London for Christmas even worse, and she phoned her mother at the last minute to tell her she would spend the holiday at Walsham after all. Besides, she suddenly felt a surge of nostalgia for her old habitat, the flat landscape of her childhood under a mackerel-gray sky.

It had been a mistake. Her mother was as bitter as she had always been, the roots of her dissatisfaction so deep in the past as to make it impossible for her to identify them. Her general attitude was one of permanent condemnation, the edge of her bitterness concealed by her polite manner but constantly sharpened by her rancor. Life had passed her by, and she blamed everybody else for it. Unlike the landscape, Pandora's mother had not changed at all over the years.

The estate as Pandora remembered it had been a Beatrix Potter–like setting of small fields, fruit trees, kitchen gardens, and semiderelict greenhouses, their rusting frames and broken panes the shelter for many hours of games of hide-and-seek with the other children living at Walsham. Not any more. Spurred on by Harry's enthusiasm for profit, the estate had become an efficient concern, the hedges vanished to create enormous fields better suited to the new agricultural machinery. The fruit trees, no longer viable because of cheaper produce from the Continent, had been uprooted, and the land was now allocated to grain production. The kitchen garden and the greenhouses were also gone in the relentless drive to reduce staff and maintenance costs. The shoot, once Uncle Harold's main pastime as a source of private pleasure for him and his neighbors, was now a thriving enterprise let to London companies for the sake of business entertainment under the guise of gentlemanly pursuits. The estate was profitable again, but at a cost. Pandora had been warned by Camilla, Harry's wife, to drink only bottled water at her mother's house because the local wells had become contaminated by the intensive use of fertilizers.

Pandora had been glad to be asked by Camilla to help her with the catering for today's shoot, giving her an excuse to leave her mother for a while after the gloom of Christmas and Boxing Day. She had originally planned to return to London the next day, but had now decided to leave that evening if there were any trains running.

At last she reached the house and noticed the large number of cars parked outside, Harry's mud-splattered Range Rover an oddity among the BMWs and Mercedeses. A second Range Rover, much newer than Harry's, was parked next to the main entrance, its golden metallic finish dulled by the flat morning light. A uniformed driver was polishing it, and Pandora noticed the license plate: "TC 1." She was briefly amused by its vulgarity and went on around the side of the house. She came into the kitchen yard and walked past the kennels. She was expecting the noisy welcome of the dogs, but they were already out with the guns. They would not have recognized her anyway. The Labradors she remembered had probably died and been replaced a long time ago.

As she went into the house via the staff entrance, she felt the warmth on her cheeks after the numbing chill of her walk. The door on one side of the room, leading to the larder, was open, and she noticed Mrs. Thomas, the cook, rummaging through the shelves. Mrs. Thomas had worked at the house for as long as Pandora could remember, but the old woman had not changed much from the last time Pandora had been there. She was just a bit stouter, a shade grayer than before. Pandora was glad to see her, and waited until Mrs. Thomas came out of the larder, holding a jar of Branston pickle in her hand, probably, from its dusty appearance, already well past its "sell by" date.

"Hello, Mrs. Thomas! How are you keeping? I always miss your Yorkshire pudding; it's the best in the world," she said cheerfully.

"My, you've changed, girl. Must be marriage," the old woman replied, without acknowledging Pandora's effusive greeting. "How's that husband of yours? Haven't seen him since your wedding. I haven't seen *you* since your wedding, coming to that," she added in a reproachful tone.

"I know. I never seem to find the time to come here anymore," Pandora said, not answering an uncomfortable question. "Camilla asked me to come and help. Where is she?"

"Mrs. Temple-Stewart is in the kitchen," replied Mrs. Thomas. Pandora followed her along the broad corridor, the stone flags eroded into dips and mounds by generations of servants' feet. Mrs. Thomas's respectful reference to Camilla had not passed unnoticed. Pandora and Harry had never been equals in the cook's eye when they were children, and Camilla took precedence now as Harry's wife.

They went into the vast kitchen, endless pots and pans lined up on deep timber shelves. Camilla was standing by the old-fashioned Aga, taking trays of sausage rolls out of one of the ovens. She laid them on the huge table in the middle of the room, and took off her quilted oven gloves.

"How lovely to see you!" Pandora said after kissing Camilla in greeting. "You seem to have a pretty flash lot here today. I've just seen the cars outside."

"You should see the owners. I'm amazed they remembered to take the price tags off their clothes. They must have all been to Purdey's to buy the whole kit just before they came. We got a call out of the blue ten days ago, someone from London desperately trying to book a shoot at the last moment for some guy. Harry was planning to keep the day for himself, so he asked for thirty pounds per pheasant. It's twice the going rate, but they didn't seem to mind. I only hope they don't shoot each other when they try to hit the birds. Worse still, they could shoot one of the beaters. They haven't a clue how to behave."

Camilla wrapped the baking trays in large tea towels, then turned back toward Pandora.

"They'll come to the house after the last drive for a late lunch, but they are having elevenses at the lodge by the lake. Why don't you give me a hand putting these in the car? Don't worry about what we do at the other end. I've managed to convince Harry to part with some money, and we've just put a microwave oven in at the lodge." Camilla rushed out of the kitchen for a moment, and returned wearing a Barbour jacket identical to Pandora's.

"Let's go," she said. Mrs. Thomas followed them with a huge thermos of coffee in her arms.

"I hear you're running a shop now. How *splendid*," Camilla said as they drove down the narrow lane toward the lake. Pandora sensed the patronizing undertone and was about to correct her, but realized that the difference between running a shop and managing a business would probably be lost on Camilla.

"MY cousin, Pandora Lyons," said Harry, introducing Pandora to the big man at the center of the group standing by the fireplace in the lodge. "Ted Carson," he added, almost as an unnecessary, embarrassing formality.

Ted Carson held out his hand. "Pleased to meet you," he said.

"The name is Doyle now, Pandora Doyle. Harry and I haven't seen each other for years," she replied as his hand gripped hers firmly. For a moment she worried that he might remember her from her scene with Peter Wentworth-Briggs at that ghastly restaurant, but he gave her no indication of recognizing her.

"As far as I can see, it is his loss," Ted Carson said.

She smiled.

"I'm flattered, but Harry might not agree with you."

"I've read about you in the papers. If you're as successful as they say you are, I may be tempted to take *you* over," Ted chuckled. Pandora noticed both his Australian accent and his blunt charm. He spoke like a man who was used to being the center of attention, and he expected his own attentions to be more than merely acknowledged.

"You wouldn't be able to take me over. Mine is not a public company, and I can't imagine that four shops justify your interest. Are you involved in retailing?" she asked.

"No, but I'm always interested in good opportunities. I wish they were as plentiful as people seem to think, but I know one when I see her," he said, smiling.

"It might be better if you concentrated on the pheasants today, instead. A small business is a very personal occupation, and mine is not for sale, anyway," she answered casually.

Everyone else in the group was now focused on their conversation, and Pandora was glad to see Mrs. Thomas approaching, holding a tray of sausage rolls. Harry indicated to Ted that he ought to have first choice.

"After you," Ted said to Pandora.

"No, thank you. I'm not hungry," she replied.

"They're very good," Ted said to Harry after taking a large bite.

"My wife made them, but I believe Pandora helped her." Pandora was surprised by Harry's obsequiousness, so unlike him. She put it down to his thirty-pounds-per-pheasant coup, but she was annoyed by the implication that she was somehow part of the all-inclusive deal.

"There are some things women can do better than men. And vice versa, of course," Ted said, smiling. The men around him smiled in approval of his remark.

"Maybe you're right, Mr. Carson," Pandora said. "But I've found that the difference between men and women, as far as men are concerned, is usually *much* smaller than men would like it to be," she added.

The men suddenly went quiet, and Harry glared at Pandora. After a moment's silence Ted began to laugh.

"You give as good as you get," he said at last. "I like that. Please call me Ted."

"Thank you. I think that Camilla and Mrs. Thomas need some help with the coffee. Excuse me, please." As she passed a window, she saw the beaters and the loaders outside helping themselves to coffee from the thermos flasks, the dogs around them, their breath visible in the cold air.

She was helping Camilla unpack the coffee mugs when she sensed somebody standing behind her. It was Ted Carson.

"I want to apologize for what I said. I've spent too long in the outback. I would like to ask you to come with us and stand with me for the next drive. You could stay for lunch later, if you want to," he said.

"It's very kind of you, but I've got to go back home to pack," she answered. She continued to line the mugs up on the table. Maybe she was being foolish. She liked to walk with the guns, and it had been a long time since she had done so. More to the point, it was flattering to have his attention. She had learned that anyone might prove useful sometime in the future, particularly someone like Ted Carson. "But I'd love to see some shooting," she added.

"Good," he said with a smile. "I can take you back to London later if you are in a hurry."

"That's most kind, but I don't like to sit for hours on the road. I take the train when I come here; it's quicker," she replied.

"I'm going back in my chopper. You'll be in London in no time," he said gleefully.

Pandora smiled her sweetest apologetic smile.

"What a shame. It would have been so nice to go back with you, but I *hate* flying. I think I'll stick to the train, but thanks for the offer anyway." She suddenly remembered the golden Range Rover outside the hall. "I thought I saw your car outside the house. It's difficult not to notice it."

"My staff and my dog came in the Range Rover. I came in the chopper. I don't like to waste time," he replied with evident pride.

STANDING by their numbers, the guns formed a line across the open field between two woods, facing the trees a hundred yards away from them. They stood in silence, and they could hear the beaters coming through the trees toward them. The sounds of shouts and wood on wood grew louder and louder, and then the birds broke in front of them, suddenly taking flight. The firing began.

A few steps behind Ted's left shoulder, Pandora took in the scene. It was as bad as Camilla had anticipated, most of the guns firing when the birds were too low or aiming at somebody else's bird, either in brash eagerness or simply because of ignorance of the rules. Not Ted Carson, though. He was an exceptional shot, as good as Harry.

But his display was so ostentatious it was almost embarrassing to watch. He had three men standing behind him: his two loaders and his butler, who was dressed as if he had stepped out of a book by P. G. Wodehouse and was holding a portable phone, something Pandora had never seen before in shoots. The purpose of the second loader became clear as Ted handed his gun back immediately after firing his second barrel. One of the men broke the gun and held it while the other reloaded. During the quick maneuver Pandora caught Ted's eye briefly shifting toward her, surreptitiously checking if she was taking in his performance.

He was trying to impress her, and it amused her. And yet she had realized something else. In many ways, she was now as much a stranger in Walsham as Ted and his group were. She was not part of this life anymore. Her visit had underlined how far apart she had grown from Harry and Camilla, from what they represented, from their confidence based on who they were rather than what they did.

During the walk the men had talked eagerly about their work, as eagerly as she would talk about hers in London. They were slightly ill at ease in their brand-new country clothes, but no more than she had been at first in her designer outfits. They were learning the rules of the world she had left behind, as she was now learning the rules of their world.

She was no longer "one of us"; she had become one of "them." But she could not help finding the brashness of Ted Carson and his friends almost as irritating as the relaxed, and unjustified, self-confidence of the likes of Harry and Johnny. She knew she could not carry on with one foot in each world, not entirely at ease in either of them.

Now Ted was standing with a pile of birds in front of him, clearly pleased as his dog kept adding dead pheasants to the heap. Most of the birds shot by the other guns had dropped behind them, winged but not dead. Clearly familiar with inexperienced guns, Harry had doubled the number of men to pick up behind them, at the edge of the pheasant's home wood, and their dogs were now fetching the wounded birds.

"Not bad," he said to Pandora with a grin, clearly expecting her admiration.

"You are a very good shot. Have you been shooting for long?" she asked.

"Long enough. My father had a small farm in Australia. I learned as a boy" was his reply, and she felt chastened by it. She had found out that there were alternatives to being a housewife in Fulham. Equally, being a young squire in the shires or a City type at a shooting school were not the only ways to learn to handle a gun properly.

"IT'S four pounds thirty, young lady."

Pandora gave the cab driver a five-pound note. "Keep the change," she told him.

"Thank you, love," he said, looking closely at her.

"I've seen your face before, haven't I? You are a famous person!" he exclaimed.

Pandora smiled. "Not really," she answered. The press coverage arranged by her public-relations agent was obviously working.

"Don't say it, don't say it, I know who you are," he went on, closing his eyes. The tip of his tongue was just visible between his teeth as he strained to place her.

"I know, you're Selina Scott!" he said triumphantly after a pause. He leaned down and picked up a piece of paper and a pen from the luggage compartment by his side.

"Could I have your autograph, then? It's for the kids, you know," he said, both pleased and awed by his discovery.

"Of course," Pandora said. She signed herself "Selina Scott" and gave the paper back to the man. He waved cheerfully at her. "You're more beautiful than Lady Di!" he shouted as he drove away.

Amused by the incident, Pandora walked up the steps to her front door. She felt tired after the long walk with the guns, but there had been a late train, and she was glad to be home. She was looking forward to her bath, and then going to bed.

As she slipped the key into the lock she saw a man get out of a small van parked in front of her building.

"Are you Miss Doyle?" he asked.

"Yes, I am."

"Please wait a minute, miss; I have something for you," the man said.

She thought it odd that someone was delivering anything so late at night. There was nobody else in sight and she was suddenly frightened, but if the man were a burglar surely he would not give her time to open the door and get into the building.

After a moment, he approached her again, this time carrying a huge basket of white lilies.

"Take it upstairs, please," she told him after she had opened the door. She pulled the crisp white envelope from the huge white bow on the basket, tore it open and read the card as she led the way into the hallway.

> I hope you have excused my brashness, but I am a rough Australian after all. I am flying to Sydney tomorrow morning, and I will be there until February. Would you like to have dinner with me on Friday 12th in Paris? My plane will take us there, and we can come back the same evening. My secretary will call you to confirm. I hope you are free.

She did not need to read the signature to know who it was from. Only one man could offer an invitation like that, and she decided to accept it. She was flattered by his interest; no one had ever asked her out to dinner six weeks in advance. But she would tell his secretary that Mr. Carson should phone her in person when he was back. It wasn't just his shooting style which could do with some polishing.

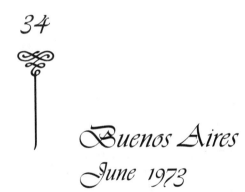

34

Buenos Aires
June 1973

Los muchachos peronistas
todos unidos triunfaremos . . .

The opening lines of the Peronist anthem suddenly filled the room. The TV screen showed the enormous crowd at Ezeiza airport, twenty miles outside the city, waiting for Perón's return after his eighteen-year exile in Spain.

Disgusted by the circuslike atmosphere, Arianne picked up the remote control and switched off the TV. She glanced at the *Buenos Aires Herald,* a habit she had acquired during her crash course in English two years ago, but threw it aside after a moment. She picked up the house phone and called the kitchen to ask for a cup of tea. After a long while, Rosinha answered. Arianne was briefly surprised, but then she remembered that the government had declared a national holiday for the day. Rosinha, being Portuguese, did not care much for these events, but the rest of Arianne's staff was probably at Ezeiza, chanting and shouting the imminent end of the stinking rich — of people like her, in fact.

Perón's return was as celebrated by most of Arianne's friends as his departure had been in 1955. They had cheered his departure out of hatred, and now they cheered his return out of fear. But their enthusiasm did not compromise the safety of either their money, wisely deposited abroad, or their children, sent to the country in anticipation of possible turmoil in the city once Perón arrived. Arianne had sent Gloria and Nana to one of her estates, a hundred miles from Buenos Aires, and now she was on her own in the almost deserted house.

She felt lonely. Gloria and Nana were the only two people she could count on. Her friendships now were merely a matter of practical interest. Even Jacques, once so close to her, had faded from view. She had seen him in Paris last year and sensed the difference. Not simply because of her money; she had lived like a very rich woman toward the end of her time in Paris. They had both been on the same side then; what she had was by the grace of Simón. But it was difficult to maintain a friendship with a makeup artist when she had crossed the Atlantic in her own jet, and was supposed to have dinner that night with a cabinet minister.

Many men had courted her since Simón's death, but she was not interested. Besides, they would want to marry her sooner or later, either because of her money or just because of the prestige attached to catching her. Simón's letter to her had put an end to that prospect, and there was no point in starting fires that she would have to put out.

Living as she was in the small circle of Buenos Aires society, her love life or lack of it became a popular topic during her early days in the city. The venom of some of the men she turned down, the vanity of those who claimed success for the sake of their image, and the envy of some of the women had combined into her simultaneous reputation as both a *femme de glace* and a nymphomaniac. The lack of firm evidence of the latter dampened the interest, her essential coldness eventually the likely explanation. Failure is not an enticing prospect, and men stopped asking her out after a while. She found herself having to rely for male company on a small circle of rich homosexuals, who provided her with regular escorts to the theater or the opera, but did little for her feeling of isolation, a feeling that overwhelmed her today.

Weakened by her introspective mood, she allowed herself to think about Paul Liehr. After her visit to "San Simón" three years ago, she had found herself eagerly waiting for reasons to visit the estate. When she began inventing them, she realized that she was close to making a fool of herself, and put a stop to it. From then on, Paul reported to her on the phone when necessary, and she had learned to dismiss her feelings on the rare occasions when personal contact was unavoidable. She sensed that attraction played no part in his respectful attitude toward her. Everybody took notice of the fact that she was a woman, of her attractiveness, bar the one person whom she would have liked to. In a way, she was glad he didn't. Life was easier if she was in full control of everything, her business as well as her emotions.

But it wasn't easy today, and she suddenly felt a compelling need to see him. She waited around her home for a while, forcing herself to look at her tapestries and paintings. Then she went to the library and picked out a book at random. She sat in one of the leather armchairs and began to read, but flung the book down on the coffee table after a while.

It was absurd. She was fretting like a schoolgirl because today she felt like seeing one particular man. Her mind was instantly made up. She picked up the phone again and called her pilot. Half an hour later she was at the Aeroparque, and then she was airborne, completely oblivious to anything else other than the fact that soon she would have her wish.

At the opposite end of the city, many miles away, the Peronist rally had reached fever point, scuffles breaking out everywhere between right-wing and left-wing supporters. "Perón, Evita, the country is Peronist," chanted one side; "Perón, Evita, the country is socialist," replied the other. The noise was deafening, but even the roar of a million voices could not drown the firing of automatic weapons when the shooting finally broke out.

Nobody would ever know which side started it, nor how many died in the massacre that followed. Men, women, and children ran in all directions, but the bullets also came from all directions, mowing them down. Hundreds of white doves escaped from the huge cage at the side of the main stage. They were to have been released when the leader, the hero of the day, made his appearance in front of his cheering supporters, but now they flew over the carnage.

The volcano of violence, rumbling for so long, had erupted. It would burn the country for nearly ten years.

AS the plane landed, Arianne realized that she had forgotten to warn the staff that she was coming. There would be no car to take her to the house. No matter. The house was not quite a mile away from the landing strip, and it was a fine day. She would enjoy the walk through the park.

After a while she began to catch glimpses of the house in the distance, and only then did she wonder what she was going to say to Paul. She ran through possible topics for discussion in her head, but they had already discussed them all. As she reached the casuarina wood she thought of a possibility, its implications both tempting and frightening.

She had to fly to the United States next month. She would tell him that she was thinking about introducing new bloodlines to the stud farm, and he should come with her to advise her.

The possibility of a few days away with him, if only for part of the time, made her heart beat faster. She decided to take a shortcut to the house by walking through the fountain garden, hidden from view by a circular yew hedge. She wanted to see Paul as soon as possible.

She saw him sooner than she expected. As she walked onto the broad white gravel path around the fountain, she noticed a couple sitting on one of the stone benches at the far end of the garden, the man's arm around the girl's shoulders. It was Paul.

He jumped to his feet, as did the girl.

"Nobody warned me that you were coming, Señora," he said apologetically. The girl realized who Arianne was, and looked fixedly at her feet.

"May I introduce Anna Rauch," he said after a pause. "She is . . . a friend."

Arianne nodded to him graciously, ignoring the girl.

"I'm only here for a moment, Paul. I suddenly decided to come to 'San Simón' because I urgently needed . . . some papers I left in my bedroom last time I was here. I'm going back now." She left abruptly without saying good-bye. It was not the awareness of her obvious lie, evidenced by the fact that she held nothing in her hands, which made her walk away. It was much worse. Her violent trembling confirmed to her that she was hopelessly in love.

THE front page of the company's July newsletter was largely taken up by a message of welcome to General Perón, accompanied by a photograph of Señora de la Force, the chairman, greeting the general at his home. The announcement of Paul Liehr's elevation to the main board after his brilliant management of "San Simón" was one among many others on the second page.

The announcement said that Mr. Liehr would now take up residence in Buenos Aires.

35

Paris
February 1988

*T*HE wine waiter carefully poured the Château Margaux, just enough to fill the bottom of the glass. Ted took a sip of his wine, closing his eyes and pursing his lips. Pandora had seen wine experts go through similar motions, reminding her of mouthwash commercials on television. He nodded his approval, and the waiter began to fill their glasses.

"How much is your turnover these days?" Ted asked suddenly.

Pandora toyed with her *émincé de veau et sa Chartreuse de poivrons rouges* until the waiter went away.

"Is that what you usually ask girls you take to Paris for dinner?" His question took her by surprise, since he had not mentioned business, either his or hers, until then. She found his abrupt change of tone as gauche as it was direct, almost as gauche as she had found the air hostess in his plane, her pale blue uniform buttoned with golden T's.

"Answering with another question is an obvious tactic," he said. "I can try to seduce you, or we can discuss business. Either would suit *me*. I would prefer the first option, but I suspect that you might be the kind of woman who does not succumb on the first date as a matter of principle. I like you enough to be prepared to wait."

"You seem to take for granted that there is something to wait for." However blunt he might be, she could not avoid being somehow flattered by his rough-edged admiration, although she was not going to acknowledge it. "I can't see why you should be interested in my line of business, though. I thought you were mainly into brewing."

"I'm involved in other things as well. I've just bought a computer company in America. They distribute a range of office furniture on the East Coast, and they own a string of large showrooms in most major cities. The business is a dead duck, though, but it's not the right time to sell it and I'm thinking of alternative uses for the showrooms."

She was not interested. Expansion into the United States, or any other country, for that matter, was out of the question for a business the size of hers, at least at present.

"I might be interested someday, but not now, and the food here is too good to let it get cold for the sake of your empty showrooms and my turnover. I'll only say that it is certainly less than yours but more than you think," she said.

He chuckled. "You are right. This is not the place for hard talk. I should have said it earlier, but you look gorgeous tonight. I like your dress; I hope I'll see the label someday." It was the dress she had bought for Geraldine's party, her most glamorous evening outfit, and it was clearly making an impression on him.

"You don't seem to waste time. Maybe we ought to go back to our business conversation," she replied with a weary smile.

"I've told you that I have little time to waste and I'm going to New York for a week tomorrow. But let's change the subject if you like." He took a sip of his wine, and immediately embarked on a knowledgeable explanation of the merits of this particular vintage.

"Unfortunately, all good things are expensive, but it's just a matter of preference. For instance, I'm sure you don't find what you pay for scent outrageous. What would you imagine a bottle of scent this size would cost?" he asked, holding up the wine bottle. The patronizing tone in his voice grated on her.

"I wouldn't know. I don't drink my scent," she said after a moment. He was visibly nonplussed. "The only reason I can think of for your comparison is that you want to find a way to let me know that this bottle costs hundreds of pounds, which I already knew." His embarrassment was immediately obvious, and she regretted her catty remark.

"I love the Place de la Madeleine; it always reminds me of an

Impressionist painting," she added, briefly looking out of the window next to their table. "I'm very grateful for your wonderful invitation." She smiled at him. He was now sitting in stony silence, but after a while he smiled too.

"You *are* a classy lady. It shouldn't surprise me. I hear you are related to the Earl of Felmingham. I met him shooting not long ago."

It would have been simpler to refer to him as Lord Felmingham, but Ted's tone showed that he liked the full title rolling off his tongue. It made her feel awkward on his behalf, but he was trying to make up for his faux pas by taking innocent pride in his social progress.

"He is my second cousin, on my mother's side. I hardly ever see him." It occurred to her that he must have carried out some pretty thorough research on her background if he was aware of such a distant relationship. "Use what you've got, that's the secret" had been Geraldine's advice. He found her attractive, and aspired to what she represented to him. She did not find him unattractive, and he could be useful. Perhaps there was more common ground here than she had been prepared to admit at the beginning of the evening.

She talked for a while about the English side of her family and her days as a deb. At first she was pleased by his interest, until she realized she was playing up to the role he expected of her. There was not much difference, only a matter of degree, between his earlier, coarse boasting, and her seemingly casual display of social connections now. They served the same purpose, but at least he had made his reasons for displaying his power absolutely clear. She knew what her own motive was, and she didn't like it. It was one thing to see the point in Geraldine's advice, quite another to start behaving like Geraldine.

"All this talk about friends and relatives must be very boring for you. They aren't very interesting, really," she said, hastily trying to bring the conversation to an end.

"Are you being sincere, or just patronizing? It's the easiest thing in the world to emphasize what you've got, and then dismiss it as if it's of no consequence. If we're going to play games, then at least let's play by the rules," he replied.

She thought for a moment.

"You're right to ask the question, but wrong about the reason. I just wanted to change the subject. But since you mention rules, perhaps we ought to clarify who's laying them," she retorted.

He laughed.

"It's too complex a question for our first evening out. But the fact that you ask it gives me hope for the future, and there's no need to play games tonight. I took your point earlier, and I'm not trying to seduce you." He looked away for a moment to catch the waiter's attention, and she felt both relieved and disappointed by his words. He turned back to her.

"Not yet," he added with a smile as the waiter presented the dessert menu.

IT was nearly seven o'clock, and almost everybody else in the office had gone home. Pandora was still rattled by her last meeting.

Soon after Christmas, one of her friends from her school days had come to see her, to ask for a job. She had said that now that her children were at school she wanted something to do, and Pandora had offered her a job as an assistant in one of her shops. The manager had phoned her in the morning to tell her that Mrs. Harrison had been caught stealing goods from the stockroom. "I would have handled the problem myself, Miss Doyle, but I know that Mrs. Harrison is a friend of yours . . ." Pandora told her to ask Mrs. Harrison to come to her office at the end of the day.

Dismissal was the only option. Even if she were to move Charlotte to another branch, the problem would probably arise again. But the fact that the outcome was inevitable had not made the conversation less difficult. Charlotte had been tearful at first, then angry, then tearful again, and Pandora could not help feeling sorry for her. Charlotte had gone at last, but the scene had been very unpleasant. From now on it would be wiser not to get involved in dismissing staff if it could be done by somebody else. She understood why generals stay away from the front. Her own battle had just begun; she wouldn't last long if she made a point of walking among the casualties and getting upset by their wounds.

Her phone rang, and she answered it. She immediately recognized the Australian drawl.

"Hello, I'm back. I'm glad you haven't gone away yet. Are you free this weekend?"

"Why?" she asked.

Ted chuckled.

"No questions. You have to tell me now if you are free or not."

Her first inclination was to say no, but it dawned on her she was glad to hear his voice.

"Yes, I am free."

"Good. I'm having some friends to stay in my house in Hampshire. I would love you to come," he said. "I'll pick you up at half past nine tomorrow morning. We're going in the chopper." He had not waited for her to accept, but she decided to let it pass.

"I've told you I don't like flying in helicopters," she said.

"I'm sure you'll learn to love it. I look forward to seeing you. Oh, and I've bought something in New York for you. Sorry, there's somebody else on the other line, and I can't keep him waiting. I'll see you tomorrow," he said before ringing off abruptly.

As she put the phone down, she wondered if she had been wise to accept. After a while, she switched off the lights and left the office. At least she was no longer worrying about Charlotte.

"THAT'S my home," Ted shouted in order to be heard over the roar of the helicopter, pointing at the endless spread of slate roofs and gables below them. As soon as he heard him, the pilot tilted the helicopter slightly toward Pandora's side, to give her as full a view of the ground as possible.

"It's very beautiful; it reminds me of Blickling," she said. She noticed Ted's blank look at the comparison. "Blickling is a lovely house near Walsham. It is one of the great stately homes of England," she added.

Now pleased by the effect the house seemed to have on her, Ted tapped the pilot's shoulder.

"Let's have a quick tour of the estate from the air, Freddy," he said. "I want Miss Doyle to see everything." The unexpected extension of the flight made Pandora regret her admiration.

Once they landed, Ted insisted on having a walk around the house before going in: he clearly wanted to show off his domain. It was said to have been built for Anne Boleyn, and had had a succession of distinguished owners ever since. Ted had bought the estate from the Duke of Barnsbury and had immediately embarked on a massive restoration program. "I employed only the best people," he boasted. The Victorian wing had been demolished, and the park restored at great expense to its original layout. "I've added a couple of polo fields," he told her as they finally went inside the house.

The other guests were already waiting for them in the Great Hall, some playing backgammon while others read the *Financial Times* or the *Daily Telegraph*. The women were all blond, or had become so, and were dressed in designer slacks and silk shirts, their chunky gold jewelry as new as the bags they had casually flung on the sofas. The men wore City shirts with the sleeves rolled up, cashmere sweaters thrown over their shoulders, or brand-new country tweed jackets over Viyella shirts. They all wore trousers pressed to a razor-sharp crease. Pandora had upgraded her usual country wardrobe of jeans and a sweater for the occasion, but now she realized that she had underplayed her hand. Everybody else seemed to have just arrived from a very sunny corner of the world by way of Bond Street.

Ted introduced Pandora to his guests. There was a Greek man whose name Pandora was not able to catch, accompanied by Melissa Harvey, whose name she did not need to catch because her life was a permanent feature in the gossip columns. Her last marriage had been to a very rich industrialist who had been knighted just before their divorce. "I'm Lady Harvey, but just call me Melissa," she told Pandora with a smile.

There were also Norman Bragg and his wife. He was a property developer originally based in the north of England. His roaring success in shopping mall developments had triggered his equally successful move to the London Docklands, where "Bragg"-emblazoned cranes were now an everyday sight. His wife looked as perfectly suburban as a golf course, and equally well groomed.

Pandora was surprised to see a face from her old days. Nick Aston-Jones used to be the boyfriend of one of the girls at Mrs. Ogilvy's shop when Pandora worked there. She had lost touch with both of them. He was accompanied by Olivia Treadwell, the notorious journalist, whose ability to outrage her readers was second only to her skill in infuriating those she wrote about. She was now riding high on the success of *Seduction*, her recently published novel. Pandora was puzzled by the unlikely pair.

"Nick! It's been such a long time! What are you doing these

days?" she asked, as Ted led the other guests toward the seats around the monumental fireplace, where his butler waited by a huge refectory table, its top almost invisible under the bottles and glasses on silver trays.

"I'm a publi-*shah* now." His career might have changed, but his accent had not. Pandora instantly understood his connection with Olivia. *Authors and publishers, wheelers and dealers, we all have something to sell to each other these days,* she thought. They chatted for a while, and then joined the others at the far end of the room.

"YOU'RE very lucky to have caught a man like Ted," Melissa suddenly said to Pandora.

They were leaning on the white painted rail around the polo field, while Ted and Vlasos Kalomeropoulos rode up and down, practicing their cut and pulled strokes. Pandora had learned the Greek's name during lunch, at the same time she had learned that Melissa was a well-coiffed viper.

"You are wrong on two counts. I haven't 'caught' Ted and, if I had, it would be *his* good luck as well as mine," she replied tersely, her eyes fixed on the riders.

Melissa seemed suddenly absorbed in checking her nail polish.

During lunch Pandora had worked out the reasons behind the gathering. Norman Bragg owned one hundred acres of redundant docks on the Thames, and Ted and Vlasos were joining him in redeveloping them. Nick was there because his publishing house had recently been taken over by one of Ted's companies, and Nick was being considered for a top position in the larger group. He had presumably brought Olivia along as a party decoration. Pandora glanced at the ancestral portraits hanging on Ted's paneled walls, unlikely to be members of the Carson family, and wondered what the elegantly dressed squires and ladies would have made of the group under their painted eyes. Perhaps they had been as concerned to get their hands on somebody else's property during their time as this crowd was.

"I think I've sorted out that planning problem we discussed last week, Ted," Norman Bragg had announced in the middle of lunch. "I've engaged Sheridan Crabtree as senior design consultant for the project. The bloke is a bit weird and he charges as if he were Boris

Becker, but the geezer knows his way around the Prince of Wales. He even *knows* the Prince of Wales; can you believe it? He has stuck columns on everything, so it's going to look *really* posh."

Ted turned toward Pandora.

"Norm is talking about our Docklands project. It's a very big development: flats, houses, offices, and a shopping mall, all first class. Maybe you could do the show houses." She noticed that he had chosen briefly to explain the project to her before replying to Bragg, making her party to the conversation. It could be sheer politeness, but it pleased her nonetheless.

"I'm glad to hear that, Norm. We don't want another hiccup like when we employed those high-tech architects we used last time. We don't want to rub the planners the wrong way. Will you do the show houses for us?" he asked Pandora.

She smiled. "I'd love to, but I met Sheridan Crabtree in New York and we may not be on the same wavelength. So far as I can tell, he does not even approve of electric lighting in houses. In any case, it would only be worth my while if I open a branch in your shopping mall. Otherwise it's too far away for potential clients."

Ted leaned toward her and patted her hand.

"That's the spirit," he said approvingly, almost possessively. Pandora remained still for a moment, then moved her hand away and turned toward Bragg.

"What stone will they be using for your columns?" she asked. Bragg seemed surprised, then he laughed.

". . . The lady has expensive taste, Ted. We won't use *real* stone; glass-reinforced plastic looks the same and it's cheaper."

Pandora did not like either his tone or the fact that he had obviously forgotten her name. She was about to reply but Ted spoke first.

"The lady is called Pandora, Norm. Don't forget it," he said sharply. "I guess you don't like our plastic columns," he said to her, as Norm joined in the conversation at the other end of the table.

"I wouldn't know. I haven't seen them," she replied. "But if you're going to bother, you might as well do the thing properly."

He seemed amused by her comment.

"Are you talking about the columns or about you and me?" he said very quietly, so that only she could hear him.

She smiled.

"About the columns. Truth is always better, in either case," she replied.

"But much more expensive, in *this* case."

"Are you still talking about the columns?" she asked in mock innocence. He laughed.

"I was, but I've suddenly remembered I've got a present for you, and now I'm not sure. I hope you'll like the present at least." He turned to the table at large.

"We'd better get a quote for real stone, Norm," he said loudly, his hand over Pandora's. This time he moved it away before she could react.

Afterward they all sat in the library, where the Braggs soon announced that they were going for a walk around the park, while Nick, who had polished off an extraordinary quantity of claret during lunch, stumbled up the stairs toward his bedroom for an urgently needed nap. Olivia said that she had some work to do and also went upstairs, probably to transcribe everything that had been said during lunch for future use in her next novel, and Pandora found herself stuck with Melissa. After ten minutes of listening to her monologue on traveling and shopping, Pandora guessed that Melissa's sex life would be the next subject. She was about to say that she would also like to go to her room for a while when Ted asked them to come along with him and Vlasos, to watch them practice.

Once Vlasos and Ted left them by the edge of the polo field and the two women were alone, her fears about likely topics of conversation were proved accurate. Melissa immediately launched into an account of her colorful experiences during the time between her ex-husband and Vlasos, whom she had met last summer in Sardinia. "I *adore* Vlasos. He would do anything for me, but we had our moments. After the stock market crash last year he went limp on me, darling. As limp as cooked rhubarb! I tried *everything,* but it was no use. Luckily the market picked up after a while, and so did he."

Pandora remained silent.

"I hear that Ted is like a tiger in bed," Melissa said quietly.

Pandora decided that she was not going to be an item in next week's columns.

"You should ask Ted, because I haven't got the faintest idea," she replied.

Melissa raised her eyebrows.

"You mean . . . ?"

"Yes, I mean that," Pandora said tersely.

There was genuine puzzlement in Melissa's voice now.

"But darling, why not? Ted is a terrific guy . . ."

Ted and Vlasos had dismounted, and they were handing their ponies to the grooms. Pandora climbed under the rail and began to stride across the field toward them. It would have been difficult for her to answer Melissa's last question. She had a point.

SITTING at the dressing table in her room, Pandora finished taking off her makeup. She was ready to go to bed when she noticed that she had forgotten to bring from London the book she was reading. She checked the books neatly piled on the bedside table for an alternative, but they were the standard issue for guestrooms in English country houses: a biography of Lord Mountbatten, a novel about the last days of the Raj, a best-selling thriller, somebody's boring account of the Second World War, and Joyce Grenfell's diaries, resting on an equally neat pile of out-of-date issues of *Country Life* magazine. She had put together many rooms like this during her early time as an interior decorator, and she could remember the last-minute rush to the bookshop in Sloane Street to achieve a lived-in, comfortable atmosphere.

After dinner, Olivia had given Ted a signed copy of her new novel, followed by a hard sales pitch about how riveting it was, and how horrified booksellers had been by the sexy bits. "Dynamite, *real* dynamite," she stressed. Olivia had stopped only when Nick had reminded her that they were reprinting it, and the book was momentarily unavailable in any bookstores. Pandora was curious about it, and remembered that Ted had left his copy on one of the tables in the library. She decided to go downstairs to fetch it.

It had been immediately after dinner when the main reason for her reluctance toward Ted, the answer to Melissa's question, became clearer to Pandora. Ted had asked her beforehand to act as his hostess tonight, and as soon as coffee was finished Pandora stood up, the signal to the other women around the table to follow her to the drawing room, leaving the men to drink port and smoke cigars. Olivia protested loudly at what she called a troglodite custom, but followed the others after a moment. The loftiness of the drawing room underlined the awkwardness of their situation, a small group of women waiting for the men to grace them with their presence.

They did not have to wait long, because soon they heard riotous laughter from the dining room, followed by Ted's voice booming across the hall, calling them to come and see. As they reentered the dining room Pandora noticed that the men had taken off their dinner jackets and Nick was squatting on the floor, his head thrown back, an open bottle of port clenched between his teeth, his arms stretched out to keep his balance. The men began to clap their hands and Nick started his Cossack dance around the table, gulping down the port at the same time. The shouting grew louder and louder until he completed his round, the bottle now empty. His bet won, he stood up and grinned, only to pass out immediately on the floor. Ted beckoned his butler and told him to carry Mr. Aston-Jones upstairs. Amid much laughter, they all moved to the library nearby for coffee, but the scene made Pandora wonder if her main role here, Nick's role as well, was to give credibility to a coarse, high-budget replica of the world she was trying to leave behind.

She had just switched on the lamp and picked up Olivia's book when the door opened and Ted came in. He was still in his evening clothes. She had not bothered to put on her dressing gown, and felt embarrassingly vulnerable in her thin nightdress.

"How did you know I was here?"

"I realized I had forgotten to give you your present, and went to your room." Ted was holding a small rectangular blue box. He gave it to her, and she opened it. It was a bracelet, a simple line of square diamonds. She saw the name Tiffany in gold letters on the white lining of the box. He had bought it in New York. She closed it, and gave it back to him.

"It's wonderful, but it's too much. I can't possibly accept it. It would make me feel . . ." She was going to say "cheap," but it would offend him, and she didn't want to do that. He put the box on the table and looked at her.

"From my point of view it's a little thing, but there you are. As I told you in Paris, it all depends on one's values. But it wasn't meant the way you think.

"You don't like my friends," he said after a pause. There was no reproach in his voice. It was a matter-of-fact statement.

"You're right, I don't."

He didn't seem to find the conversation uncomfortable, but she did.

"Is it because you don't like them, or because they show you something about yourself that you don't like?"

"I thought we were talking about *your* friends," she said angrily.

He smiled.

"I like it when you are angry. I wouldn't miss my sleep just to discuss my friends, though. You know what we are really talking about, and you've seen enough to know if you want me or not. Since you're in business, you must know that it pays to make up one's mind quickly. I'm not the waiting type."

"We are not talking business here," she retorted.

"Maybe not, but we are talking about personal decisions. I've never seen any difference between them."

It was what Arianne had said to her in Venice, and he had been right on one score. She had not liked his friends because they showed her what she could become, maybe had become already. But her stay at Walsham had equally shown her that she no longer belonged in Harry and Camilla's world. At least Ted represented the future.

The question was whether she wanted him around her. She was not interested in a fling for the sake of it, and she could not go back to being an appendage to somebody else's life, as she had been with Johnny. But the frantic pace of her work life contrasted with her loneliness outside the office. She would be thirty soon, and she could not spend the rest of her life trying to avoid the issue. She could not deny that it was flattering to have a man like him by her side, and if there had to be somebody, well, it would not have to be on his terms alone. Not anymore.

Her mind was made up, but she still found it difficult to give her answer.

"What are you expecting me to say?" she murmured at last.

"You've said it." His arms around her waist, he kissed her. She was beginning to return his kiss when they suddenly heard a loud buzzing.

"What's that?" she asked.

He laughed.

"That's my butler setting the burglar alarm. There are sensors under every door, and we won't be able to leave this room until seven in the morning, when he switches it off. Don't worry, there are plenty of sofas around." He took her hand and led her away from the bright light, toward the comfortable half-light beyond.

36

Buenos Aires
June 1975

THE limousine, escorted by a Ford Falcon in front and a second Falcon immediately behind it, made slow progress in the busy traffic. The escort cars were chauffeur-driven, each carrying three men with submachine guns. The mirrored windows blocked all sight of the limousine's interior, where Arianne de la Force sat in the back between two bodyguards, their Magnum .44's on their laps. But those were dark days in Buenos Aires, a city scarred by violence, and the rich and powerful took elaborate precautions to protect themselves, especially after the spectacular kidnapping of the Born brothers by guerrillas a year before, followed by a sixty-million-dollar ransom demand. It was the first in a wave of kidnappings, against the background of open war between right- and left-wing paramilitary groups.

Arianne and others like her had been forced to surround themselves with bodyguards in order to maintain a semblance of normal life. A false sense of security spread at first, and some partygivers briefly took pride in the fact that the number of bodyguards gathered outside often exceeded the number of guests inside the house, the evidence of their social standing. But pride was soon overwhelmed by the dreadful suspicion that the bodyguards, an unrivaled source of inside information about security arrangements, could be bribed by the guerrillas to facilitate the kidnapping of their employers. It was unnerving to rely on the loyalty of men for hire.

After the Born kidnapping, Arianne's security advisors had insisted that Gloria be sent out of the country. Arianne had refused point-blank, but she had made the mistake of mentioning their suggestion to Nana, who became obsessed with the possible risk to the child. Again and again Nana told Arianne that she would hold her responsible if anything were to happen to Gloria, and after two months of relentless pressure, Arianne finally gave in. Gloria had been sent to Paris with Nana, and she was now at a convent school. Arianne missed her, but once she got used to it she realized that it was a relief to know that Gloria was out of danger. She was looking forward to her trip to Paris tomorrow. For the first time, business was not the only reason behind her going away. She had taken a villa in Cap-d'Ail for the summer. Gloria and Nana would spend the school holidays there, and she would stay with them for as long as possible.

As the convoy approached its destination and the limousine slowed down, the bodyguards in the escort cars jumped out. By the time the limousine came to a standstill, they had formed a double line on both sides of the entrance to the building. Arianne got out without any delay, and walked swiftly into the relative security of her office. She paid no attention to her grim guard of honor. She had become accustomed to them.

HER mind made up, Arianne returned the papers on her desk to the leather folder in front of her. It was time for the board meeting. She would announce her decision then. It would hurt Paul, but she had no choice. In spite of so much time having gone by, she still found it hard to make decisions she knew would upset him, but the business must be her priority.

After her initial impulse, she had half-convinced herself that nothing but business imperatives were behind her decision to bring Paul to Buenos Aires. He had run a very large estate brilliantly. It was only natural to promote him, and she had expected him to live up to her expectations. But soon after he joined the board it became clear to Arianne that while he was a very good leader of people, he was a very poor manipulator of them. A board position required the skill of planting one's own ideas in the minds of fellow directors so that they took root and developed as if they were their own, the ability to form alliances, to leave markers to be called up when necessary. Paul was an open character, incapable of dissembling. This had no bearing on business decisions because she was the final arbiter, but it isolated him from his colleagues.

For a while she had expected that, when they were thrown into close proximity by his move to Buenos Aires, their personal relationship would inevitably develop. She could not but believe that, once they were in daily contact, it would be a matter of time before he was attracted to her. She had endeavored to consult him at all times, for them to be together as often as possible, until people in the company began to talk about her favoritism toward him, which did not bother her nearly as much as Paul's lack of inclination to justify the gossip. She was forced to accept that she had been misled by a silly fantasy, and his lack of response was perhaps the best outcome.

". . . AND the problem is that you don't understand the point!" Paul Liehr said angrily to his colleague. Everybody's eyes turned to the head of the table, waiting for Arianne's reaction, but she remained silent.

The board had been discussing future policy for the "San Simón" estates, in view of the country's plummeting economy. The more general view was that the time had come to trim down, liquidate cattle stocks, and cancel any plant expansion projects, which would only create hard currency commitments at a time when the peso was going through the floor, with no stop in sight. Paul had been advocating the opposite: land prices had fallen dramatically, making it possible to expand stocks at very low real cost. It would take only a small upturn in international beef prices, which would generate additional dollar earnings, to absorb the initial losses.

". . . and you will have to sell the dollars at Mrs. Perón's official rate of exchange. At the present rate, even this company could not afford it," another director said from the far end of the table.

Arianne decided to put an end to the squabble. There had been too many similar episodes in the past, and there was no point in delaying the outcome.

"Gentlemen, I've listened to what you've all said. Paul has made his point very well, but I have to agree with what is clearly the general view." She avoided Paul's eyes as she spoke. She knew that her perfunctory compliment would not have made any difference to him, and she knew how strongly he felt about anything concerning "San Simón" and its future.

She looked at him at last, but he was not looking at her, and it didn't matter anymore.

"Let's move on to the next point," she said to the table at large. Tomorrow she would go away, and she would leave all this behind her for a while. She looked forward to it.

ARIANNE had just finished taking some of her jewelry out of her bedroom safe and packing it into her travel case when the phone rang. She would be leaving for the airport in half an hour. As she picked the phone up, she noticed on the bedside table the photograph of herself as a child in Rio, and slipped it into her case as she tucked the receiver under her chin. It was the housekeeper.

"Security just phoned to say there is a gentleman at the gates to see you, Señora. His name is Paul Liehr, and he says it's very urgent."

"Please let him in and show him to the library." Arianne was momentarily dumbfounded by Nelly's announcement. She could not think of any possible reason for the visit here, and she dared not imagine one either. She rushed to the mirror for a last-minute check before going downstairs.

Paul was standing by the fire, his back to the door, and she paused before entering the room. She was used to seeing him, but it had always been in the neutral surroundings of her office, where she could pretend that ultimately he was no different from the hundreds of others she employed. But now he was in her home, and they were alone. His presence here suddenly turned her tapestries and paintings into a lifeless collection of woven and painted figures, only underscoring the reality of this man quietly waiting by the fire. She forced herself to go into the room.

"This *is* a surprise," she said with a perfectly gracious smile. "Please sit down," she added, pointing to the sofa near the fire as he turned around.

"Thank you, but I won't be long. I know that you are busy, and I don't want to keep you. I'm sorry to drop in like this, but I had to see you. I have something to tell you." He spoke faster than usual, rushing out his words, as if he were embarrassed. No, it wasn't embarrassment; it was as if he were almost overcome by what he had to say, she thought, and her heart jumped in expectation of what she wanted to hear. She stood next to him. She was too close to the fire, but she didn't mind.

"What is it?" she asked anxiously.

"Here is my resignation," he answered, pulling an envelope out of his jacket pocket.

She felt as if the ground had suddenly given under her feet. It was work after all that had brought him here. She had assumed too much from his manner, but there was only anger behind it, and it suddenly occurred to her that her position had shielded her from other people's anger to the point where she was no longer able to recognize it. She looked away to conceal her disappointment, then took the envelope. She was about to open it but suddenly changed her mind.

"I want to know why." She endeavored to speak with her chairman's voice.

He turned his face away from her, and leaned on the mantelpiece.

"You know why. I've been very unhappy since I came here. There's no reason for my staying with the company any longer. It was only you . . . your support that kept me." His voice was almost inaudible now. "I've accepted a job in Patagonia."

"Are you saying that you've stayed here only because of me?" She was now more aware of his physical presence than her own. She had heard him, and she wanted to be sure. She could not face another disappointment. But she looked at his face, and realized that her question was pointless. She regretted it.

"I don't think my reasons for staying here make any difference now," he said calmly. "I know that my decision is the only sensible one, for you as well as for me."

For a second she thought of pressing her point, to make him say what she wanted to hear, but she knew he wouldn't say it. Wrapped up in her own concerns, too aware of her own situation, she had failed to understand his. She had expected him to climb to her, not realizing that, even for her, some things were out of reach. She forced herself to smile.

"You're right. It is unnecessary to dwell on the reasons for your decision. I regret it very much, but I accept it. I just want to let you know that, if you ever change your mind, you can always go back to 'San Simón.' " She knew she meant it, but she also knew her tone made it sound like the expected farewell from a chairman endeavoring to keep up appearances.

Paul held out his hand, and she could see he was relieved that their meeting had come to an end. *It's the last time I will see him,* she thought, suddenly dreading the fact. There had to be a way to delay the moment.

"I'm on my way to the airport," she said. "Why don't you come with me? There are a few things I need to discuss with you, and it won't take very long. My driver will take you back to the office."

He thought for a moment. It was plain he would have preferred to go now, but she knew he could not turn down her suggestion.

"If you wish," he said tersely.

"The car is waiting outside. I have to go upstairs for a moment. I won't be long," she said, walking briskly toward the door. At least in one small way she had forced him to do what she wanted.

AS their convoy drove away from the house, Arianne glanced at the huge gates closing behind them, to avoid looking at Paul. She was as uncomfortably aware of his presence next to her as she sensed he was of hers, and she briefly regretted her whim. But she would be with Gloria and Nana tomorrow, and all this nonsense would soon be forgotten. She turned toward him and began to fire questions about the business, his answers equally brisk.

They crossed the Avenida Callao and were now heading toward Recoleta. She could see the tower of the Pilar Church in the distance, its white-and-blue tiled top gleaming in the winter sun. Suddenly, a group of policemen diverted the traffic, and forced Arianne's convoy to turn into a side street, along the flank of the Alvear Palace Hotel. As they slowed down on the steep incline toward the Río de la Plata, Arianne saw a procession coming up the road toward them. It was Corpus Christi Day, a carefully observed religious event in Buenos Aires, and the full-size image of Christ on the Cross carried by devout men surrounded by priests and nuns was just one of the many to be seen around the city that day. The street was too narrow for the cars to bypass them, so they pulled to the side to allow the procession to continue toward the church.

As the nuns approached, Arianne noticed their suntanned faces, but it was too late. The image of Christ crashed to the ground as the terrorists disguised as priests and nuns suddenly pulled their guns out of their wide sleeves.

"Look out!" the driver managed to shout. Paul pushed Arianne to the floor and fell on top of her. Unable to see, she could only hear the roar of machine guns and the shouting around her.

If Arianne's bodyguards had been less professional, the outcome would perhaps have been different. Three of them held the advance of the bogus policemen from their rear, while the others fired their automatic weapons at the guerrillas before they could break into her car and snatch her away. The gun battle went on for a short while, until the attackers ran toward their getaway cars.

Almost suffocated by Paul's weight, Arianne kept her eyes tightly shut until she heard the gunfire cease. Just as she was opening them, a shattering of glass cascaded on top of her and Paul, as one of the bodyguards smashed the window on her side to release the lock. The door was opened, and she could see the horror of the scene outside. What had been an elegant street just a moment ago had become a panorama of destruction. The marble shopfronts were scarred by bullets, and the smashed crucifix lay on the ground, surrounded by bleeding bodies. She could hear the police sirens in the distance, getting louder.

Paul did not move. The bodyguard pulled him up and laid him on the seat, his blood slowly seeping into the velvet upholstery. Free at last, Arianne knelt on the floor. The broken glass cut into her knees, but she did not feel it. She was staring at Paul's face. For the second time in her life she was facing the dead body of a man she loved, and it was all her fault again. She had forced him to come with her. Now she had nothing but her grief and her guilt.

She began to scream. She thought she would never stop.

37

London
September 1988

PANDORA flung the file down on her desk. She leaned back in her seat and closed her eyes. Every week her public relations agency sent her copies of any press clippings relating to either the business or to herself, although the difference was becoming less and less apparent. "The magic of Doyle"; "Doyle bucks the trend"; "Pandora Doyle and Ted Carson: the dynamic duo." It went on and on, the copy on the financial pages sometimes as colorful as the gossip columns. At first it had been thrilling, but now she had to fight the temptation to dump the file into the wastepaper basket.

The business had grown beyond anyone's expectations, certainly her own. The licensing arrangements had been a great success, and Doyle shops would soon be found in every major city in Britain. But regardless of what the press hype efficiently organized by her p.r. agency said, the economic climate had begun to bite. The consumer boom was being curtailed by the government's efforts to damp down inflation; interest rates had started to climb, and mortgage repayments would soon trim down disposable income. It had become necessary to run just to stay in the same place, and expansion into America, unlikely as it had seemed a few months ago, could now be the answer. No one was more eager than Ted for the move to take place.

To expand into the United States meant raising further capital at a time when the dollar was on an upward trend against the pound. If the business there did not perform as expected, it could jeopardize her home base as well. Expansion into America also meant finding suitable premises at once. Ted's offer of a partnership solved both problems at a stroke, and her financial advisors had enthusiastically supported it. She knew she would not be able to delay indefinitely.

She was aware of Ted's ulterior motives. Ever since their affair had begun, he had relentlessly tried to intervene in her business, at first with friendly advice, and then through more determined moves. Earlier on, Pandora had told Ted about Arianne's role in setting up her company, and then she found out that he had approached Arianne through his New York bankers to buy her out of Doyle. A major confrontation followed, although it proved unnecessary when Arianne's lawyers notified Ted that Mrs. de la Force was not interested in his offer. Nevertheless, the episode made Pandora uncomfortably aware of a side of Ted she had disregarded until then.

The desire to own and to control everything around him was ingrained in Ted's nature. What he was like had been clear to her from the beginning, and she accepted that there had been an element of calculation on her side when they had begun their affair. Ted was a visible symbol of her achievement, an enviable scar to heal the wound left by Johnny, but she found herself in a better version of the same trap.

Unlike Johnny, Ted had no apparent trouble in a relationship with a woman who had her own interests. If she had decided to play tennis during her marriage, Johnny would have told her that she was wasting her time because she was no good at it, then he would have stood behind her during her lessons, holding her arm and giving constant instructions until she stopped playing through lack of confidence. Ted was a bigger, more intelligent man. He would have been perfectly happy for her to play tennis whenever she wanted, for as long as she wanted, provided that he owned the court and sat in the umpire's chair. Maybe it was just a matter of not letting him buy the court.

Otherwise he was obviously very fond of her, and she was fond of him. There were no fireworks, but Pandora found very few fireworks in her life at this point. Her work, which had started in a frenzy of excitement, was less and less a source of personal satisfaction. Her business was a much larger organization now, and she had been forced to delegate most of the jobs she enjoyed in order to concentrate on policy and financial decisions. Her days were now taken up by long meetings on financial matters, stock control, manufacturing and delivery schedules. She was simply supervising others doing what she had originally done herself. Her initial passion had imperceptibly given way to a sort of contentment. Perhaps it was inevitable, and there was no reason why contentment should not also be her aim in her personal life.

Ted's desire to please her was obvious, and tonight was yet another example. She had talked him into sponsoring the forthcoming production of *Das Rheingold* at Covent Garden, and they had been asked to the Royal Box by Lord and Lady Woodfall to see *L'Italiana in Algeri*. Lord Woodfall was one of the main fundraisers for the Opera, and he obviously knew this particular sponsor: two acts were as far as Ted's patience would go. Unfortunately, the sponsorship was in the name of the property development company, and Vlasos and the dreadful Melissa had also been invited.

She stood up. It was time to go home and change.

THE Rolls-Royce turned into Floral Street, closely followed by a Bentley. Pandora fixed her eyes on the road ahead to avoid the intrigued gaze of the operagoers on their way to the main entrance on Bow Street, momentarily distracted by their opulent caravan.

Both cars stopped outside the discreet side entrance and the drivers let their passengers out. Pandora and Ted waited for a moment until Melissa managed to negotiate her voluminous skirts out of the car door, then they led the group into the small foyer, where Lord and Lady Woodfall were waiting for them. Lord Woodfall shook hands with the men, introducing them to his wife, and Ted then introduced Pandora and Melissa to the Woodfalls.

"Aren't you Serena's daughter?" Lady Woodfall asked Pandora.

"Yes, I am. I still remember when Mummy and I went to stay with you, although I must have been very small."

Lady Woodfall smiled.

"Your mother and I were at school together. Such a long time ago. She was so beautiful. You look very like her." Pandora knew she didn't, but either Lady Woodfall's memory was failing or she was adept at small talk. She thanked Lady Woodfall and held onto

Lord Woodfall's arm as they began to climb the graceful stair winding its way around the foyer.

"What a handsome man," Melissa said appreciatively, staring as they walked past it at the silver-framed portrait on the wall showing a distinguished middle-aged man in a light-gray double-breasted suit. A brief silence ensued, broken by Lord Woodfall.

"He's Sir John Tooley, our last director. We owe him a great deal," he said, clearly uncertain of how to respond.

Vlasos cast a daggerlike glance at Melissa.

"He's probably not rich enough for you," he barked.

"I *adore* Rossini," Lady Woodfall immediately interjected to no one in particular, in a voice loud enough to drown any other conversation, and they all agreed that Rossini was wonderful. A liveried porter opened the double door facing them on the landing, and they entered the antechamber to the Royal Box. A table for six was already laid in the middle of the room and a waiter stood by a small round table in the corner, where a drinks tray and glasses had been set out for them.

Pandora sensed Ted's disappointment at the modest elegance of the room. Melissa's reaction was plain to see. She had obviously expected something out of Imperial Vienna, not a room reminiscent of a small drawing room in a provincial hotel suite. Her eyes were fixed in disgust on the electric fire glowing in the fireplace at one end of the room.

"It's rather . . . charming," she said finally, with more tact than Pandora had come to expect from her. She walked to the fireplace and admired herself in the mirror above the mantelpiece, quickly retouching her hair.

"What would you like to drink?" asked Lord Woodfall.

"I would *adore* a glass of champagne," Melissa said. Lord Woodfall glanced at the drinks tray and whispered something to the waiter. The man rushed out, probably on his way to the foyer bar.

"I'm sorry, but we don't seem to have any here. It won't be a moment."

"You could have given her ginger ale; she wouldn't be able to tell the difference." Vlasos laughed loudly as Lord Woodfall handed him a whisky. Ted went red in the face.

"I hear your garden is glorious," Pandora said to Lady Woodfall, who gratefully launched into an explanation of her restoration work in the last few years.

Champagne glass in hand, Melissa joined them, and the conversation took off at last, the men on one side of the room discussing business while the women exchanged views first on gardens, and then interior decoration. Lady Woodfall praised Pandora on her remarkable achievement.

"You girls are all doing something worthwhile these days," she said; "it's simply wonderful. I'm ashamed to say that the only thing I do is collect porcelain. What do you do, Melissa dear?"

"I collect alimony," Melissa replied.

Luckily the first bell rang.

"I think we ought to take our seats now," Lord Woodfall said to the company at large. "We'll have dinner here during the interval."

"Is there only one interval?" Melissa asked anxiously.

"I'm afraid so, but we will have just one course. Everybody seems to be on a diet anyway," replied Lady Woodfall.

Her hopes of a triumphal stroll through the Crush Bar dashed, Melissa sulkily followed Lady Woodfall and Pandora into the box just as the second bell rang. At last they all sat down, the guests quickly studying their programs to get some idea of the plot. The lights went down and the overture began. After a while, Pandora noticed Vlasos was losing his hopeless fight to keep his eyes open. She decided to keep a regular check on Ted. At least he was within reach of her elbow.

"MARVELOUS, just marvelous," Melissa exclaimed as the waiter served her coffee. The conversation had focused again on the opera.

"Most enjoyable, the singers are very good," added Ted. Pandora hoped he would not expand on his comment.

Fortunately Lady Woodfall launched into an explanation of the merits of Marilyn Horne's voice, referring to other roles she had heard her sing in the recent past. The door suddenly opened, bringing her monologue to a momentary halt.

A man in his early thirties walked in. He was wearing a plain cotton suit and no tie, but he did not seem ill at ease among the black-tied company.

"I'm sorry to barge in like this, Uncle Jack, but I saw you in the distance and I thought that I ought to say hello. I hope you still remember me."

"Andrew! What a surprise!" Lord Woodfall said, introducing him to their guests. A waiter brought a chair, and the man sat next to Lady Woodfall.

"Andrew left London a few years ago," she explained. "What are you doing these days, dear?"

He smiled.

"I'm running a bird sanctuary in the Seychelles. Most unprofitable, but very rewarding." He pulled out a tie from his pocket and showed it to his aunt. "I was looking more respectable earlier on, but it is very hot where I am."

"I know. It can get frightfully hot in Covent Garden sometimes. It's such a relief when the curtain opens and there is that wonderful rush of cold air," Lady Woodfall said sympathetically.

He laughed. "You have to be in the front stalls to feel it. I'm afraid I can no longer afford seats as good as yours. My seat is so high up you almost need an oxygen mask."

Ted, sitting next to Lady Woodfall, turned toward the newcomer.

"Why did you choose the Seychelles?" he asked. "Isn't it a god-forsaken part of the world?"

The bell rang, and Andrew stood up. "Precisely for that reason," he replied. "I used to do something completely different after Cambridge, but I became more and more involved with environmental work, until I realized it was really what I wanted to do. It's too long a story, and I have to climb back up to my seat." He turned to his aunt. "I'm here for a while. I'll come and see you at home, if I may," he said, then kissed her good-bye. He waved absently at the rest of the group, as though he scarcely noticed them, and left.

Obviously amused, Lord Woodfall shook his head.

"My nephew is an unusual chap. He used to work for me at the bank, but then he decided to go away and live in the middle of nowhere."

"He probably came across Melissa at a party," Vlasos said from the other end of the table. Eyes glaring, Melissa rushed through the polished mahogany door at one side of the fireplace and disappeared into the toilet. She came back a moment later, her lip gloss as shiny as the satisfaction on her face.

"Now I can say I've been to the Queen's loo!" she told Pandora. "It's very quaint, all paneled and ancient. You ought to see it." The discreet coat of translucent powder on Lady Woodfall's cheeks was not enough to conceal her sudden blush. She instantly stood up, plunged into a quick explanation of the plot of the final act, and led them all back into the box.

PANDORA cast her eyes for the last time over the neatly typed report and the accounts covering the last quarter, then signed the short covering note clipped to the front of the document. It was a slightly warmer variation of the "Please find enclosed . . ." type of letter she signed many times a day. With reluctance, she had given up her attempts to develop a more personal correspondence with Arianne. They were occasionally in touch over the phone, but their conversations after Venice had made clear that Arianne was wary of talking about anything other than business matters. It was almost as if, having shown too much of herself then, she was now busily rebuilding the impenetrable wall around her.

Pandora regretted it. She owed so much to Arianne, and she hoped that the bond between them would not fade away. She glanced at the letter again, then opened a drawer and took out a small sheet of her personal stationery. "I hope everything is well. I'd love to hear from you," she wrote. She attached her message to the top of the report, placed it in her "Out" tray, and carried on with signing the rest of her mail.

38

Formentor, Majorca
July 1975

IT was midafternoon, and the hotel was quiet. Most of the guests had retired to their rooms for their after-lunch siesta. There were a few people milling around the lobby, but the bar was empty. The barman was polishing glasses at the far end of the counter, and Charles Murdoch tapped on it to catch his attention.

"A beer. Make sure it's cold," Charles snapped at him. The barman was surprised by the order. Until then Mr. Murdoch had always asked for champagne. He poured Charles an ice-cold San Miguel and went back to his tasks. Experienced barmen know when to leave their customers alone.

Charles was deep in thought. He was down to his last three hundred dollars, and there was no prey in sight. He could get a refund for his return ticket to New York, but he didn't like the idea of giving up his escape route. The idea of selling his gold watch was out of the question.

He now bitterly regretted having annoyed that German woman. He had met her at the casino in Monte Carlo, where her diamonds caught his eye. He did not mind the fact that the diamonds sparkled against lizardlike skin, nor that the woman's waistline had become a long-forgotten memory; he was prepared to service a brick wall if the rewards were right. It had been easy enough to pick her up. They had spent a few days in Monte Carlo, which had been ruinous for him since he was paying his own hotel bills, but it had been worth it. The woman had asked him to come with her to her villa in Formentor, giving him a chance to go for the kill.

He had learned early in his career that, in order to make his efforts worthwhile, the last thing to do was to mention money in the early stages of an affair. It put women on their guard. It was far more productive to wait until the right moment came along, when the illusion of a relationship had been created, and then mention some worthy educational project he would love to undertake, were it not for his limited resources. A year in Florence studying restoration of frescoes seemed to be particularly effective with his clients. Like him, they knew nothing about it, but it probably made them feel good to sponsor his cause, and a generous check usually followed his plea for help. After showing more than adequate gratitude, he always made it clear that the money was a loan, to be paid back as soon as his circumstances allowed.

If the target proved unresponsive, then he relied on his second line of attack. He traveled with an assortment of jeweler's tools and paste diamonds in various sizes and shapes; he would substitute some of the fake diamonds for the woman's jewelry before parting company. It could be even more lucrative than cultural sponsorship at times, but it could also lead to trouble with the police, and Charles wanted a quiet life. His problem was that his understanding of a quiet life was a very expensive one, and his money never seemed to last for long.

Things had progressed smoothly with the German woman, and by their second night together in Formentor he endeavored to bring his performance to an even higher standard than usual, in preparation for his request for educational assistance. He had been too successful. Brought to a frenzy of pleasure, the woman began to shriek, waking her Chihuahua from his sleep in one corner of the bedroom. Believing that his mistress was being attacked, the dog leapt on them and sank his teeth into Charles's thigh. Blinded by pain and rage, he had grabbed the ratlike creature and flung it away, but he miscalculated his strength. The dog flew out of the second-floor window, landing in the swimming pool below. Nothing worse happened to the damn animal other than shock and a slight chill, but the woman became hysterical and threw Charles out of the villa on the spot. He had now been in the hotel for nearly two fruitless weeks.

The real money was in the villas nearby, and their occupants seemed to keep to themselves.

Eager for anything to take his mind off his problems, he began to listen to the conversation between one of the waiters and the barman. He understood a little Spanish from his early days in New York, when he had been surrounded by Puerto Rican neighbors, and managed to pick up a word here and there, enough to guess that it might be useful to join in.

"What are you talking about?" he asked.

"Pedro was just saying that a huge yacht has anchored outside the cape. Apparently the world's richest widow is on board," the barman told him.

Charles stood up. It was nearly five o'clock, and he had to change. There was no time to lose. He signed his bill and left the bar.

THE sight of Cape Formentor, the sheer white rock faces rising to the sky from the vivid blue waters, is one of the wonders of the Mediterranean. But for Arianne, lying in a deck chair on her yacht a quarter of a mile away, it was just a fuzzy outline.

She was waiting for another day to go by. Since leaving Buenos Aires weeks ago, she had lived in a daze of Scotch and Valium. She was in no state to face Gloria and Nana in Cap-d'Ail, and had flown directly to her yacht. When the captain had asked for their destination, she had tried to focus on the nautical chart and pointed at Cyprus, farthest away from where they were. Once they reached the island, she looked at the map again. Majorca was at the other end of the chart now, so that was where she wanted to go next.

She would never come ashore, ever. The shore was a place for pain, and she wanted to spend the rest of her life like this, floating aimlessly between sea and sky. Radio and telex messages were brought to her daily from the bridge. She would crumple them in her hand and throw them into the sea without reading them, watching them sink slowly in the wake of the yacht. Unlike her memories of Paul.

She noticed that the outline of the coast was becoming clearer. Time for another pill. She struggled to get it out of the box and took a sip from the whisky tumbler by her side to wash it down. It was nearly empty, but a steward immediately refilled it. Good man, she thought. It was nice to have good men around her. She lay back in her chair. It would soon be time for something. Lunch, dinner, she wasn't sure, and she didn't care. She felt the wind on her face. She liked it. The wind blew things away.

"Blow, blow, the wind blows," she told the nice man nearby.

"Yes, Madame," the steward said impassively.

She raised her eyes toward the sky, but the bright light made her dizzy and she closed them. She could hear the wind, only the wind. And then she heard something else, someone shouting. She opened her eyes again and saw the steward rushing to the other side of the deck.

"Help!" It was a man's voice, but she couldn't tell where it came from. The steward threw a lifebelt overboard, and two sailors joined him to pull at the rope. After a moment, she saw a man climb on board. He was wearing only very brief white swimming trunks, and he was coughing up water.

Her sailors helped the man to his feet, holding him until he seemed able to stand on his own. The man looked at her, then staggered across the deck and knelt by her side.

"I'm Charles Murdoch," he told her. "I can't tell you how grateful I am. You've saved my life." He meant it. The boatman he had hired on the beach to take him to the tip of the cape had warned him that the tide would be strong, and his plight had become more real than he had intended. He was an exceptional swimmer, but it had been a close call.

"It's nice to save a man's life. *Very* nice," she mumbled, taking a long sip from her glass. Charles stared at her. The woman was drunk, but even so, she was ravishing. Maybe it was his lucky day after all.

But she wasn't saying anything, she was just staring at him with glazed eyes. Charles decided to stand up to give her a chance to appreciate how tall and handsome he was, then he collapsed into the deck chair next to her. It would be dangerous to give the impression that he had already recovered enough to be sent back to shore.

"I'm still a bit weak. I'm sorry if I'm delaying your cruise," he said apologetically.

Arianne waved her hand dismissively.

"Don't worry, I'm not in a hurry. I've plenty of time. Nothing but time. All the time in the world . . ."

She felt euphoric. Here was a nice man by her side, a man from the sea. He came from the sea, and he would soon go back to the sea. Like a fish. She enjoyed talking to a fish.

"You're a fish!" She giggled suddenly. Charles forced himself to laugh. She liked his laugh. He was a friend.

"Maybe," he replied. "But you are a truly lovely lady," he added.

"Yes, I'm lovely. *Veeery* lovely. So lovely that any man that gets close to me drops dead. Don't drop dead, fish," she said, helping herself to another pill. Charles caught her hand to stop her. The woman was clearly mad, but he didn't want her to fall asleep just yet.

"Those are no good for you. You should have something to eat," he said, taking the pill away.

"You care for me, fish. A caring fish, I like that. I have plenty of pills in my cabin, though. Lots of wonderful pills." She waved her hand toward the portholes a few yards away from them. "But you're right; we should have something to eat." She tried to stand up but she stumbled. Charles put his arm around her waist and helped her regain her balance.

"Why do you say that men who get close to you drop dead?" he asked as they made slow progress toward the dining room. He was almost dragging her along. He knew little about her, and he panicked for a moment. She couldn't be Mafia, could she? She didn't sound Italian or American, but it was better to find out more about her before going too far.

"Because they do, fish, they do. The first one . . . the first one had an accident, the second one died of disappointment, and the third one . . . the third one . . ." She began to cry, then almost as suddenly, she started to laugh. "It's funny to die of disappointment, isn't it? I told him that I couldn't have children, and he died. Right there. Just like that."

Charles half-listened to her drivel. The woman stank of whisky. She was not going to make it through dinner, and he could not afford for her to fall asleep, as she was likely to do any minute now. It was still light enough for him to be taken to shore as soon as she collapsed and her staff took her to bed. He had seen the motorboat on board. He had to act now. It would make all the difference in the morning.

As they walked past the door leading to her stateroom, he pulled her close to him and began to kiss her. She offered no resistance and, after a moment, he picked her up in his arms and carried her inside.

THE sun poured through the windows of the cabin, and the polished silver frame around the photograph on the bedside table shone in the light. It was the first thing Arianne saw when she opened her eyes. The figures were in sharp focus for the first time in ages. She had probably forgotten to take her pills last night. She stretched her hand toward the drawer when she heard a noise next to her. She turned around and saw a naked man quietly snoring by her side.

She jumped out of bed and realized she was naked as well. She had no idea who he was, nor could she remember anything about last night, other than a vague recollection of talking to someone about fish. But the scene was eloquent enough, and the thought of a stranger touching her made her feel sick. She rushed to the bathroom, turned on the shower full force, and scrubbed herself until her skin burned. She stood under the shower for a long time, the water mixing with her tears.

She came out at last and returned to the cabin. She did not look at the bed; she could not bear the sight. She could not bear the thought of her last weeks either, of what she had become. She had seen the yacht as her cocoon, but it had become her jail. She had to get out of here. She quickly threw on some clothes, picked up her address book, and rushed out of the cabin. She ran to the drawing room and made a couple of ship-to-shore calls. Then she rang the bridge, and asked the captain to come to see her without delay.

"I'm leaving now," she told him as soon as he entered the room. "Please have the boat ready to take me to shore immediately. I won't be coming back. Take the yacht back to Monte Carlo." She paused for a moment, then turned her face away from him.

"I had a . . . guest last night. Once I'm gone, wake him up and take him to shore." She hated herself for having to say the words, for her unnecessary humiliation.

"Yes, Mrs. de la Force. Is there anything else?"

"No, that's all." She noticed that he had not needed to ask where the guest was.

"MUMMY, look!" Gloria shouted before diving off the edge of the pool. Arianne was soaked by the splash and laughed.

"You are a little pest, and I'm going to catch you!" she yelled. Gloria was delighted at the prospect of the chase, and Arianne was about to dive in after her when she saw the maid approaching.

"There's a gentleman to see you, Madame. His name is Charles Murdoch. He says it is about Mr. de la Force."

The man's name meant nothing to Arianne. She had spent ten days in Paris catching up with business matters before joining Gloria and Nana in the villa at Cap-d'Ail a few days ago, and he had probably been sent by the Paris office, although anyone there should know better than to refer to Simón after all these years.

"I'm sorry, darling, I have to go into the house for a minute." Gloria continued to splash as hard as she could as Arianne put on her beach wrap.

"Show him to the study. I'll be there in a moment," she told the maid.

The man was already sitting down, but he stood up and held out his hand when she came in. He smiled broadly. There was something proprietorial about his attitude, almost as if he were the host and she were the guest. Other than the fact that he was very handsome, his face meant nothing to her at first, but then she froze. He noticed it.

"Hi! I'm the fish. I'm glad you remember me," he said. "It's a pity you don't want to shake hands, but I can understand."

"How did you know where to find me?" she asked frostily.

He smiled again, and she was repelled. Her instinct was to leave the room at once, but she knew that he must be here for a reason.

"I'm a very persistent man. I have my ways." His eye fell on the drinks tray at the corner. He walked over and poured himself a Campari and soda.

"Would you like anything?"

"I don't drink during the day."

He raised his eyebrows, and then returned to his seat.

"I suppose you must be wondering why I'm here. It's very simple. I think we ought to take up where we left off. It was a very pleasant night, and it would be as much in your interest as in mine."

She went to the door and opened it.

"I think it's better if you leave now; otherwise I'll call my security staff."

He sat back and took a long sip of his drink before replying.

"I don't think you would like your servants to hear what I have to say."

The old fear took over, but she instantly dismissed it. He could not possibly have found out about Ruben's murder, but she was curious now. She closed the door and went across the room to sit behind her desk, as far from him as possible.

"I knew you would be sensible," he said. He made himself comfortable before continuing.

"I have to confess that I had never come across a woman like you before, and our conversation intrigued me. I found out who you were, and decided it would be useful to do some more research. I went to Madrid, and had a most interesting time reading old newspapers at the Argentine College library in the University. I found out that your husband died of a heart attack on your wedding night. From my experiences with you the other night, I can understand that."

She was enraged by his coarseness.

"I read the Argentine papers at the time, and there's nothing you can tell me that I don't already know. If that's all you have to say, there is no point in continuing this conversation. I would like you to leave now."

"What I've got to say won't take very long." He took another gulp of his drink, then looked at her long and hard. "Please have a little patience." She found his politeness even more unbearable than his attempts at intimacy.

"Finding out about your husband's death threw your comment about one of the men close to you dying of disappointment into a very different light. You said it happened when you told him that you were unable to have children. It made sense to me that the only man who could have been so affected by the news was the one who married you." Arianne hoped her face showed nothing. She couldn't see what he was getting at, but she was becoming anxious.

"I can understand one of the world's richest men being bitterly disappointed by the news," the man went on. "According to his obituary, he was not a young man, and he had no children. As his wife, you were his heir. Having seen your yacht, and having read about the size of his business, I can also understand why you didn't want to disappoint him *before* the wedding. It's just my guess, but I would say you only told him after he had married you."

She was alarmed now. He was wrong about her reasons, but he was clever. "Get to the point," she said impatiently.

He glanced at his cheap watch. He still regretted the loss of his old one, but it had been a wise decision to sell it to pay for his expenses in Madrid.

"It will take me only a minute to finish. It cost me some money, but I consulted a Spanish lawyer who is very experienced in Argentine law. It seems that a marriage where one of the parties withholds information relevant to the intentions of the marriage from the other is not valid in Argentina. The creation of a family is considered one of the intentions of marriage there, and your husband married you in that belief, although you knew it wasn't possible. That means your marriage is void, and your husband's estate should have gone to his sisters, not to you. I imagine that they would be interested in my little discovery, but I would prefer to deal with you."

Her immediate reaction was to stand up and throw him out, but she sensed that he was probably right about the legalities. He wouldn't be stupid enough to start something like this without being certain of his ground, and a medical checkup would prove that she was barren. But there was no evidence that she hadn't told Simón about it before their marriage. There were no witnesses, and it would be her word, her almighty word, against Simón's sisters, seconded by this rat, assuming that any lawyer would want to represent them. They had no money, and therefore little prospect of getting their hands on hers.

She relaxed a little. In a moment he would be out on the street, where he belonged. She started to say "Get out!" but the words never came. She had remembered something else.

There *were* witnesses. Hundreds of them. Her mind raced back to their wedding party, when Simón had told whoever cared to listen that they were going to have a child as soon as possible, boasting about the son she would soon give him. They all knew Simón's overwhelming pride. He would never have boasted about anything if it would lead to a loss of face. Her lie would still have to be proven in court, but the evidence was strong enough to tempt a greedy lawyer into taking up the case. The first thing any lawyer would do was check up on her background. If this man had been able to find out what he had merely by reading newspapers and having a consultation with a Madrid lawyer, she could not afford to have detectives in Paris and Rio digging up the rest.

"How much do you want?"

He left his seat and came to her. He sat on her desk and crossed his legs with nonchalance, as if he were at home. Arianne wished she could wipe that awful smile off his face.

"It's not exactly money I need. My price is that we spend the rest of our lives together. From now on I can't afford to lose sight of you. As you said, men who get close to you drop dead. I'm not suggesting for a second that you might be tempted to take a contract out on me after this conversation, but it would be much more unlikely if I publicly become your live-in lover. If I were to die in suspicious circumstances, you would then be the prime suspect. But this is a morbid conversation, and completely unnecessary. Let's say that I like your life-style, and I would love to share it with you. We've got on very well so far." He saw the flash in her eyes. "Don't worry, I wouldn't want you to do anything against your wishes. I'll live my life discreetly in that respect, and I'll never embarrass you. But I want your answer now. There's a flight to Buenos Aires tonight; I wouldn't want to miss it."

His price rocked her. Even at arm's length, she wasn't going to spend the rest of her life with this vermin. She needed time to find a way out.

"I'm amazed at your audacity. I've never heard such rubbish in my life and — "

He interrupted her. "We are wasting time. You have an hour to decide. I'll be waiting for your call at the bar at the Miramar." He stood up and walked to the door. "If I were you, I would think twice before making inquiries," he said before leaving the room.

Her hand went to the telephone as soon as the door closed behind him, but she paused for a minute, then dropped it back in its cradle. He was right. She couldn't make any inquiries with anyone in Buenos Aires without setting off suspicions, followed by rumors. Once the validity of her marriage was questioned, it would only be a matter of time before the de la Force family decided to try their luck in court.

The option was to hand over Simón's estate to his family now. But even if she were prepared to consider losing everything she owned, she could not afford the consequences. Once she relinquished control of the estate, the lawyer retained by Simón, whoever he was, would then release the information about her to the Brazilian police. She would not only lose her money; she would go to jail, and she couldn't face losing Gloria. Simón's letter with its threat of disclosure had originally trapped her for ten years. Those years would soon run out, but now the same threat had been extended indefinitely by the possibility of her past being dug up by Simón's family if Charles went to them with his information. She was trapped, and she knew it.

She sat in silence for a long while, until she picked up the phone at last and asked the operator to connect her to the Miramar. The conversation that followed took less than a minute. She was to pay the price for many years.

NANA locked the door to her room, then took a suitcase from under her bed, and began to pack her belongings. Nana could not understand why Arianne had allowed this man Charles to move in with them a year ago. She did not like him, not one bit, and Arianne did not seem to like him either. They were together in public, but they lived totally separate lives at home. Arianne had not loved Simón, but at least Nana could understand why she had married him. This Charles was nothing but a good-looking leech.

He was worse than that. He was the worst thing anyone could be in Nana's eyes. He upset Gloria. Not by his actions, because he hardly took any notice of the child. In fact, he seemed to go out of his way to avoid her. But ever since his appearance Gloria had become impossible, and Arianne had begun to avoid her as well. It was difficult to deal with a child who constantly shouted that she hated her mother and the man she had chosen to live with, but sending Gloria away to boarding school in Switzerland, as Arianne had just done, was cruel. Nana had learned to respect Arianne for her loyalty and her kindness. But now she had chosen to send Gloria away, and the only explanation was that Arianne wanted to make her own life as easy as possible.

Nana knew that Gloria would grow up away from her now. The child was as effectively gone from her as her own daughter was, and Nana's life had become simply a matter of waiting for time to pass. She had told Arianne a moment ago that she wanted to live somewhere else, away from them all. Arianne had been adamant at first, but she had eventually relented, and had asked her where she would like to go.

Nana's choice had surprised Arianne. She did not want to live in Paris, or even in France. There were too many memories there. Nana chose "La Encantada," Arianne's holiday home in Punta del Este. The hills and the sea reminded Nana of her childhood home, and she could live there on her own most of the time. Arianne assured her that she would make a point of going to Punta del Este with Gloria during her Christmas school holidays, which coincided with the beginning of the Argentine summer.

She would still be able to see her granddaughter, and she would live on her own, away from this madness. If it weren't for the fact that she blamed her for Gloria's unhappiness, Nana could almost be sorry for Arianne. But she had chosen her life. She had chosen her husband, and she had chosen this man. Arianne was a strong woman, and life had put her in a position where she could choose whatever or whomever she wanted. She had made the wrong choice, but it was her privilege.

39

*London
November 1988*

$\mathcal{P}$ANDORA had had a particularly tough day at work. There were distribution problems in the Midlands, the postal strike was a nuisance, and a large shipment of her new chintz collection made in Taiwan had been ruined in the containers, either in transit or at a port somewhere. She had been screaming in the phone at some man at the other end of the world when exhausted, and fed up, she had finally slammed the receiver down. It was half past seven: the Friends of the Earth lecture on their work to save the seals in the North Sea, their immune system weakened by industrial pollution and now struck down by a virus, had begun at six-thirty. If she hurried, she could still catch the end of it.

Ted was in New York, and his absence made a difference: he was a reassuring, comforting presence. He could also be overwhelming and overprotective, but she could live with that. As she scanned every aspect of their relationship, she was convinced it was a good one, and she should count herself lucky. But, in spite of her reluctance to admit it, she was glad to be on her own when he was away. *Maybe I just needed a breathing space,* she thought as she parked her car near University College.

By the time she walked into the building, the lecture had just finished, and people were coming out of the lecture hall into the foyer. She was on her way to the exit when someone tapped her on the shoulder. She turned around.

"Hi, remember me? I'm Andrew Macadam. I met you at Covent

Garden a few months ago. You were having dinner with my aunt and uncle. I'm sorry, but I can't remember your name."

She had not really taken notice of him at the opera, although she remembered his exuberant interruption of a stilted evening. Many people glowed with vitality and health, but his was not the kind that comes from sweaty sessions on Nautilus machines and tanning salons in a City basement, but from the sun and sea. His eyes were the same faded blue as his jeans, his lean frame did not require shoulder padding, and he was very attractive.

"I'm Pandora Doyle. I remember you, but you looked different then."

He laughed.

"Other than the fact that I was wearing my only suit, I can't think why. Maybe you've begun to see people differently now."

"Maybe," she said. Perhaps he was right.

"I have to go back to the Seychelles tomorrow morning. Lack of time makes one bolder. You look so great that I would ask you to dinner right now, but it is too soon, we hardly know each other, and you would be forced to pretend that I am a nuisance. Why don't we talk for at least five minutes, and then I'll ask? Tell me why a smartly dressed, beautiful woman comes to dull lectures about seals."

He had the engaging directness of a child, with none of the condescension that usually goes with good looks. His admiration rang true, and Pandora felt flattered.

"I am a sponsor of this project," she told him.

"Rich, attractive, and with a conscience; you are very unusual."

"Why are *you* here, and what makes you think I'm rich?" she replied, aware of her defensiveness for no apparent reason. At worst, he was just being candid.

"I used to share a flat long ago with the guy who gave the lecture. Why do I think you are rich? It's the way you stand; you stand like a rich person. When I was in banking, I could work out the exact worth of anyone, give or take a million, by the way they walked. I haven't done it for a long time, so I am out of practice. I haven't seen you move yet, but stationary . . ." He crossed his arms and looked at her in mock concentration. "I would put you in the five-to-ten million league. Precisely how rich are you anyway?"

Pandora felt distinctly uncomfortable, then annoyed. The question was much too personal for a ten-minute acquaintance, and she decided to end the conversation there and then.

"I haven't got the faintest idea, and it's none of your business anyway," she replied coolly.

"You *are* rich, I knew it. What a pity, that means you are probably a complicated person. Still, we can have a simple dinner."

"Why should I have dinner with you? I don't know anything about you."

"A very good reason to have dinner together. Then I can tell you all about myself. I left London five years ago, but there must still be some nice Chinese place around here, discreet lights, music from the mysterious East, good food, bill under ten pounds. Do you have any suggestions?"

The conversation reminded her of her early days in London, when most people she knew had very little money. The unexpected invitation suddenly appealed to her, adding an innocent touch of spice to an otherwise dreary day. It would be fun to listen to his story, and then she would never see him again.

"I don't think we could eat anywhere that cheaply, unless your story is very short. They'll throw us out because they will want the table long before the end. Can you stretch the budget? Otherwise I can pay."

"Don't be deceived by my walk; I *really* don't have much money. Still, I don't take money from women, even London millionairesses. How about going Dutch?" he asked.

"It's a deal," said Pandora.

"Where are we going?"

"Well, I don't know any cheap Chinese restaurants anymore, but I know a nice Indian one. It's the only Indian restaurant with an Austrian decor, and the food is not bad. It's called the Moti Mahal. It's in Chelsea, but I've got my car here. I'm parked in Russell Square."

"Sounds fine. Let's go," he said cheerfully.

As they left the building, Pandora thought of Ted. For God's sake, we are only having dinner, she told herself, half-listening to Andrew's comments about the lecture. They reached her car. Her black 911 Porsche was one of the prides of her life, but now it seemed too ostentatious. He got in without comment, and she sensed that the car had just not registered with him. Some people don't react to things because they don't know what they are, others because they just don't care. Long ago, she used to know people like that.

She started driving down Southampton Row. He was too tall for the car and his leg was almost touching the gearshift, his hand resting on his thigh, his long brown fingers slightly spread over the top, and she felt ill at ease, too conscious about his presence for her comfort. She forced herself to speak to break the mood.

"So, where are you now?" she asked, glancing at him out of the corner of her eye.

He smiled.

"I was saving my story for later, but I can start now if you want. We have enough time to make it worthwhile."

The narrow gap in the seats kept them apart, but he moved slightly and their shoulders touched briefly, no more than a second. The air around her felt suffocatingly close. Luckily she had to concentrate on weaving her way through the traffic around St.-Mary-on-the-Strand, toward Trafalgar Square.

"I left the bank five years ago. I realized that we were all either trying to get rich quick to be able to do something else after we were burned out, or trying to stab each other in the back to reach the top. I didn't want to be at the top, and what I wanted didn't require that much money anyway. My dream was cheaper than a farm in Wiltshire and expensive schools for children I don't even have yet."

"What was this dream of yours?" she asked. She swerved to avoid an idiotic motorcyclist, and her hand touched his leg as she changed gears. For an instant, all her senses were on the outside edge of that left hand. She stared ahead, holding the wheel tightly, and drove straight on down the Mall, the huge flags on either side waving gently in the night breeze.

"I was always interested in birds as a child. So I packed in my job, sold my flat, bought the whole collection of Penguin Classics, and took myself to the Seychelles. I own a little hotel on one of the islands, I'm writing a book on tropical birds, and I work on bird conservation with a small team of great people. I don't need something like this," he said, pointing at Buckingham Palace, "and I would have probably lost my job by now, anyway. Many of my friends did a year ago, after the Big Bang went wrong." Pandora remembered the stock market crash, and briefly wondered about Johnny. He had suspended his alimony payments as soon as her name began to appear in the papers. Maybe that was the reason, but she didn't want to find out.

"But aren't you bored?" She was genuinely curious now.

"Boredom is having nothing to do, or doing something you don't like. I have plenty to keep me busy, and I love it. It doesn't make me much money, but that doesn't mean it's boring. The people around here" — he nodded toward the Eaton Square terraces that they were passing — "must be bored far more often than I am. They don't have to fix their own roofs."

"It sounds rather self-indulgent to me. It must be a very pleasant life, but does it give you any sense of achievement?"

He looked at her sharply. "Probably not in the sense you mean, but we've been able to reintroduce the Black Paradise flycatcher, which was almost extinct when I arrived, and there's a lot more to do. I work fourteen hours a day, but I never use a telephone." His rebuke chastened her, and she kept silent for a while.

At last they turned off the King's Road into Smith Street, and miraculously she found a parking space in a cul-de-sac near the restaurant. She was glad to get out of the car, to put some space between them as soon as possible. She started to walk toward the restaurant when she felt his hand on her arm.

"I'm sorry if I sounded angry," he said gently. She smiled.

"And I'm sorry for sounding dismissive," she replied, then moved ahead to avoid his eyes. They walked into the restaurant, but they couldn't get much farther than the bar. A crowd of young men in pinstripe suits and their miniskirted dates blocked their way, loudly ordering white wine. The manager saw her and came over.

"Miss Doyle, you haven't booked, and there won't be a table for at least another forty minutes. I am so sorry." The man wrung his hands.

She almost didn't hear him. Andrew was standing behind her, their bodies pressed together by the crowd, his warmth so near to her skin, his breath on her neck. Aware of nothing else, she did not move immediately, then turned around and made an effort to look at him, in spite of her confusion.

"I live around the corner. Maybe we could go home and have a drink, and then come back in forty minutes."

"Fine," he said. Nothing else.

They walked toward St. Leonard's Terrace without saying anything. As they turned the corner he took her hand, holding it tightly. They reached her gate. He stopped and glanced at the front of the house. The wisteria was bare for winter, and she wished he could have seen it in full bloom. He stared at her house for a moment.

"Not bad," he told her admiringly.

"Your dream was a tropical island; mine was a house in St. Leonard's Terrace."

"Mine is cheaper."

"Mine is easier to get to from work," she said, standing outside the door and pretending to search for her keys. Her mind clicked into focus as she stopped talking, and she was suddenly filled with apprehension. She didn't know him at all, and she had been carried away. This had never happened to her before, and until tonight she would have found the idea inconceivable, this loss of control over a man who was almost a complete stranger. She forced herself to think of Ted, but it made no difference. Then she felt his hands on her shoulders, and she raised her eyes. Yes, it was inevitable.

"I think you should open the door," he said at last, holding her gaze.

They walked in and faced each other in the half-light coming through the open door. She did not dare to close it, but he pushed it shut and they were in darkness, each of them as aware of the other as if in broad daylight, the space between their bodies almost palpable.

They remained still for a moment, the silence only broken by their breathing. Then his arms were around her, his lips on hers.

THE ringing of the phone filled the room, and Pandora woke up. She stretched her arm to pick up the receiver; she had no idea of the time, only that the sun was pouring through the window. She also noticed that Andrew was gone.

She picked up the receiver. She thought it was her morning call, but it was Tessa, her assistant. Her shrill voice was the last thing Pandora wanted to hear.

"Pandora, are you all right? Mr. Thomas is already here!"

"I'm sorry, there was a burglar alarm going all night, and I haven't had much sleep. I probably didn't hear the phone earlier. I'll be there in a moment." She put the phone down, turned to the other side of the bed, and touched the hollow in his pillow. Only then did she see the piece of paper by the bedside. "Flying back this morning. Address on back. Come on the next plane. We will have all the time in the world."

She didn't want all the time in the world, she wanted *him*. Everything she was or wanted to be had been shaken by their few hours together, everything she owned a poor substitute for what she had found. It had not been a revelation but a confirmation of a certainty, sensed from the moment they had sat next to each other in her car. She went through the day as if it were happening to somebody else, remembering him and their time together, fighting the temptation to take the next plane to find him.

But then there was another day, and then another, all of them filled with things to do, people to see, decisions to be made. And Ted was back.

Her longing grew weaker day by day. First she was able to force her mind away from thoughts of him for a few moments, then a few hours, until eventually she knew that it was just a wonderful, fading memory. Real life was different, and she had worked too hard to find her place in it. Dreams could be dangerous.

40

Punta del Este
September 1988

I<small>T</small> was a cold September morning in spite of the sunshine, and Arianne raised her collar. The men lowered the coffin into the freshly dug grave in the Maldonado cemetery and she dropped into the open trench the bouquet of white roses she was carrying. She walked away before the priest finished his blessing. She did not want him, or anyone else, to see her tears.

As quietly, as silently as anything else she had done, Nana had walked into the sea one week ago. The body had been found on the island in the middle of the bay three days later. Nana had left no message of farewell, no explanation, but it was not necessary. Arianne had phoned her ten days ago, to tell her about Gloria's wedding and the birth of her baby girl.

Arianne had been reluctant to let Nana know about Gloria's wedding. Gloria and Charles had left Venice the night of the ball, before Arianne had had time to speak to her daughter. She had heard nothing from Gloria or Charles afterward, other than friends' gossip that they had married and were living in Connecticut.

Much as she wanted to make contact with her daughter, Arianne thought it would be better to wait until Gloria's feeling of triumph would be tempered by the realization of her mistake. Otherwise any contact between them would be nothing but an exchange of recriminations. She had also been restrained by the hope that Gloria would make the first move, but after months of silence she knew that it would be up to her to establish contact. She had avoided speaking to Nana because she knew that while Nana would say nothing to her, she would blame her for Gloria's appalling marriage.

When she heard through friends of the birth of Gloria's child, her wish to contact her daughter was overwhelming. Perhaps as a rehearsal of what would be the more difficult conversation, she had phoned Nana instead to break the news. Now she realized the depth of her mistake. She should have realized that Nana would see Gloria's marriage to Charles as her own ultimate failure. Gloria had always been the center of her grandmother's life.

Gloria and her child were now all Arianne had, the only ones left to chase away the ghosts. Ruben, Florinda, Simón, Paul, and now Nana had gone from her. But Nana's death gave Arianne a reason to phone Gloria at last, to share her grief. It was not an excuse; it was an inescapable need. She could not wait to get back to New York, to make contact with her daughter at last, and to see the baby. Nothing else mattered.

"GOOD afternoon, Miss Gloria," the butler said courteously, holding the door open for Gloria and the nanny behind her, carrying the baby in her arms. His tone was casually polite, as if he still saw Gloria every day. She looked around, and felt as if she had never been away. She was home.

"Good afternoon, François. Please show Rosie to your sitting room," she said, introducing the nanny. "I'm sure she would love a cup of tea." She deliberately avoided any mention of the fact that she had been away for a long time, and took Mercedes from the nanny. She carefully rearranged the folds of the little girl's wrap, then turned toward the drawing room as the others walked away. It was then that she saw Arianne standing at the far end of the gallery, witnessing the scene. At any other time she would have thought that her mother was playing her usual power games, letting Gloria come to her; now she guessed her mother was as eager as she was for a reconciliation, but equally frightened about their meeting. The two women walked slowly toward each other, until Arianne opened her arms at last and embraced her daughter and her grandchild.

"My darling, I'm so glad to see you at last!" Arianne's arm was around Gloria's shoulders, and there were tears on her face. Arianne gingerly pulled the wrap away from Mercedes's face.

"She is the only one who is entitled to cry here, and look how well she's behaving. She is lovely!" Arianne held out her arm in a silent request for the baby, and Gloria handed her over with a smile. Arianne gently cradled the sleeping child, kissing her cheek and nuzzling her downy head.

"Let's go to my bedroom," she said. "Mercedes will be much more comfortable on my bed." They walked into Arianne's dressing room, where Gloria noticed an enormous box of diapers, another box full of baby lotions, and an array of soft toys on a chest of drawers.

"I did some shopping this morning, just in case," Arianne mumbled, then laughed, hugging Mercedes to her. They walked into the bedroom and Arianne very gently laid the baby down on the silk bedspread, meticulously arranging the matching cushions around Mercedes. The two women stood by the edge of the huge four-poster, watching over the small bundle for a moment, until Arianne squeezed Gloria's hand.

"She seems all right. Let's sit down by the fireplace; we can keep an eye on her from there," she said, ringing the bell by the bed. After a moment, François appeared with a tea service, laid it on the low table by the fireplace, and left the room. Mother and daughter were suddenly conscious that the easy part was over. Now they had to address each other, and Arianne concentrated on serving tea, grateful for the temporary distraction.

She had rehearsed her speech many times during the last few days. Now the time had come to say it, to put an end to twenty years of silence or half-truths, to own up. She would have to explain who she really was, what she had been. But that was easy, or easier than the rest, at least. Nana, the real Arianne, Gloria as a baby, Charles, her whole past had to be unfolded and exorcised, once and for all. She was facing the hardest task of her entire life. She handed a cup to Gloria and sat next to her on the small sofa. She closed her eyes for a moment, then began to talk, staring fixedly ahead.

"I've never been so happy as I am right now. Seeing you has made me realize how much I've missed you. There are so many things I want to tell you, things which concern both you and me, and you are entitled to know them. Whatever may come out of it, I want you to know that I've always thought of you as my daughter. You are, and have always been, the most important person in my life. I'll always, always, love you, no matter what. If a lie is a distortion of what we really feel, then I have never really lied to you, but I want to tell you about myself, about Nana, about . . . you . . ." She felt the tears welling in her eyes and stopped, unable to speak for a moment. She was about to continue when she felt Gloria's hand gripping hers.

"Mummy, please don't go any further. I know what you want to say will be very painful for you, and it really doesn't matter anymore. You *are* my mother and I love you; the rest makes no difference. I learned many things during this year we've been apart, about myself as well as you, and Mercedes taught me anything else I needed to know. Now that I have a daughter I can understand you at last. You owed me nothing but love, and you gave me that in the best way you could. I tried to hurt you, but I hurt myself more . . ." Gloria stopped.

"I want you to forgive me . . . ," Arianne murmured after a while.

"And I want you to forgive *me*," Gloria replied. They remained still, and Arianne felt flooded with a mixture of surprise and joy as they sat side by side, their hands clasped together. Until a moment ago she had thought it was essential to spell out the truth about her life, because she had seen it as an obstacle between Gloria and herself. Now Gloria had shown her it was not necessary. Once acknowledged, love became a truth in itself, more powerful than mere facts.

"There's something else I want to tell you, something I hadn't realized until now. I'm proud of you. Very proud . . ." She briskly composed herself, stood up and walked to the bed, beckoning at Gloria with a mockingly stern face.

"I hope you have not forgotten about her. Obviously I have to keep very close watch on this child . . ." Gloria walked to her side, and both women looked down on the sleeping baby.

"I'm sure that you will." She laughed.

*   *   *

"HOW much did she give you?" Charles asked anxiously as Gloria walked into the sitting room. He was long past pretending. Ever since their marriage he had been meeting all the bills, and his funds were nearly exhausted. The rent was crippling. He had counted on Arianne's softening up soon and chipping in so that she could visit Gloria during her pregnancy, but the bitch had proved tougher than he thought, and the hospital bills after the birth had been shocking. Shortly afterward he had had to fire the cook and the live-in maid, and they had to make do with a cleaning woman twice a week. Now that winter was setting in it would be possible to fire the gardener as well, but life could not go on like this indefinitely.

Charles had heard through a friend of Gloria that the last surviving sister of Simón de la Force had died in Argentina. Charles's hold on Arianne had come to an end. He was no longer able to blackmail her, and any attempt by him to ask for money would put her on her guard about keeping Gloria as her sole heir. Everything depended on that.

Gloria looked at him.

"Sometimes I think you ought to crawl back into the sewer you came from," she said slowly. "Unfortunately for you, I didn't ask my mother for any money."

"How did it go, then?" he asked, trying to soften his tone.

"Fine," she replied. She did not want to talk to Charles about her mother, any more than she had wanted to talk to her mother about Charles. Gloria now wished she had listened to her a year ago. Her marriage was a shambles. Charles's sole concern was her money, her prospects of money. He still put up a good show, hardly ever mentioning the subject, but the birth of Mercedes dispelled whatever was left of Gloria's naiveté. Charles would have cared more for a prize dog than he did for his baby.

"Mummy has asked us to spend Christmas with her in Punta del Este," she told him. "I couldn't possibly say no, and I have accepted on your behalf, but I want you to stay here. I won't be coming back. I will talk to the lawyers tomorrow. I want a divorce."

Charles was thunderstruck, then furious. The girl was a spoiled brat. It took one visit to her mother for her to want to run back home. More to the point, it upset his plans. He did not want to divorce her until the settlement was worth his while, which would mean at least half of her mother's money. But she had to get it first.

"Gloria, you are talking nonsense. I can understand how distraught you must be after an emotional reunion with your mother, but this is not the time to review our marriage. We have to give each other time. You owe it to our daughter."

The mention of the child enraged her.

"You don't give a damn about Mercedes! If you're counting on the prospect of a fatter settlement the longer we stay together, then forget it. Mummy told me she plans to set up her whole estate as a trust for Mercedes in Liechtenstein. The trust will look after me for life, at the trustees' discretion. I don't think you will rate very highly in their opinion. The arrangement will be in place by next year. Frankly, it's not worth your while to hang around."

Charles was barely able to conceal his alarm. His whole scheme hinged on his certainty of Arianne's attachment to Gloria, but it had never crossed his mind that their child would give Arianne a reason to bypass her daughter altogether when settling her estate. It would be easier for him to look into the Queen of England's handbag than to probe into a Liechtenstein trust. He needed time, and he had to keep calm.

"Gloria, I'm truly sorry to hear what you've just said. You have totally misjudged me, but I'm not going to argue with you. Have you discussed the divorce idea with your mother?" He hoped that his voice did not betray his anxiety.

"No, I haven't." She regretted it now, but she had been restrained by a remnant of pride. She could not bring herself to admit openly to her mother during their first meeting after so many months that she had been entirely wrong about her marriage.

Charles struggled to conceal his relief. Perhaps everything was not lost. He lowered his eyes and spoke as if with great difficulty.

"I find your decision extremely painful, but I will not put any obstacles in your way. However, Mercedes is my daughter as well as yours, and I need some time to adjust to the idea that I won't see her so often anymore. Let us have at least one Christmas all together, and I promise you that I will agree to a divorce on whatever grounds you want once we are back in New York. But don't talk to the lawyers yet. It would be impossible to have even the illusion of a

happy family occasion if we are already entangled in legal proce-
dures. And I would ask you not to tell your mother about your
decision until the New Year, to give us one last chance to work
things out. I don't think that's asking too much, do you?"

Gloria hesitated for a moment. It was hard to believe that
Mercedes was so important to him, but, after all, she was his daughter. It did not matter a great deal, anyway. It was only two months
until Christmas, and his cooperation would make things easier afterward.

"I agree," she said finally. "But I will move to the other side of
the house until then." She left the room without looking back.

Charles sighed with relief. Sleeping on his own was almost a blessing. He needed peace and quiet to make his plans.

AWAKE in her bed, Arianne relived the day time and time again.
The joy of seeing Gloria and her baby had been as sweet as she had
anticipated, clouded only by Gloria's obvious unhappiness. They
had both tried their best to be at ease with each other. Perhaps it
would have been easier if she had been able to explain to Gloria the
true nature of her past relationship with Charles, but it would have
meant dwelling on the subject of her past again. Gloria had given
her the chance to leave it behind her, for her own sake as well as
her mother's.

While holding Mercedes in her arms, she had realized that she
wanted Mercedes to be a part of her life from now on. But she had
ruled out further visits in New York for the time being. It would
not be possible to avoid the subject of Charles indefinitely. Gloria's
marriage would soon come undone, but she did not want to be seen
as instrumental to Gloria's inevitable decision. There had been too
much rancor in the past because of what Gloria judged to be Arianne's interference in her life. It would have to be Gloria's own
choice to bring her marriage to an end.

But Arianne wanted to create at least a semblance of normality in
their relationship, and she had thought of Christmas in Punta del
Este as the best possible option. Charles and Gloria could stay on
the yacht, well away from the house, and Charles could sail or
water-ski during the day, while she and Gloria spent time in the
house with the baby.

Her eagerness to see Mercedes had momentarily blurred the implications. But now she realized that the three of them thrown together again would be an impossible situation. She had to find other people to stay with them, to defuse the situation by turning it into a social gathering.

She went to her desk and began to scan her address book. There were hundreds of names, but they were all either too close to her past with Charles, or not close enough to justify an invitation for Christmas.

The answer struck Arianne suddenly. Pandora Doyle. Arianne felt close enough to her to share this awkward moment, and Pandora was a monument of discretion. Pandora had mentioned that Ted Carson was her boyfriend when he had approached Arianne to buy her out of Pandora's company; the episode had made Arianne think that he was probably cut from the same cloth as Simón, but that was Pandora's concern, not hers. Pandora and Ted Carson, the perfect solution to her dilemma. They would be ideal guests for the occasion.

THE bright sunshine filtered through the window, casting blue, red, and amber spots on the gray tiled floor. The stained-glass picture of Santa Teresa, a plaster image of the Holy Mother, and a small wooden crucifix were the only ornaments in the simple room. Sister Rosario sat on one side of a scrubbed pine table, facing Florinda.

"It has not been easy to find you a job with your record, Florinda," she said sternly. "But I have watched you during your years in prison, and I believe that your repentance is sincere. You know that the Mother Superior took an interest in your case. It was only because of that that you were released early. Now we have been able to find you something, and you must not let us down."

"Thank you, Sister Rosario. I just want a job to enable me to get on with my life," Florinda said quietly, her eyes cast down in humility.

"You must go to the Hotel Praia dos Morros, in San Corrado, and ask for Maria Gálvez. She is in charge of the cleaning staff, and she is expecting you." The nun gave a piece of paper to Florinda. "Here's the address. May God be with you, my child."

Florinda leaned forward and kissed the nun's hand.

"Thanks to you I've learned the ways of Our Lord, Sister Rosario. I hope that one day you'll be proud of me," she mumbled.

As soon as she was outside, she ran along the cloister toward the street. She wanted out of this damn place fast. It was almost as unbearable as the jail where she had rotted for nearly twenty years. She had been out for almost a month, and she had spent most of it saying prayers with the stupid nuns and cleaning their latrines.

But it had been worth it. Now she was free at last, free to find Silvia, wherever she was. She had rotted in jail for years because of her sister. If she could find her, she would make her pay. If only she could find her . . .

41

Punta del Este
December 1988

ARIANNE was enjoying the car trip from "La Encantada" to the Montevideo airport, where she would pick up Pandora in a couple of hours. She could have sent someone else, but she had been glad to have an excuse to get away from the house.

At long last she sensed that things were taking a turn for the better. Charles, Gloria, and Mercedes had arrived from New York that morning, but they were resting on the yacht after the overnight flight. Pandora had phoned at the last minute from London to say that Ted Carson was not coming with her after all. But at least there would be somebody else to defuse the atmosphere in the house, and that was all that mattered. Arianne stretched out her legs and leaned back against the soft leather upholstery. As the car sped down the Interbalnearia road toward Montevideo, she could catch occasional glimpses of the sea through gaps in the thick pine forests along the coast.

The death of Inés de la Force a few weeks ago had at long last canceled Charles's hold over her. For twelve years she had waited as Simón's sisters died, one by one. In any event, next June it would be Arianne's twentieth wedding anniversary. Under Argentine law, the matter would simply lapse through the passage of time. Charles would be better off to take whatever he could get from her in a divorce settlement with Gloria. Three or four million dollars was as much as she was prepared to pay for the sake of seeing him off without further trouble to her or to her daughter. Otherwise, she would just let her lawyers loose on him.

It was now a matter of dealing with the future: hers, Gloria's, and the baby's. Her money was truly hers at last, and Gloria and Mercedes would become the center of her life.

Yes, things were taking a turn for the better. It was a sunny afternoon, and she almost felt like singing. For a moment, she thought of the chauffeur's reaction, but then she began to whistle loudly, amused by the chauffeur's surprised glance in the rearview mirror. She didn't care; she was Mrs. de la Force, after all.

THE plane gathered speed, ready for takeoff from Rio de Janeiro airport on the last leg of its journey from London to Montevideo. Pandora looked out of the window, anxious for distraction.

Her eyes fell on the vaguely Gothic church on top of a mountain nearby, an incongruous sight against the dramatic outline of Rio's *morros,* the church's spires reminding her of monasteries on the Rhine. But the light, the mountains, the trees, everything was different. It was another world, so unlike the one she knew. Maybe her problems would seem different, less urgent, from here.

Her most pressing difficulty was in front of her eyes, the large diamond on her finger. She had turned the stone inward as soon as she left Ted yesterday afternoon, but it felt uncomfortable after a while, and the ring was too valuable to take off and drop into her pocket.

Ted must have sensed something after his return from New York three weeks ago, because he had begun to talk about the need to "work on their relationship." They had agreed to meet at his flat yesterday evening, to go to the airport for their overnight flight to Montevideo. Pandora had arrived early. They sat on the sofa facing the fire, making small talk, when he suddenly changed the subject.

"I need to know your decision about expanding into America. I can't hold the shops for you indefinitely."

"I've told you I'm worried about taking on such a big financial commitment now," she replied.

"There's a painless way for you to raise the money."

"Such as?"

"By becoming Mrs. Ted Carson, of course." He pulled the ring out of his pocket and slipped it onto her finger. "I would have no trouble financing the expansion of my wife's business."

She stared at the ring, avoiding his eyes.

"I . . . I can't give you an answer now," she said at last.

"Why?"

"Because I've been married before, and it takes more than a ring. It's not as simple as that." It wasn't, and it had little to do with her previous marriage. A couple of months ago her answer would have been an unequivocal "yes," but her meeting with Andrew had shattered her comfortable contentment.

"I know. I've been married too, and at least *you* don't have to pay alimony. But that isn't any reason not to try again."

It might not be for him, but she was full of doubts.

"I have to think about it," she told him.

Ted stood up.

"If you need to think about it, then the answer is 'no.' " He was clearly upset.

"If I knew the answer, I would give it to you now. The fact that you already know what you want on this particular score doesn't mean that I do. I have to think about it." She also stood up, and faced him.

"Perhaps it would be better if I go to Arianne's alone. I want to be able to do my own thinking in peace and quiet, otherwise you would influence my judgment. You can be very persuasive, sometimes more than you think," she said flirtatiously, trying to sound as lighthearted as she could.

He frowned for a moment, then he smiled.

"You're right," he said. "Maybe being on your own with Arianne de la Force might help my cause. She didn't do badly marrying a rich man."

Pandora raised her eyebrows. "Maybe she didn't, but I don't imagine you're keen on following in her husband's footsteps. Nor would I want you to."

Ted laughed, then took her in his arms. She felt so safe she almost said "yes" there and then, but something held her back. Now, seven thousand miles away, she wondered if she had been right to postpone her decision.

The screen at the front of the cabin showed the plane's progress on a map of the region. They had just crossed the border between Brazil and Uruguay. They would reach Montevideo within an hour. She had a week of peace and sunshine ahead of her to make up her mind.

ALONG *the baseboards, don't miss the socket plates on the wall, up the door frames, then the furniture. Feather duster in hand, Florinda went around the hotel room, just one of many she had to do on that floor alone, mentally repeating the instructions from her new boss like a mantra. The woman was a dragon. She toured each of the rooms and ran a white cotton glove over all the flat surfaces. Any evidence of dust was enough to send her into a tantrum. Florinda hated her, but at least she had a small room in the attic, shared with another maid, and the salary was just enough to survive on. Otherwise, she would have had to go back to the slum or, even worse, lodge with the nuns again. She had to stick to this job for a while and avoid being fired if she was to get a reference.*

Her hatred of her boss was almost a relief, a distraction from her growing, relentless obsession with her sister. It was intolerable to have to live like this, watching her every step, not being able to take anything from the rich cretins staying in the hotel. Money, cameras, jewelry, were sometimes carelessly left around in the rooms, just begging to be stolen, but she couldn't run the risk. In the meantime, her sister was probably having a good time.

But maybe she wasn't. Silvia had always been a weakling, only good for lying around and letting Ruben or Florinda look after her. Without either of them, she was probably starving. The thought of her sister dressed in rags, trying to survive in the favela on her own, comforted her, but only briefly. It was also possible that she had found another sucker to keep her. She could be lying on the beach right now, while Florinda was scrubbing floors. She ground her teeth in anger and began to make up the bed, savagely beating the pillows into shape, imagining them to be Silvia.

Emptying the wastepaper basket was the last task on her list and the only one likely to yield some slim reward; perhaps a not quite empty scent bottle, or a discarded lipstick. Florinda did not find anything as useful as that this time, but at least there was a copy of Brazilian Vogue, and she decided to have a break. She locked the door, then sat down in the armchair and flicked through the pages.

The sight of rich women flaunting their opulent homes, of beautiful girls wearing clothes she could never afford, made her furious. Whores, they were all whores, undeserving of their good fortune. She was half-looking at a feature on paintings and their prices, their obscene prices, when the photograph of a woman caught her eye. The face seemed familiar; at first she thought the woman might be one of her former employers, but after some thought she decided it was somebody else. She had seen that face, a long, long time ago. Not with that confident, knowing expression, certainly not dressed like that, but she knew she had seen that woman before.

The revelation hit her like a blow in the chest. It was Silvia. The caption gave her name as Arianne de la Force, but Florinda had no doubt. It was her sister. She walked to the mirror, placed the magazine on the dressing table, and took a look at herself, pulling back the loose skin on her face, smoothing away the lines brought on by bitterness and poverty as much as the passage of time. It was the same face. Silvia looked younger, less worn, but so would Florinda if she had clothes and jewels like that.

She began to read, and found out that the "fabulous Mrs. de la Force" was said to have bought a painting by someone called Manet for fifty-five million dollars. She was described as enormously rich and shy of publicity. Her South American connections were mentioned, and also the fact that she only left her European or New York homes to spend Christmas at her magnificent house in Punta del Este.

Florinda tore the magazine into shreds in her rage. While she had rotted in jail Silvia had been living like a queen, having everything she wanted and more. But now she knew where to find her. The bitch would pay, at last. She would have to give Florinda money for her silence, lots and lots of money. Then she would kill her. Only that would be adequate compensation for Florinda's years of suffering.

Her wages would be paid tomorrow, the day before Christmas Eve. They were enough to cover the bus fare to Uruguay, and it would take her only three to four days to reach Punta del Este. She would be there just in time.

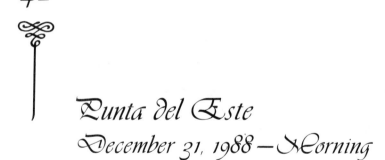

42

Punta del Este
December 31, 1988 — Morning

THE maid came into the room on tiptoe and quietly drew the curtains.

"You don't have to be so careful, Corazón; I'm already awake," Pandora said from her bed.

"I haven't brought your breakfast, Miss Doyle, because Mrs. de la Force told me to ask you if you would like to join her downstairs."

"Please tell Mrs. de la Force that I will join her as soon as I'm ready. It won't take me long," Pandora told the maid as she jumped out of bed.

"Mrs. de la Force is having breakfast on the terrace," Corazón announced very formally before leaving the room.

Under the shower, Pandora thought that it would be the first time Arianne and she had had breakfast together since her arrival a week ago. Pandora had managed to conceal her annoyance with Arianne when she casually mentioned, on the way from the Montevideo airport, that Charles, Gloria, and their baby would be spending the holiday with them. The reason for the invitation was suddenly clear to her. But she was in Arianne's debt, and she resigned herself to her role as peacekeeper. Her worry was unfounded. Pandora had been quickly taken up by the local set, who provided an endless stream of invitations to parties, yachts, and yet more parties, invariably declined by Arianne, and she found herself spending very little time in the house.

Her hostess had been a model of sociability compared to Charles, though. Pandora had seen him for any length of time only during her first evening there, supposedly the Christmas celebration dinner, although it was hard for Pandora to enter into the Christmas spirit in this beautiful summer weather. Arianne had been at her sparkling best then, mostly talking to Gloria about people they knew, while Charles concentrated on Pandora. His performance was as polished as she remembered from Geraldine's party nearly two years ago. Only Gloria had shown any signs of discomfort, her tension underlined by Charles and Arianne's apparent ease. From then on she had seen Charles very rarely, and only from a distance.

Having come to terms with the awkwardness of the situation, she was thoroughly enjoying her stay. The social merry-go-round had postponed any thoughts about her own problems. It had been easy to fool herself into believing that there weren't any in a setting like this.

She came out of the bathroom and dressed quickly, then left her room through the French doors leading directly to the terrace.

Sitting under a large white umbrella by the balustrade facing the lagoon, a pool of shadow on the huge stone terrace edged by white geraniums in terra-cotta urns, Arianne held Mercedes in her arms. Ten yards away, the nanny stood against one of the pillars of the gallery, keeping respectful watch on her charge. A maid appeared, carrying a silver breakfast service, the polished surfaces almost incandescent in the morning sun.

"Perfect timing," Arianne said to Pandora with a smile. The maid placed the breakfast tray on the table.

"Would that be all, Señora?" she asked.

"Yes, Alma, thank you." The maid left, and Pandora sat down.

"Would you mind pouring the coffee?" Arianne asked, clicking her fingers for the baby, who tentatively tried to grab them. "I can't let go of Mercedes. The nanny is dying to have an excuse to take her away from me. Please help yourself to whatever you want." Arianne managed to balance the child on her lap while she buttered her toast, but in the meantime Mercedes dipped her little fingers into the strawberry jam and then rubbed them all over Arianne's white shirt.

"Naughty girl!" She laughed. The nanny came toward them but

Arianne waved her hand, dismissing her. Pandora smiled at the scene.

"You're obviously besotted," she told Arianne.

"She's the best thing that's happened in my life in a very long time. I've learned a few things recently, mainly to care only about what really matters."

"How can you tell? It's not always easy."

Arianne glanced at her.

"You *always* can. We may not want to face it, but it's there to see." She noticed Pandora's hand.

"You complimented me on my rings the first time we met. Now it's my turn. We haven't really spoken since you've been here, so why don't you tell me all about it now? Then I can go on holding Mercedes and her nanny won't have any excuse to whisk her away from me."

Pandora fidgeted with her ring for a moment, then looked up.

"Ted has asked me to marry him."

"And you don't want to."

Pandora sighed. "I wish it was as clearcut as that. I know I would have preferred to carry on as we were. He is forcing me to make a choice, to commit myself, and I'm not sure I want the commitment. It's very difficult to be anything other than Mrs. Carson if you marry a man like that. On the other hand, I'm not sure if I want my work to be the most important thing in my life either. It fills most of my time, I enjoy it, and I'm very proud of what I've achieved, but I still have to go home at the end of the day."

"I would say that what you don't know is how to get out of your dilemma," Arianne said, struggling to release Mercedes's sticky grip on the long gold chain around her neck. "You probably think it's an offer you can't refuse. Or shouldn't. From my experience, beware of offers you can't refuse. They always turn out to be more expensive than you thought." She called the nanny.

"Mercedes needs a new diaper," she said as the nanny took the baby. She wet a napkin in her water glass and rubbed it on a damp mark on her white trousers.

"If *Vogue* could see me now," she sighed mockingly. Both women laughed, then Arianne suddenly became serious.

"You're going back tomorrow, and I wanted to talk to you before you left. I'm very grateful for what you've done for me by coming here. I'm sure you understand why I asked you."

Pandora smiled.

"I think I know what you mean, but I'm the one who has every reason to be grateful. I must confess that I was surprised to find Gloria and Charles here. But it was pretty clear that you didn't want to talk about it, and perhaps some things are better left unsaid."

"That's a *very* British reaction," Arianne laughed.

"I *am* very British. I saw it as a problem in New York, but now I take it as a fact of life. And there's no need for you to apologize, not after what you did for me last year."

"I just invested some money, and that only because I knew it was a viable business. There was little risk. Now that you have your own money, you must have realized that it is very important in some ways, but it's not everything. You gave me something that night in Venice at least as important to me as the money was to you."

Pandora tried to remember their conversation then, but she could find no clue.

"My only recollection is that I didn't make much sense that evening, I was so worried by my own problems. What did *I* give *you?*" she asked, genuinely puzzled.

Arianne took a sip of her coffee before replying.

"I'll follow your advice about certain things being better left unsaid. It doesn't matter. I just wanted to let you know I'm grateful, particularly in the circumstances." Her tone indicated to Pandora that there was something else on her mind.

"If you are talking again about Charles and Gloria, I hope my being here has been helpful. Charles certainly seems to keep himself out of sight. Maybe he's embarrassed, and can't face you."

Arianne shook her head.

"He's up to something. If only I knew what it was. He's been going for long walks in the park every day, and he's not the walking type." She briskly clapped her hands. "Enough of that subject. Let's talk about tonight. The Cullens have asked us to join them at the New Year's Eve party at La Terraza. Gloria and Charles will be going, but dinner on Christmas Eve was enough for me. You and I can have dinner here alone tonight, and then you should go to the party without me. My driver will take you there, and he can wait to bring you back."

"I'll stay here with you if you don't want to go."

"Absolutely not. I'm tired of parties, but you have to start the year doing something more exciting than keeping me company. Maybe you'll meet the man of your dreams there, although I have the feeling you already have."

"What do you mean?" Pandora asked, taken aback.

Arianne smiled enigmatically.

"Don't be so defensive. I was only referring to your ring," she said.

CHARLES looked around for the last time. He was sure he was alone, but he had to be cautious.

It hadn't taken him long to locate the generator house during his first walk, discreetly concealed by landscaping at the bottom of a slope. Luck was on his side. A recent storm had brought down a few pines at the edge of the forest on top of the hill, and his only concern now was to confirm, during his daily strolls, that they remained in place. It was most unlikely that the trees would be removed today. Nobody liked hard work between Christmas and New Year, certainly not on New Year's Eve.

He had not been fooled by Arianne's flawless performance since they had arrived. He knew she would not show herself in public with him and Gloria, particularly somewhere as conspicuous as the party at La Terraza. It had only been a matter of getting that English girl out of the house tonight, and his suggestion to the Cullens to ask her along as well had taken care of that. Arianne always gave the staff the night off after serving dinner on New Year's Eve. Later she would be alone in the house.

He had made sure that there would be nobody else on the yacht as well. That morning he had told the captain that the staff could have the night off. More than pleased, he began the long walk back toward the house.

A breeze rustled the pines on top of the hill, a hundred yards away from where Charles had been a moment ago. The branches creaked, startling Florinda, and she took cover among the fallen trees. After a while she was reassured that she was alone, and loosened her grip on the handles of the small bag she had brought with her from Rio.

As soon as she had arrived three days ago, after the back-breaking bus journey, she had checked the Punta del Este telephone directory, where she found the listing she was looking for: "A. de la Force, 'La Encantada.' " But there was no address. She was eventually told at the post office that "La Encantada" was twelve miles away, on a hill near Punta Ballena. She had to go back to the Onda bus station and take the next Punta del Este–Montevideo bus, stopping at Punta Ballena. The fare took most of what was left of her money, but money would soon be no problem.

She found the house at last, after a tiring walk uphill. She was awed by its magnificence, but she did not linger to take in the view. Her first concern was to find a hiding place before nightfall. The forest was a long way from the house, and clearly a place nobody went to. She slept outdoors, the chill of the night biting into her.

She stalked the house during the next two nights, scavenging the garbage cans for food, and drinking water from the fountain on the terrace. One evening she caught sight of her sister in the window at the top of the tower; her joy at discovering where she slept almost canceled out the surge of rage she felt at the sight of her. She was also able to confirm that there was only one other woman staying in the huge house, sleeping at the opposite end from the tower. She had to hope that her sister would be alone tonight; she knew from her days as a maid that even the rich gave their staff the night off on New Year's Eve. If her sister went to a party, she would wait for her return. She had waited long enough; a few more hours would make no difference.

She opened her bag and pulled out the gun she had stolen from the manager's office before leaving the hotel. The feel of the polished metal filled her with pleasure. The gun was almost identical to Ruben's.

43

Punta del Este
December 31, 1988 — Evening

CHARLES checked the time once again before going into the galley. It was nearly nine o'clock. From the bottom step he could see Pepa putting the finishing touches to the dinner trays laid on the long stainless steel top.

"I'm sorry to disturb you so late, Pepa. I know you're about to go home, but I've just noticed that I'm missing my American Express card. I may have left it in the pocket of the shirt I gave you to be laundered this afternoon." He flashed his most ingratiating smile. "Could you find it for me now? I would do it myself if only I knew where to look." The laundry was on the lower deck, so it would take Pepa a few minutes to get there and back.

"Of course, Señor. I won't be a moment," Pepa said.

"Don't hurry. I don't want you slipping down the stairs in a rush. I can wait," he said. As soon as Pepa left, he pulled a bottle of Seconal out of his pocket. He had asked for beer with dinner that evening. The beer mug made his dinner tray easy to identify.

Gloria had ordered gazpacho. He quickly sprinkled the contents of two Seconal capsules into the bowls on Gloria's and the nanny's trays, stirring them until he could see no trace of the powder in the soup. By the time Pepa returned, he was inspecting the spice rack on the wall.

"Here's your card," Pepa told him. Charles slipped it into his pocket.

"I'm so glad you found it," he said. He had known that she would. He had put it there on purpose. Pepa picked up Gloria's tray and Charles courteously stood aside to let her go first.

THE clock struck eleven. Their dinner over, the two women were alone in the dining room, lingering over coffee.

"Do you have a wish for the New Year?" Arianne asked. She noticed Pandora's expression, and smiled. "Don't worry, I'm not expecting you to disclose your secrets. But it's your first New Year's Eve here, and it is very easy to see shooting stars in the summer sky in this part of the world. Look for one, and make your wish. It will come true."

Pandora raised her eyes. "Just like that?" she asked.

Arianne smiled.

"You have to help your wishes come true, but it's better to have some support from above."

Pandora suddenly felt very lonely.

"I do have a wish," she said after a while, "and I'll tell you what it is. I hope I'll see someone again."

Arianne stood up and picked up the wine bottle from the silver wine cooler.

"Probably not the same someone who makes that ring feel so uncomfortable on your finger," she said as she refilled Pandora's glass before going back to her own seat. "There's truth in wine, so why don't you tell me about him?"

"I met him in London not long ago. He lives in the Seychelles, and he went back the next day. It's probably just a fantasy of mine," she explained, rather apologetically.

"You shouldn't dismiss fantasies so lightly. They give us something to achieve. If nothing else, they're the spice of life, after all. Do you love him?"

"I wish I knew; it would make everything so much easier. How can you tell if you love someone after only a few hours together?"

Arianne seemed suddenly pensive.

"Time has nothing to do with it," she replied after a while. "You don't love someone simply because you spend your life with that person. Love is not a habit, but you have to make allowances for the fact that I am a tempestuous South American," she said jokingly. Then she became serious. "Don't analyze love, just let it happen," she murmured.

"Even if it means giving up everything else in your life, and puts in question everything you value or is important to you?"

"Yes, if it *is* what you really want. What we really want is what counts in the end," Arianne said in a voice that reminded Pandora of their conversation in Venice.

"You're entitled to think I have no right to ask you this, but what you're saying is very important to me, and I'm asking for my sake, not yours. It is more than obvious that you don't love Charles. Now that I know you better, I guess you never did. If, as you say, loving a man is so significant in one's life, why did you ever choose him?"

Arianne left her chair and walked to the French doors. She stared at the clouds gathering over the moon, her back to Pandora.

"Because I couldn't afford not to. We have to make our choices along the way. They make certain things possible, but not everything. What matters is not to discover that what you left behind counted more in the end than what you've got. There are personal prices you can pay, and others you simply can't afford. That's ultimately what I discovered through our conversation in Venice, although it wasn't so clear at the time. You helped me then and that's the reason why I'm so grateful to you, why I decided at the time to help you."

Pandora wondered what she had said that could have affected Arianne so much, but she was no more able to remember the full conversation than she had been over breakfast.

"I think you ought to go now," she heard Arianne say. "You should be there before midnight, and it's a long way from here. La Terraza is past the casino in San Rafael."

Pandora stood up. "Are you sure you don't want me to stay? I don't like to leave you all alone on New Year's Eve."

Arianne smiled. "Most certainly not, particularly after all you've told me. The last thing you need is to be left alone with your thoughts, and I'm tired. I just want to go to bed.

"But we can toast the New Year early," Arianne said, walking across the huge room toward the sideboard. She took a champagne bottle out of the silver bucket and opened it. The cork shot out, falling at Pandora's feet.

"There's a local superstition that if you are single and a champagne cork falls on you, you'll get married soon," Arianne said, pouring the wine into two champagne flutes.

"You aimed the bottle at me, so it doesn't count." Pandora laughed. Arianne handed her a glass.

"It's an innocent game and you have to cheat sometimes, if you are going to get what you deserve," she said. "Happy New Year," she added, raising her glass. The identical emeralds on her fingers sparkled in the candlelight.

"Happy New Year," answered Pandora. She hoped it would be. "Do *you* have a New Year's wish?" she asked.

Arianne smiled.

"I think I've already got mine. Gloria told me this afternoon that she'll start divorce proceedings as soon as we are all back in New York." Her happiness as she spoke was plain to see.

"I'm delighted, for you as well as her," Pandora said. They sipped their champagne, then Arianne put down her glass.

"Time for you to go. Have a wonderful time, and remember to look for shooting stars."

They walked across the dark hall, the Moorish tiles gleaming in the light from the waiting car outside, visible through the glass doors.

Arianne waited until the car drove away. She turned toward the stairs to her bedroom, but stopped when she heard a noise outside. Probably the wind knocking over one of the chairs on the terrace, she thought. But she was suddenly uneasy, conscious of being on her own in the huge, dark house.

She remembered Simón's gun, lying in the bottom drawer of her desk. It was silly, but perhaps she should get it.

CHARLES hummed softly as he drove along the empty coastal road, trying not to think about the knot of tension in his stomach. He saw the lights of a car coming toward him in the distance, so he pulled to the side and ducked his head down until he heard it drive past, then he went on.

The early part of his plan had worked as he had expected, and Gloria and the nanny were both asleep in their cabins, slumped on their beds. He would tell Gloria tomorrow morning that she had been sleeping so soundly he had hated the thought of waking her up for the sake of a party. He might even take a Seconal himself, and let them find *him* asleep in his bed later.

He came to the side road, almost a track, leading to "La Encantada." He turned off the car lights and began to drive uphill until he reached the gates. He parked at the side of the road, behind the huge shrubs, and picked up the shoulder bag from the back seat.

He walked until he was in sight of the house. The only lights were in Arianne's bedroom, outlining the louvered shutters, and in the hall downstairs, but the entrance lights were left on during the night at all times.

He turned left, and began to walk toward the forest. After a while he reached the top of the hill, and came to the fallen trees. A sea wind had begun to blow, and the trees creaked around him. Good. It would be one possible explanation in the morning.

He waited for half an hour, then he gently shoved the small, bushy pine along the ground until it began to roll downhill, crashing against the building at the bottom of the slope. Charles followed it, pushing it tight against the ventilation grate in the lower section of the wall, a dense mass of pine needles blocking the outlet for the power generator's exhaust. Choked by its own fumes, the engine soon stalled.

Charles ran toward the house. "La Encantada" was now in complete darkness. It was one o'clock. He would give Arianne half an hour to fall asleep, then he would make his final move.

THE party at La Terraza was in full swing. After the rush of champagne toasts, hugs, and kisses one hour ago, the dancing had continued with a vengeance in the main building, in the gardens, and around the floodlit swimming pool. Pandora was one of the few who did not join in.

Charles and Gloria had not appeared, and she was worried. Arianne had said she thought Charles was up to something, and Pandora regretted having left her alone. There was no point in staying any longer now that it was well past midnight. She would ask the driver to take her back to the house right away.

She walked across the lawn, down the stone steps leading to the car parking area, the wind blowing her hair. In spite of her worries, she could not avoid being momentarily struck by the view in front of her, the infinite horizon of sea gleaming in the moonlight, under the stars. She had reached the bottom of the steps when she saw a single shooting star flying brightly across the night sky under the Southern Cross.

By the time she reached the car she had made her wish.

HALF past one, time to go. Charles stood up and walked across the silent courtyard. He opened the front door with his key and slipped into the house. He collected a small brass candlestick from one of the hall tables, and paused for a moment at the bottom of the stairs, but he heard no noise. He began to climb.

He reached the door at the top, and waited again. Everything was quiet. Gently, very gently, he opened the door a fraction and peered into the room. In the moonlight filtering through the shutters he could see Arianne asleep on the bed.

He took off his shoes and lifted the heavy wrench out of his bag. He went into the bedroom; the room reeked of Arianne's scent, making him as aware of her presence as if the lights were on. He walked on tiptoe until he almost reached the edge of the bed, holding the wrench high, ready to knock Arianne unconscious. Suddenly he stopped. The only noise he could hear was the beat of his own heart, but he was terrified.

He had to regain his calm, otherwise he might not knock her out at first, and he had to be careful not to crush her skull. It must all look like a terrible accident. Details were crucial, and he had to avoid making mistakes. Perhaps it would be better to set up the scene first. He put the wrench in his pocket and, walking backward step by step, his heart pounding with every creak of the floorboards, he returned to the landing. Arianne did not stir.

He pulled out a screwdriver and a large tin of floor wax from his bag and laid them on the floor. He loosened the screws in the door handle on the bedroom side of the door and put the screwdriver away, then he picked up the tin of wax and the candlestick. Back inside the bedroom, he carefully placed an open book by Arianne's side, as if she had been reading, then he put the candlestick on the bedside table. He was moving in slow motion, but he could feel sweat trickling down his forehead. He paused for a moment, waiting for his heart to slow down, then he opened the tin of liquid wax and poured the thick contents on the valance and the floor under the bed, the solvent fumes filling the air. Once it was empty, he slipped the tin inside his shirt. The scene was set: it would be just a mishap, someone falling asleep while reading by candlelight, not at all uncommon around here during power cuts at night.

He was ready at last, but suddenly the room fell into pitch darkness. The wind had gathered the clouds, and there was no moonlight. He needed a little light to aim his blow accurately, otherwise he might break her nose. Even a provincial doctor would notice that. He thought of going back to his bag to get the torch, when Arianne stirred. He didn't dare move; the creaking floorboards might wake her up. Time was running out. He grabbed the wrench, searched in his pocket for his lighter, and lit the candle. Able to see again, he raised his arm and brought the wrench down on Arianne's head.

An explosion deafened him, then he screamed in agony. The bitch had gone to bed with a gun, and the bullet had shattered his kneecap. His hand flung backward in the spasm of pain, sweeping across the table, and knocking the lit candle to the floor, into the pool of wax. Flames immediately leaped around the bed. Charles began limping toward the door when the gun went off again, slamming into his back. Suddenly he was short of breath, and his legs gave way. He managed to drag himself across the room, his blood oozing onto the floor. He tried to make it through the half-open door but he couldn't. He collapsed in front of it, his inert weight pushing the door shut.

The flames climbed up the paneled walls so lovingly waxed over the years. They spread onto the ceiling, and Charles could hear Arianne screaming somewhere behind him. She sounded a million miles away, but she must have been next to him, because her feet kicked at him, trying to shift his body while she pulled desperately at the door handle. He thought she screamed again when the handle came loose in her hand, but maybe he just imagined it. He could just see, but as if he was underwater, like a fish, a fish surrounded by fire and smoke, lots and lots of smoke. Arianne collapsed on top of him; by now his sight was dimming, until all he could see was the section of the wall in front of him, where a painting of a woman was being destroyed by the flames. He knew he had seen that painting before, but where . . . ?

The fire turned every surface into a sheet of flames. The portrait on the wall was soon only a pile of ashes, like everything else in the burning room.

"GO faster!" Pandora urged the driver as the car raced through the open gates. The wind suddenly broke the cloud, and at last she saw "La Encantada" ahead of them, the top of the tower wrapped in flames. The car stopped in the forecourt, and Pandora ran inside the house.

For a second, everything looked as she had left it. Then the insidious smell of smoke and the horrifying screams from the tower shattered the illusion of calm. She rushed up the stairs. She did not think about herself; her only thought was for Arianne.

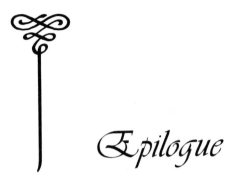

Epilogue

44

Punta del Este
January 1, 1989

PANDORA'S memories of that terrible night would never fade. She would eventually learn to keep them at bay, wild animals pinned in a corner, but that morning they were as real as the view, a part of it. The fire had been brought under control, but the smoke was noticeable in the distance, a tracery on the cloudless sky. "La Encantada," only yesterday another monument to Arianne's power, was now her tomb, as it would have been Pandora's had the firemen not appeared seconds after she lost consciousness.

She was alone on the terrace of the just-opened café. She stirred her coffee mindlessly as she gazed at the view. It was so perfect: the bay rimmed by an endless line of pale sand, the pine forest bordering the coastline, the mountains behind fading into a lavender haze, and then the sky, a shimmering pale cobalt blue, reflected in the water, a flawless backdrop for a carefree summer, or so it had seemed to her until a few hours ago. The men were rich, the women good-looking, the world as it should be when the living is easy.

Soon the island in the middle of the bay, a couple of miles from the shore, would be festooned with big white yachts, the scene for long lunches on deck under white awnings, served by white-jacketed waiters, while the Rivas, glistening black against the foam of their wakes, pulled the water-skiers across the bay. She had been part of that life and she had loved it, but now it was over.

As she picked up her coffee cup, the sunshine brought out shards of light from her ring. Until yesterday, her work, Ted, Andrew, had seemed an unsolvable conundrum, but she had decided last night, at the party, to turn down Ted's offer of marriage. Her midnight wish had been that she could be with Andrew again, but that had been before the horror of "La Encantada." Now it hardly mattered at all. Arianne was dead. Like a shooting star, she had made Pandora's wishes possible, and now she was gone. Perhaps it was only sensible to go back to London and continue with her life as she had left it, to find comfort in certainties.

She noticed a car approaching slowly from the harbor. It was one of Arianne's cars. Charles or Gloria must have sent for her, or maybe the police. She shuddered to think about what would happen next. The statements, the inquest, the trial that would inevitably follow if her suspicions were correct. When she was discharged earlier that morning from the Maldonado Infirmary, she had been told that the police might want to contact her during the day. She couldn't bring herself to return to the house, and told the nurse that she would be at the harbor café, having breakfast. Maybe she ought to go to the bus terminal, a few blocks away, take a bus to Montevideo now and board her flight to London that afternoon before the police could find her.

What could she tell them? She knew that Charles had murdered Arianne, but she could not prove it. Arianne had told her about her suspicions, and she knew his mind better than anyone else. Suddenly, the memory of her friend overshadowed everything else.

The police would want facts, and she tried to remember every detail of the night before. The clue to Arianne's murder could be somewhere in her memory. But there were many facts about Arianne that she did not know. Now she never would.

Charles must have been clever enough to cover his tracks, or else the police would be swarming over the yacht by now. But the yacht was there, a few hundred yards away, and nothing disturbed its peaceful rolling in the morning swell. Gloria would get her mother's money at last. Even if she divorced Charles, as Arianne had hoped she would, he would be entitled to a massive settlement. Life would go on.

Maybe that was the best one could hope for. Arianne's example had been one of the determining factors behind her wish to prove herself, and Arianne's money had made her business a reality. Her doubts were based on nothing but a crazy fantasy about a man she hardly knew.

She stared at her diamond, a beacon of security. Was she going to be silly enough to give up a man like Ted? But it wasn't Ted she wanted by her side now to comfort her, it was Andrew. Yet Andrew was so far away . . . For all she knew, he would have forgotten her by now. What did she *really* want? She had spent the last two years trying to answer that question, but it didn't matter now. The only thing that really mattered to her was to do whatever she could to help catch Arianne's murderer.

The car was very close now. She could not bring herself to face Charles, and there was no time to call the waiter. She stood up and dropped some money on the table, ready to leave. The car stopped a few yards away from her table and the driver got out.

Pandora looked away. She did not want Charles to see her face, a mask of impotent rage, any more than she wanted to see his, glowing in triumph. But she was instantly ashamed by her reaction. She owed it to Arianne to face him. She might not be able to prove anything, but she could at least confront him with the truth. She raised her eyes at the approaching figure, then froze in disbelief.

It was Arianne, walking toward her with the same elegant ease, the same smile on her face as when she had walked into her New York drawing room two years ago. Pandora's grief, so overwhelming until a second ago, was instantly canceled by her joy at seeing Arianne, alive and beautiful, as if nothing at all had happened last night. Pandora ran toward her. There were tears in her eyes as she embraced her friend.

"I thought you were dead!" she cried again and again. Arianne smiled and put her arm around Pandora's shoulders.

"Never believe anything until you actually see it happen," she told her.

They walked back toward the table, and Arianne began to talk as soon as they sat down.

"I wasn't in the house when the fire broke out. I went out for a while. The firemen were already there when I came back. They told me that you had been taken to the Maldonado Infirmary, so I went there immediately. I was told you were asleep, and that you would be discharged in the morning. Then I went to the yacht, to check on

Gloria and Mercedes. Everybody was asleep, and I spent the night there. I spoke to the hospital a little while ago, but you had already checked out. They told me where to find you."

Pandora gripped Arianne's hand.

"But what happened last night? I heard screams from your room!" Even in her confusion, Pandora noticed that Arianne's face showed a mixture of emotions, as though she couldn't quite bring off her usual perfect performance.

"I can't tell you everything in one sentence. Please be patient, and I'll explain."

"I just want to know who was in the room when I tried to open the door. Then tell me the rest."

Arianne remained silent for a moment.

"It was . . . it was someone who was close to me in Brazil when I was very young. I was getting ready for bed when she rang the bell, and I let her in. She was obviously in great distress, and I felt sorry for her. She had come to see me to ask for money. I don't know why, but she needed it there and then. It wasn't much, just a few hundred dollars, but I keep hardly any money in the house. I thought I could cash a check in the casino, and I told her to wait for me. I stupidly forgot that the casino would be closed on New Year's Eve. I spoke to the security men, but they obviously couldn't help me. Then I went back to the house, and I've already told you the rest. The police assume that Charles was in the house for some reason, and that he found her in my bedroom. He must have thought she was a thief; I don't know what happened, but the police are satisfied that nobody else was involved. The chief of police is a charming man. He's gone out of his way to minimize any inconvenience for me, and he told me there was no need for me to identify the woman's body. Apparently she was burned beyond recognition. They will try to formally identify her through her dental records, but they have so little information on her that it is almost certainly an impossible task . . ." Arianne's hands fluttered in urbane despondency, as if the chief of police's predicament was her own. "I explained to the police that, other than the fact that her name was Silvia, I remember little or nothing about her, and I have no idea where she was living. My gardener has been kind enough to identify Charles's body in the morgue, to save Gloria and me any distress."

"Is Charles dead?" Pandora tried to take it all in.

"It's very sad, but he was apparently shot by this woman. She must have had a gun, although I didn't see it. Perhaps Charles disturbed her while she was trying to steal my jewelry. The police think the woman set the room on fire to destroy any evidence, but she was unable to get out."

Pandora was momentarily speechless. The whole thing was too preposterous. She was perplexed by Arianne's glossing over Charles's presence in the house. She was sure Arianne was not telling her the true story, but it no longer mattered. Her friend was alive, and that was all she cared about.

"I'm glad I won't have to speak to the police after all. But I will stay here with you for as long as you need me," Pandora said.

But Arianne wasn't listening. She closed her eyes and her hands gripped the edge of the table, her lips tightly drawn, her mouth turned into a thin, trembling line. After a moment she opened her eyes again, and sighed. She then started to speak again in a quiet but determined voice.

"No, it wasn't like that at all. I'm ashamed that I've tried to deceive you, but old habits die hard. In Venice . . ." She stopped for a moment, then continued. "Let's not make things unnecessarily complicated. Truth matters, and I owe you the truth." She took a long sip of water from Pandora's glass, then leaned forward, her eyes focused on the far distance.

"I had a sister. I hadn't seen her, or heard from her, since I left Brazil many years ago. Last night, after you'd gone, I heard a noise. It frightened me, so I decided to look for Simón's old gun, but as soon as I found it I realized I was being absurd. I wouldn't know how to use it in any case, so I went to my bedroom. I was looking at the portrait of Madame Claire when I heard the door open . . ."

"Was the painting in your bedroom?" Pandora interrupted Arianne, in spite of her curiosity to know the rest of the story. The painting had brought about their first encounter, and she wanted to know what had happened to it.

"Yes. As I told you in New York, at first I didn't know where to hang it. But over the last few months I grew more and more fond of that portrait, because I came to see the similarity between that woman looking at herself in the mirror and me. We were both busy admiring ourselves until something else, something more urgent, made us look back at reality. She and I had become relevant to the world only because we were worth a lot of money. It sounds silly, but I came to see her as my alter ego, and I decided to bring the painting with me to Punta del Este." Arianne's mouth curved into a dry little smile. "But I'm still here and I'm still worth a lot of money, while poor Madame Claire is a pile of ashes."

"Better than the other way round," Pandora said. "Please go on."

"I suddenly heard the floorboards creak. I turned around, and found myself facing my sister again, a gun in her hand . . ."

"DON'T move!" said the woman.

Arianne's first shock of fear was overtaken by the feeling that she had seen her before, this ghastly, demented woman pointing a gun at her, her face splattered with mud, pine needles in her hair. Suddenly she froze.

"I knew you would recognize me," Florinda said with glee. "I'm sure you're thrilled to see your long-lost sister. I don't look as good as you do, you whore, but I haven't changed that much." The hatred in her voice made Arianne shiver. Even if she had tried, she would not have been able to move. She stood still, staring at her sister, a nightmarish reflection of herself.

"I know what you are thinking, little sister: that I look like shit. Unlike you, I never found someone to keep me, and I've spent years in a putrid jail, paying for a murder you committed. Yes, I was found guilty on your behalf. But you can put that right at last," she said.

Arianne felt the same rage she had experienced over twenty years ago, when she had faced Florinda at Ruben's office. As then, her sister was now out of control, a gun in her hand. She was infuriated by Florinda's allegation that Ruben's death had been her responsibility. That was a lie. As then, Florinda could only understand her own hatred. But it would be pointless to confront her with the truth now.

"What do you want?" Arianne asked quietly. Even in her fear, she registered the implication of what Florinda had said. Ruben's murder, the root of all her troubles, was a closed case at last.

"Money!" Florinda barked. "Lots of it."

"How much?" she asked calmly. She had to keep Florinda talking, at least until the rage in her eyes diminished. She was acutely aware of her sister's finger on the trigger.

"Now I want a hundred thousand dollars. The rest we can talk about later."

Arianne sighed.

"Do you think I keep that sort of money around the house? There's my jewelry," she said, pointing toward the case on her dressing table. "You can take that."

Still aiming the gun at her, Florinda walked to the table and pulled the case open. She gasped at its contents.

"I'll take this, all right," Florinda said, her fingers raking through the jewels. She glared at her sister. "And the money. You must have money in the house; you have one minute to think where you're going to find it."

"I really don't have much money here. You can look in my purse if you want. I assure you I don't keep any elsewhere in the house, and I can hardly go to the bank now."

Florinda thought for a moment.

"Maybe you are telling the truth," she said. She grabbed a handful of jewelry and thrust it uncomfortably close to Arianne's face.

"While you were wearing these, I've been cleaning up the shit of rich bitches like you in Rio and São Paulo, and I know only too well that people like you don't keep any real money lying around." She laughed hoarsely. "You are afraid of being robbed by scum like me." Her voice became more shrill as she spoke, her rancor taking over.

"It's a pity you don't have the money, but your jewels are enough. We'd better say good-bye." She aimed at her sister's head and was ready to pull the trigger.

"Wait!" Arianne shouted. Florinda smiled grimly.

"I knew you would think of something. Guns have a way of making people think," she said.

"I could try to cash a check at the casino. They know me there. But it will take me more than an hour to get there and back."

Florinda raised the gun.

"Do you think I'm stupid? You're planning to come back with the police! We have wasted enough time already." She took aim again.

"I don't want the police involved in this. Please don't shoot!" Arianne cried.

Florinda thought for a moment, then laughed.

"You're right. You wouldn't like your friends to find out who your sister is. I don't think the police would do you much good. I think you should go to the casino."

Hardly believing her luck, Arianne pulled her checkbook and the car keys from her bag, Florinda watching her every move. She could only think about the next minute, when she would be out of this room. She was almost ready to leave when Florinda stopped her.

"Not so fast. We have plenty of time. Don't count on your friend coming back. I have enough bullets for two."

"What do you want now?" Arianne asked, trying to conceal her despair. Maybe Florinda's agreement to her proposal had simply been a cat-and-mouse game to let her think that she would survive after all, but she was not going to break down in front of her sister, as she used to do. She wasn't going to give her that last satisfaction.

"I told you that I've been a maid for years. Now it's your turn to find out what it's like." She waved the gun at Arianne, pointing toward the bathroom.

"Run my bath, cow!" she shrieked.

Arianne walked into the bathroom, Florinda behind her. She turned the taps on.

"Don't forget the bubble stuff; I like that," Florinda told her. Arianne reached toward a huge bottle of Chanel bath foam on the ledge and sprinkled some of it into the water.

"All of it," said Florinda, prodding painfully at Arianne's ribs with the gun. "And don't forget to put in something that smells nice as well." She picked up the largest bottle of Arianne's Bal à Versailles scent, and sniffed it.

"Nicer than this," she said with a grimace, pouring the scent into the sink. Arianne picked up a bottle of Floris bath oil and emptied it in the bath, by now filled with a mountain of suds. When the bath was ready, Florinda removed the cord from Arianne's dressing gown and grabbed her arm, pushing her back into the bedroom.

"Now take off those pretty clothes you are wearing," she ordered. *Arianne hesitated.*

"Do what I say!" Florinda screamed. Arianne undressed, fighting her shame. Florinda flung the dressing-gown cord at her.

"Tie your feet together. Tightly." Arianne sat on the floor and did as she was told. Florinda then wrenched Arianne's hands behind her back and tied her wrists with a stocking. Arianne lay on the floor and Florinda prodded her with her foot.

"Now roll toward the door. I want to keep watch on you from the bath." Arianne followed her instructions, and struggled until she was lying across the bathroom entrance. Florinda stepped on her as she walked into the bathroom.

"You make a nice doormat," she said as she flung her cheap cotton dress on the floor. She lay in the bath for a long time, trying every soap in the large silver dish. At last she got out, luxuriantly rubbing herself dry with Arianne's monogrammed bath sheet. Florinda returned to the bedroom and put on Arianne's clothes, then sat at the dressing table and pinned her hair back, like Arianne's. She stared across at Arianne's face, then made herself up with her cosmetics. Finally satisfied, she picked up her gun again and released Arianne's hands, noticing the emerald rings on her sister's fingers for the first time. She pulled them off, and slipped them onto her own.

"You can untie your own feet; I'm not your maid," she barked. "Now put on my dress."

Even in the overpowering steamy atmosphere, drenched in scent, Arianne could smell her sister's filthy dress as she pulled it over her head. Florinda took her by the arm and led her toward the mirror, then she pulled the pins out of Arianne's hair and messed it up with her fingers.

"There you are! I'm you and you are me. We are not very different after all, are we? In fact we are not different at all." Arianne looked in the mirror, and was repelled by what she saw, as if the last twenty years of her life had never existed.

Florinda yawned.

"Enough of this game. On your way now. And don't get ideas about finding a gun somewhere, or coming back with someone to help you. I'll be waiting for you outside, under cover. You come

back with the money, on your own, and stand in the middle of the courtyard, with your hands up, where I can see them. You have an hour and a half, not more. Otherwise I'll leave the house, but I'll come back and shoot you later, or that lovely baby I've seen you playing with. So get going . . ."

Arianne ran down the stairs. Florinda watched her from the landing, until she heard the car start. Holding the gun, she made herself comfortable on her sister's bed, and prepared for a long wait.

Her gaze was caught by the silver-framed photograph on the bedside table. She picked it up and looked at it for a moment. It had once been hers, and she had treasured it. Like so much else, Silvia had taken it from her. Now she could have it back, but she didn't want it. It meant nothing to her after all these years. She flung it onto the table, the glass shattering into daggerlike shards.

She lazily stretched out her arms, admiring the emeralds on her hands. They were her rings now. The gleam of the emeralds was as pleasant as the touch of the silk shirt on her skin, and she sighed in contentment. She felt really good after the hot bath, and she closed her eyes for a moment . . .

"I SUDDENLY heard the floorboards creak, turned round, and found myself facing my sister, a gun in her hand. . . ." Arianne suddenly shifted her eyes away from Pandora, and remained silent for a while.

"There's something else I ought to explain to you," she said at last. "Something I've never told anyone else before. There was a man in Rio, a man whom I loved very much. I may have . . ." Arianne's voice was almost a murmur now. Pandora took one look at her agonized face and interrupted her before she could continue.

"I just want to know what happened last night. Anything else is in your past, and I have no right to know it. It would make no difference to me, anyway," Pandora said firmly.

Hearing her, Arianne was reminded of Gloria's almost identical words during their reunion in New York. She leaned across the table and affectionately held Pandora's hand in hers.

"I thought I owed you the truth," she said quietly.

"There are no debts in friendship. Even if you hadn't told me what really happened last night, you would still be my friend. No other woman has ever had so much influence on me, and you're the one entitled to call in debts — " Pandora noticed that Arianne was nearly crying now, and she stopped midsentence.

"Did your sister ask you for money?" she asked once Arianne had calmed down.

"Yes," Arianne whispered.

"And the rest of the story is just as you told me before?"

"Yes. I have no idea what Charles was doing in the house, but I'd rather not know."

"I think we both know." Pandora called the waiter, then faced Arianne again. Their eyes locked for a second, in silent agreement to leave last night behind them now.

"Do you want me to stay and help you sort it all out?" Pandora asked. Arianne shook her head, only her warm smile belying her usual cool composure.

"I'm very touched by your offer, but it's really unnecessary. There's no point in you staying here any longer. The house is a mess, and I have to arrange for builders and decorators before leaving for New York. Gloria, Mercedes, and I will be flying back as soon as possible. This is obviously a shock for Gloria, and I want to spend as much time as I can with her from now on."

Arianne settled the bill.

"Shall we go? Your side of the house was not touched by the fire, and Corazón has packed your bags. I've arranged for your luggage to be taken to the airport; I'll drive you there myself. There's no need for you to delay your departure." She paused for a moment, a mischievous glint in her eyes. "Please don't think that I'm in a rush to get rid of you, but I'm sure there are better ways for you to use extra holiday time than by keeping me company."

They climbed into the car, and drove away. The smoke was still visible as they approached Punta Ballena.

"It's a nuisance, but I hope the house will be clear of the smell by next summer. I want to sell 'La Encantada.' " It was all Arianne said.

"What about you? What are you going to do now?" Arianne asked. Pandora took a deep breath.

"You told me yesterday that we always know what's right in our hearts. It is true. You also said that one should only be concerned about what truly matters; suddenly seeing you alive after thinking that you were dead has made me realize there are very few things that are really important. Once I'm back in London, I'll have to decide if I want to continue with the business or not. I might well sell it, but your investment is secure no matter what, I promise you. I'm sure you'll make a good profit," she told Arianne.

"I'm always good at that, at least," Arianne replied.

They remained silent until they reached the airport. They parked outside and Pandora walked toward the Aerolineas Argentinas counter. Arianne's driver was already there with her luggage.

"How do I get to the Seychelles?" she asked the girl in the pale blue uniform. The girl was used to passengers asking about the next flight to Buenos Aires, not to places she had never heard of. She opened a thick manual and looked through it for a while before replying.

"It's a *very* long journey. You have to fly to Johannesburg first. We have a flight there this afternoon. If you catch the plane to Buenos Aires now, you'll probably make it." Pandora handed over her credit card, and the girl busied herself at her computer terminal. Pandora left Arianne at the counter and walked to the kiosk nearby, where she bought a small box of chocolates and a brown envelope. She emptied the chocolates into the nearest bin, then wrote an address on the envelope and gave it to Arianne.

"Would you mind sending this back to Ted by registered mail from New York?" Pandora asked, dropping her diamond ring into the box. "I'll phone him from somewhere along the way."

Arianne took the box and slipped it inside the envelope. She smiled in amusement.

"You seem to be solving your problems," she said.

"And so do you." Pandora took her ticket and the boarding card. "I owe it to myself to find Andrew, and then I'll see what happens. Either I'll find out that he was just a fantasy of mine, or that he is important to me. But I have to give it a chance."

They walked together toward the boarding gate; the plane was fifty yards away. Pandora stopped and faced Arianne.

"What will *you* do?" she asked.

"Oh, I'll always have plenty to do; don't worry. Don't forget I have Gloria and Mercedes now. Can you believe I'm a grandmother!" Arianne replied, joy dancing in her honey-colored eyes. They laughed until they reached the gate, where they suddenly became silent and stood face to face.

They hugged each other for a long moment, the morning sunshine casting their shadows behind them. Then Pandora turned toward the waiting plane, and began to run. She ran toward her future now, without looking back.

Acknowledgments

Research is inevitable in any novel, particularly when, as in this case, the characters lead infinitely more eventful lives than their author does. It involves traveling and the compilation of information from many sources. But none of these can be as helpful to the author as the patience and kindness of those knowledgeable on a particular subject. I am grateful to John Alexander, Kin Coombe, Robert Hancock, Debbie Hutton, Nora Jaureguiberry, Julio Nuñez, Mandy O'Flynn, Rolando Paiva, Neil Shaw, Juan Suaya, Saxon Tate, and Mary Wiggins for their most valuable advice and help.

I am also grateful to Lynn Nesbit, my agent, and to Fredrica Friedman, my editor. In many ways, *Sugar and Spice* is as much their book as mine.